GHOST
FORCE

GHOST FORCE

PATRICK ROBINSON

 HarperLargePrint

An Imprint of HarperCollins*Publishers*

www.harpercollins.com

HarperLargePrint
An Imprint of HarperCollins Publishers
10 East 53rd Street
New York, NY 10022.

ISBN: 0-06-112073-1

Printed in the U.S.A.

This Large Print Book carries
the Seal of Approval of N.A.V.H.

AUTHOR'S NOTE

For this, my ninth techno-thriller, set in the future and, hopefully, sailing perilously close to the wind, I needed to be more careful than usual with my sources.

For reasons that I hope are obvious, I would not wish to implicate any senior officers, either naval or military, on either side of the Atlantic, within the many politically lethal issues contained in these pages.

I decided therefore to accept no direct advice or instruction from anyone; rather, I based the story on the strongly held views mentioned to me by so many commissioned officers over several years.

This book involves a new journey to the cold South Atlantic, and the ever-vexing questions surrounding the ownership of the remote Falkland Islands. And I have inevitably drawn on the mountain of knowledge I received from the Task Force Commander of the 1982 war, Admiral Sir Sandy Woodward, whose autobiography I helped to write fourteen years ago.

This time, however, I did not go to him with every twist and turn in the road, nor did I drive him mad for detailed explanations of the myriad of high-tech naval data at which he is a world-acknowledged master and commander, and I remain ever the layman.

I plowed a lonely furrow, distilling many, many highly controversial opinions into my own story. I hope its subliminal message will be enjoyed by serving, and indeed, retired, officers. With perhaps a chilling lesson for the kind of politician we all despise.

Any mistakes, and wayward opinions, either technical, tactical, or strategic, are mine alone. And nothing should be laid at the door of any present or past Commander, naval or military, whose acquaintance or friendship I have long valued.

This applies to perhaps a dozen people, but in particular it applies to Admiral Woodward, who, on this occasion at least, remains shining-white innocent of any involvement with my occasionally acid-dipped pen.

—PATRICK ROBINSON, 2005

CAST OF PRINCIPAL CHARACTERS

United States Senior Command

Paul Bedford (President of the United States)

Admiral Arnold Morgan (Private Adviser to the President)

Admiral George Morris (Director, National Security Agency)

Lt. Commander Jimmy Ramshawe (Personal Assistant, Director NSA)

Admiral John Bergstrom (SPECWARCOM)

Central Intelligence Agency

Agent Leonid Suchov (Deputy Chief, Russian Desk)

United States Navy SEALs

Commander Rick Hunter (Assault Team Leader)

Lt. Commander Dallas MacPherson (2 I/C, Explosives)

Chief Petty Officer Mike Hook (Explosives)

Petty Officer First Class Don Smith

Petty Officer First Class Brian Harrison

Seaman Ed Segal (helmsman)

Seaman Ron Wallace (helmsman)

Chief Petty Officer Bob Bland (Military Breaking and Entering)

Captain Hugh Fraser (CO, USS **Toledo**, SEAL team insert commander)

United Kingdom Political

The Prime Minister of Great Britain

Peter Caulfield (Secretary of Defense)

Roger Eltringham (Foreign Secretary)

Commander Alan Knell (Conservative Member of Parliament, Portsmouth)

Robert Macmillan (Conservative MP)

Derek Blenkinsop (Labour MP, East Lancashire)

Richard Cawley (Conservative MP, Barrow-in-Furness)

Sir Richard Jardine (Ambassador to the United States)

United Kingdom Armed Services

General Sir Robin Brenchley (Chief of Defense Staff)

Admiral Sir Rodney Jeffries (First Sea Lord)

Admiral Mark Palmer (C-in-C Fleet)

Admiral Alan Holbrook (Task Force Commander)

Captain David Reader (CO, HMS **Ark Royal**)

Major Bobby Court (Company Commander, Mount Pleasant)

Captain Peter Merrill (Commander Immediate Response Platoon, Falkland Islands)

Sgt. Biff Wakefield (RAF Rapier Missiles, Mount Pleasant)

Brigadier Viv Brogden RM (Commander Landing Forces, Falkland Islands)

Lt. Commander Malcolm Farley (CO, Royal Navy Garrison, Mare Harbor)

Captain Mike Fawkes (CO, HMS **Kent**)

Captain Colin Ashby (CO, HMS **St. Albans)**

Commander Keith Kemsley (CO, HMS **Iron Duke**)

Captain Rowdy Yates (CO, HMS **Daring**)

Commander Norman Hall (CO, HMS **Dauntless**)

Captain Colin Day (CO, HMS **Gloucester**)

Captain Simon Compton (CO, submarine **Astute**)

United Kingdom 22 SAS

Lt. Colonel Mike Weston (CO, Hereford HQ)

Captain Douglas Jarvis (Team Leader Fanning Head Assault)

Combat Troopers: Syd Ferry (Communications); Peter Wiggins (Sniper); Joe Pearson; Bob Goddard; Trevor Fermer; Jake Posgate; Dai Lewellwyn

Lt. Jim Perry (Team Leader SBS, Lafonia)

Russian Senior Command

The President of the Russian Federation

Valery Kravchenko (Prime Minister)

Oleg Nalyotov (Foreign Minister)

Gregor Komoyedov (Minister for Foreign Trade)

Boris Patrushov (Head of FSB, Secret Police)

Oleg Kuts (Energy Minister)

Admiral Vitaly Rankov (C-in-C Fleet, Deputy Defense Minister)

Russian Navy

Captain Gregor Vanislav (CO, **Viper K-157**)

Siberian Political and Oil Executive

Mikhallo Masorin (dec.) (Chief Minister, Urals Federal District)

Roman Rekuts (New Leader, Urals Federal District)

Jaan Valuev (President, OJSC Surgutneftegas Oil Corp.)

Sergei Pobozhiy (Chairman, SIBNEFT Oil Corp.)

Boris Nuriyev (First VP Finance, LUKOIL Corp.)

Anton Katsuba (Oil Ops Chief, West Siberia)

Argentina Senior Command

The President of the Republic

Admiral Oscar Moreno (C-in-C Fleet)

General Eduard Kampf (Commander Five Corps)

Major Pablo Barry (Commander Marine Assault, Falkland Islands)

Principal Wives

Diana Jarvis (Mrs. Rick Hunter)

Mrs. Kathy Morgan

UK Prime Minister's Principal Guests

Honeyford Jones (pop singer)

Freddie Leeson (soccer player), wife Madelle (former nightclub employee)

Darien Farr (film star), wife Loretta (former TV weather girl)

Freddie Ivanov Windsor (restaurateur)

GHOST FORCE

PROLOGUE

As a general rule, Admiral Arnold Morgan did not do state banquets. He put them in the same category as diplomatic luncheons, congressional dinners, state fairs, and yard sales; all of which required him to spend time talking to God knows how many people with whom he had absolutely nothing in common.

Given a choice, he would rather have spent an hour with a political editor of CBS Television or the **Washington Post**, each of whom he could cheerfully have throttled several times a year.

It was thus a matter of some interest this evening to witness him making his way down the great central staircase of the White House, right behind the President and his guests of honor. The Admiral descended in company with the exquisitely beautiful Mrs. Kathy Morgan, whose perfectly cut dark green silk gown made the Russian President's wife look like a middle-line admin clerk from the KGB. (Close. She had been a researcher.)

Arnold Morgan himself wore the dark blue dress uniform of a U.S. Navy Rear Admiral, complete with the twin-dolphin insignia of the U.S. Submarine Service. As ever, shoulders back, jaw jutting, steel-gray hair trimmed short, he looked like a CO striding toward his ops room.

Which was close to the mark. In his long years in service as the President's National Security Adviser, he considered the White House **was** his ops room. He always called it "the factory," and he had conducted global operations against enemies of the United States with an unprecedented free hand. Of course, he had kept the President posted as to his activities. Mostly.

And now, with the small private reception for the Russians concluded in the upstairs private rooms, Arnold and Kathy stood aside at the foot of the stairs, alongside the Ambassador and a dozen other dignitaries, while the two Presidents and their wives formed a short receiving line.

This was deliberate, because the Russians always brought with them a vast entourage of state officials, diplomats, politicians, military top brass, and, as ever, undercover agents—spies, that is— badly disguised as cultural attachés. It was, frankly, like seeing a prizefighter's goons and bodyguards dancing a minuet.

But here they all were. The men who ran Russia, being formally entertained by President Paul Bedford and the First Lady, the former Maggie Lomax, a svelte, blonde Virginian horsewoman, fearless to hounds, but nerve-wracked by this formal jamboree in support of U.S.-Russian relations.

So far as President Bedford had been concerned, the presence of Arnold Morgan had been nothing short of compulsory. Although the telephone conversation between the two men had been little short of a verbal gunfight.

"Arnie, I just got your note declining the Russian banquet invite…Jesus, you can't do this to me!"

"I thought I just had."

"Arnie, this is not optional. This is a Presidential command."

"Bullshit. I'm retired. I don't do State Banquets. I'm a naval officer, not a diplomat."

"I know what you are. But this thing is really important. They're bringing all the big hitters from Moscow, civilian and military. Not to mention their oil industry."

"What the hell's that got to do with me?"

"Nothing. 'Cept I want you there. Right next to me, keeping me posted. There's not one person in Washington knows the Russians better than you. You gotta be there. White tie and tails."

"I **never** wear white tie and tails."

"Okay. Okay. You can come in a tuxedo."

"Since I don't much want to look like a head waiter, or a goddamned violinist, I won't be wearing that either."

"Okay. Okay," said the President, sensing victory. "You can come in full-dress Navy uniform.

Matter of fact, I don't care if you turn up in jock-strap and spurs as long as you get here."

Arnold Morgan chuckled. But suddenly an edge crept back into his voice. "What topics concern you most?"

"The rise of the Russian Navy, for a start. The rebuilding of their submarine fleet in particular. And the exporting of submarines all over the world."

"How about their oil industry?"

"Well, that new deepwater tanker terminal in Murmansk cannot fail to be an issue," replied the President. "We're hoping they'll ship two million barrels a day from there direct to the USA in the next few years."

"And I guess you know the Russian President already has terrible goddamned problems transporting crude oil from the West Siberian Basin to Murmansk..." Arnold was thoughtful. And he added slowly, "...And you know how important that export trade is to them."

"And to us," said President Bedford.

"Give us a little distance with the towelheads, right?"

"That's why you gotta be at the banquet, Arnie. Starting with the private reception. Don't be late."

"Silver-tongued bastard," grunted Admiral Morgan. "All right, all right. We'll be there. Good morning, Mr. President."

Paul Bedford, who was well accustomed to the Admiral's excruciating habit of slamming down the phone without even bothering with "good-bye," considered this a very definite victory.

"Heh, heh, heh," he chortled, in the deserted Oval Office, "that little bit of intrigue on a global scale. That'll get the ole buzzard every time. But I'm sure glad he's coming."

Thus it was that Arnold and Kathy Morgan were now in attendance at the State Banquet for the Russians, gazing amiably at the long line of incoming guests entering the White House.

So many old friends and colleagues. It was like an Old Boys' reunion. Here was the Commander of the U.S. Navy SEALs, Admiral John Bergstrom, and his soignée new wife, Louisa-May, from Oxford, Mississippi; Harcourt Travis, the former Republican Secretary of State, with his wife, Sue. There was Admiral Scott Dunsmore, former CNO of the U.S. Navy, with his elegant wife, Grace. The reigning Chairman of the Joint Chiefs, General Tim Scannell, was with his wife, Beth.

Arnold shook hands with the Director of the National Security Agency, Admiral George Morris, and he greeted the new Vice President of the United States, the former Democratic Senator from Georgia, Bradford Harding, and his wife, Paige.

The Israeli Ambassador, General David Gavron, was there with his wife, Becky, plus, of course, the silver-haired Russian Ambassador to Washington, Tomas Yezhel, and the various Ambassadors from the United Kingdom, Canada, and Australia.

Arnold did not instantly recognize all of the top brass of the Russian contingent. But he could see the former Chairman of the Joint Chiefs, General Josh Paul, talking with the Russian Foreign Minister, Oleg Nalyotov.

He vaguely knew the Chief of the Russian Naval Staff, a grim-looking, ex-Typhoon-class ICBM Commanding Officer, Admiral Victor Kouts.

But Admiral Morgan's craggy face lit up when he spotted the towering figure of his old sparring partner, Russian Admiral Vitaly Rankov, now C-in-C Fleet, and Deputy Defense Minister.

"Arnold!" boomed the giant ex-Soviet international oarsman. "I had no idea you'd be here. They told me you'd retired."

Admiral Morgan grinned, and held out his hand. "Hi, Vitaly—they put you in charge of that junkyard Navy of yours yet? I heard they had."

"They did. Right now, Admiral, you're talking to the Deputy Defense Minister of Russia."

"Guess that'll suit you," replied the American. "Should provide ample scope for your natural flair for lies, evasions, and half-truths..."

The enormous Russian threw back his head and roared with laughter. "Now you be kind, Arnold," he said in his deep, rumbling baritone voice. "Otherwise I may not introduce you to this very beautiful lady standing at my side."

A tall, striking, dark-haired girl around half the Russian's age smiled shyly and held out her hand in friendship.

"This is Olga," said Admiral Rankov. "We were married last spring."

Admiral Morgan took her hand and asked if she spoke any English since his Russian was a little rusty. She shook her head, smiling, and the Admiral took the opportunity to turn back to Vitaly and shake his head sadly. "Too good for you, old buddy. A lot too good."

Again the huge Russian Admiral laughed joyfully, and he repeated the words he had used so often in his many dealings with the old Lion of the West Wing.

"You are a terrible man, Arnold Morgan. A truly terrible man." Then he spoke in rapid Russian to Mrs. Olga Rankov, who also burst out laughing.

"I understand we are sitting together," said Arnold. "And I don't believe you have actually met my wife, Kathy."

The Russian Admiral smiled and accepted Kathy's outstretched hand. "We have of course spoken many times on the telephone," he said. "But believe me, I never thought he'd persuade you to marry him." And, with a phrase more fittingly uttered in a St. Petersburg palace than a naval dockyard, Vitaly added with a short bow and a flourish, "The legend of your great beauty precedes you, Mrs. Morgan. I knew what to expect."

"Jesus, they've even taught him social graces," chuckled Arnold, carelessly ignoring the fact he was a bit short in that department himself. "Vitaly, old pal, seems we both got lucky in the past year. Not too bad for a couple of old Cold Warriors."

By now the guests were almost through the receiving line and a natural parting of the crowd established a wide entrance tunnel to the State Dining Room. Within a few moments, President and Maggie Bedford came through, escorting the Russian President and his wife to their dinner places, with all of the guests falling in, **line astern**, as Arnold somewhat jauntily told Vitaly.

The President took his place next to the former KGB researcher directly beneath the Lincoln portrait. Maggie Bedford showed the boss of all the Russians to his place next to her at the same table, and everyone stood until the hostess was seated.

The banquet, on the orders of Paul Bedford, was strictly American. "No caviar, or any of that restaurant nonsense," he had told the butler. "We start with Chesapeake oysters, we dine on New York sirloin steak, with Idaho potatoes, and we wrap it up with apple pie and American ice cream. There'll be two or three Wisconsin cheeses for anyone who wants them. California wines from the Napa Valley."

"Sir," the butler ventured, "not everyone likes oysters…"

"Tough," replied the President. "Russians love 'em. I've had 'em in Moscow and St. Petersburg. Anyone who can't eat 'em can have an extra shot of apple pie if they need it."

"Very well, sir," replied the butler, suspecting, from vast experience, that Arnold Morgan himself had been somehow in the shadows advising Paul Bedford. The tone, the curtness, the sureness. Morgan, not Bedford.

As it happened, there had been one short conversation when the Oval Office called Chevy Chase to check in on the menu content. "Give 'em American food," Arnold had advised. "Strictly American. Big A A A. The food this nation eats. We don't need to pretend sophistication to anyone, right?"

"Right."

And now, with the apple pie just arriving, the Strolling Strings, a well-known group of U.S. Army violinists, began to play at the rear section of the room. It was a short mini-concert, comprising all-American numbers, such as "Over There!"…"True Love" (from **High Society**)…a selection from **Oklahoma**…"Take Me Out to the

Ball Game"…and concluding with "God Bless America."

Finally the President rose and made a short speech extolling the virtues of the Russian President and the new and close trade links developing between the nations.

The guest of honor then stood and echoed many of the Presidents' statements, before responding with a formal toast "to the United States of America."

At this point the entire room stood up and proceeded toward the door that led out to the Blue Room, where coffee would be served, followed by entertainment in the East Room, and then dancing to the band of the United States Marines in the White House foyer.

Everyone was on the move now, except for one guest. Mikhallo Masorin, the senior minister from the vastness of Siberia, which fills one-twelfth of the land mass of the entire earth, had suddenly pitched forward and landed flat on his face right in front of Arnold, Vitaly, Olga, and Kathy.

In fact, the huge Russian Admiral had leaned forward to break his fall. But he was a fraction of a second too late. Mr. Masorin was down, twisted on his back now, his face puce in color, gasping for breath, both hands clutched to his throat, working his jaws, writhing in obvious fear and agony.

Someone shouted, **"Doctor! Right now!"**

Women gasped. Men came forward to see if they could help. Arnold Morgan noticed they were mostly Americans. He also considered Mr. Masorin was very nearly beyond help. He was desperately trying to breathe but could not do so.

By now two or three people were shouting, **"Heart attack! Come on, guys, let the doctor through..."**

Within a few minutes there were two doctors in attendance, but they could only bear witness to the death throes of the Siberian head honcho. One of them filled a syringe and unleashed a potent dose of something into Mr. Masorin's upper arm.

But there was no saving him. Mikhallo was gone, in rapid time, dead before the Navy stretcher bearers could get to him. Dead, right there on the floor of the State Dining Room in front of his own President and that of the United States.

President Bedford asked one of the doctors if the Siberian could be saved if they could get him to the Naval Hospital in Bethesda.

But the answer was negative. "Nothing could have saved this man, sir. He was gone in under four minutes. Some heart attacks are like that. There's nothing anyone can do."

Of course, only those few in the immediate vicinity realized that one of the Russian guests had actually died. More than 120 other dignitaries quickly became aware than someone had been

taken ill, but were unaware of the fateful consequences of the heart attack.

And the evening passed agreeably, although
the White House Press Office did feel obliged,
shortly before eleven p.m., to put out a general
press release that the Chief Minister for the Urals
Federal District, Mr. Mikhallo Masorin, had suffered a heart attack at the conclusion of a State
Banquet, and was found to be dead on arrival at
the United States Naval Hospital in Bethesda,
Maryland.

Admiral Morgan and Kathy made their fare-
wells a little after midnight, and Arnold's driver
picked them up at the main entrance and headed
northwest to Chevy Chase.

"Terrible about that poor Russian, wasn't
it?" said Kathy. "He was at the next table to us,
couldn't have been more than fifty years old. Must
have been a very bad heart attack..."

"Bullshit," replied Arnold, not looking up
from an early edition of the **Washington Post**.

"I'm sorry?" said Kathy, slightly perplexed.

"Bullshit," confirmed the Admiral. "That was
no heart attack. He was writhing around on the
floor, opening and shutting his mouth like a goddamned goldfish."

"I know he was, darling. But the doctor **said**
it was a heart attack. I heard him."

"What the hell does he know?"

"Oh, I am so sorry. It entirely slipped my memory I was escorting the eminent cardiovascular surgeon and universal authority Arnold Morgan."

Arnold looked up from his newspaper, grinning at his increasingly sassy wife. "Kathy," he said, formally, "whatever killed Masorin somehow shut down his lungs instantly. He could not draw breath. The guy suffocated, fighting for air, which you probably noticed was plentiful in the State Dining Room. But it was beyond his reach. Heart attacks don't do that."

"Oh," said Kathy. "Well, what does?"

"A bullet, correctly aimed. A combat knife, correctly delivered. Certain kinds of poison."

"But there was no blood anywhere. And anyway, why should the CIA or the FBI or whatever want to get rid of an important guest at a White House banquet?"

"I have no idea, my darling," said Arnold. "But I believe someone did. And I'll be mildly surprised if we don't find out before too long that Mikhallo Masorin was murdered last night. Right here in Washington, DC."

CHAPTER ONE

**0830, WEDNESDAY,
SEPTEMBER 15, 2010**

Lt. Commander Jimmy Ramshawe, assistant to the Director of the National Security Agency in Fort Meade, Maryland, had both his feet and his antennae up. Lounging back in his swivel chair, shoes on the desk, he was staring at an item on the front page of the **Washington Post**.

TOP RUSSIAN OFFICIAL

DROPS DEAD IN WHITE HOUSE

**Siberian political chief
suffers fatal heart attack**

"Poor bastard," muttered the American-born but Australian-sounding Intelligence officer. "That's a hell of a way to go—in the middle of the bloody State Dining Room, right in front of two Presidents. Still, by the look of this, he didn't have time to be embarrassed."

He read on, skimming through the brief biography that always accompanies such a death. The forty-nine-year-old Mikhallo Masorin had been a tough, uncompromising Siberian boss, a man who stood up for his people and their shattered communist dream. Here was a man who had brought real hope to this 4,350-mile-long land-mass of bleak and terrible beauty, snow fields, and seven time zones—one-third of all the land in the Northern Hemisphere.

Mikhallo was adored in Siberia. He was a politician who stood up fiercely against Moscow, frequently reminding his Russian rulers that the oil upon which the entire economy was built was Siberian. And it was the natural property of the Siberian people. And he wanted more money for it, from Central Government. Not for himself, but for his people.

The Urals Federal District is one of the three Siberian "kingdoms" that make up the huge area. The others are the Siberian Federal District, thousands and thousands of square miles between the Yenisei River and the Lena River, and then the Russian Far East. The Urals Federal District is easily the most important because that's where most of the oil fields are located.

Mikhallo Masorin was a towering figure, standing stark upon those desolate plains of Western Siberia, the freezing place that the locals claim was "forgotten by the Creator," but beneath which lie the largest oil fields on earth.

And now Mikhallo was gone, and Jimmy Ramshawe's hackles rose a lot higher than his shoes on the desk. "Streuth," he said quietly, taking a swig of his hot black coffee. "Wouldn't be surprised if a bloody lot of people were glad he died. None of 'em Siberian."

At times like this, Lt. Commander Ramshawe's instincts of suspicion, mistrust, misgivings, and downright disbelief sprang to the fore. And a few harsh lessons issued to him by the Big Man fought their way to the front of his mind…**whenever a major politician with a lot of enemies dies, check it out…never trust a goddamned Russian…and never believe anything is beyond them, because it's not…the KGB lives, trust me.**

"Wouldn't be the biggest shock in the world if the old bastard calls on this one," he said, refilling his coffee cup. And he was right about that.

Three minutes later his private line rang. Jimmy always thought it betrayed an irritable, impatient tone to its modern bell when the Big Man was on the line. And he was right about that too.

"Jimmy, you read the **Washington Post** yet? Front page, the dead Siberian?" Arnold Morgan's tone reflected that of the telephone.

"Yessir."

"Well, first of all, you can forget all about that heart attack crap."

"Sir?"

"And stop calling me 'sir.' I'm retired."

"Could've fooled me, sir."

Arnold Morgan chuckled. For the past few years he had treated Jimmy Ramshawe almost like a son, not simply because the young Aussie-American was the best Intelligence officer he had ever met, but also because he both knew and liked his father, a former Australian Navy Admiral and currently a high-ranking airline official in New York.

Jimmy was engaged to the surf goddess Jane Peacock, a student and the daughter of the Australian Ambassador to Washington, and Arnold was very fond of both families. But in Jimmy he had a soul mate, a much younger man, whose creed was suspicion, thoroughness, tireless determination to investigate, always prepared to play a hunch, and a total devotion to the United States, where Jimmy had been brought up.

He might have been engaged to a goddess, but Jimmy Ramshawe believed Arnold Morgan was God. Several years ago Admiral Morgan himself had been Director of the National Security Agency, and ever since had continued to consider himself in overall command of the place.

This suited Admiral George Morris, the current Director, extremely well, because there was no better advice available than that of Admiral Morgan. And the system suited everyone extremely well: the ex–Carrier Battle Group Commander

George Morris, because Arnold's input made him look even smarter, and Jimmy because he trusted Arnold's instincts better than he trusted his own.

When Admiral Morgan called the NSA, Fort Meade trembled. His growl echoed through Crypto City, as the Military Intelligence hub was called. And, essentially, that was the way Arnold liked it.

"Jimmy, I was at the banquet, standing only about ten feet from the Siberian when he hit the deck. He went down like he'd been shot, which he plainly hadn't. But I watched him die, rolling back and forth, fighting for breath, just like his lungs had quit on him. Wasn't like any heart attack I ever saw..."

"How many you seen?"

"Shut up, Jimmy. You sound like Kathy. And listen...I want you very quietly to find out where the goddamned body is, where it's going, and whether there's going to be an autopsy."

"Then what?"

"Never mind 'then what.' Just take step one, and call me back." Slam. Down phone.

"Glad to notice the old bastard's mellowing," muttered Jimmy. "Still, Kathy says that's how he's talked to at least two Presidents. So I guess I can't complain."

He picked up his other phone line and told the operator to connect him to Bill Fogarty down at FBI headquarters. Three minutes later the top Washington field agent was on the case, and twenty minutes after that Bill was back with news of the fate of the corpse of Mikhallo Masorin.

"Jimmy, I walked into a goddamned hornet's nest. Seems the Russians want to take the body directly back to Moscow tomorrow afternoon. But the Navy is not having it. Masorin is officially in their care while the body's in the USA. He died on American soil, and they're insisting the formalities are carried out here, including, if necessary, an autopsy."

"What do the Russians think about that?"

"Not a whole hell of a lot," said Bill Fogarty. "They are saying Masorin was an official guest of the President in the United States, and they should be afforded the diplomatic courtesy of treating his death as if it happened in their own embassy, where he was staying. They want to take the body home as soon as possible."

"Will they get their way?"

"I don't think so. Under the law, a foreign national who dies in the USA is subject to the correct procedures of the United States. If something has happened to a high-ranking Russian official, it is within the rights of the United States to demand the most exhaustive inquiries into the cause of death until we are satisfied that every avenue has been explored. Even then, the body is released only on our say-so."

"Sounds like the Russian President is asking for a major favor."

"And some people here at HQ think they're gonna get it. But I still think the will of the U.S. Navy will prevail. And they have the body still at the hospital at Bethesda."

"Bill, I'm gonna make one phone call. And I have a hunch it's going to end all speculation. After all, anyone who was in the White House at that time must be a suspect if there is a question of foul play. And that must include the President and all his agents and officials. That body's not going anywhere for a while, except the city morgue."

Lt. Commander Ramshawe thanked Bill Fogarty and immediately called the Naval Hospital, leaving a message for the duty officer to call him right back at the NSA. That took two full minutes, and it established that the body of the number one political commissar in all of Siberia would be leaving for the morgue inside the hour. An autopsy would be carried out this afternoon. The Russians were, apparently, not pleased.

Jimmy hit the buttons to Chevy Chase.

"Morgan, speak."

"Sir, the body of Mr. Masorin will be at the city morgue in a couple of hours. The Russians are trying to kick up a fuss and get permission to remove it back to Moscow. But that's obviously not going to happen."

"Doesn't surprise me any, Jimmy. Tell the pathologist we're looking for poison of some kind. I'm damn sure it wasn't a heart attack."

"You think one of our guys got rid of him?"

"Well, that's what it looks like. But you never know with the Russians. A short, sharp murder in the White House gives 'em marvelous cover. Because they can feign outrage at this disgraceful breach in American security, while they make their getaway home, to that god-awful country of theirs."

"You mean they might have killed their own man?"

"It's happened before, both in and beyond the old Soviet reign. But let's not get excited. We'll wait 'til we hear the autopsy report. Then we'll take a very careful look...hey, well done, kid...but I gotta go. I'd better talk to the Chief."

4:00 P.M., SAME DAY

Lt. Commander Ramshawe's veteran black Jaguar pulled into the parking lot behind the city morgue, and headed straight into one of the VIP reserved spaces. This was an old ruse taught him long ago by Admiral Morgan...**no one, ever, wants to tangle with a high-ranking officer from the NSA. Park wherever the hell you like. Anyone doesn't like it, tell 'em to call me.**

Inside the building, the area where the autopsy had been conducted was busy, despite the fact the FBI had denied the Russians entry. There were two U.S. Navy guards on the door, three White House agents outside in the corridor, and the Chief Medical Officer from Bethesda was in attendance. The coroner, Dr. Louis Merloni, was there, and the autopsy was carried out by the resident clinical pathologist, Dr. Larry Madeiros. No details of the examination had yet been released.

Jimmy showed his NSA pass to the guards and was admitted immediately. Inside he said firmly, "Dr. Madeiros?"

And the pathologist walked over and held out his hand.

"Lt. Commander Ramshawe, NSA," said Jimmy. "I would like to talk to you for a few minutes in private."

"No problem, sir."

They walked to an adjoining office across the wide examination room, and almost before they had time to sit down, Jimmy Ramshawe said, "Okay, Doc, gimme the cause of death."

"Mikhallo Masorin died of asphyxiation, sir."

"You mean some bastard throttled him?"

"No. I don't mean that. I mean he was given a substance, a poison of some type, which caused the transmission of nerve impulses from the brain to the muscles to be seriously impaired. In the end to the point of limpness. When this process hits the chest muscles, breathing stops."

"Jesus Christ."

"This diagnosis tallies with the accounts of the two doctors who attended Mr. Masorin. The victim was wide awake and aware of what was happening, until he lost consciousness."

"You don't think he was poisoned by something in his food?"

"No. I found a very fine puncture mark on the back of his neck, right side. I think we will find he was injected with the poison through that hole."

"Do we know what the poison was yet?"

"No idea. All the bodily fluids are still in the lab. That's blood cell counts, bone marrow, liver, kidneys, and all biochemical substances found in the body. It'll take a while, but I'm pretty sure we're going to find something very foreign deep inside that corpse."

"The bloody corpse was very foreign," said Jimmy cheerfully. "That makes the poison amazingly foreign."

"Unless it was American," replied the doctor, archly.

"Well, yes. I suppose so," said Jimmy. "When will you know?"

"You can call me on my cell at 10 o'clock. I'll let you know in confidence what we've found. Thereafter the report will be issued first thing tomorrow morning to the hospital and medical officer of record in Bethesda, and then to the FBI and the White House agents.

10:00 P.M., SAME DAY
AUSTRALIAN EMBASSY
WASHINGTON, DC

Jimmy excused himself from the Ambassador's dinner table and walked into the next room, then punched in the numbers on his cell phone that would connect him to Dr. Larry Madeiros.

"Hello, sir. It was curare, and quite a sizeable shot of it. A most deadly poison originating from South America."

"Kew-rar-ee," said Jimmy. "What the hell is it?"

"Well, curare is a generic name for many different poisons made from the bark and roots of forest vines," said the doctor. "The main one's called Pareira, and the lab technicians here think that's the one. Five hundred micrograms of that stuff will cause death in a few minutes. And Mr. Masorin had more than that."

"Jesus. And this poison could have shut down the transmission of nerve impulses from the brain, like you said?"

"Absolutely. This is the classic poison that will unfailingly achieve that. I've checked it out briefly, and it seems it's a favorite of the professional assassin."

"Steady, Doc, old mate. This was a White House State Banquet. There weren't any professional assassins walking around there."

"As you wish," said Dr. Madeiros formally. "But that is very much the history of this particular poison."

"Well, thanks anyway, Doc. You've been a big help."

Jimmy clicked off, and instantly dialed Admiral Morgan's number.

"You were dead right, sir. Someone hit Masorin with a lethal shot of poison injected into his neck. More than five hundred micrograms, according to the pathologist..."

"Know what it was?"

"Yup. Curare, a special type called Pareira."

"Wait a minute, Jimmy. I got a book of poisons here. I was waiting for your call. Lemme check this out...yeah, right, curare, a known poison since the sixteenth century, a gummy substance used to tip hunting arrowheads by Indian tribes up the Amazon River in South America.

"Says here it comes from the region now known as Peru, Ecuador, Brazil, and Colombia... Sir Walter Raleigh returned home in 1595 with the first sample of curare ever seen in England. I guess it's kinda well known, but rare."

"Sir, I'll alert Admiral Morris what's going on. And then I guess we'll let the rest of the investigation take its course. It's not really our business anymore, is it? Civilian matter now, right?"

"Exactly so, Jimmy. But I'm sure as hell glad we know what's going on. No heart attack. Murder."

From an official point of view, inquests, coroners, and autopsies are a pain in the rear end. They are inevitably public and must be entered in the public record. Thus it was that on the morning of Thursday, September 16, the FBI announced to the world that the death of the Siberian Minister, Mikhallo Masorin, was indeed suspicious.

Traces of the lethal poison, curare, had been found in the body, and the investigators were now treating the case as a murder inquiry, since suicide was out of the question.

MURDER IN THE WHITE HOUSE, bellowed the **New York Post**. SIBERIA BOSS ASSASSINATED thundered the **Washington Post**. All of it on the front page, in specially reserved end-of-the-world typeface.

And while the maelstrom of a frenzied media swirled around the Russian visitors, the President's Aeroflot state airliner took off right on time for Moscow from Andrews Air Force Base on Thursday evening. The body of Mikhallo Masorin was not on board.

For some reason, best known to neurotic news editors, the U.S. media, including the twenty-four-hour news channels, leapt to the conclusion that somehow an American had been responsible for the Siberian's death. Perhaps it was just too farfetched that the Russians would choose the White House as a theater to assassinate one of their own.

The American media, to a man, jumped on the story as if an American-based terrorist, possibly a Chechen rebel in disguise, had fired some kind of poison dart into the neck of Mr. Masorin, who had subsequently died while dining with the President of the United States and 150 of his closest friends.

The media grilled the FBI, grilled the Washington Police Department, grilled the White House Press Office. It took three entire days before it truly dawned on them all that no one had the slightest idea who had killed Mr. Masorin, and that there were no Chechen rebels in attendance at the State Banquet.

Of course they were not to know of the massive rift that now existed between the President of the United States and the President of Russia, who had almost begged Paul Bedford to allow him to take the body home to Moscow.

It was not within the realm of Russian understanding that the Boss of the United States could not do anything he pleased. The finer points of a Western democracy still eluded them, that when it comes to the absolute crunch, the law of the land remains sacrosanct. Especially when all the great institutions of law and order are certain of the correct procedures. Not to mention the United States Navy.

Mikhallo's body was going nowhere until the investigation was complete. Someone had plainly murdered him. Possibly inside the White House. And until that someone was identified, the corpse of the Siberian Minister was staying right here in the home of the brave.

Jimmy Ramshawe was thoughtful. He sat in his colossally untidy office, surrounded by mounds of paper, all in neat piles, so many of them, well, they crowded out his desk, clogged his computer table, and turned the carpeted floor space into a death trap.

There was one dominant thought in his mind... **the Big Man thinks the bloody Ruskies killed Masorin in the White House because no one would ever dream they would pull something off quite like that.**

"I know that's what he thinks," he murmured. "He has not said it, but he was sure as hell the first person to suspect murder. And he's never once suggested an American may have been responsible."

What Jimmy knew was that the Russian President would shortly be landing in Moscow and that his public relations machine would be full of venom. All aimed at the lapsed, decadent security arrangements in the United States...**which has somehow caused the death of our beloved brother, sorry comrade, Mikhallo Masorin.**

"And a right crock of shit that is," he muttered, a bit louder in the empty room, with all the inherent charm of an Aussie swagman. "I'm with the Big Man on this one. And I consider it's in the interest of the United States of America to find out what the hell's going on...I'd better go and see the boss."

Admiral George Morris, a portly ex–Naval Battle Group Commander with the appearance of a lovesick teddy bear, but a spine of blue-twisted steel, listened attentively.

He scarcely betrayed even a flicker of surprise when Jimmy delivered his punch line..."Sir, I think Admiral Morgan believes the Russians bumped old Mikhallo off, right there in the bloody State Dining Room."

"Yes, he does," replied Admiral Morris. "So do I. Want some hot coffee?"

Jimmy blinked. "Yes to the coffee, sir. But the Big Man has not yet made any accusation—how do you know what he thinks?"

"He just told me, 'bout fifteen minutes ago."

"Streuth."

"Jimmy, Admiral Morgan knows more about the Russian mind-set than any man I ever met. And I've known him for over thirty years, most of them as a pretty close friend. And there is one view of his which ought never to be discounted."

"What's that, sir?"

"That even after President Reagan forced them to take down the Berlin Wall, even after President Reagan made them dismantle the old Soviet

Union, a coupla years after he'd gone, in 1991, all of the old instincts for brutal central control exist in the psyche of Russia's new leaders.

"It's going to take decades to get rid of them. Barbarous actions, poisoning and assassinations, all aimed at crushing dissent, stamping out free expression. Drastic measures, and they all thrive today in Russia. It's an integral part of an insidious political culture.

"Remember, Jimmy, it was Stalin himself who said very simply, 'If you have a man who represents a problem, get rid of the man. Then there's no problem.' Both Arnie and I believe Mikhallo Masorin was the embodiment of just such a problem. Would he really secede from Russian rule and take his oil with him?"

"Not anymore he wouldn't," said Jimmy, "and no bloody error."

"Both Arnold and I would like you to bear that in mind during the course of your investigations. And by the way, we would like you to continue with them, on a full-time basis for the next couple of weeks. We really ought to find out what the hell's going on."

"Christ, sir. Mind if I take a swig of the coffee. That's a bloody lot to digest."

Admiral Morris smiled. "Take a look at some of the really suspicious deaths that have taken place in the past, say, forty years. And you might start with Georgi Markov."

"Who's he, sir?"

"He was a Soviet expert with the BBC in London—a good journalist with excellent contacts behind the Iron Curtain. He wrote some really hair-raising stuff about the Soviets and the KGB. I believe he was a good friend of Alexander Solzhenitsyn. He was a real thorn in the side of officials in the Soviet embassy in London..."

"And what happened to him?"

"Why don't you go and look it up accurately. Late seventies. I remember it, but not well enough."

"Righto, sir. I'll get right on it."

Lt. Commander Ramshawe retreated to his lair and moved into the Internet. It took him ten minutes to find a reference...**Georgi Markov, Bulgarian dissident working for the BBC... assassinated on a London street, 1978...later discovered to have been jabbed by an umbrella, its steel tip containing a deadly poison, almost certainly curare.**

A later article by the former KGB colonel and renowned British double agent Oleg Gordievsky stated categorically that Markov had been assassinated by a KGB agent. And what's more, that assassination was carried out with the approval of the head of the KGB, Yuri Andropov, later the General Secretary of the Soviet Union.

"Streuth," said Jimmy Ramshawe for the second time in a half hour. "One bloody surprise after another."

He trawled through all manner of disappearances, of politicians, dissidents, and others deemed whatever the Russian is for pain in the ass, before alighting on the big one...so big it forever blighted the name of the Russian leadership, and it did not even work.

Viktor Yushchenko, the opposition leader in the infamous Ukraine election of 2004, the hugely popular pro-European who was spectacularly poisoned but never died in the September before the election.

His face, hideously pockmarked and disfigured, was shown to the entire world, just a few weeks after he had looked perfectly normal. The murder attempt had taken place at a political dinner with Ukraine security services, and the evidence of poisoning by dioxin was overwhelming. At least it was considered so by the doctors who treated Viktor in Vienna. They asserted the levels of dioxin in his blood were more than one thousand times above normal.

It was also obvious that his stance as a pro-European, pro-democracy candidate was a serious danger to Moscow, with its love of state control. Here was a man, and here was a problem. And Joseph Stalin himself had instructed them how to be rid of it. Viktor Yushchenko was lucky not to have died, and everyone knew the new Russian secret police, the FSB, had been responsible for this attempted murder.

It was also a timely reminder that the old, vicious KGB methods of elimination were alive and well in modern Russia. Not just alive, and not just well, but ruthlessly woven into the fabric of Russian politics, where they've been since the 1920s, when the KGB first built their laboratories to develop special poisons to use against dissidents.

Jimmy Ramshawe was gratified to note that Viktor Yushchenko eventually became President of the Ukraine, and that his health slowly returned to normal. But his ordeal demonstrated once and for all that modern ideas of political freedom and human rights have never taken root in Russia, and probably never will.

At least, that was the view of Admiral Arnold Morgan and his cohort Admiral George Morris. "And who the bloody hell am I to argue with those two?" muttered Jimmy. "They got me. The ole Ruskies most definitely took a pop at Mikhallo, and this time they didn't fuck it up."

By now, Admiral Morris had left for a meeting at the Pentagon, and Jimmy elected to spend the rest of the afternoon trying to find out just what Mr. Masorin had done; something so bad the heavies from Moscow had decided to take him out, right after dinner in the White House, damn nearly in full view of the entire world.

Jimmy Ramshawe picked up his telephone and asked to be put through to CIA headquarters in Langley, Virginia, extension 4601.

"Hi, Mary, is Lenny in this afternoon?"

"He sure is, sir. You want to speak with him?"

"Would you just ask him if I can come and see him, right now?"

"Hold a moment...yes, that will be fine. Mr. Suchov said the usual place, say, forty-five minutes?"

"Perfect, Mary. Tell him I'll be there."

Six minutes later Lt. Commander Ramshawe's black Jaguar was ripping down the Spellman Parkway heading south. He cut onto the Beltway at Exit 22 and aimed the car west, counterclockwise, and stayed right on the great highway that rings Washington, DC, until it crossed the Potomac River on the American Legion Memorial Bridge.

Seventeen miles along the Beltway had taken him fifteen minutes, and now he picked up the Georgetown Pike for two miles, straight into the CIA headquarters main gate, where a young field officer from the Russian desk met him and accompanied him to the parking area near the auditorium.

Jimmy thanked him and walked through to the CIA's tranquil memorial garden, pausing just to gaze at the simple message carved into fieldstone at the edge of the pond—**"In remembrance of those whose unheralded efforts served a grateful nation."**

Like most senior Intelligence officers, a place in Jimmy's soul was touched by those words—and visions instantly stood before him of grim, dark streets in Moscow or the old East Berlin or Bucharest, of men working for the United States, alone, in the most terrible danger, stalked by the stony-faced agents of the KGB. Always the KGB, with their hired assassins, knives, and garottes.

"I just hope the nation is bloody grateful, that's all," he said as he walked in the sunlight toward the blue-painted seat by the pond where he always met Leonid Suchov, perhaps the most brilliant double agent the West ever had.

He smiled when he thought of Lenny. A stocky little bear of a man, who walked lightly on the balls of his feet, Lenny hardly ever stopped smiling, and would slide a knife between your ribs as soon as look at you. Which was the principal reason he was still alive and not buried somewhere in the bowels of Lubyanka. Even Lenny had lost count of the KGB agents he had somehow eluded. Or worse.

Lenny was Rumanian by birth, but lost both of his parents, schoolteachers in Bucharest, when he was twelve. Typecast as dissidents, they were grabbed by KGB thugs and never seen again. Lenny, however, had a major talent to go with his profound hatred of the Communist Party, Moscow, the Iron Curtain, and everything to do with that monstrous regime.

Lenny was a champion wrestler. Never quite good enough to win an Olympic medal himself, he became a world-class coach and was part of the team that helped steer the great Vasile Andrei to the Greco-Roman heavyweight gold medal for Rumania at the Los Angeles Games in 1984.

For aficionados, the name Andrei still brings curt, knowing nods of respect. In each of his four bouts in L.A., the mighty Rumanian defeated his opponent in less than four and a half minutes, an almost unprecedented feat of strength and skill.

And Lenny was right there heading up the coaching squad. The only difference was, the others went home to Rumania, whereas Lenny Suchov was spirited out of the Olympic village and then flown in a United States Navy helicopter to Vandenberg Air Force Base north of Santa Barbara, and thence to Washington.

His disappearance was of course a huge embarrassment to the Rumanian Olympic authorities, and exquisitely so to staff members of the KGB, who had recruited Leonid many years before as a full-fledged spy, passing information directly from any Western city in which the Rumanian wrestling team competed.

They were not, of course, to know the jolly little wrestling giant, with the handshake like a mechanical digger, had been working diligently on behalf of the CIA for twenty years. And his eminence in Rumanian and Soviet sports circles afforded him untold privileges at the tables of the most powerful party officials behind the Iron Curtain.

He inflicted untold damage on all the Eastern European secret police services, exposing their agents, their networks, their radio bands, codes, addresses, and phone numbers to the CIA field chiefs. He was directly responsible for at least fifty assassinations conducted by the CIA in those brutal days of the Cold War.

And to each victim he drank a silent toast to Emile and Anna Suchov, his far-lost parents. And no one ever suspected him. As a matter of fact, neither the Soviets nor the Rumanians suspected him, even after he had defected in Los Angeles.

They even issued a statement confirming that Leonid Suchov had left the Rumanian Olympic organization in order to marry an American and take up a private coaching career with one of the major American universities. They expressed their gratitude for all that he had done, and wished him well in the future.

Meanwhile, back at CIA headquarters the beloved wrestling coach from Bucharest was installed as deputy head of the Russian desk, at one of the biggest salaries ever paid to a former agent.

And here he was at last, moving swiftly around the pond, light on his feet, a big smile of greeting across his swarthy features.

Christ, he still walks like a pooftah, thought Jimmy. **But I'd bloody hate to remind him.**

"Jimmy Ramshawe! Where you been?" Lenny's smile lit up the entire memorial garden.

"Stuck at that factory in Maryland," he replied. "Trying to earn an honest living."

"There's no honesty in our line of business," said the Rumanian. "You know that. I know that. We just gotta stay cheerful, hah?"

Jimmy grinned. "By the way, my dad sends his best," he said, producing the first white lie of the day. Admiral Ramshawe was very fond of Lenny, having known him for several years, since the Sydney Olympics, when both men were official guests of the Australian government, Lenny for infinitely more sinister reasons than Ramshawe senior.

"Okay, Jimmy, now you tell me what you need. As if I don't know. You wanna talk about the late Mikhallo Masorin, right?"

"How the hell did you know?"

"Mostly because I guess by now you have worked out the Russians took him out, not the Americans, eh?"

"How do you know that?"

"Jimmy…this is my business. You didn't believe that heart attack nonsense, did you? Right at the beginning?"

"Well, no. But only because Admiral Morgan told me he didn't believe it either."

"Phew! That Admiral. He's something, right? Doesn't miss a trick."

"Really, Lenny, I've come to ask if you have any idea why they wanted him dead?"

"They've wanted him dead for months and months, Jimmy. I'm surprised he lived so long."

"You are?"

"Of course. To them he is one of the most dangerous men in the entire country, a perceived enemy of the state, a threat to the Moscow government."

"You mean some kind of a traitor?"

"No. Some kind of a patriot...come on, let's walk for a while. I don't like static conversations. Someone might be listening."

Both men stood up and walked slowly to the edge of the pond. "Jimmy, do you have any idea how important the oil industry is to Russia?"

"Well, I know it's pretty big."

"Jimmy, Russia holds the world's largest natural gas reserves, and it's the second largest oil exporter on Earth. Only Saudi Arabia can pump more crude onto the world market. The World Bank thinks Russia's oil and gas sector accounts for twenty-five percent of GDP while employing only one percent of the population. Russia has proven oil reserves of more than sixty billion barrels. That's three million a day for sixty years."

"Beautiful. But what's that got to do with poor old Mikhallo being hit by a poisoned dart from a bloody blowpipe?"

"Everything. Because darn near every barrel of that oil is in Siberia. And old Mikhallo is effectively the boss of the western end of Siberia where nearly all of it is. In the West Siberian Basin just east of the Urals, that's Mikhallo's land.

"And out there they think he's God, and he's sick to death of the enormous taxation levied by Moscow on what he calls **his** people's oil. He's sick of Moscow, period. And he's sick of the price gouging, the way Moscow wants all the oil cheap, cheaper, and cheapest. Worse yet, the major oil companies and the other political leaders in Siberia also thought Masorin was God.

"And Russia lives in fear that a man like him will one day rise up and take it all away, and the country will collapse economically. And remember, Siberia has another ready market right on their doorstep, China. And Beijing will pay much more generously for the product. Moscow faces ruin if these Siberian bosses, both oil and political, cannot be brought into line."

"Lenny, those are what you might call bloody high stakes."

"Jimmy, those are the highest stakes on this planet. And I'm assuming you understand the pipeline problems?"

"Not really, but I guess they have a pretty damn big one pumping all that oil over the biggest land mass in the world."

"It's a truly colossal system, Jim. The biggest in the world. The Southern Druzhba—that's the export line west of Moscow—runs oil right across the Ukraine, north into Prague, and southwest across Hungary and Croatia to the Adriatic oil port of Omisa. The same system branches to Odessa on the Black Sea and the Caspian.

"There is a branch farther north, the Baltic Pipeline System, running oil to the ports of Butinge and the new tanker terminal at Primorsk on the Gulf of Finland. Siberian oil flows everywhere, across Estonia, Latvia, and Lithuania.

"And the new northern pipeline all the way to the new terminal at Murmansk up on the Barents Sea is one of the engineering marvels of the modern world. Right out of the West Siberian Basin, it's over twelve hundred miles long through terrible country, mountains and marshes, ice fields, and shocking climate."

"And then some bloody upstart threatens to turn the tap off, right?"

"You always had a way with words, young Ramshawe." Lenny grinned. "But you're right. Some bastard suddenly threatened to turn the tap off. Mikhallo may not have been absolutely serious, but Moscow has no sense of humor at the best of times."

"And didn't I read somewhere about the row over the Far Eastern pipeline?"

"You sure did. The key to that is the Siberian city of Angarsk—that's a place on Lake Baikal to the north of Mongolia. It used to be the end of the oil pipeline, but then they extended it, right around the lake for twenty-five hundred miles to the Siberian port of Nakhodka on the Sea of Japan, and a new market, okay?"

"Gottit," said Jimmy. "More big profits for Moscow, right?"

"Right. But somewhat sneakily, the East Siberian government moved ahead with a fifteen-hundred-mile new pipeline directly into the inland Chinese oil city of Daqing. The Chinese built and paid for a huge length of it, and the Siberians pretended it was all part of the general expansion of the Russian oil industry. But if push came to shove, we know who would control, and service, that particular stretch of pipeline.

"The fact is the Siberians now have a direct line into one of China's comparatively rare, but extremely well organized, oil complexes, with excellent pipelines to transport the product everywhere. And China will take damn near all the oil it can get its hands on. And they'll pay the price. That scares Moscow."

Lt. Commander Ramshawe was thoughtful. "I suppose," he said slowly, "it's kind of a natural marriage. China's got a zillion people and hardly any resources, Siberia's got a zillion resources and no people."

"Precisely so," replied Lenny Suchov. "And no one knows quite what would happen if the Siberians, who would most certainly have been led by the brilliant but dead Mikhallo Masorin, declared autonomy from Moscow, and elected to go their own way. Russia would be virtually powerless. You can't fight a modern war in a place that big. And anyway Russia does not have the resources for that kind of operation.

"Siberia could shut down the oil for a while, and get along just fine. Moscow, and Russia with it, would perish. You still wonder why Mr. Masorin is no longer alive?"

"I sure as hell don't. In fact it's a bloody miracle he lasted so long."

"Considering the mind-set of his enemies, that is exactly so," said Lenny. "Moscow could easily negotiate a better deal for Siberia and make everyone happy. But the Russian government is no good at that. They see a problem and instantly try to smash it. Kicking down the door, even if it's unlocked."

"And what will happen now?"

"Who knows? But I imagine there is seething anger in Siberia. They will have guessed what happened to their leader, and I imagine they will begin to level huge demands on Moscow. Always with the unspoken threat...**whose oil is it**

anyway, and do we need interference from Central Government in Moscow?

"They will surely point out that all the other independent states from the old communist block are thriving, why not us? **And we're bigger than all the rest put together, including yourselves.**"

"Jesus. Moscow will not love that," said Jimmy, unnecessarily.

"No, Jimmy, they will not. They most certainly will not."

The two men continued their slow walk around the memorial garden, in silence. Eventually Lenny said, "Have you finished with me? We just took delivery of some surveillance film from the White House. There was a camera on that dinner and we might just see who delivered the fateful attack on Mr. Masorin."

"Probably just one of their goons," said Jimmy. "And it's dollars to doughnuts he's safely tucked up in bed in Moscow by now."

"I agree. But we may recognize him. Or I may. And we'll slip his name into one of our little black books, hah?"

"Yeah, I guess so. But thanks, Lenny, for the geopolitical lesson. It's bloody unbelievable how much trouble the oil industry causes, eh?"

"Especially since it's mostly owned by despots, hooligans, and villains…"

Jimmy chuckled, and then, almost miraculously, his guide from the Russian desk arrived to walk him back to the parking lot.

"Bye, Lenny, stay in touch."

And Jimmy watched the double agent from Bucharest, on little spring-heeled steps, still smiling as he made his way back into one of the most secretive buildings on Earth.

0800 (LOCAL), MONDAY, SEPTEMBER 20 WESTERN SIBERIA

Winter had arrived early on the great marshy plains above the oil fields. And the road up to Noyabrsk was already becoming treacherous. Two hours out of the industrial oil town of Surgut, heading north, a mere four hundred miles south of the Arctic Circle, the huge articulated truck from the OJSC oil giant had its windshield wipers flailing against the vicious snow flurries that would soon turn the ice-bound landscape milk white.

Temperatures had crashed during the night and the great wheels of the truck thundered over ice crystals already forming on the highway. In the passenger seat, Jaan Valuev, President of the OJSC Surgutneftegas Corporation, sat grimly staring into the desolate emptiness ahead, clutching his arctic mittens.

Jaan was a Siberian by birth, a billionaire by choice, from Surgut way back south on the banks of the Ob, the fourth largest river in the world. His mission today was secret, and he traveled in the truck to preserve his anonymity. Out here in the purpose-built dormitory towns that surround the oil rigs, the icicles have ears and the clapboard walls have eyes.

Jaan Valuev wanted no one to know of his presence in Noyabrsk. So far only the driver knew he was on his way, except for Boris and Sergei. And the big truck kept going, fast, the speedometer hovering at 120 kilometers, great tracks of pine and birch forest occasionally flashing past, but mostly just bleak white flatland, bereft of human life, the icy wilderness of the West Siberian Basin.

They came rolling into Noyabrsk shortly before nine a.m. The weather, if anything, had worsened. The sky was the darkest shade of gray, with lowering thunderheads. The temperature was–10C, and malicious snow flurries sliced down the streets. The locals call them **bozyomkas**, and, as **bozyomkas** go, these were on the far side of venomous.

They say there is no cold on this earth quite like that of Siberia, and those gusts, 50 mph straight off the northern ice cap, howling in off the Kara Sea, shrieked down the estuary of the Ob River and straight into downtown Noyabrsk. That's cold.

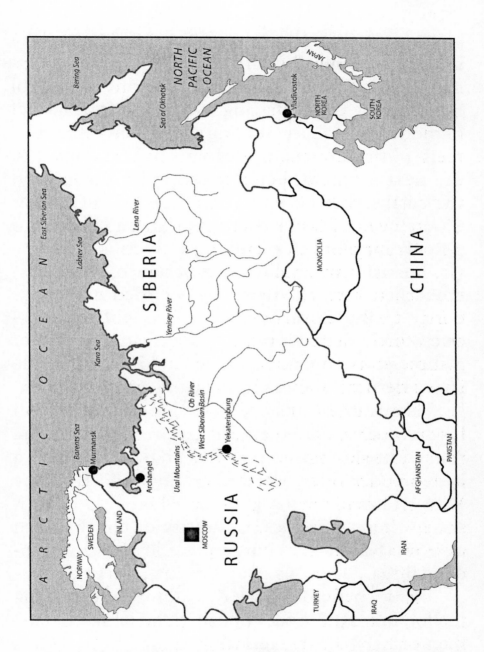

Russia, showing the dividing line of the Ural Mountains. To the east lie the vast plains of Siberia, all the way to the Pacific Ocean.

In the wild lands beyond the town, men were already struggling with the drilling pipes, man-handling the writhing hydraulics, trying to control them, heavy boots striving to grip the frozen steel of the screw-drill rig, forcing the pipe into the steel teeth of the connector mechanism that joins it to the next segment, lancing two miles down, into the earth. Jaan's corporation alone, OJSC, drills ninety of these wells every year and accounts for 13 percent of all Russian oil production.

The fifty-two-year-old Siberian oil boss dis-embarked from the truck and nodded his thanks curtly to the driver, who had brought the mas-sive vehicle to a halt outside the main doorway of a three-storey wooden office building on a side street right off the main throughway of the town.

Jaan hurried inside, brushing the snow off his fur coat as he entered the warm corridor. He walked briskly upstairs to the first floor, where a large wooden door bore the lettering SIBNEFT, the Russian name for the gigantic Siberian Oil Com-pany, whose refineries in the city of Omsk, down near the Kazakhstan border, and in Moscow, pro-duce 500,000 barrels of oil product every day.

Inside, behind a large desk, in front of a roar-ing log fire, sat Sergei Pobozhiy, the fabled Chair-man of SIBNEFT. Neither man had been to this oil frontier town for at least two years, and they gave each other great bear hugs of recognition. Sergei had arrived by helicopter from the city of

Yekaterinburg, which stands, in its infamy, in the foothills of the Urals.

The next visitor, who arrived at 9:30, had traveled up from the same city, also by helicopter. The mission was too secret for the men to travel together. Like Sergei, Boris Nuriyev, first Vice President of Finance at the colossal, restructured LUKOIL Corporation, had traveled alone in the corporate helicopter.

Boris Nuriyev was a stranger to Jaan and Sergei, but all three of them were Siberian-born, and all three of them had been close friends with the late Mikhallo Masorin. They shook hands formally and sat down with black coffee to await the arrival of the fourth and final member of the meeting.

He came through the door at 9:40, direct from the rough little Noyabrsk airport, having landed in a private corporate jet directly into the teeth of the wind, and was almost blown off the runway. The government car that picked him up was a black Mercedes limousine, with chains already fitted to the tires. The automobile was a gift from the Chinese government.

Roman Rekuts, a big man well over six feet three, issued no bear hugs, mainly because he might have crushed the spines of the other men. But Jaan, Sergei, and Boris each shook hands warmly with the last arrival, welcoming the new head of the Urals Federal District, the man who had replaced Mikhallo Masorin. A Siberian-born politician, he had served under Masorin for four years.

Sergei Pobozhiy motioned for Roman to remove his coat and to sit in the big chair behind the desk. The SIBNEFT boss poured coffee for them all, and suggested that the new Urals Minister begin proceedings. Nothing written down, just an informal chat among four of the most influential men in Siberia.

"Well," he began, "I understand we are unanimous that Moscow agents assassinated Mikhallo Masorin. The American newspapers confirm the findings of the autopsy, and the coroner in Washington is expected to deliver a verdict that he was murdered by person or persons unknown.

"I imagine the Russian security contingent that traveled to the United States with the President will maintain the Americans must have done it. But of course no one is going to believe that. At least the Americans won't, and neither will we.

"Gentlemen, we are discussing here a matter of approach. And we should perhaps decide among ourselves what it is we want. And the short answer is plainly revenge, and then money. The taxes on Siberian export oil levied by Moscow are very high, and we do not get even a reasonable share of it.

"It would obviously suit us much better if the oil corporations—your good selves, that is—paid a higher tariff to Siberia, and made Central Government pay a higher price for domestic oil, and then share some of their huge export tax revenues with the country of origin. That's us."

"Of course, we are not really a country," said Boris thoughtfully. "We are, and always have been, a part of Russia."

"A situation that could probably be changed," said Sergei. "Let's face it, Siberia really is a separate country. The Urals form a great natural barrier between us and European Russia. We're talking a twelve-hundred-mile range of mountains stretching north-south all the way from the Arctic Circle to Kazakhstan. That's a barrier, a true break point. Enough to discourage anyone from using force against us."

"True enough," said Jaan. "And the Russian government knows it has no possibility of suppressing us by force. Even the mighty army of Germany never penetrated the Urals. We're safe from invasion, and the Chinese love us, so we don't have that much to fear. If we demand financial justice, Moscow essentially will have to give it to us."

Sergei, who, with Masorin gone, was probably the most militant of them, suddenly said flatly, "We could just round up the other two Siberian Federations and inform Moscow that we do plan to secede from the Russian Republic. Just like the smaller countries did from the Soviet Union.

"We ought not to do this in any spirit of malevolence, and we should inform them we would like to continue with trade agreements, much like the status quo. But in the absence of cooperation from Moscow, and in light of their compliance in the murder of the leader of the Ural Federal District, we intend from now on to call the shots financially on our own oil, and increase our trade with China."

"To which they will say, No, out of the question," said Roman, mildly.

"Then we issue our first veiled threat that there may be some interruption in production," replied Sergei.

The room fell silent. The snow squalls lashed against the double-glazed windows, and the wind howled.

"You hear that weather out there?" said Sergei. "That is our greatest strength. Because you have to be Siberian to work out here, to cope with the terrible conditions. I know we ship in labor for the rigs from Belarus and other cold climates. But the bedrock of our workforce is Siberian. Without native labor the entire oil industry would collapse. No one else is tough enough to stand it."

"Gentlemen, how serious are you about a declaration of independence?" Roman was pensive.

"Not very, I don't think," said Boris. "But I think we all believe the threat would send a lightning bolt through the Russian government. And that would quickly bring an agreement that the Siberian Federations deserve more from the treasure that lies under their own lands. It's really the only compensation the people have."

"I believe the intention of opening up increased trade with China would really frighten them," said Jaan. "We already have shortages and bottlenecks on the pipelines. If Moscow thought we intended to ship more and more oil down the new pipeline to China, I think they'd be very nervous. Especially if we were getting a much better price for it."

"And of course we ought not to forget the new tanker terminal in Murmansk," added Boris. "Right now we're shipping one point five million barrels of Siberian crude a day to the United States directly from the Barents Sea to the U.S. East Coast. Moscow would hate to jeopardize that, and Murmansk is a real outpost, way down at the end of a very long pipeline. Everyone knows they're what the Americans call 'low man on the totem pole.'

"Any shortages up there would infuriate them. But they already know the danger. And they know the sympathies of the big oil corporations are very much in favor of the Siberians. Especially as so many of us **are** Siberians. The truth is, Siberia not only owns the oil, Siberia also controls it."

Outside, the ice storm continued to blow out of the north. Sergei stood up and placed another couple of logs on the fire, saying quietly as he did

so, "Moscow is fifteen hundred miles from us—
and if we decide to increase our production to
China, there's nothing they can do about it. Except negotiate, on our terms. And the murder of
Mikhallo has not helped their cause, both in this
room and out there among the people."

"Gentlemen, I think this calls for a summit
meeting, in the next ten days. Is that likely to be possible?" Roman was getting down to brass tacks.

"Yes. I think we could manage that," replied
Sergei. "Say four or five top oil executives, ourselves and perhaps three more, plus four or five
major Siberian politicians, Roman and the other
two Federation leaders, plus two Energy Ministers from the Ural Federation and maybe Mikhail
from the Far East."

"Place?" said Roman.

"Well, it can't be out here," stated Boris. "We'll
be lucky to keep this little gathering under wraps,
even if we get out the moment the weather slows
down. I'd suggest Yekaterinburg, because it's bigger, more anonymous, and we can arrive from
several different directions. It doesn't matter if
any one of us is recognized, so long as no one
knows we're meeting together."

"It's important we show Moscow a united front
that truly represents the will not only of the Siberian oil industry, but that of the people," said Roman. "They can't assassinate us all, can they?"

"I suppose not," muttered Sergei.

0800 (LOCAL), SAME DAY
WASHINGTON, DC

Lenny Suchov was on the secure line from CIA headquarters early. Lt. Commander Ramshawe took the call.

"Guess you heard the verdict, Jimmy. It's in all the papers this morning."

"Sure did. Murder by persons unknown."

"Well, I called you for two reasons. First of all we got a picture of the guy who probably shot the curare into Mikhallo's neck. Only from the back. But he's a big guy, and he's leaning over talking. We've checked every inch of the surveillance film. No one else got that close all evening, at least not while Masorin was dining.

"The FBI are making formal inquiries at the Russian embassy, showing them our film, but the guy is back in Russia. And word is the White House does not want this to go much further. We got major oil trade agreements with Moscow, and the new export route from Murmansk is working well and profitably for everyone.

"Guess the President doesn't want to piss 'em off any more than we already have."

"That'd be right," said Jimmy. "Anyway, in the end, it's nothing to do with us really. It's a Russian murder and a Russian matter...what else?"

"One of our guys in the Siberian oil fields thinks something is brewing up there, politically."

"Yeah?"

"Apparently, earlier today—"

"You can't get much bloody earlier…"

Lenny chuckled. "They are nine hours in front…"

"Oh, yeah, that's different. Carry on."

Lenny laughed out loud. "Pay attention, young Ramshawe," he said. "Otherwise I have you assassinated…as I was saying, one of our guys was out at the little airport in Noyabrsk when a private jet landed, bearing none other than Boris Rekuts. That's the new political chief who's replaced Masorin as boss of the Urals Federal District.

"Anyway, our man tracked him into the town and saw him go into the SIBNEFT offices, where he stayed for three hours. Our guy sat in his car, just up the street, in a snowstorm, and saw Jaan Valuev leave the same building—he's the billionaire who runs OJSC, one of the biggest oil companies in Russia. Our man did not see anyone else leave, and he waited until dark at four p.m. But Valuev was picked up by an articulated truck, right across the street."

"Is all that significant?" asked Jimmy.

"Well, they were in these small SIBNEFT site offices. You know that's the enormous Siberian Oil Company. We got the biggest man in the business, Jaan Valuev, sneaking in and out of articulated trucks, and the political boss of

Western Siberia showing up for just three or four hours. Sounds like a serious powwow to me."

"You think it has something to do with Masorin?"

"I've no doubt they mentioned it. But the Siberian oil establishment is restless at the moment. They're sick of Moscow, dying to trade more with China, and when two or three very big cheeses start meeting in secret, in the wilds of the western Siberian plains, it's good to know."

"I guess it is," said Jimmy. "And I'm going to record all of this in my files. But I'm not quite sure why."

"If Russia suddenly attacks its Siberian colonies and causes a World War, you'll be glad I call you, hah? Glad to know Lenny was still steering you straight!"

"I'm always glad of that, old mate," replied Jimmy. "Dad's coming down to Washington for a couple of weeks soon…will you have dinner with us?"

"That would be very nice…good-bye now…how you say? Old mate."

1530, MONDAY, SEPTEMBER 27
EASTERN FOOTHILLS OF THE URAL
MOUNTAINS

The city of Yekaterinburg lies 1,130 miles east of Moscow. It is a city of a million souls, a light, airy, modern place with wide avenues, parks, and gardens, many of its historic public buildings constructed in the same fawn-and-white stucco as those in faraway St. Petersburg.

Some of the more elegant architecture of the old city, dating back to the 1720s, has been preserved; not, however, the Ipatiev house, which stood on a piece of land opposite the cream-and-turquoise tower of the Old Ascension Church. The house is long gone, bulldozed on the orders of Leonid Brezhnev. Today there is just a stark white memorial cross among a copse of trees.

It marks the spot where, on July 17, 1918, Czar Nicholas II, his wife, son, and daughters were slaughtered in the basement of the merchant Ipatiev's residence, gunned down, bayoneted, and bludgeoned by the secret police squad that guarded them on behalf of the Bolsheviks.

The name Yekaterinburg will always stand as a symbol of those brutal, violent murders, and, as if to make sure no one ever forgets, there stands a statue, right in the middle of Central Avenue, the former Lenin Street, of Yakov Sverdlov, organizer of the killings.

Not a hundred feet from the statue, in another basement, the lower floor of an office building owned by SIBNEFT, there was taking place one of the most secret meetings ever conducted in Yekaterinburg, certainly since the days leading up to the death of Czar Nicholas and his family.

At the head of a long polished oak table sat Roman Rekuts, the towering figure who now virtually ruled western Siberia. At the far end sat Sergei Pobozhiy, the Chairman of SIBNEFT, flanked by his two coconspirators, the billionaire Jaan Valuev from OJSC Surgutneftegas, and the powerful LUKOIL Financial Vice President, Boris Nuriyev.

The First Minister of the Central Siberian Federal District was there, in company with the new Chief Executive of the Russian Far East, who brought his Energy Minister, Mikhail Pavlov.

Roman Rekuts had brought his new deputy with him, and Sergei Pobozhiy was accompanied by his West Siberian Chief of Operations, the grizzled, beefy ex-drillmaster on the exploration rigs, Anton Katsuba.

Every one of the nine men in the room was Siberian-born. And not one of them failed to be attracted by the prospect of a clean break with Moscow. Of forming a new Republic of Siberia, a free and independent state with its own flag and currency. Even Yekaterinburg had its own flag, a white, green, and black tricolor, and there was talk of a Urals franc.

But the meeting was collectively certain of one sacrosanct rule—they must keep their close ties to Moscow in the oil business, retaining, however, the freedom to trade with their anxious, more affluent industrial neighbors to the south and east, in the People's Republic of China.

There had been instant camaraderie in the boardroom since the meeting began, as men with similar stated aims pointed out the advantages of freedom to both the corporations and to the people of Siberia. They had begun at 3:00 p.m. and intended to proceed until dinner, which would be taken at the big table, before proceeding with the final draft of their communiqué to Moscow.

The meeting ended early, however, shortly after 4:30, when the double doors to the boardroom were booted open and an armed Soviet-style guard in military uniform bearing no insignia aimed his Kalashnikov straight at the defenseless head of Roman Rekuts and opened fire, pumping three bullets in a dead straight line across his forehead.

In a split second four more guards were in the room. They cut down Sergei Pobozhiy with a hail of bullets to the neck and chest, and blew away Jaan Valuev, who was hit by eight AK-47 bullets to the throat and neck.

Boris Nuriyev stood up and held his hands out in front of him, in the fleeting mini-seconds before he was gunned down with a burst to the chest that caused him to fall forward, bleeding onto the rough draft of their demands to Moscow.

Anton Katsuba, seated in the center of the table opposite the guards, crashed his way under the table and seemed to vanish from everyone's mind, but the big man made a stupendous comeback, rising out from under the seats like a rogue elephant and clamping a mighty fist on the wind-pipe of one of the attackers.

By now he was the only one of the nine left alive, and he grabbed the guard's rifle and opened fire. No one was ready for this, and he actually killed two and wounded three before he was himself cut down in a hail of bullets from the other six.

The room was a total bloodbath, the carpet awash, the walls splattered. Blood flowed over the table. It was a grotesque insurrection, a near copybook repeat of the events of July 17, 1918, in a subterranean room not so far away from the old Ipatiev basement.

The one difference was that these modern soldiers of the Republic of Russia would have no need for the bayonets that were used to finish the Czar and his family. There was no need to plunge the steel into the bodies of the oilmen and the Siberian politicians as the guards had done to finish Nicholas, and the Empress Alexandra, the little boy Alexi, and the Grand Duchesses Marie and Olga, and Tatiana and Anastasia.

The ripping slugs of the clasp-loaded modern AK-47s were a lot more efficient than the old service revolvers of the early twentieth century. Not one of the original nine men who had assembled in this room was breathing.

And outside the room, there was pandemonium. The Russian Army, which had screamed into Central Avenue from the headquarters just outside the downtown area, had sealed off the entire throughway. Outside the building there were three large Army trucks plus one military ambulance.

Stretcher parties were running in through the main doors. Everyone working in the building remained at their desks. Armed guards were posted on every door. Huge green screens were erected to shield the main entrance from the public, and they continued to the rear of the trucks. Soldiers with body bags were sprinting down the stairs to the basement. A team of soldiers with ladders, paintbrushes and rollers, cans of paint, and ammonia were descending the steps in single file.

Everything from the room was being removed, eleven dead bodies, three wounded guards, the big table, carpets, chairs, papers. Everything. Behind the screen outside the door the Army trucks were being loaded, engines revving.

The first of them, the one containing all of the bodies, was under way less than twenty minutes after the opening burst of fire had cut down Roman Rekuts. It swung out of Central Avenue heading north, directly toward the arctic tundra northeast of the Ural Mountains on the estuary of the Ob River.

The truck containing the bloodstained carpets and furniture was next, roaring up the snowy street and again heading north. The ambulance was next, then the final truck, containing the screens and a dozen infantrymen in the back to assist with the burning and general destruction of the evidence when finally they reached their destination in the frozen north in the small hours of the morning.

This was the Russian military at their most thorough. No one would ever know the fate of the nine men who had sought freedom for their homeland of Siberia to trade their oil without the heavy yoke of the Russian government around their necks.

Perhaps even more sinister, no one would ever know how Moscow found out the meeting was taking place. But, as they say in the Siberian oil industry, even the icicles have ears and the wooden walls have eyes.

MIDDAY (LOCAL), TUESDAY, SEPTEMBER 28 PRIVATE RESIDENCE OF THE RUSSIAN PRESIDENT MOSCOW

There were just three visitors this morning: the Commander in Chief of the Russian Army, East of the Urals. The head of the FSB, who was rapidly developing a reputation comparable to his many predecessors. And the Russian Energy Minister, Oleg Kuts.

"Anyone heard anything?" asked the President.

"Not a word, sir. It seems no one knew who was in the meeting, no one knew what had happened, no one saw the cleanup, and no one's heard a word since. So far, that is."

"Good," said the President. "Very good. Please congratulate your Commander on a very skillful job, very well executed."

"I'll make a point of it," said the Russian General, kicking the heels of his jackboots together with an exaggerated, sharp crack.

"No word from inside the oil industry, I trust?"

"Nothing, sir," replied Oleg Kuts. "But that's understandable, since it seems no one has any idea who was in that room. I don't suppose anyone will realize they're missing for another twenty-four hours at least."

He turned to the sallow-faced, fortyish head of the FSB. "Your men found out anything?"

"Not really, sir. Except that at least six of the men in the basement traveled to Yekaterinburg by completely different routes. None of them traveled together, and they used private aircraft and helicopters, cars, and two of them at least finished the journey on the Trans-Siberian Railway, one from the east, one from the west."

"A very secret meeting, eh?"

"Yessir. Highly classified."

"We were certainly on the right lines then?"

"Most definitely, sir."

"But in my view this all leads to one inevitable conclusion, gentlemen…we can't go on doing this sort of thing. And I truly do not know how long we can keep the lid on Siberia. In the end they are going to try again, because the temptation of riches from China is simply too great. And we cannot go on putting people in jail whenever they become too powerful, as we have done in the past, eh?"

"Or...er...eliminating them, sir."

"Exactly so. The fact is, we need to home in on at least one major foreign oil supplier who is not in Siberia. We cannot have all our eggs in that one huge basket."

"I know, sir. But these days, everyone who has any oil whatsoever is desperate to hang on to it and reap the reward. Yes, we may have to use our powers of persuasion."

The President smiled. "Perhaps, Minister, you should conduct an immediate study...and find a new supplier, with substantial reserves, who might be...shall we say...vulnerable?"

CHAPTER TWO

Jaan Valuev, for the past six years, had led something of a double life. As the hard-driving boss of OJSC he was the very picture of a New Russian industrialist, a suave, well-tailored chief executive, presiding over the fortunes of an oil giant with income of more than $6 billion a year, annual growth of 17 percent, and 100,000 employees.

His wife had died four years earlier, and at fifty-two Jaan still lived in the grand mansion on the edge of the city of Surgut where they had brought up their two children. Both boys were now studying engineering at the Urals State Technical University in Yekaterinburg, the alma mater of Russia's first President, Boris Yeltsin, and his long-suffering wife, Naya.

This university is the largest east of the Ural Mountains. It once boasted twelve graduates on the Central Committee of the Communist Party. Jaan Valuev was its biggest private benefactor, and unlike all of the other Russian oil chiefs, he also heavily supported social programs in his hometown of Surgut. Generally speaking, Jaan Valuev had been a pillar of Siberian society.

But there was another side to him. Instead of the traditional lavish dacha on one of the more scenic coastlines of the Black Sea, Jaan preferred western Europe. He owned a spectacular beachfront estate two miles east of the Marbella Club in Andalusia, southern Spain, and kept a permanent $300-a-night suite at the superb Hotel Colon on Cathedral Avenue in the heart of Barcelona.

He owned an opulent white-fronted Georgian house in The Boltons, off London's pricey Brompton Road, and a twenty-acre country estate in the hills above the Thameside village of Pangbourne in Berkshire. He had found his way into this glorious English countryside through his great friend, the urbane multimillionaire publisher, hotelier, and soccer fanatic John Madejski, the Chairman of Reading Football Club and owner of the towering modern stadium on the borders of the M4 motorway.

It was this love of soccer that hurled the two men together. In 2009, upstart little Reading had fought their way into the upper echelons of the English Premier League and ended up playing mighty Barcelona in front of 60,000 people in the European Champions League at the Noucamp Stadium in Spain's second city.

And who should emerge that day, almost shyly, as the great new power in the Barcelona club? The billionaire behind some of the biggest player transfer deals in the history of Spanish football—Jaan

Valuev. Barcelona beat Reading 4–1, but the Siberian and the English tycoon became instant pals, and Jaan bought a house just a couple of miles from the imposing Madejski estate in Berkshire.

By 2010, Jaan Valuev was Chairman of Barcelona FC, following in the footsteps of another Russian oil tycoon, Roman Abramovich, who famously bought and recharged the batteries of Chelsea Football Club, in West London, with close to half a billion dollars, which purchased some of the best players in the world.

And tonight, Tuesday, September 28, Barcelona were in London, for their European Champions League game against England's greatest football club, Arsenal, founded in 1883 and a byword for excellence and sportsmanship in a sometimes tarnished world game.

Barcelona versus the Gunners, in the ultramodern new Emirates Stadium, in the heart of North London. Here was a game to be savored by aficionados all over the world. And 60,000 fans, 8,000 from Spain, were already making their way across London by taxi, bus, and train to watch this clash of titans, the Champions of the Spanish League against the Champions of England's Premiership.

Inside the marble halls of the Emirates Stadium, arrangements had been made for a sumptuous VIP dinner at 8:45 p.m., immediately after the game. The Arsenal Chairman would host it, and among his guests would be the Barcelona Chairman, and his buddy John Madejski, who was rumored to be preparing a sensational bid to buy Arsenal Football Club in partnership with Jaan Valuev.

But these awesome financial shenanigans were all taken in good heart, and the game was under way right on time, with the stadium packed and both teams free of injury. There was only one blight on the big game landscape: Jaan Valuev, whose body was currently lying burned in a mass grave deep in the icy wastes of the arctic tundra in northern Siberia, naturally had not turned up.

The seat next to John Madejski was empty, and it was still empty when Barcelona scored, and still empty when the teams came in for halftime. The Barcelona Deputy Chairman, Andre di Stefano, was absolutely mystified.

"I have an e-mail from his secretary, dated yesterday. He was flying in today directly from Yekaterinburg in a private jet owned by Emirates Airlines. I have the flight arrival time, but the airline guys say he never boarded the plane."

"Well, where the hell is he?" asked the Reading Chairman.

"Tell you the truth, we thought you'd probably know."

"I haven't spoken to him since Sunday, and he said he'd see me here for a glass of wine before the kickoff."

"So unlike him," said Andre. "To have informed no one he wasn't coming. Something must have happened."

"Well, it's close to midnight in Russia," replied John Madejski. "His office is shut, and I tried his mobile twenty minutes ago and it was switched off...so perhaps he had to fly somewhere else first, and will get here for the second half. That's a huge business he runs."

"I still think it's totally unlike him to vanish without informing anyone...but...maybe a girl-friend?" di Stefano chuckled.

"What! Instead of watching the game against Arsenal? No chance," replied Madejski.

And the second half kicked off without Jaan Valuev. And Arsenal scored three times to thunderous roars that could have been heard in Piccadilly Circus six underground stops away.

The game ended and the dinner began, with places rearranged to close the gap left by the absent Siberian soccer chief.

At the end of the evening, as John Madejski slipped out of the stadium to where his chauffeur, Terry, had the big blue Rolls Bentley waiting, a reporter from the **London Daily Telegraph** approached the Reading Chairman for a quote about the game. But what he really wanted was a quote about the rumored bid to buy Arsenal.

John Madejski, of course, was far too wily to fall for that. "It was a wonderful game," he said.

"Played with great spirit. We saw four superb goals and Arsenal deserved it." As an afterthought he added, "Tell you the truth, it was a little disappointing for me, because Mr. Valuev was unable to get here…and that was a shame. He would have loved it, even though his beloved Barcelona lost."

And that was sufficient for the football writer. Not for tonight's report. That was already filed. But for tomorrow's follow-up to the biggest game of the season:

SIBERIAN OIL BILLIONAIRE
MISSES BARCELONA'S BIG ONE
Mystery of Jaan Valuev's Arsenal No-Show

The following report pointed out the reason Jaan missed the game was because of the protracted speculation that he and John Madejski might be scheming to buy Arsenal Football Club.

They quoted Madejski as saying "Rubbish." And the Barcelona club as saying they were not privy to all of their Chairman's travel arrangements. No, they had not heard from him since the defeat in North London.

Yes, they were quite certain he would be back in the director's box for the game against Spanish rivals Real Madrid at the Birnabau Stadium in the Spanish capital a week from Saturday.

1100, FRIDAY, OCTOBER 1
NATIONAL SECURITY AGENCY
FORT MEADE, MARYLAND

Lt. Commander Jimmy Ramshawe was in heaven. Or, as near to heaven as an organizational hell such as his own office permitted. A colleague from the National Surveillance Office, just returned from Europe, had dropped him off a pristine copy of yesterday's **London Daily Telegraph.**

This was a fairly regular occurrence up here on the eighth floor behind the massive one-way glass walls of the OPS2B Building. Lt. Commander Ramshawe's voracious appetite for top foreign newspapers was well known.

Leaning back in his swivel chair, feet on the desk, he sipped a cup of fresh coffee before reaching for his newspaper and turning to his favorite pages. As it happened there was not much going on in London to interest him, and he kept wandering through the newspaper until he finally landed on the sports pages.

And one word jumped straight out at him: **Siberian**. Right in the headline. If the word had been set in smaller type he'd most certainly have missed it.

But there was no missing this. SIBERIAN OIL BILLIONAIRE.

"Hallo," said Jimmy. "One of the late Mr. Masorin's mates. What's he done to get himself in with the bloody football players?"

One minute later: "Christ, the bugger's vanished. Those Siberians aren't having much luck lately."

On nothing more than pure reflex, he picked up his phone and called Lenny Suchov.

"Lenny, you seen anything about this Siberian oil guy gone missing?"

"Funny you should mention that. We just got a highly classified report in from our man up in Noyabrsk pointing out the Chairman of SIBNEFT has vanished—not been seen for two or three days.

"Our guys think he may have been snatched by agents of Moscow, and put in the slammer, just like they did to poor old Mikhail Khodorkovsky, the biggest Yukos oil shareholder, six years ago.

"Anyway, how did you find out about it?"

"I've just read it in the **London Daily Telegraph**."

"Impossible. This has only just broken. It's not even in the Russian newspapers yet."

"Maybe not, but the old Siberian was supposed to be at a football game coupla nights ago in London and he never showed."

"A what!"

"A football game. He's the Chairman of Barcelona."

"What the hell are you talking about? The missing Siberian is called Sergei Pobozhiy. And he's supposed to be at SIBNEFT's northern site office near the oil field in the West Siberian Basin. Not at a football game."

"What do'you say his name is?"

"Sergei Pobozhiy."

Jimmy grappled with the London broadsheet. "Well, that's a different guy. My man's called Jaan Valuev. He's the boss of some Russian oil company, but it doesn't say here which one. Anyway it does say he's vanished."

"Christ, Jimmy, that's two missing and one dead in the last couple of weeks, all major Siberians...what the hell's going on?"

"Beats the hell outta me, old mate."

"Okay, I'll get another couple of field agents on this. Tell you what. I'll keep you posted. But this isn't anything military, or to do with national security. Give me a call in an hour, and I'll tell you where we stand."

11:30 A.M., SAME DAY
MOSCOW

The President of Russia, a big, burly, sallow-faced former deputy head of the Soviet secret police, the KGB, missed the old sledgehammer rule of the authoritarian Central Government more than most.

He rubbed along adequately with both houses of the Russian Parliament—the Federation
Council and the Duma—but as the elected Head
of State he had enormously broad powers, including the appointment of his deputy, the Prime
Minister, and all government ministers.

Some Presidents of the Russian Federation
are more approachable than others. This one was
very remote, yearning in his heart for the old days
of the Politburo, the huge brutal power of the Soviet machine, which could deal with "trouble"
instantly and ruthlessly. This President was not
really a committee man.

If anyone had found out what had been perpetrated at the oil summit in Siberia, the President
might very well have faced a career-ending onslaught in the Parliament. But this President held
power, like so many of his recent predecessors,
with an iron grip. The Duma and the Federation
Council found out what he wanted them to know.

Russia was ruled from this grand suite of offices where the President now sat, sipping coffee
at the head of a highly polished table. With him
were just four men, gathered here in the domed
rotunda on the second floor of the Senate building, today the ultimate seat of Russian power, situated on the east side of the Kremlin.

The great yellow-and-white, triangular, eigh-
teenth-century neoclassical edifice stands east of

Peter the Great's Arsenal building, alongside the old 1930s Supreme Soviet. It is situated behind the ramparts that flank the Senate Tower, directly behind Lenin's tomb.

Like the current Russian President, Vladimir Ilych Lenin both lived and worked in the Senate, a measure of history adored by the reigning President. But perhaps the leader in 2010 liked even better the fact that during World War II, this rotunda hosted the Red Army Supreme Command, under Stalin.

The President was relaxed in this cradle of Russian history, feeling as he always did in the rotunda a vast sense of confidence, impregnability, and destiny. The men who depended entirely upon him for their exalted positions and grandiose lifestyles were apt to treasure his every word.

It was almost impossible to imagine the old days, when Politburo members occasionally vanished for incurring the wrath of their Communist Party leader. Almost impossible. Not quite.

The President smiled at those whose undying trust he enjoyed. There was the Prime Minister, Valery Kravchenko, who like himself was a native of St. Petersburg. There was the current head of the FSB, Boris Patrushov; the Energy Minister, Oleg Kuts; the Minister for Foreign Affairs, Oleg Nalyotov, who literally strutted around in his vast authority, pompously occupying the office once held by the great Andrei Gromyko.

The last man at the table, placed to the right of Nalyotov, was Gregor Komoyedov, the former Moscow oil executive who now occupied the critically important Ministry for Foreign Trade. Above them all fluttered the white, blue, and red horizontal tricolor of the Russian Federation, high atop the flagstaff at the pinnacle of the rotunda.

Twelve hundred meters to the south, the Moscow River flowed icily eastward, lazily as Russian history. And beyond the great Senate Tower, in Red Square, a thousand tourists stared up and over the Kremlin ramparts, most of them gazing at the towering gilded dome of Ivan the Great's Bell Tower, still the tallest structure in the Kremlin, and once the tallest building in Moscow.

From the wide windows of the rotunda, the Russian President and his colleagues could see the riotous colors, the greens, the yellows, and the bloodred livery of St. Basil's Cathedral with its twisting domes jutting skyward to the south of the square.

One glance through those windows could engulf the mind with visions of the stark and tumultuous history of Russia. Every man at the table sensed it, especially the President. And they sensed it every time a highly classified meeting was invoked. As ever, for former middle-line government officials elevated to the grandeurs of power, destiny beckoned.

"Gentlemen," said the President, "first of all, I think we owe a vote of thanks to Boris Patrushov, to the quite brilliant way he first located, and then dealt with, that treasonous and seditious conference that took place in Yekaterinburg. I think our mutual role model, the late First Secretary, Leonid Brezhnev, would have been very proud."

The head of the new secret police looked modestly down at his notes, and said quietly, "Thank you, Comrade. But I should say our success was entirely due to the very alert observation of our little mole in the office of the Chairman of the Siberian Oil Company. The rest was routine for me. That conference represented a threat to the Russian people. A threat to the bedrock of our economy. It had to be extinguished."

"Absolutely correct," interjected Oleg Nalyotov. "The consequences of their proposed actions were unthinkable for any Russian not resident in Siberia."

The President nodded. "However," he continued, "the Siberian threat remains. They are a vast Russian protectorate, which, at the top at least, suspects it no longer needs our protection. I think it is likely that such an intention, to secede from the Motherland, may very well occur again, though probably not for a while.

"We have probably silenced it for maybe five or six years. But we have not killed it, any more than we could ever kill it. The will of the Siberians, to profit and prosper from the oil and gas that lies beneath their godforsaken frozen soil, will surely rise again.

"But first I would like to deal with more immediate matters. The...er...termination of the careers of the treacherous men who gathered in Yekaterinburg on Monday. Plainly they will be missed. Probably already have been..."

Foreign Minister Nalyotov intervened. "With respect, Comrade, the Western press has already picked up a lead on the disappearance of Jaan Valuev, the Surgutneftegas President...apparently failed to turn up at some soccer game...caused questions in sports circles...now we have formal inquiries from foreign media asking if he's been found."

The President nodded, very seriously. "Nothing else?" he asked.

"Well, they seem to think Sergei Pobozhiy, the Chairman of SIBNEFT, is mysteriously vanished. I think Gregor Komoyedov might have some information."

The Energy Minister nodded and said, "Very little, I am afraid. But I understand there have been some serious inquiries inside the corporation as to his whereabouts. The Chairman does not often go missing, and I did hear they were talking to his wife. That'll be public knowledge in twenty-four hours."

"Plainly," said the President, "we must move on this. I think the best course of action would be an accident in a military aircraft deep in the tundra. We need not give details, as the mission was highly classified. But I have drafted a press release, which should be issued directly from the military. It should begin something like this…

"With deep regret we announce the loss of a Russian Air Force jet, which disappeared over the arctic tundra somewhere north of the Siberian oil fields earlier this week. Unfortunately, the aircraft was known to have been transporting several important personnel from the Russian national oil and gas industry, as well as several senior Siberian politicians. Severe weather conditions have made the search for bodies almost impossible.

"Their ultimate destination was Murmansk for an international conference at the new tanker terminals. Air Force helicopters are currently in the search area but no wreckage has yet been found, and we have no information on the cause of the crash. Because of the classified nature of the mission, the Air Force will not be releasing the names of any of their own personnel.

"Families of the deceased executives and politicians are currently being informed. The government and the military authorities are treating the incident as an accident that occurred in flight, though there will of course be a thorough investigation into the possible reasons for the jet to have gone down."

"Excellent," said Boris Patrushov, with the clear relief of a man who had just ordered and masterminded a dozen cold-blooded murders of innocent Russian civilians. "It'll take a few days and a few awkward questions. But we'll alert the military media authorities on the procedures we expect them to adopt.

"And we'll make it known that the government would prefer this very sad incident to be treated with care and sensitivity. Sensationalizing the death of such men will incur the anger of the authorities. It might also be a good idea to bestow some kind of decorations or medals on these men who died in the service of their country."

"Very good idea," said the President. "Perhaps the Cross of the Russian Federation for the civilians, and regular combat medals for the pilots."

"Perfect," offered Boris. "And of course in the end we'll blame the appalling weather and the impossibility of landing the aircraft after an instrument failure, and an apparent problem with the hydraulics."

"Yes, I think that will see our little problem off very nicely," said Prime Minister Kravchenko. "Very nicely indeed."

"Meanwhile," continued the President, "I think we should discuss the heart of the problem."

"Which is?" asked Kravchenko.

The President looked concerned. He glanced up and said, "What would become of Mother Russia if ever the Siberians were to succeed in going their own way? They certainly would not be the first of our satellites to do so. But they would be, by a long way, the most dangerous.

"And even if they demanded or took a far greater license in deciding the destination of their own oil and gas...well, that could prove nearly fatal for us. Because they would almost certainly turn to China, and a close, cozy relationship between those two, right down at the ass end of the fucking Asian continent, would not be great..."

"Neither financially, geographically, nor diplomatically," mused Kravchenko. "World sympathy would immediately swing to Siberia, the poor freezing underclass of the old Soviet Union... never had anything, never been fairly treated by Moscow...struggled with the world's cruelest climate for centuries...and now the bullies of the Kremlin want to suppress them yet again—"

"Yes," interrupted the President. "I think that was quite sufficiently graphic. And I think I speak for everyone when I say we might one day simply lose control of that Siberian oil. We won't be ruined…there'll still be riches and reward for the Russian government. But it won't be like now. The goose's golden eggs will become a bit more…well, brassy."

The Russian President stood up and pressed a bell for the Senate butler to come through and bring them coffee and sweet pastries. He stood before a gigantic portrait of the elderly Catherine the Great, accompanied by her brown-and-white whippet, and specified the precise texture of thick dark coffee he required, and the precise sweetness of the pastries.

Then he sat down and began to outline a plan of such terrifying wickedness and subversiveness, each of the four officials who were listening were stunned into silence.

"We are going to need a new supply of oil," he said. "From somewhere in the world where there are ample reserves, billions of barrels of crude, which we can seize control of. I know it's not going to be easy, and that anyone who has it wants to keep it. But there is a new and very serious player in the game…China. And within a few short years they are going to want every last barrel they can lay their hands on."

He hesitated for a moment as the door opened and the butler came in with their coffee. He nodded respectfully and set the large silver tray down on an antique sideboard beneath a gigantic nineteenth-century painting of the Battle of Balaklava fought in the Crimea in 1854.

Turning to Energy Minister Kuts, the President said, "Oleg, read to them those stats you gave me yesterday, will you? I think everyone will be interested, and I would like my memory to be refreshed."

"Certainly," replied Kuts, shuffling his files. "I should perhaps begin by stating there are more than fifty-six million cars, vans, and sport utility vehicles rolling down China's highways at this very moment. That accounts for probably sixteen percent of the world's energy consumption— that's second only to the U.S., which gobbles up twenty-four percent.

"By 2020 it is estimated that China will be very close to that twenty-four percent—probably using eleven million barrels a day, plus three point six trillion cubic feet of natural gas. And that's likely to put their backs to the wall.

"Hardly a day passes without some kind of power outage in China, especially in the winter, when their aging pipelines occasionally fail. Their electricity grid grows more decrepit every year. Output is rapidly declining in the big northeastern fields around Daqing, and their reserves in far western China mostly lie beneath the high, dry deserts.

"That means their best shot at claiming those reserves, deep beneath the surface, is going to be very, very expensive.

"That's why, even as we speak, China is out there scouring the globe for new opportunities in oil exploration. They will naturally try to crowd their way into neighboring Siberia with promises of a huge market for local oil. In the meantime, they will be pushing forward, financing and trading, to open up oil exploration fields in Australia, Indonesia, Iran, Kazakhstan, Nigeria, Papua New Guinea, and the Sudan.

"Gentlemen, China calls it **supply security**, and the name of that game is diversification. They're in it up to their elbows, we're lagging far behind. We're too dependent on Siberia. We must raise our sights. And I think you will find our most esteemed leader has some very advanced views on that.

"Yesterday I briefed him as well as I could on the global situation. Who has new oil? Where are the big new fields? Is anyone vulnerable to persuasion? If not, how **can** we persuade them? During the next few minutes, gentlemen, you will hear why our President may one day be talked of in the same breath as Brezhnev, Gorbachev, and Yeltsin. The great visionaries of our time."

The President smiled. "Thank you for those generous words, Oleg. I'm grateful for them, and I'm grateful to be here among old and good friends who share my concern for the future.

"And I would like, if I may, firstly to outline the very obvious difficulties that lie in much of the world's oil exploration countries. Take the Middle East...well, we may make some headway, but mostly in Iran. The rest of the Gulf, the principal Arab producers, are always in the hands of the Americans.

"The Saudis, the Emirates, Iraq, Kuwait, Bahrain, and Qatar are all encompassed by the USA—particularly after the Presidency of George W. Bush. None of them move without an okay from the White House.

"Indonesia was up for grabs. But the Americans are strong there and the Chinese are getting close. The Brits are running out of North Sea oil altogether. Europe is devoid of all resources except coal. The USA will never relinquish any of the oil from the Alaskan fields, and Mexico and Venezuela prefer to deal with Washington. Thanks again to President Bush."

The Russian President rearranged his papers. "Which brings us to two of the biggest strikes of this century so far—the one in South Georgia, which lies deep in the middle of the South Atlantic, about four meters from the Antarctic Circle, and those two huge new oil fields on the Falkland Islands."

"The Falkland Islands!" exclaimed Oleg Nalyotov. "That's more hopeless than all the other places put together. It's a British Colony that twenty-eight years ago was the scene of one of the most vicious little three-month wars in modern history.

"I'm sure you all remember. The Argentinian military seized it, claimed it, and occupied it. And before you could say **Nyet,** the Royal Navy assembled a battle fleet and charged down the Atlantic and did what they said they'd do.

"Literally, the Brits blew 'em off that island with guided missiles and bombs. They landed a force of ten thousand and fought for the place as if they were defending the coast of Sussex. Some terrible Admiral they had put the big Argentine cruiser, the **General Belgrano,** on the bottom of the Atlantic, drowned more than three hundred sailors.

"My general advice would be don't fool with the Brits. They get very touchy. And I happen to know it's Exxon and British Petroleum who are going to develop those oil fields. That's a U.S.-UK alliance. We should be wary of those, especially when there's a lot of money involved."

The President looked up and nodded. "My dear Oleg," he said patiently, "you do not think for one moment I intend to become involved in a fight with either of them, do you? Frankly I'd rather fight the Siberians, or the Chinese for that matter.

"But there is one rather hotheaded little nation that might very easily be happy to do our dirty work for us. I believe it's called Argentina, and they are not afraid of anyone when it comes to those islands. The Malvinas, they believe, belong to them. The very word **Malvinas** drives them mad in Buenos Aires.

"Grown men, military officers, beat their breasts and start raving about how proud they would be if their own sons fought and died for the islands. One of the Argentine admirals in the last conflict stated he would die a happy man if the blood of his son, killed in combat, was to seep into the soil of the Malvinas. There is no reason in that country, just passion…**Viva las Malvinas!** All that nonsense.

"Their claim is essentially ludicrous, utterly dismissed by London. But with a little clandestine help from us, they might just go at it again. You know, capture the islands, which are scarcely defended, seize the oil, expel the oilmen from Exxon and Shell. And allow us the rights—in return for a generous royalty.

"We then put in two big Russian oil companies, build them a tanker complex, and sit back and take our cut, in the form of taxes on the oil exported to the Gulf Coast of the United States. Works for everyone, correct?"

"Sir, it is my duty to warn you that the Americans would be absolutely furious and might use military force against the islands."

"Thank you, Prime Minister Kravchenko. But I don't think you are right. The Americans might be furious, but in the end they would do a deal. The Brits, however, would not. They'd attack the islands, just as they did in 1982."

"You really think so?" said the PM. "The Royal Navy all over again, bombing and blasting the islands all over again. British troops, fighting and dying in the frozen hills of that awful, weird little place?"

"Yes, Comrade. I think they might," said the President. "But this time they would most certainly lose. And there would be absolutely nothing they could do about it. Everyone involved in our military knows it. Great Britain's Labour governments have weakened their war-fighting capability to a truly stupendous degree.

"They do not have the troops, they have savagely cut out some of their best regiments, merging them, closing them. They have cut back their Navy, selling many ships and scrapping others. They've reduced their air combat force to virtually nothing. The Brits would be a pushover.

"And, since they don't have Margaret Thatcher anymore, the Argentines would crush them. Especially with a little help from us. If I was their Defense Minister I would not even think about trying to recapture the Falkland Islands, should Argentina decide to claim them."

The Russian press release was issued by the Russian Air Force in Moscow at midnight, too late for the television news channels, and very late for the morning newspapers, which are inclined to print earlier on Friday nights because of various weekend supplements and magazines.

The release, scarcely changed from the precise wording written by hand by the Russian President that morning, reached the international wire agencies shortly before one a.m. on Saturday.

It was still Friday afternoon in Washington, around five p.m., and there was plenty of time to develop the story. However, East Coast newsrooms had much more on their minds than an obscure military air crash in northern Siberia, where a few oil execs may have perished.

And it was greeted, generally, with a thunderclap of disinterest. The **Washington Post** and the **New York Times** carried a single column, a two-inch-long mention of the accident in their foreign news roundup, well inside the paper. No one thought it worth a follow-up. The CNN twenty-four-hour news channel never mentioned it; neither did the main newspapers in Philadelphia or Boston.

On the other hand, over on the eighth floor of the National Security Agency, Lt. Commander Jimmy Ramshawe took one glance at the release from Moscow and damn near rammed the ceiling with the top of his head as he blew directly upward out of his office chair.

"H-o-o-o-o-l-e-e shit!" he breathed. And the words on the sheet of copy paper jumped straight out at him...**Siberia...oil...death...air crash...no trace...no details...Whoa!**

Having almost walked into the wall with excitement, he reeled around and hit the buttons to the former assassin in the CIA, Lenny Suchov.

"I know, I know, Jimmy, I just got it. How **about** that? Something's going on right here. I am certain of that."

"Hey, that's a pretty sharp deduction—for a bloody spook," said Jimmy, once more sounding like Crocodile Dundee.

"Oh, you mean I was clever enough to work out there may be a connection between the death in the White House and those deaths in the Siberian tundra?"

"I should bloody say so, old mate. The Ruskies obviously wiped out a top Siberian oil exec in the State Dining Room right here in Washington. And now they might have done a whole bloody planeload of 'em somewhere northeast of the Urals."

"My thoughts completely," said Lenny. "Crudely but effectively stated. However, it's still very much a Russian affair—nothing to do with us. But I think it's our duty—mine at least—to take a look at something as sinister as this. We ought to know what's happening."

"I agree, Lenny. But I'm not sure where to start. I suppose I could get U.S. Air Force Intelligence to find out precisely which aircraft from which base somehow took off and never returned. I could have someone get inside the rescue operation and find out how many Russian aircraft are on the case..."

"Jimmy, I think that might prove a waste of time."

"What does that mean?"

"Because, if there is something sinister, there will be no aircraft and no air crash."

"Gimme that one more time?"

"Jimmy, let us assume our general deductions are on the right lines. Someone near or at the top of the Russian food chain wanted those Siberian execs eliminated. Firstly, they would have found a far more efficient, quiet way of achieving that objective.

"Secondly, they would not have bothered to sabotage a damned expensive military aircraft, and effectively murder two or three Russian Air Force officers, in a totally unnecessary way. It's not the way they operate. It's completely out of character.

"No, young Jimmy. This aircraft crap is a cover-up. And quite a noisy one. They'll be aware that within a few days there'll be people all over the place trying to solve what the stupid newspapers will call **the mystery of the missing Russian jet**...and they'll have to offer a measure of cooperation.

"But, Jimmy, they won't care who wants to investigate. Because no one will ever find anything. There's nothing to find. I'm sorry to disillusion you...but the Air Force jet is a decoy. Doesn't exist. But neither, I am afraid, not now, do all those oil chiefs."

"Jesus. This is like listening to Sherlock Holmes. You're more bloody devious than the Russians..."

"That, Lt. Commander Ramshawe, is what I believe your government pays me to be."

Jimmy chuckled. "Well...former genius of the Black Sea wrestlers...what the hell do we do now?"

"You sit tight. I'm going to get some field agents on the case, simply to find out who died in Siberia. I'm looking for names. The whole list of who's suddenly gone missing. Then we can sit down and try to join up the pieces. Jimmy, this may have much more to do with your area of operations than you know. But for the moment, sit tight."

"Sit tight? I'm not sitting bloody tight. I'm phoning the Big Man, right after I contact Admiral Morris."

He said good-bye to the spymaster from Langley and punched in an e-mail message for Admiral Morris, his boss, to contact him from the West Coast, where he was attending a conference with the FBI in San Diego. He informed the Admiral that something had come up re the White House murder, and he was proposing to have a chat with Arnold Morgan.

Jimmy then called Admiral Morgan and quickly realized he had done so at a bad time.

"Christ, Ramshawe. It's nearly four bells, I **never** take phone calls on the last dog-watch. I'm trying to get ready for the evening."

"Sorry, sir. But something's come up you'll want to know about…"

"How the hell do you know what I want to know about…?"

"Well, sir, I think…"

"Think, think, think. The whole damned world's thinking, mostly crap. I'm not interested in what you think. Call me with facts, fine. Not goddamned thoughts, hear me?"

"These are bloody facts, Admiral, otherwise I wouldn't have called…"

"That's entirely different," the Admiral harrumphed. "But I'm still busy. Can these facts wait, or is the entire goddamned planet on the brink of war?"

"Not exactly, sir. I guess they can wait."

"How long can they wait?"

"Not long, sir. This is important."

"All right, all right. Now listen. In precisely two hours I have to meet Mrs. Kathy Morgan in Le Bec Fin, one wildly expensive restaurant in the heart of Georgetown on one of the most expensive streets in the free world...I suppose you wanna come?"

"Jeez, Admiral. That would be great." But he added after a sudden flashback on the Admiral's excellent taste in French wine, "So long as I don't have to pay."

And then, realizing this might be the precise moment to push his luck to the absolute brink, he asked, "Can Jane come?" He knew of course that Kathy adored his fiancée, the Australian Ambassador's daughter Jane Peacock, but was nonetheless aware that Arnold's answer might not be precisely orthodox. Arnold's answers usually weren't.

"Can Jane come?" he rasped. "Oh, sure, why not check whether there's any other members of her family at a loose end tonight...few cousins, aunts, maybe a coupla neighbors?

"How about your mom and dad, could they make it down from New York in time? Got any visiting uncles from the goddamned outback, might fancy a bowl of kangaroo soup at a high-class establishment at about twenty-five bucks a spoonful—bring the whole goddamned lot if you like. I'll remortgage the house."

Jimmy by this time was falling about laughing. "Actually, I meant just Jane, sir," he eventually said.

"'Course she can come," grunted the Admiral. "Eight bells, Le Bec Fin. And don't be late. My best to your dad." Bang. Down phone.

Jimmy called Jane at the embassy and told her he'd pick her up at 7:45. Then he spoke to Admiral Morris, who was very thoughtful about the Russian press release and what Lenny Suchov had said. "Good plan to run it past Arnie...I'm sorry I can't join you."

Jimmy resisted the temptation to inform his boss that the merest suggestion of another guest at the table might have sent Arnold into a paroxysm of mock indignation. Instead he just said, "I'll give him your best, sir. And it sure will be interesting to hear what he thinks about the old Ruskies."

"Jimmy," concluded Admiral Morris, "we know what he thinks about the Ruskies. But this press release from their Air Force will get his attention."

"It better," replied his assistant. "Otherwise I might find myself with the biggest dinner check I ever saw."

EIGHT BELLS
LE BEC FIN
GEORGETOWN, WASHINGTON, DC

It was raining steadily when Jimmy Ramshawe's black Jaguar came whipping through the puddles and pulled up right outside the entrance to the restaurant. A doorman immediately stepped out with an umbrella and motioned for Jane to jump out.

Then, somewhat surprisingly, he motioned for Jimmy also to disembark. "Admiral's orders, sir, we're to park the car for you…you are Lt. Commander Ramshawe, aren't you?"

"That's me, old mate."

"Yes, I thought I was correct."

"What did the Admiral actually say?"

"He said when some kind of a black English racing car comes speeding up the goddamned road, let the beautiful blonde in the passenger seat out first, then bring the Australian driver in, and park the car."

"Sounds just like him."

"Yessir. Remie will take care of you right inside the door."

The maitre d' steered them to the back of the restaurant where Admiral Morgan and Kathy were quietly sipping glasses of superb 2001 Meursault, which had set the Admiral back almost $100.00. The bottle of white burgundy was in an ice bucket set in a raised stand on the floor at the end of the table.

"Hi, kids," said Arnold, standing to greet first Jane, then Jimmy, while Kathy climbed to her feet and hugged Jane.

The waiter had already placed two extra wineglasses on the table, and the Admiral dipped into the bucket and pulled out the bottle, splashing it out generously. Never occurred to him either of his guests could possibly want anything else. And he was dead right about that.

"That, Admiral, is outstanding," said Jimmy.

"And your new information better be of the same quality." Arnold grinned. "Delicate, yet with a powerful core, with deep promise of greater things to come…"

"Would you ever listen to his rubbish?" said Kathy, her inbred Irish intonations bubbling to the fore. "He's got more blarney than my grandma, and she lived there, a mile from the castle!"

"Now, Kathryn," said the Admiral, "I want you and Jane to have a nice little chat while I listen to the considered intelligence of young James. That's why he's here."

The Lt. Commander said nothing. He just produced the sheet of paper with the press release from Moscow and handed it to Arnold Morgan.

The Admiral read carefully, his eyebrows slowly raising. "Holy Mary, Mother of God," he breathed. "Those bastards have knocked down a planeload of Siberian oil chiefs—two weeks after murdering another in the White House."

"Not quite," said Jimmy. "No plane."

"Huh?" said the Admiral, looking, for once, baffled.

And Jimmy recounted the thoughts of the retired assassin, Lenny Suchov.

Without hesitation, Arnold Morgan said, "He's absolutely correct. They'd never destroy a perfectly sound military aircraft when they could achieve the same ends with a handful of carbine bullets. Plus, the nonexistent air crash makes a perfect cover story—which no one will ever crack. Because it never happened."

"Right up there in the tundra," said Jimmy. "Inside the Arctic Circle, northern Siberia, where the ground is always frozen, and where a blizzard could cover all traces of any air crash in a couple of hours. It would never be seen again."

"Do we expect the CIA to come up with an accurate list of the big-deal oil execs who have apparently perished?"

"That's in motion. Lenny Suchov's on the case. He thinks there's one or two very important Siberian politicians involved. And he's absolutely sure the Russian government had 'em all shot."

"The question is, why?" said Arnold. "What has the Siberian oil industry done to deserve all this?"

"Who knows? But Lenny thinks it's a problem that occasionally comes to the surface. A kind of undercurrent in Siberia that the local population does not get a fair share of the wealth that lies under their land. That's mostly oil and gas. But also gold, and the largest diamond fields on Earth."

"He thinks these guys may have been planning to break free of Moscow, at last?" asked

Arnold. "He thinks the Russians just put down a goddamned revolution?"

"He thinks something was brewing up there. And he feels the full list of who was apparently killed in the air crash will provide some important clues."

Arnold was pensive. He took another luxurious pull at his Meursault de luxe, as he called it, and said, quietly, at least quietly for him, "Listen, you guys…that's all three of you. I'm going to tell you something about the Russians. You all remember the Cold War, which you doubtless assumed was all about the rampant spread of communism and missiles.

"Well, ultimately it wasn't. The great fear in Russia, always has been, was the starvation of its people. Could the gigantic collective farms ever produce enough grain and vegetables to feed the population?

"Mostly the answer to that was no. Year after year there were dreadful failures of the crop, and year after year they just somehow muddled along, suffering the most awful privations, sometimes buying from the West.

"But the great fear of the free world, during the 1960s through the 1980s, was that a First Secretary of the Communist Party might suddenly believe a vast number of his people might starve to death.

"**That** was the great fear of the West. That a Russian leader may be faced with telling his people there was nothing to eat. At that point, to avoid the total collapse of Soviet Communism, that leader must find food.

"And, kids, there's only one way for any national leader to get food. He either needs to buy it, or steal it from someone else.

"And that, ladies and gentlemen," concluded Arnold, with a flourish, "was the fear: that Russia would marshal its massive Red Army, and march into western Europe in search of food.

"We thought they might rampage through Poland and a defenseless Germany, and then the Low Countries, ransacking farmlands and shipping grain home to the Soviet Union. The only way to have stopped them was probably a nuclear showstopper on Moscow—and we all know where that might have led."

"Sir, are you suggesting what I think you are?" said Jimmy.

"I'm suggesting that yesterday's Russian grain crisis is today's Russian oil crisis. If somehow they lost the Siberian product, I do not know what would happen. But I know this. The Kremlin has been nurturing for several years a user-friendly, modern face.

"And for them to take action this savage, this darned drastic…well, they sure as hell know something about Siberia that we don't. And whatever that may be, it sure scares the bejesus out of them."

"Wow," said Jimmy, unhelpfully. "You think they might rampage through someone else's oil fields with that Army of theirs?"

"No, I don't. But I think these events must lead us to think that Russia is very worried about her oil industry in Siberia. And I think that may lead the Kremlin to start searching far afield for new supplies, something that Russia has not needed to do in the past.

"Siberia, and to an extent Kazakhstan, have always provided enough. But if Siberia demanded independence, I think we'd find Russia in a global expansionist mood."

"Christ, I'd sure hate to wake up and find out they'd conquered Saudi Arabia or somewhere," added Jimmy.

"I don't think we'll find that, kiddo. But we got to watch them, and watch their movements internationally. We got enough trouble with China trying to buy up the entire world's oil supply, without the goddamned Ruskies joining in."

"Well, sir, Lenny's going for the passenger list from the nonexistent aircraft in the tundra. It'll sure be interesting to find out precisely who the Kremlin admits is no longer alive."

Arnold smiled and passed around the menus. "Order anything," he commanded. "I've ordered us another bottle of this Meursault because I know

Kathy will probably have fish. For us, my boy, I've ordered an excellent bottle of 1998 Pomerol—remember, all of you, that was the year the frost and rain hit the left bank of the Gironde and the great chateaux had a very difficult time.

"But on the right bank, the sun shone sweetly and the harvest was bountiful, and the wine all through St. Emilion and Pomerol was rich and plentiful…"

"Jesus," said Kathy, "would you listen to him? He thinks he's at the Last Supper."

"I hope to hell he's not," said Jimmy. "This is just great—and all because the ole Kremlin staged one of its periodic mass murders."

"Every cloud," replied Arnold, philosophically, "somehow has a silver lining. Even that big bastard darkening the east side of Red Square."

0900, MONDAY, OCTOBER 4
RUSSIAN NAVAL HEADQUARTERS, MOSCOW

Three of the four men who attended the meeting in the rotunda of the Senate were now seated around a much smaller table in company with the President: Prime Minister Kravchenko, Foreign Minister Nalyotov, and the Energy Minister, Oleg Kuts.

"Very well," called the President, "send for Admiral Rankov, will you?"

A Navy guard turned smartly on the marble floor of the grandiose room and marched toward the huge double doors. Moments later, the mighty figure of Admiral Vitaly Rankov strode into the room. The veteran Naval Commander, in his new status as Deputy Minister of Defense, wore no uniform.

He was dressed in a dark gray suit with a white shirt and military tie, and he still looked as if he could pull the bow-side five-oar in a Russian Olympic eight, which he once did.

Despite a passion for caviar served on delicious blinis, and Siberian beef topped with cheese, plus all manner of desserts, Vitaly Rankov somehow remained fit, and for a very big man, trim. This had much to do with a lifelong iron regimen on his ergometer, the killer rowing machine used by international oarsmen the world over.

With his eyes glued to the flickering computer as he hauled himself into Olympic selection, Vitaly could stop that digital clock at 6 minutes and 18 seconds for 2,000 meters. That's world-class, and that was his regular time in the run-up to the 1972 Olympics in Munich.

Today, at sixty, the towering Vitaly Rankov fought a daily battle to "break seven"—the young oarsman's mantra—and even this morning, fighting through the final "yards" on his stationary machine in his basement, he hit the 2,000-meter line in 6:58. Nearly killed him. But here he was.

"**Dobraye utra**—good morning, Admiral," greeted the President of all the Russians.

"Sir," replied Vitaly sharply, pushing his great shock of gray curly hair off his forehead. He took the chair left vacant on the President's right and nodded to the other three Ministers, all of whom he knew relatively well.

"As I mentioned to you on the telephone," said the President, "this is a matter of the utmost secrecy. Nonetheless, our Intelligence Service leads us to believe the forces of Argentina are preparing to launch another attack on the Falkland Islands, some twenty-eight years, I believe, after their last disastrous attempt."

This was of course the biggest single lie the President had told this week, but it was only Monday, and it was essentially kids' stuff compared with his record last week.

As it happened, the young Lieutenant Commander Rankov had received his first command, of a missile frigate, back in 1982. And like all of his colleagues he had watched with rapt fascination as the Royal Navy fought that epic sea battle off the Falkland Islands, during which they lost seven warships, including two Type-42 destroyers. Two remain on the bottom of the ocean; the other, HMS **Glasgow**, took a bomb amidships, straight through her hull and out the other side.

Admiral Rankov, as it happened, knew a great deal about that war in the South Atlantic. And he looked quizzically at the President. Then he said sternly, "I'm not sure the result would be the same today, sir. The British have been very, very shortsighted about their war-fighting capability. The Argentinians may be successful this time."

The President nodded, and continued, "At present we are only discussing a sudden, preemptive strike, which would certainly overrun the very flimsy British defenses of the islands. But I would like your opinions upon the likely outcome if the British again sailed south with the intention of blasting the Argentinians off their territory."

"Sir, that is a very complicated question. Mainly because we do not know the relative strength of the Argentinian fleet, nor its land forces. However, we do know they are quite formidable in the air."

"Vitaly, if I may take a worst-case scenario," said the President. "The Argentinians occupy the islands, and the airfields. Their Marines are in tight control. There is no internal resistance. The British send down an aircraft carrier packed with fighter-bombers and whatever guided-missile frigates and destroyers they have left, okay? Who wins?"

"Sir, all battles depend to a large degree on the will and brilliance of the overall commanders. In 1982 that Royal Navy Admiral outsmarted them, held his nerve, made no real mistakes, and in the end clobbered them. He was the first Admiral whose fleet ever defeated an Air Force.

Knocked out more than seventy Argentina fighter-bombers."

"Yes. I read that during the weekend," mused the President. "But, Vitaly, could you put your finger on perhaps one single aspect of the war at sea that cost the Argentinians victory? One critical path along which they failed?"

Admiral Rankov pondered the question. He was silent for a few moments, and then said, "Sir, the critical path for the Argentinians was always simple: take out either of the Royal Navy carriers, before they have established an airfield ashore, and the operation is over. You always need two decks in case one goes out of action even for a couple of hours—otherwise you lose all the aircraft you have in the air."

"Why so important?"

"Because that would have robbed the British land forces of adequate air cover. That would have meant the Army would have refused to go ashore. Because without air cover they would have had Dunkirk all over again, being pounded by Argentine bombs instead of those of Hitler."

"Hmmmm," said the President. "And why did the Argentinians not go for the carrier? And end it?"

"Mainly because they couldn't get to it. The South Atlantic is a very, very big place, and that Royal Navy Admiral was a very, very cunning Commander. He made damn sure they would never reach it. He never brought the carrier within range, except at night, when he knew the Argentinian Air Force did not fly."

"Well, if the same war happened again, how would they get to the carrier this time?"

"With great difficulty, sir. Unless they had a very quiet, very skillfully handled submarine that could locate and track it. But that's extremely hard to do, and I don't think the Argentines have the skill."

"Does anyone?"

"Possibly. But the Royal Navy Commanders are traditionally very good at this type of thing. Getting in close to a ship of that size would be damn near impossible. All carriers are permanently protected by an electronic ring of underwater surveillance. I suppose the Americans might get in and perhaps fire a torpedo, but even that's doubtful."

"How about our Navy? Could we do it?"

"The issue is, sir, could we do it without getting caught and sunk? I would not put my life savings on it. 'Specially against the Royal Navy...but you know, sir, I think the problem this time might not be quite so grave. Because I think modern advancements in rockets, missiles, and even bombs is so great, any commander would prefer to sink a carrier from the air.

"The damn things carry about a billion gallons of fuel. If you get in close enough, with a modern supersonic sea-skimming missile, that's the trick."

"And where would that leave the Argentinians—same as before?"

"Not if they could get a submarine in, maybe seven miles from the carrier, and take an accurate GPS reading on its precise position on the ocean. Then they could vector their fighter-bombers straight at it."

"And do they have **that** submarine capacity?"

"I don't think so, sir. The Royal Navy would almost certainly locate and sink them."

"If Argentina were to recruit an ally, to help them with this critical aspect of submarine warfare, who do they need?"

"The USA, sir."

"How about China?" asked the President, shrewdly trying to keep his Admiral off his own critical path.

"China! Christ, no. The Brits would pick them up before they reached Cape Town."

"How about France?"

"Possibly, but they lack experience. The French have never fought a war with submarines."

"Neither have we."

"No, sir. But I'd still make us the second choice if I were the C-in-C of the Argentinian Navy. We still have top flight commanders, and we probably have the ship that could do the job..."

"Oh, which one...?"

"Well, I'd go for one of our Akula-class nuclear boats myself. Hunter-killers, about ninety-five hundred tons, packed with missiles and torpedoes, excellent radar and sonar. The most modern ones are ten to fifteen years old, but lightly used, and very quiet."

"Where do we keep 'em?"

"Oh, there's a couple in the Pacific Fleet, two more in the Northern Fleet up near Murmansk."

"Do you know the ships personally? I mean are they ready to go?"

"One came out of refit last spring, sir. She's on sea trials right now, just completing. A very good ship, sir. I went out in her a month ago."

"Aha, and what's her name, this Akula-class hunter-killer?"

"She's **Viper**, sir. **Viper K-157.**"

"Thank you, Admiral. That will be all for the moment."

4:30 P.M., MONDAY, OCTOBER 11
FLORIDA GARDEN CONFITERIA
CORDOBA AVENUE DISTRICT,
BUENOS AIRES

It was always a favorite haunt of the military junta that ruled Argentina so spectacularly badly in the late 1970s and very early 1980s. It made for a kind of clamorous escape from the fierce undercurrents of unrest that were edging the great South American Republic of Argentina toward outright revolution.

It was a sanctuary from the hatred of the populace, a sanctuary with sweet tea, sugary pastries, and piped tango music. And it still stands today, still frequented by Argentinian military personnel, right next to the venerable old Harrods building, that far-lost symbol of a far-lost friendship.

The Generals and the Admirals always met here pre-1982 to indulge in military plots and plans against the British government. At that time they were just working out ways to look better, to stem the engulfing tide of the seething, restless middle classes. They were trying to stay in power. So unpopular was the junta that they really needed a rabble-rousing foreign policy to hang on to their limousines.

And in so many ways the year 2010 was not much different. The shattering defeat of 1982 still rankled with the populace down all the years. And the visions of the Falkland Islands—their very own Malvinas—still stood stark before them; high, wide, and handsome, very British and now chock-full of oil.

The inflamed, reckless ambitions of a junta of long ago was just as virulent in 2010, but now it lurked in the minds of a new breed of Argentinian military officer, better equipped, better trained, and better educated.

Which was why, on this cool, sunlit Monday afternoon, two senior Argentinian officers, one a General, the other an Admiral, plus a medium-rank Cabinet minister, were sitting quietly at a corner table in the **confiteria**, awaiting the arrival of a Russian emissary on an obviously secretive mission.

The appointment had been arranged by the Russian embassy, but it was stressed their official would not be in residence there. And the Russians had stressed they preferred the meeting to take place somewhere discreet.

And now the Argentinians waited, staring out through the wide windows onto tony Florida Avenue, down which their visitor would probably walk from the Claridge Hotel.

And they were not kept waiting long. At 4:32 p.m., the stocky, quietly dressed Gregor Komoyedov arrived. He was in his mid-fifties, wearing a dark blue suit, white shirt, and dark red tie, and carrying, as arranged, a copy of the **New Yorker** magazine. He stepped into the crowded **confiteria** and stared around. The Argentinian Minister, whose name was Freddie, turned and held up his hand. The Russian nodded and made his way through the throng to the corner table.

Freddie stood up and introduced General Eduardo Kampf and Admiral Oscar Moreno. All three of them were wearing civilian clothes, and they each shook the hand of the Russian Minister for Foreign Trade, whom the President had selected for this mission on the basis of his superior worldliness.

"I expect you would like some coffee, being a Russian," General Kampf said and smiled.

"That would be very civilized," replied the Russian. "Perhaps we should speak in English, your second language, I believe...?"

"No problem," replied the General. "And I should confirm we are extremely anxious to hear your business here—your embassy was very close-mouthed about it...for a minute we thought you might be declaring war!"

"Ah, you military guys, that's all you think about. My own background is deep in the Russian oil industry, strictly commercial. To us, war is unthinkable, mainly because it gets in the way of making money!"

Everyone laughed. Mostly because the Argentinians were not yet aware of the colossal insincerity of that remark. But old Gregor was a wily Muscovite wheeler-dealer from way back. He knew how to coax a subject along gently.

The coffee and pastries arrived, and, at a nod from the Admiral, the piped tango music began to play a tad higher. "I don't think we will be overheard," he said. "And I am looking forward to your proposition."

Gregor smiled. "But how do you know I have one?"

"Because you would not be here otherwise, having flown halfway around the world, on obvious orders from the President, in a dark and clandestine manner."

"Well, let me begin by assuming you all know of the recent massive oil strikes in the Malvinas," he said, skillfully banishing the British name for the islands from his vocabulary.

All three Argentinians nodded.

"And I imagine you continue to feel the same sense of injustice you had in 1982. After all, the oil is yours by rights, and most fair-minded people in the world understand that. How London can possibly proclaim they own those islands, eight thousand miles from England, and a mere three hundred miles off your long coastline…well, that's a mystery no one really grasps. But the British have some inflated views of both their past and their present."

"The Americans understand," said General Kampf.

"They'll understand anything they choose to," said Gregor Komoyedov. "Just so long as there's a good buck in it for them, ha?"

"They're going to make a good buck in the Malvinas," added Freddie. "We understand Exxon are in there already in partnership with British Petroleum."

"I did hear," added the Russian, "there was some talk the Argentinian military might be assessing the possibility of a new campaign against the Malvinas—a sudden, brutal, preemptive strike, and an occupation of the islands that could easily withstand a counterattack from the Royal Navy?"

"I wish," replied Admiral Moreno. "But no one's told me."

"Well, perhaps I transgress into military secrets that are none of my, or my country's, business."

"Perhaps you do," said the Admiral. "But we would all prefer you to go on talking…"

"If, for instance, you did find yourself owning the oil, you would find a very willing partner in the Russian government, to help you drill, pump, and market it, in the most profitable way.

"We could do for you what the Americans did for the Saudi Arabians. We have the know-how. And our pipeline techniques are probably second to none, since we pump directly out of the West Siberian Basin. And we are used to working in extreme weather conditions.

"No one could help you quite like we could. We would take over the operation completely, and pay you a generous royalty for every barrel. We would allow you to oversee the daily output, and we would build you a tanker terminal in order to maximize the exports. Our aim would be the U.S. market along their Gulf Coast."

"The snag is, of course," replied Freddie, "we do not own the Malvinas, nor have I discerned any anxiety on our government's part that we should own the Malvinas. I mean, we do get periodic bouts of anger from the media, that our birthright to those islands has somehow been grabbed away from us by an outmoded colonial power.

"And we do hear outbursts from politicians, that we should again try to negotiate a treaty with the British, which would ultimately make the islands ours. But nothing definite…no, nothing definite at all."

The table fell silent. Admiral Moreno signaled for more coffee, and since Gregor Komoyedov was plainly enjoying the sweet little pastries, he signaled for a few more of those as well.

And the sugar intake further galvanized the man from Moscow. "Gentlemen," he said, "do you have any idea what recent London governments have done to the British military? They have decimated their regiment system, the one that has terrified their opponents for about three hundred years. They have cut down on the numbers of armored vehicles, tanks, and artillery. Much of their equipment, including combat clothing, is out of date. Even their small arms are suspect.

"The Royal Navy has been beaten down, their fleet reduced to a pale shadow of that which faced down Hitler on the high seas. It would be fair to say the Royal Navy High Command is almost heartbroken at what has befallen it.

"A series of incompetent politicians has progressively castrated the military in Great Britain. And we watch them very carefully. They do not have one single operational interceptor in their fleet, or their Air Force. They are unable to put a survivable Carrier Battle Group together, not even to face a Third World Air Force.

"When we heard—perhaps wrongly—that there was talk here of a new offensive against the Malvinas, we were absolutely certain about one thing...if the Argentinians attempt it, they will achieve it. But perhaps I have, as they say, jumped the gun."

"You study these matters," said General Kampf. "You think our military, our Navy, and our Air Force have the capability to capture the Falkland Islands?"

"Yes, we do, with one or two gaps."

"Such as?" asked Admiral Moreno.

"We think your Achilles' heel may be the lack of a top-class attack submarine that could range in close to the Royal Navy's carrier, running deep and quiet, perhaps revealing her position to your very fine fighter pilots."

"You may be right about that," replied Oscar Moreno. "But remember, our Achilles' heel last time was the range of our aircraft. We could not refuel them sufficiently to get them round the back, to the east of Woodward's Battle Group.

Therefore he could concentrate his defenses to the west. I think this time we may have the range…but I cannot be absolutely certain. Failing to hit the Royal Navy carrier could still cost us a new war."

"Not if you had just a modicum of underwater assistance from Mother Russia." Gregor smiled. "That would seal your overwhelming victory. Very probably on the first day of the war."

And with that, Gregor Komoyedov stood up and wished them all good-bye, in classic Russian, **"Da svidaniya."** Adding, quietly, "Just a few things to ponder, gentlemen. If you would like to talk further I suggest Moscow. Perhaps your C-in-C would like to arrange something with our Ambassador here in Buenos Aires.

"Just mention the code word…**Viper K-157.**" He stepped toward the cafe door and added, flamboyantly, his arms spread wide apart, **"Viva Las Malvinas!!"**

And the instant, rousing cheers of his fellow cafe patrons echoed unmistakably in the ears of the wily Gregor Komoyedov as he stepped outside, summoned his waiting taxi, and rode twenty-four miles to Ezeiza Airport and an Aeroflot flight. Big European Airbus. Private. Not one other passenger. Direct to Sheremetyevo-2, the sprawling international airport that lies twenty miles to the northwest of Moscow.

CHAPTER THREE

0900, MONDAY, OCTOBER 18
THE KREMLIN
MOSCOW

General Eduardo Kampf and Admiral Oscar Moreno had spent a comfortable night in the sumptuous private apartment of the President of Russia, right here in the Senate Building.

Their journey from Buenos Aires had been conducted with such precision—private aircraft, government cars, darkened windows, no uniforms—it would be reasonable to surmise that absolutely no one knew the two top Argentinian commanders were in Moscow, save for those who were supposed to know.

General Kampf was commander of Argentina's Five Corps, headquartered at Bahia Blanca, close to the naval base at Puerto Belgrano, 280 miles southwest of Buenos Aires. General Moreno was Commander in Chief Fleet, a position once held by the hawkish Argentinian patriot Admiral Jorge Anaya, the man who had taken his nation to war in the Falkland Islands twenty-eight years ago.

For the past week, both men had been cloistered in the Casa Rosada, the Presidential Palace on the Plaza de Mayo in Buenos Aires. Each morning in company with the President of Argentina, plus the most trusted Ministers, the officers had taken coffee out on the great columned balcony, before which a one-million-strong crowd had once stood and roared, **M-a-a-l-v-i-n-a-s!! M-a-a-l-v-i-n-a-s!!** when news of the Argentinian troops landing on the Falklands had finally broken in the spring of 1982.

Today, once more consumed with the thrill of potential conquest, General Kampf and Admiral Moreno sat in front of the President of Russia and his ever-faithful Navy Chief, Admiral Vitaly Rankov, in the grandeur of the enormous rotunda.

Both Argentinians had served in the 1982 war against the British: Kampf as a young Lieutenant hopelessly trying to defend the garrison at Goose Green in the face of the rampaging, slightly desperate Second Battalion Parachute Regiment; Moreno as a Lieutenant on board one of the old ex-U.S. destroyers trying to protect the doomed **General Belgrano**. Both men had wept at the Argentina surrender on June 14, just ten weeks after the war had begun.

But now, cradled here in the immense stronghold of Russian military power, things were looking sweetly different. And the huge wintry sun struggling into the gray skies high above the onion domes of St. Basil's Cathedral cast a sense of righteousness upon them all.

Of course the Malvinas are yours...what rights do the British have to them...? Who do they think they are? And the oil? That huge field probably begins under mainland Argentina.

And here was the towering figure of this confident veteran Russian Admiral, laughing loudly at what he called the wreckage of the Royal Navy... **"Destroyed, willfully, by its own government! Ha ha ha!** Gentlemen, there is no way you can lose this battle.

"Firstly, I doubt the British could raise a battle fleet. Secondly, they hardly have an air strike force to put in an aircraft carrier. And thirdly, if they can find a few tired old Harrier jet fighters, with a little help from us, you'll sink the carrier. And the Harriers will all run out of fuel and fall into the sea. Checkmate. **Ha ha ha!** Poor bastards."

Even the President laughed, and he was taking this entire conversation very seriously. "Vitaly," he said, "I want you to explain to our guests exactly why we can make such a difference to the Argentinian strategy if, and only if, the British elect to sail once more for the South Atlantic and fight to recapture their islands."

"Las Malvinas are not," interjected Admiral Moreno, "their islands. They are ours."

"Of course," replied the President, smiling. "Thoughtless of me. I meant, should they wish to try once more to capture Las Malvinas."

"General Kampf," said Vitaly, "as a senior military commander of land troops, you of course understand better than any of us, no one would dream of putting ashore an army several thousand strong on a fortified island, as the Malvinas will most certainly be, without proper air cover. Correct?"

"Absolutely not, Admiral," replied General Kampf. "That would be suicide. The troops would be strafed to pieces with no reasonable prospect of hitting back. Every man on the beach would be at the mercy of enemy air attack, and there'd be no British supply lines. The men would be cut off from their ammunition, food, shelter, and hospitals. For them to fight on would be impossible. I doubt any land force commander would attempt anything so crazy."

"And would the British High Command be aware of this?"

"Of course. They'd never do it. Neither would anyone."

"So," exclaimed Vitaly, "you have a short sharp war, with only one single objective. Take out the Royal Navy carrier. Then they have no air defense for the men they intend to land on the beaches."

"Correct. No carrier. No landing. The Malvinas are ours."

Admiral Rankov stood up, walked around the table, and shook the hand of the Commander of the Argentine land forces. "General...how the Americans say? We sing from the same hymn sheet!"

"But, I think these facts finally dawned on the Argentinians last time and they were unable to hit the carrier." The President had covered this conversation before, and he knew the answers. He was just feeding Admiral Rankov the lines he wanted repeated.

"Oh, this time it will be very different," replied the Russian Admiral. "You see, sir," he said, turning to his ultimate boss, "fighter aircraft are like motorbikes with wings. They go very fast and run out of fuel in less than ninety minutes. We do have extra tanker refueling now, but a run of way more than one thousand miles from the air base at Rio Grande is still very, very difficult. Not much time to waste searching vast, empty seas for a wandering aircraft carrier.

"Only just time for a fast one-shot strike on a known target, turn around and try to make it home on what's left in the tank. Last time, the Argentine Air Force pilots were often unaware of the damn carrier's location, and that Royal Navy Admiral was amazingly smart keeping it out of the way.

"The trouble was, Argentina had no effective submarine that could creep around, locate the carrier, and silently stay with it. They still don't have a ship good enough to do that. But we do.

"The Russian submarine can send a satellite communication to our friends in the Argentine air control rooms that will put their fighter jets bang on target with accurate readings. Either that, or slam a wire-guided torpedo straight into the hull of the carrier. Whichever's easiest. The Royal Navy carrier will be history on the first day. The British these days simply don't have the muscle to stop it."

"You hit it underwater? Or we hit it from the air?" asked General Kampf.

"Oh, probably from the air," said Vitaly. "But possibly from underwater. Our submarine would need to close to perhaps seven thousand yards to get a hit, and the British destroyers and ASW frigates would probably find us and make life very hot. A couple of active homing torpedoes make a very great...er...hullabaloo in the water.

"But your Air Force can launch an armada, and the Royal Navy may hit some of them, but they won't hit them all. Most definitely not. Your guys will get bombs and missiles into that fleet, the carrier will explode, tons of jet fuel, many sailors will burn or drown. But that's war. That's defeat. And the British forces will have no alternative but to go home to England, while you throw a victory party in Port Stanley.

"I come, bring Red Army choir, and good Russian vodka. Celebrate for both our great countries.

Ha ha ha! Then we both make huge profits, hah? Make stupid Americans pay top dollar for beautiful Argentina oil. Siberian traitors go fuck themselves. Ha ha ha!"

The Russian President looked sharply across at Rankov, as if warning him of the danger of that last statement. But it was clear the Argentina military men had neither noticed nor understood. And just then the door opened and the ebullient figure of Gregor Komoyedov came exuberantly through the rotunda's enormous wooden doors.

"My friends!" he cried. "How are my friends from the **confiteria**? So good to see you again. We partners yet? Or do I come back later?"

He bounded over to Admiral Moreno and gave him a mighty Russian bear hug and a kiss on both cheeks. Then he did the same to Eduardo Kampf. Then he stood back with a great beaming smile.

"Well," he said, repeating the question, "we partners, eh?"

The President looked very slightly perplexed, as if Gregor might be slightly rushing his fences.

But both General Kampf and Admiral Moreno stepped forward, and they took each one of the three Russians by the hand.

"Oh, yes," said Admiral Moreno. "We are most definitely partners."

"Pastries!" yelled Gregor. "Someone bring the sweetest, most lovely pastries for my friends from the southern oceans. And coffee. And vod-ka. The finest vodka!"

And the boss of all the Russians, smiling broad-ly, stood up and walked to the door to arrange the delivery, doubling up as the Kremlin butler, for the first and only time of his entire Presidency. He could have kissed Gregor Komoyedov, that old Moscow smoothie.

Back in Buenos Aires, at the highest level of government, nothing was quite as innocent as General Kampf and Admiral Moreno had made out to the Russians. **What...us? Reinvade the Falklands? Hadn't really thought about it... not really one of our priorities...Argentine government has said nothing.** And would you be interested if we could help? **Well...er...that's interesting. But we're quite unprepared for anything like that.**

As Admiral Morgan might have put it, Bullshit. They'd thought about it, all right. In fact there was a group of Argentinian military officers who had thought of hardly anything else for a quarter of a century. They'd seethed over the sheer humiliation of the war in the South Atlantic in 1982, of 15,000 Argentinian troops and commandoes surrender-ing to a couple of hundred British paratroopers. They'd seethed all right. And not one of them had ever forgotten or forgiven their imperious, victori-ous former friends from Great Britain.

And curiously, the Florida Garden **confiteria** was the known headquarters of the renegades, right there on Cordoba Avenue in Buenos Aires, the very place where the Russian Trade Minister Gregor Komoyedov had charmed the jackboots off the two Argentinian officers. Well, metaphorically, he had.

The wide, bright cafe, with its bubbling fresh ground coffees, superb sweet pastries, and loud piped tango music was the meeting point of the civilian informants and the military top brass— the ones who really cared about their missing islands. They called themselves the **Malvinistas**.

The British, of course, with a rush of good intentions after Margaret Thatcher's great triumph, maintained for some years a tri-Service force, with a joint headquarters, under the rotational command of a two-star officer. This remotest of garrisons of the British armed forces was meant to be a stern deterrent to the Argentinians not to try anything rash in the foreseeable future, and also to provide reassurance to the Falkland Islanders that Aunt Maggie's boys would come charging back at the drop of a tin hat.

For a start they built a new airfield, at Mount Pleasant, thirty-five miles west of the tiny capital city of Stanley, located at latitude 51.49.22 South, 58.25.50 West. It was laid out on high ground, at an elevation of 242 feet, with two runways, one 8,500 feet in length, over one and a half miles of flat blacktop. They also built a fine military complex, for their shore-based troops—with a gym, swimming pool, shops, messes, and club facilities. They even built a church.

But, as relations with Argentina began to improve, the threat of a renewed attack on the islands lessened. And Great Britain's government saw an opportunity for severe cuts in the military presence. They began to make significant force reductions, and as the years passed they cut back the little garrison in the Falklands, to the bone.

With pressures mounting for British military presence in parts of Africa, the Balkans, Afghanistan, and the Middle East, the Falklands very nearly slipped out of the equation altogether.

In Whitehall, the "mandarins" who run the Civil Service would cheerfully have closed the entire thing down, but for the moral requirement to reassure the Falkland Islanders that Great Britain really did have an enduring interest in their future.

The other brake on outright British detachment from the islands and their inhabitants was the impressive structure of the Falkland Islands Memorial Chapel, at Pangbourne Nautical College, due north of Portsmouth Dockyard in the English County of Berkshire.

This church was built as the ultimate symbol of British naval and military skill, and courage, in a modern war. It stands as a reminder of the sacrifices made in the South Atlantic, and inside its portals, on two high granite walls, the name and rank of every man who died in the battle is carved into the stone—250 of them.

Even the most self-seeking political economist could scarcely recommend cutting all military ties with the islands, thus sending a message to every one of those families that it had all been in vain. The British didn't really mean it, or any longer need it. They all died for nothing. Names carved in granite for a cause made of gossamer.

And so, the garrison remained. Because the government reluctantly accepted it had to remain. They cut it back to near useless operational capabilities. And soon it was regarded, by all of those who served there, as the Forgotten Force, stranded in the South Atlantic for months at a time, vulnerable to an attack by just about anyone with a couple of spare missiles.

Even the discovery of oil, major oil, did not penetrate the minds of the bureaucrats and politicians. Safe in the ironclad security of their own jobs, they whiled away the years in Whitehall, preparing to claim their even more secure retirement pensions, while scowling even at the mention of the very expensive Falkland Islands. Even the Saudis understood the drastic need to protect their oil with a heavy armed presence. Not, however, Britain's Labour government.

Left largely to its own devices, operationally stripped to its bare minimum, the garrison was working for a government that believed Great Britain could not possibly be caught out again. Not so long as the new Mount Pleasant Airfield (MPA) was functional and capable of handling a rapid reinforcement force at the first sign of danger.

But the 2010 government appeared to have forgotten entirely that on May 21, the opening day of the 1982 war, it took about three minutes and one British thousand-pound bomb to render Argentinian takeoffs and landings from the Falklands virtually impossible for fast-jet aircraft, for the entire duration of the war.

Right now, in the autumn of 2010, there was just a company group of the Third Rifles, 140 men rotating every nine months. They consisted of just a small HQ and three rifle platoons. They had a few heavy machine guns but absolutely no mortars or antitank weapons.

The savagely diminished presence of the Royal Navy was sufficient to bring joy to the heart of Admiral Oscar Moreno. There was one aging Fleet Auxiliary ship whose sole purpose was to resupply groceries and fuel to South Georgia, the other British protectorate in the South Atlantic, some 1,100 miles away, southeast.

And there was the 1,400-ton patrol ship, HMS **Leeds Castle**, which was designed for a 30mm gun with a range of seven miles, a platform for a Sea King helicopter, and facilities for a detachment of Royal Marines. The helicopter was missing and so was the detachment of Royal Marines. But the gun was still there.

Both ships were stationed in Mare Harbor, a windswept little bay five miles to the south of the airport, where the Royal Navy's tiny HQ is based.

A few years back it was decided that a heavily armed frigate, packing a lethal, modern, can't-miss guided-missile system, was essential for the defense of the islands. But these days, the islands received only an occasional, irregular visit from a Royal Naval frigate on task 4,000 miles to the north in the Caribbean, essentially looking for drugs.

The Royal Air Force presence had also been scaled right back. They kept a VC-10 refueling tanker and a search-and-rescue Sea King helicopter. But they no longer had any lift capacity. For stores and supplies, the work had been contracted out to a civilian firm, which normally operated on oil rigs.

A decade ago the Royal Air Force was forced to withdraw from service a flight of four Tornado F3s owing to the prohibitive cost of continuing a service line for obsolete fighter aircraft. At the time it was intended they would be replaced by the air defense version of the new Typhoon (the Eurofighter), which was still not operational, despite having been the RAF's top priority program for twenty years.

It was not considered possible to send Typhoons to the Falklands. And the Ministry of Defense in Whitehall considered this an acceptable risk.

They decided only one thing mattered: making sure the international airfield at Mouth Pleasant stayed operational. And for that they installed a Rapier missile system, manned by RAF personnel. That was two towed launchers, each mounting eight missiles for short-range air defensive cover across the airfield. The Rapier missiles had a maximum range of around three miles and a ceiling of under 10,000 feet. Its surveillance radar was good for about twelve miles.

Literally thousands of evenings were spent by Argentinian military personnel in the Florida Garden **confiteria**, most of them gleefully, discussing the British defensive capability in the Falkland Islands.

They were older now. Mostly in their fifties and sixties. But these were pilot officers who had somehow bailed out of downed fighter aircraft at 600 mph. There were others who had been pulled out of the Atlantic after the **General Belgrano** was sunk; still others who had fought and been wounded on the freezing mountainous terrain of East Falkland—and perhaps above all, there were the officers who had surrendered their beaten troops, unforgettably, humiliatingly, on the melancholy morning of June 14, 1982.

That was the core of the **Malvinistas** who met in the cafe on Cordoba Avenue in downtown Buenos Aires. They were men who believed there would be a next time. They were men who knew that the future attack must be a swift, violent strike, without warning. Surprise was everything.

This was nothing remotely like the gung-ho amateurish group that had cheerfully gone into a major war against one of the best high-tech naval machines in the world. By the time General Kampf and Admiral Moreno returned from Moscow, the Argentine military had identified and selected a small group of carefully chosen officers and briefed them to begin detailed planning. Information was released strictly on a need-to-know basis.

This was a burgeoning Argentinian force no longer packed with conscripts who knew nothing of combat. It had a command and staff structure based on the United States model, and its doctrine was based solidly on lessons learned in 1982.

Conscription had been abolished in 1995, and since then a 55,000-strong regular army had been built, half the size, devoid of rookies and four times more professional than any battalion that had tried to take the Malvinas twenty-eight years earlier. It was infinitely better equipped, better organized, and better trained. Worse yet, for the Brits, this Argentinian High Command knew just about everything there was to know about the troops they regarded as occupying forces in the Malvinas.

The prime reason for this was the oil. The advent of exploration, drilling, and recovery of the crude, particularly in the North Falkland Basin and the Special Co-Operation Area in the southwest, had opened up the region, wide, in the 1990s.

Most of the oil consortiums involved had established small bases in the Stanley area, and there had long been a regular flow of personnel to and from the islands. Many of them arrived on the Santiago-based Lan Chile Airline, which flies Boeing 737s regularly between Punta Arenas and Mount Pleasant.

This had enabled Argentinian agents to move freely in and out of the country for several years, observing the British garrison forces, identifying their strengths, and many weaknesses, their equipment, their base area, their routines, their patrolling patterns, and other military activities.

In the Florida Garden **confiteria** they knew more about the British Army and Royal Navy in the South Atlantic than the Ministry of Defense knew in London. And Messrs. Kampf and Moreno had been telling a lie of the most majestic proportions when they first had asserted to their Russian visitor, Gregor Komoyedov, that no one in Argentina had given much thought to another assault on the Malvinas.

And now, armed with highly detailed charts and notebooks, General Kampf and Admiral Moreno were in conference in Bahia Blanca, the Five Corps headquarters, where the principal military capability for the whole of southern Argentina is located.

With them was General Carlos Alfonso, the Army Chief of Staff, and Admiral Alfredo Baldini, the Chief of Naval Operations, and the Air Force Chief, General Hector Allara, a former Mirage attack pilot over Falkland Sound in 1982.

All five men thought they could be ready any time in the new year. And all five men believed their attack should begin when the visiting Royal Navy frigate was well and truly on her way home, steaming hard toward the Caribbean, at least five days out of Mare Harbor.

General Allara was especially keen on this aspect of the strategy since his French-built Mirage jet fighter had been hit and destroyed by a Sea Dart missile launched from HMS **Coventry**, north of Falkland Sound, in the hours before the British destroyer was sunk by Argentinian bombs.

Hector had bailed out into the water, and these many years later, no one was more aware than he that a well-handled Royal Navy guided-missile ship represented a serious opponent. He saw no reason to tangle with one, unless it was unavoidable. Sitting still, and waiting for the British frigate to leave town, was, in his view, the most agreeable option.

Five Corps had under its command the First Armored Brigade, stationed inland to the northeast at Tandil; the Eleventh Mechanized Brigade, stationed far south on the coast at Rio Gallegos, 490 miles directly west of the Falklands; the Sixth Mountain Brigade at Neuquen, deep inland in northern Patagonia; and the Ninth Mechanized Brigade at Comodoro Rivadavia, which stands on the coast 360 miles north of Rio Gallegos.

Thus Five Corps had a light armored battalion, medium artillery, air defense, army aviation and engineering, signals and logistics. And it had its one-third share of Argentina's 256 main battle tanks, 302 light tanks, 48 reconnaissance vehicles, 742 armored personnel carriers, and 6 attack helicopters.

The Corps's infantry division was armed with the most modern recoilless rifles, submachine guns, general-purpose machine guns, Browning M2 heavy machine guns, mortars, and antitank guided missiles. Five Corps's artillery carried a formidable range of howitzers. They had low-altitude surface-to-air missiles, Bofors aircraft guns, and a whole range of other antiaircraft guns.

More important, they knew how to use the entire arsenal. And right now their commanders were beginning to move their operations south, to the coastal regions down toward the Falkland

Islands. This applied particularly to the Argentine Air Force, which realized it must once more, for the second time in twenty-eight years, reactivate its sprawling Rio Grande air base in Tierra del Fuego, the 1982 home of Commander Jorge Colombo's heroic Second Naval Fighter and Attack Squadron.

The base lies right on the coast at the mouth of the river, forty-two miles southeast of the Bay of San Sebastian, a big inlet, twenty miles across.

This was the base for Argentina's French-built Dassault-Breguet Super-Etendard, the single-seat naval attack aircraft that delivered the 650-knot, radar-homing half-ton antiship missile, the Exocet—the one that incinerated the Royal Navy's Type-42 destroyer HMS **Sheffield** on the fourth day of the 1982 war.

The Super-Es, especially modified with extra gas tanks fitted under one wing, had an 860-mile range—sufficient to get well within striking range of the seas around the Falkland Islands.

Back then, the Rio Grande base was the start point of the Exocet missile's deadly journey, but this time the strategy would be very different. Because this time the Argentine forces would hold the airfield at Mount Pleasant. Or, at least they would if General Kampf had anything to do with it.

But any attacking air force needs a home base, on native soil. And Rio Grande would once more be home to a squadron of the fabled French-built

Super-Es, and there the pilots and ground crew would live, work, and train as one from November, until it became clear that Argentina not only owned and controlled the Malvinas, but there was no one on the horizon still planning to do anything about it.

Right now the entire operation was just about as highly classified, utterly secret, as anything can ever be in a South American country. But Argentinians talk, and they talk with emotion, fervor, and optimism. Which was why, back in the Florida Garden **confiteria**, rumor was rife there was to be a new assault on the Malvinas.

By eleven p.m. on Friday, October 29, a crowd had gathered before the Casa Rosada Presidential Palace on the Plaza de Mayo. It was not yet in the tens of thousands, but it certainly numbered several thousand. And, as the weekend throb of the tango began to permeate hundreds of bars and clubs in Buenos Aires, there was, very suddenly, a rapidly spreading sense of heightened expectation and hope.

And even as the moon rose above the dark, faded elegance of the old city, an ever-rising, rhythmic roar of unbridled passion could be heard from the Plaza de Mayo. It was a cry from a thousand hearts, a hymn to the slain Argentinian warriors of 1982...**Viva las M-a-a-l-v-i-n-a-s!! Viva las M-a-a-l-v-i-n-a-s!!**

1200, MONDAY, NOVEMBER 2
NATIONAL SECURITY AGENCY
FORT MEADE, MARYLAND

Lt. Commander Jimmy Ramshawe normally placed South America about eighth on his list of priorities. Nonetheless, he always enjoyed reading English-language newspapers from foreign capital cities. Sometimes he took a few days to get to them, but he always got to them.

Today he was scouring the **Buenos Aires Herald**, the English-language daily that specializes in politics and business news and is renowned for its outspoken editorials, written fiercely against whoever seemed to be screwing life up for the Argentinians.

During the Dirty War of the 1970s and '80s, the **Herald** was so unremitting in its condemnation of military and police abuses that its editor had to go into hiding after threats against his family.

Of all the newspapers Jimmy Ramshawe was not really interested in but could not afford to miss, the no-punches-pulled **Buenos Aires Herald** stood right at the top of the list.

And right now he was preoccupied by one particular story that should have been confined to the business section, but was given enormous prominence on the front page of the paper. The headline read:

OIL STRIKE ON PATAGONIA COAST
HIGHLIGHTS MALVINAS OUTRAGE

"Hullo," muttered James. "The bloody gauchos are at it again." This was a statement of such astonishing unawareness that even Jimmy, with his Aussie brand of outback humor but high intelligence, was moved to reconsider.

"Tell the truth, I'm not so sure what a bloody gaucho is, except he rides a horse, carries a knife, eats a lot of beef, and doesn't give a rat's ass about anyone."

As a description of the native Argentinian horsemen and cowboys, there was an element of truth in this. However, the badly missed point was the gauchos didn't give a rat's ass about the oil strike either. This was a matter for the big hitters of Argentinian business.

The **Buenos Aires Herald** had published a story that speculated, with much authority, on a possible rich seam of oil and gas discovered a few miles to the north of the Patagonian port of Rio Gallegos. It had absolutely nothing to do with the Argentinian naval base located in that city.

Rio Gallegos had long been a seaport for the export of coal from the huge mines found 150 miles west of the city. There had also been oil discoveries in the region, of sufficient volume to justify a sizeable refinery in Rio Gallegos. But according to the **Herald**, this new discovery was right on the coast, stretching out under Argentina's coastal waters.

They quoted an executive from the Argentine state oil company, who said:

It cannot be a mere coincidence that the Patagonian oil fields plainly run from the coalfields to the coast, and then in a dead straight line to the Malvinas, where the biggest oil and gas strikes in recent years have been confirmed.

The **Herald** reasoned:

If that is true, then the oil fields on the islands MUST be the property of Argentina, since we are the clear and rightful owners of the Malvinas, and the ONLY country with coastal waters and seabed above the oil.

Argentina's claim on the islands has always been correct and unchallengeable politically, even the British understand that. It now appears to be unchallengeable geologically. The rock strata that has housed the oil for thousands of years is purely Argentinian, not British.

Their absurd claim to own the Malvinas would be as if we claimed

their North Sea oil because a few Argentinian families had settled on the east coast of Scotland.

Until now, the oil companies have always stated the oil on the Argentine mainland and the oil in the Falklands are separate issues. However, last month's new discovery north of Rio Gallegos has joined up the last dot in a long chain of Argentinian oil fields. The oil is ours, obviously ours. All of it.

And what is our government, and indeed our military, doing about it? THEY OWE THE PEOPLE AN EXPLANATION...VIVA LAS MALVINAS!!

"Christ," said Jimmy.

In an entirely separate story in the business section there was a long article about the financial ramifications of the new strike—the likelihood of 500,000 barrels a day, the need for yet another huge refinery in Rio Gallegos, and the prosperity that would occur in southern Patagonia.

On the editorial pages, there was a piece by the editor of the **Herald**, pointing out the new strike had made the Malvinas even more difficult to reclaim. The British were now backed by the giant American oil corporation that had joined BP in the oil fields southwest of Port Stanley. They would likely dig in even more fiercely, probably even refuse to negotiate further.

"The British government has never been anything less than dogmatic, unreasonable, and forever obdurate," he raged. **"Perhaps now is the time for Argentina once more to consider the military option."**

"Christ," repeated Jimmy. And then, slowly, "I'm telling you, that oil business causes more bloody trouble on this planet than any other issue in the entire history of mankind. Except religion."

He pulled up a map on his big computer and punched in the buttons that would reveal the coast of southern Patagonia and its proximity to the Falkland Islands.

"I'll say one thing," he muttered, "it is a bloody straight line, and no error."

He pondered the story, trying to work out whether it had anything to do with the United States and its national security. And the answer was clearly no. **If the ole gauchos wanna fight the Brits over those rat-hole islands again, well, let 'em. It really is not our business.**

Nonetheless, he logged all the data in his special computer file, the one designed purely as a reminder to him, any time he wanted to check a global issue.

But the impending row over the Falklands stayed on his mind, and at the end of the afternoon he made a copy of the articles in the **Buenos Aires Herald**. Then he posted them off, regular mail, to Admiral Morgan. He just scrawled "FYI" at the head of the first sheet and left it at that.

Seven days later, however, on Monday, November 9, there were two developments that caught his interest. The first was a memorandum from Ryan Holland, the veteran career diplomat from Mississippi, who was now the United States Ambassador to Argentina. His communiqué had been sent directly to the State Department, but was then forwarded to the CIA and the NSA.

It read:

Continued Friday and Saturday night disturbances in the Plaza de Mayo. That's the huge square in front of the Presidential Palace in the center of Buenos Aires. The crowd appears to grow in size every night. On Saturday the police estimate there were 12,000 people, all chanting Viva las Malvinas!!

I mention this because there have been no such demonstrations here for many years. I cannot understand this sudden rise in public indignation over those damned islands. Though I did notice a hot editorial in the Herald **the other day, claiming the oil recently dis-**

covered on the Falkland Islands was in fact the property of Argentina.

The Herald's **editor, a nice enough guy with a plainly hysterical streak, was actually recommending the use of military force again. I expect it will all blow over, but those crowds were very substantial, and loud, getting louder. At no time did the President appear on the balcony of the Palace, and there was no indication of any official action being contemplated.** Ryan Holland, Ambassador to Argentina.

One hour after Lt. Commander Ramshawe read the communiqué, his direct telephone line rang. Admiral Morgan on the line.

"Hey, Jimmy, thank you for the cuttings from Buenos Aires. Very interesting. Just remember it's easy to dismiss stuff, easy to say it's not our business. But remember last time, we ended up standing up to our armpits in that mess. The Brits and the Argentinians were really slugging it out, fighter-bombers hitting the Atlantic by the dozen, warships hitting the bottom of the Atlantic. It was a very nasty, bitterly fought war...and the USA was right in the middle of it, helping Ronnie Reagan's best friend Margaret Thatcher to win it..."

"Sir, I was only about four years old at the time."

"Well, you should have been paying attention."

"Yessir. But I'm definitely paying attention now. I just read a communiqué from our Ambassador in Buenos Aires…"

"Ryan Holland, right? Cunning old guy. Doesn't make many mistakes, and more important, doesn't waste a lot of time on rubbish."

"Nossir. Want me to tell you what he says?"

"Sure. Always listen to Ryan Holland, my boy. He usually knows what he's saying."

Jimmy read. And at the end of it, Arnold Morgan was very thoughtful. "Kinda fits with what the **Herald** was saying, right? Growing indignation about the Brits' claim, not only on the islands, but also on the oil."

"Well, presumably we supported that claim in 1982, so we're kinda stuck with it now, huh?"

"Yes. We are. That's why these observations in Buenos Aires may well be important."

"Well, Ryan says he is not seeing anything official."

"It doesn't need to be official, does it?" said Arnold Morgan. "Argentina has spent a lot of time being ruled by a military junta. And officers from all three services have enormous influence in that country.

"In 1982, a couple of Admirals were almost entirely responsible for that war. And if there was anything similar going on right now, it would be very difficult to run the plotters to ground. Doesn't mean it isn't happening though, does it?"

"No, it doesn't. Just as the United Nations search team couldn't find Saddam's nuclear program in Iraq, didn't mean he didn't have one, did it?"

"No, Jimmy. It did not." The Admiral spoke thoughtfully. "It meant the UN guys could not find it. That's all. **Can't find** and **doesn't exist** are not the same. And only a left-wing politician could think they were."

"Do you think we ought to do anything?"

"Well, not in a big hurry. But I would not be surprised if something was brewing. And it might not hurt to have the CIA check out the military bases along that southern coast of Argentina. Just in case. Just in case they pick anything up."

"Okay, sir. I'll get right on it, and anything shakes loose I'll keep you informed."

"Right, and get some reading done on the 1982 war in the South Atlantic. You never know, you might be glad of the knowledge someday. Read Admiral Sandy Woodward's book. It's the most accurate and interesting account."

"Okay, sir. See you soon."

For the following few days, Jimmy Ramshawe tried to understand the causes and results of the Argentine decision to make a military landing on the Falkland Islands twenty-eight years ago. It was, he decided, pretty damned obvious they decided to go for it after a slashing British government defense review in 1981 that saw both Royal Navy aircraft carriers **Hermes** and **Invincible** sold to India and Australia, respectively.

It was also, he considered, a blinding error of judgment on Argentina's behalf: to misjudge both the dates upon which the carriers would actually **leave** England and the fact that Margaret Thatcher was a very determined Prime Minister—a lady of whom President Reagan once said, "She's the best man they've got."

Anyway, so far as Jimmy could see, it was a total screwup, bound for failure from way back, and a lesson for those determined to pick a fight with someone much tougher than they look.

It was a quiet time, globally and politically, coming up to Christmas, and no one was getting wildly excited about anything, not even the Palestinians. Jimmy's studies were seriously interrupted only twice, both times by Lenny Suchov over at CIA headquarters in Langley, Virginia.

The first time was to reveal the Russians never did issue another formal press release about the Siberians who had died in the plane crash in the tundra. At least they did not issue one that named the dead. They only announced the wreckage had not been found, and there were elements of doubt about who was and who was not on board. The military authorities therefore considered it "inappropriate" to make any formal statement about the disaster.

As Lenny had predicted, no one in the media felt much like braving the arctic weather and conducting their own search in northern Siberia. Especially as the government had cordoned the entire area off, banned private aircraft, and banned private investigations.

"All that," said Lenny wryly, "to prevent a search for an aircraft that was not there in the first place. Clever, hah? No one could get caught doing one single wrong thing."

This left, of course, only the missing, and their distraught families. And three days after his first call, Lenny was back on the line with a report, meticulously put together by the CIA's men in Moscow and Yekaterinburg. It contained the names of nine people who had just vanished.

But the list was distinguished by one fact: none of their families knew of any flight that would have taken their husbands, sons, fathers, or brothers away to the far north. No one knew anything about any conference in Murmansk. And it was most unusual for any of them, apparently, to travel by Russian Air Force jet.

These were extremely distinguished men, all of them occupying positions of the highest order, both corporate and governmental. It was only provincial government, but this particular province was bigger than the USA. These were very important men.

There was Sergei Pobozhiy. Vanished. Went to his office that day, never seen again. There was Jaan Valuev, the OJSC boss. Gone. A billionaire, Chairman of Barcelona FC, and no one knows where he is, or where he had gone that day. There was Boris Nuriyev, the Senior Financial Vice President of LUKOIL, the biggest corporation in Russia. **"Where the hell was he?"** demanded Lenny, adding, **"People of that importance** cannot **just vanish, trust me. Not even in Russia."**

And where was Roman Rekuts, a bigger-than-life guy, who stepped into the snow boots of the murdered Mikhallo Masorin, and was the uncrowned ruler of Western Siberia. **"Where's he gone?"** grated Lenny. **"And what about his Chief of oil operations, Anton Katsuba? He's a really tough ex-drillmaster on the rigs. Was he really killed in a goddamned plane crash that no one can find? His wife does not think so. He never mentioned anything about a journey by air, and neither did the rest of them. They all were just going to Yekaterinburg.**

And that included, apparently, the First Minister of the Central Siberian Federal District, and the new Chief Executive of the Russian Far

East, plus his renowned Energy Minister, Mikhail Pavlov, the man who literally masterminded the Trans-Siberian pipeline. All of them vanished.

"Nine of them," yelled the excitable Lenny. "How you say? Vamoosed. And no one seems to know anything. The Air Force claims to have lost its plane, won't even name the missing aircrew. And the government wishes it could help. Yeah, right. I've known these bastards for too long."

Jimmy sat pensively listening to the irate Lenny, predictably furious at behavior from the modern Russian government that mirrored that of the old Soviet Union.

At length he said, "Lenny, are all of the families agreed the missing guys were going to Yekaterinburg?"

The CIA spymaster checked his file. "Yes, they're agreed on that."

"Okay, then whatever happened may very well have happened in Yekaterinburg, right?"

"Correct, Jimmy. And I can tell you are about to wander down the investigation path I went down, and then steal my best lines. Selfish Australian bastard, hah?"

Jimmy laughed. "Yeah, well, I was only going to mention that when the government announced the plane crash, just one day after it apparently happened, they must have been damn certain right then the guys were never going to be seen again."

"Precisely," said Lenny. "So the guys were either transported away from the city and executed, or murdered right there in the city...right?"

"Any report of anything unusual happening in the downtown area...?"

"Keep quiet, Australian bastard...I'm coming to that! Now, I have one report from our agent, and we only got the report because I asked him if he noticed anything. He did not think it important enough to mention by himself..."

"And did he?"

"He did. He remembers from his diary he was downtown in Yekaterinburg on Monday morning, September twenty-seventh because he was having his hair cut. God knows why, he's damn near bald. Anyway, usually he parks his car and walks down Central Avenue and then cuts through one of the side streets to the barbershop.

"But on this day he remembers one side street was cordoned off..."

"Did he remember which one...?"

"Silence, Australian bastard," said Lenny, routinely. "No, he didn't. But when I asked him he said he couldn't remember the name, but it was the street down the side of the big SIBNEFT office building..."

"Get outta here!" said Jimmy incredulously. "Ole Sergei Pobozhiy's place, one of the missing guys, right?"

"How the hell do you remember that?"

"Mostly because I'm an Australian bastard, I suppose."

"I wonder if you also remember my man in Noyabrsk, the one who tracked Roman Rekuts into town from the airport the week before, tracked him to another SIBNEFT office, where Sergei was also in residence..."

"Jesus. And did he know why the street in Yekaterinburg was blocked off?"

"No. But he remembered there were several big military transporters in there, and the guys guarding the barriers on Central Avenue were Army, not police. Trouble was, he might have gone down that street, but he did not need to. So he just kept going—but he noticed it was closed, right down the side of the SIBNEFT building."

"You don't think they massacred those guys right there in the building in cold blood?"

"Don't I?" said Lenny. "I am afraid you don't know them like I do."

"What time did the Russian Air Force issue that press release, the one about the plane crash?"

"Midnight, Jimmy. Same day. And you know that was deliberate, getting the story played down in Russia. I'm sure they had it ready many hours before that. I mean, Christ! The President, or at least the Prime Minister, must have been involved. And I checked both their timetables that day. The PM was watching an ice hockey game, and the President was ensconced in the royal box in Theater Square."

"Where the hell's Theater Square?"

"Moscow, James," replied Lenny, haughtily. "It's the address of the Bolshoi Theater, home of the greatest ballet company in the world. Christ, there's a few gaps in your world knowledge…"

"Well, Lenny, old mate," said Jimmy, reverting to his best Crocodile Dundee accent, "we don't get a lot of **par day durr** in the outback. Upsets the koalas."

"Fuck me," said Lenny, with mock exasperation. "Anyway, listen…what I'm trying to say is, that press release must have been agreed to sometime in the afternoon. By which time the highest level of government in Russia knew, beyond doubt, the guys were all dead, and they were not coming back. Ever."

"Guess so. By the way, is anyone kicking up a major fuss about the guys…I mean, a wife or a son?"

"I don't think anyone dares. But Mrs. Anton Katsuba is about ready to make a few demands. She says her husband never went on any journey without telling her exactly where he was going. And since she's about twenty years younger than him, a very beautiful ex-actress, you can't blame him for that.

"She's called Svetlana, and they live in Yekaterinburg. He told her there was a meeting downtown at SIBNEFT that he thought would be over late afternoon. Said he'd meet her at seven p.m. at the cinema. But he never turned up. Never called. Was never heard from again. Going to Murmansk? She told our man that was the biggest lie she'd ever heard."

"Beginning to sound like the biggest lie I've ever heard," said Jimmy.

"Anyway, my boy," said Lenny, "to return to the big picture, we plainly have a very disturbing situation between the Russian government and Siberian oil. There must have been a threat of some kind by the Siberians. A threat that apparently could not be tolerated."

"I guess that's it for now…oh, by the way, I just heard they've released Masorin's body to return to Russia."

"Have they? That's a pretty old corpse by now, Jimmy."

"Yeah, but it's frozen. Poor old Mikhallo's preserved, cold."

"I bet he's not as cold as the other nine guys, buried somewhere in northern Siberia," replied Lenny, darkly. "Stay in touch."

The young Lt. Commander replaced the phone and returned to his studies about Argentina and the Falklands War. He did not, of course, connect the two subjects, centered at opposite ends of the globe, which had thus far dominated this Monday morning in early November.

Instead he decided to familiarize himself with the Falkland Islands...**just in case the bloody gauchos make another grab for 'em.**

Three hundred and forty islands altogether. Two big ones, East and West Falkland, divided by the wide seaway of Falkland Sound. Only 320 miles from the nearest point on the Argentinian mainland. Less than 5,000 square miles, about the size of Connecticut, or Ireland. The computerized facts popped out at him.

Jimmy scanned down the screen, muttering to himself snippets of key information, in his normal, quaint Aussie phraseology...**"Been British since Captain John Strong fell over 'em in 1690. Home to a coupla thousand sheep-shaggers** (country farmers). **Nearly all of 'em Poms** (British). **A Pom colony with Her Maj Head of State. Same as Australia. Christ, Queen Elizabeth of the Falklands. When you think...her Great-Great-Granny Victoria was Empress of India. That's what I call a significant decline.**

"Still, it says here the Falklands are home to the rare and bloody fragile rockhopper penguins, not to mention the ole black-browed albatross. Wouldn't want to lose either of 'em, myself."

He came to the section on oil exploration, staring for a long while at the numbering systems used for the quadrants and blocks contained in the massive 400,000-square-kilometer Designated Zone. This is almost as big an area as Texas, and surrounds the islands completely, ending sharply to the west, where Argentinian waters begin, over the Malvinas basin.

Many licenses had been awarded, and indeed Occidental Argentina had been busy drilling in these waters, under licensing agreements with the UK and Argentine governments. To the north, fourteen companies were awarded Production Licenses, directly from London.

And to the south, in the Special Cooperation area, the governments of both Great Britain and Argentina were involved in granting drilling licenses. Although everyone knew London really controlled the whole operation, no one really cared until the big on-land oil strike in late 2009.

At that point it became very serious business, because oil located on land is about ten times easier to get at than deep-sea crude in offshore locations. It is thus considerably cheaper, and the Argentinian oil consortiums never got a look in.

Suddenly, there was no further bidding. ExxonMobil was in there, partnered by British Petroleum. Whatever oil there was immediately came under the control of the American colossus and the British giant.

By the end of the week Jimmy was clued up on the state of the Falkland Islands unrest. And since nothing was happening, he more or less permitted the subject to slip onto his personal back burner. The Siberian situation also died on him, and phone calls from Lenny Suchov dried up.

The first snippet of interesting news emerged a couple of days after the New Year, when Ryan Holland reported a massive New Year's Eve demonstration in Plaza de Mayo. A half million people had crowded into the square before midnight, and spent thirty minutes chanting **Viva las Malvinas!!** for no apparent reason.

It was just another wail of anguish from a people who believed a terrible injustice was being visited upon them. And their voices rang out, a mournful, tormented cry of fury and outrage, and shortly before midnight, they had their way.

The President of Argentina, in company with two of his most trusted commanders, General Kampf and Admiral Oscar Moreno, came out onto the balcony and faced the enormous throng of people, just as Juan Perón, and his widow Isabel, had done.

The President beckoned them to silence, and through a microphone wished them all the happiest and most prosperous New Year. He said, "God Bless you all, and God Bless this great land of ours, this Argentina, this heaven on earth..."

And the crowd rose up and chanted, shouting his name, shouting their loyalty to the Republic.

And then, as the President turned away through the great door into the palace, he did something that stunned everyone in the square. He suddenly turned back and seized the microphone again. With his clenched fist held high, he bellowed, **"Viva las Malvinas!"**

And what followed was nothing short of pandemonium, a scene of patriotic fervor unmatched in the Plaza de Mayo since General Leopoldo Galtieri had stood on that same balcony in 1982. No one ever forgot how that President faced one million people, and sent them into a patriotic frenzy that lasted for an hour, by shouting those very same words.

Viva las Ma-a-a-a-l-v-i-n-a-s!!

Ryan Holland had watched the scene on television, noticing how Admiral Moreno and General Kampf enthusiastically patted the President on the back when finally he turned back through the palace door.

And in his report, the U.S. Ambassador noted:

I thought the entire performance seemed preplanned. It was the most inflammatory action. The size of that crowd was too enormous to be ignored. And the photographs from the square were used on the front pages of all the Argentinian newspapers the following day.

Television channels led their news programs all day, and every single

headline featured the word Malvinas. As I have explained, there has been nothing but official denials in Buenos Aires. Both government and military say simply that nothing is being planned. I'm surprised we haven't heard a word from London, but then, they didn't say anything last time, remember?

But I must say, I don't really believe them. Rumors here are rife. People seem to talk of little else except the recapture of those damn islands. I have not one shred of proof, but I will be most surprised if something doesn't break loose in the next couple of months.

As it happened, something broke loose precisely six weeks later, on Sunday morning, February 13. At first light, a United States–built A4 Skyhawk light bomber from Argentina's Second Naval Attack Squadron came screaming off the runway at Rio Gallegos and out over the Atlantic to make a rendezvous with a refueling tanker forty miles off the Argentina coast.

Full of fuel, with the sun rising way up ahead, the Skyhawk's pilot, Flt. Lt. Gilberto Aliaga, set a course 110 degrees, east-southeast, for the four-hundred-mile run to the Malvinas, and opened the throttles.

Flying at 30,000 feet, the bomber took thirty-five minutes to come in sight of the jagged coastline of the Passage Islands, fifty miles ahead, guarding the western approach to West Falkland. He immediately swerved southeast, and went almost into a dive, still making six hundred knots.

He made a great sweeping loop keeping his eye on the coastline of East Falkland on his port side. Now, coming in low-level, out of the southeast, right above the waves and below the radar horizon, he "popped up" as he swung around the coastline, ripping through the radar, and taking a bearing on his target before diving back down.

Flying fast over open water, heading northwest, he flashed on his own radar, and spotted his target one and a half miles out. He released two deadly thousand-pound iron bombs, which came flashing across the surface straight into the harbor, where the only resident warship was in clear view. Instantly, he swung away to the southwest, completely undetected by anyone on land.

No one identified the bombs as they came hurtling at high speed across the water. The first anyone knew of it was when HMS **Leeds Castle**, moored alongside the jetty at Mare Harbor, exploded in a fireball at exactly 0755 on that bright, clear Sunday morning.

Actually, they did not know anything about it even then. A few Royal Navy personnel knew the ship had exploded, but they had no idea how or why. Almost everyone in the little HQ at Mare Harbor was asleep. Twenty-three others, who had been on board the ship, were dead. All of them had been instantly incinerated when the half-ton iron bombs had slammed into the hull and upperworks on the starboard side and detonated with savage force.

The blast tore the heart out of the ship, obliterated the engine room and the ops room, which is located midships, below the upperworks and the big radar mast.

HMS **Leeds Castle** was essentially for scrap. As warships go, she was very small, only 265 feet long, and the wallop in those big Argentine bombs could have sunk a man-sized destroyer. The few Navy personnel sleeping in the accommodation block were naturally awakened by the blast, and they came charging out onto the jetty, half dressed and absolutely stunned at the sight before them.

This was the only warship they had, and it was ablaze from end to end, a searing hot fire sending flames and black smoke from burning fuel a hundred feet into the air.

Plainly there was nothing that could be done, except to try and evacuate any wounded, but to board the ship would have been suicide. Anyway, no one could possibly have survived that fire. HMS

Leeds Castle, already listing badly to starboard, was doomed. And the twelve sailors who stood on the jetty accompanied by two Petty Officers and a young Lt. Commander were completely astounded at what appeared to be a gigantic accident.

But this was no accident. The forces of Argentina had been preparing for this moment for almost three months. And the remnants of the warship's crew, now struggling to locate firefighting equipment, did not know the half of it.

Just for openers, Admiral Moreno had sent a Lockheed P-3B Orion to track the 4,200-ton British Type-23 guided-missile frigate **St. Albans** as soon as it left for the Caribbean. Right now it was four days out making twenty-five knots, 2,400 miles north of the Falklands, 300 miles off Rio de Janeiro. Irrelevant.

This was a proper military operation, conducted by excellent strategists, commanding officers who had weeks earlier placed their assault crews and selected aircraft crews on immediate notice to deploy. Since mid-December they had all been sealed from the outside world, in carefully guarded camps and buildings—waiting for the highly dangerous British frigate to come and go.

The Argentinian bombers, earmarked for the attack, had been flown down from the parent bases in Rio Gallegos, where the forward tactical command headquarters had been established.

And even as the Royal Navy's makeshift damage control units finally connected their hoses to quell the fires, two French-built delta-winged Mirage III Es, proudly displaying the livery of the Argentine Air Force, came sweeping out of the skies above the northern coast of East Falkland.

Each armed with 2-X-30mm cannon and two air-to-surface missiles, they flew fast at 20,000 feet, flashing over the settlement of Port San Carlos, which had scarcely echoed to the roar of fighter-bombers for twenty-eight years.

The Mirage jets swerved overland, high above the foothills of the desolate Mount Simon, and screamed over the landlocked end of Teal Inlet, crossing the lower slopes of Wickham Heights. And at that moment, Royal Air Force Sergeant Biff Wakefield picked them up on his Rapier missile radar system, on Mount Pleasant Airfield, twelve miles to the south.

He caught two "paints" moving very fast, and he picked up a French radar transmission, precisely as Oscar Moreno knew he would. Sgt. Wakefield tracked the two "paints" even though he knew they were well beyond the reach of his own missiles.

Outside, beyond his small concrete-built ops room the two big Rapier missile launchers stood at permanent readiness. But there was no point activating them yet; the two Mirage jets were over Berkeley Sound headed out to sea and off the screens. But Biff Wakefield kept them tracked as well as he could.

What he could not know was the real danger. And that suddenly burst out of the skies north of Falkland Sound, two more Mirage III Es, rocketing over the rocky granite coast, but not on the same easterly course as the other two. This pair was heading southeast.

And before Sgt. Wakefield's three-man team had even a chance to locate and identify, the Argentinian pilots unleashed two air-to-surface bombs each, all four of them aimed at the big short-range RAF Rapier launchers to the west of Mount Pleasant Airfield.

They came homing in at more than 500 mph, blasting both launchers to smithereens, followed by both Mirage jets, which opened up with their 30mm cannons, riddling the area with shells, smashing through the window of the ops room and killing Sgt. Wakefield and both of his duty operators. Their radar surveillance was still aimed to the northeast in search of Argentina's fleeing decoys.

In the space of five minutes, Great Britain's sea defensive unit, HMS **Leeds Castle**, and the entire air defense cover system for Mount Pleasant had ceased to exist. And that was by no means the worst of it.

Ninety minutes before first light, five hundred Marines from Argentina's Second Battalion had disembarked from landing craft on the deserted coast just west of Fitzroy. They had been marching steadily for a little over two hours, and right now were positioned on a bluff overlooking the airport. They were late, cursing their luck at not making it in the dark, but nonetheless ready for their daylight assault on the British garrison.

Meanwhile, the garrison ops room on the airfield, which had been ignored in the air attack on the Rapier launchers, understood they were under some kind of attack. They could see the flames still leaping skyward from the harbor, and they of course knew they had been slammed by bombs or missiles in the past few minutes.

Captain Peter Merrill ordered his immediate response platoon stood to. They already had their weapons and ammunition to hand, and the duty officer had them deploy instantly, initially to man all prepared positions around the airfield buildings and control tower.

The Captain alerted the Company Commander, Major Bobby Court, who ordered every man in his 150-strong force to get up, dress, assemble, and draw their weapons from the armory, full scales of ammunition from the stores' color sergeant. The machine-gun section also drew their weapons, together with spare barrels, and 12,000 rounds of boxed ammunition packed into belts of 250.

Twenty minutes later, with everything and everyone loaded onto Army trucks, they began to move out of the garrison toward the airport buildings. And as they did so, they heard the opening bursts of gunfire erupt from the bluff to the west, as the Argentinian Marines began to rain down fire on the vehicles of the British immediate-response platoon.

Led by Lieutenant Derek Mitchell, they poured out of the trucks and went to ground, desperately trying to locate where the small-arms fire was coming from. They had taken nine casualties in that opening burst and the stretcher parties were not yet assembled.

It took five minutes to identify the positions of the Argentinian Marines, and Lieutenant Mitchell ordered his men to fire at will. The Argentinians could see they were up against a much smaller force, and began to advance.

The British infantry held them as best they could, but the Marines were well commanded by Major Pablo Barry, who split his force, ordering a separate company to move around onto the left flank of Lieutenant Mitchell's platoon.

That took fifteen minutes, and the moment they were in position, Major Barry ordered the Marines to fix bayonets, spread out in assault formation, and advance. By now Britain's immediate-response platoon had taken heavy casualties, and was reduced in numbers by approximately half.

Which left around twenty-five British infantrymen to face the oncoming five hundred from

all directions, and right now they were still trying to fire at the first company that had engaged
them.

With only fifty yards between the troops, the
flanking Marine assault party began to close in,
opening fire, gunning down the British troops
from this unexpected direction. Alternately they
used the bayonet to great effect. Overwhelmed
by sheer weight of numbers, not one British rifle-
man survived the battle. Lieutenant Mitchell died
from bayonet wounds to his back and lungs. The
Argentinians lost only twenty-three Marines.

Meanwhile Major Bobby Court had the rest
of his infantry company thundering into position, the big Army vehicles transporting everyone to the airport and its surrounds. They knew
things had already gone badly among the immediate-response group, but they still had two
heavy machine guns, which they carefully sited
on the flanks of their defensive position. They
might have been surprised and outnumbered,
and they might have been totally unprepared to
withstand an assault on this scale, but the Brits
were no pushover.

As the Argentine Marines began their second advance toward the airport buildings, Major
Court's machine guns raked the area, the fire in-
terlocking across the front of the company. The
invading Argentinian Marines took over fifty casualties on their first assault, retreated, and gave

the defenders time to organize a first-aid post and reserve stocks of ammunition.

Again the Argentinians attacked and were once more repulsed. And now they went to their mortars, laying down indirect fire and still trying to penetrate the wall of steel spitting from the British machine guns.

Once more they took many casualties, out there on that exposed ground, but they kept coming, using smoke bombs to disguise their advance, running forward, hurling grenades close in to the trenches, all under the cover of a barrage of mortars.

And, as before, they eventually overwhelmed the defenders by weight of numbers. Only seventeen British riflemen survived, eight of them badly wounded.

Major Pablo Barry immediately took charge, and called upon all civilians in the airport buildings to offer no resistance. The wounded were taken into the buildings, where British and Argentine medical staff administered first aid to casualties on both sides.

Major Court was badly injured in the attack and died that evening in the passenger terminal. And before he did so, the last element of British resistance was removed when a Special Forces troop of seventy-five flew in from Rio Gallegos and immediately overwhelmed the small naval garrison at Mare Harbor with one volley of light-machine-gun fire along the jetty. Only two of the seven sailors still on duty were hit, and Lt. Commander Malcolm Farley ordered his men to surrender.

Two hours later the big Argentinian C-130s began landing at Mount Pleasant, carrying troops and light vehicles of the Fourth Airborne Brigade based at Cordoba. Swiftly organized, they took it upon themselves to haul down every British flag on the airport and replaced them with the light blue and white symbol of the Republic of Argentina.

Then they turned north and drove into Port Stanley, using bullhorns to instruct the citizens to stay within their houses. As ordered, they were swift and brutal to any objections to their presence, clubbing down five islanders with rifle butts and booting in the doors of houses that seemed likely to shelter armed civilians.

At 1800, they ordered the Governor out of his residence and drove him and his family and staff to the airfield, shipping them out immediately by air, to Rio Gallegos.

At fifteen minutes past six o'clock, on Sunday evening, February 13, 2011, the Argentinian flag flew over Port Stanley for the first time since June 1982, when Britain's Second Battalion Parachute Regiment had ripped it down and replaced in once more with the Union Flag of Great Britain. It was ten o'clock in the evening in London.

CHAPTER FOUR

The most astonishing aspect of the lightning-fast Argentinian military action on that Sunday in mid-February was the failure of the British land forces to make any form of communication with their High Command. The same applied to the survivors in the Royal Navy garrison.

Under normal circumstances one would have expected Lt. Commander Malcolm Farley to have instantly contacted the closest Naval Operations base. The problem was, Lt. Commander Farley had a 1,400-ton warship on fire right outside his front door, with many dead and some wounded. The nearest help was all of 2,400 miles away—the north-heading frigate—and his home base was 8,000 miles away in Portsmouth.

The problem for Major Bobby Court was much the same. There had been a ferocious attack on the missile system that protected the airport, his men were under serious small-arms fire, and generally speaking everyone was just trying to stay alive. The nearest help was thousands of miles away, and they were all in a life-or-death fight with the Argentinians.

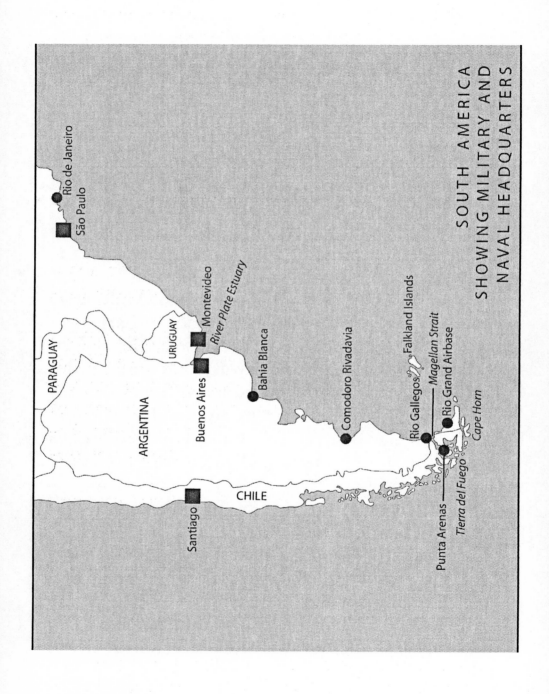

SOUTH AMERICA
SHOWING MILITARY AND
NAVAL HEADQUARTERS

Rio de Janeiro
São Paulo

Montevideo
River Plate Estuary

PARAGUAY

URUGUAY

Bahia Blanca

ARGENTINA

Buenos Aires

Comodoro Rivadavia

Falkland Islands

Rio Gallegos
Magellan Strait
Rio Grand Airbase

Cape Horn

Santiago

CHILE

Punta Arenas
Tierra del Fuego

Neither Lt. Commander Farley nor Major Court lived to make the communication, and it was not made by anyone until six p.m. (local) on a telephone in the passenger terminal at Mount Pleasant Airfield.

Sergeant Alan Peattie, who had manned one of the heavy machine guns, and somehow emerged unscathed, called the British Army HQ in Wilton, near Salisbury, where the duty officer, stunned by what he heard, hit the encrypted line to the Ministry of Defense.

That represented another duty officer absolutely stunned, and he in turn called Britain's Defense Minister at his home in Kent.

At 10:24 p.m. the telephone rang in the British Prime Minister's country retreat, the great Elizabethan mansion Chequers, situated deep in the Chiltern Hills, in Buckinghamshire to the west of London. The Defense Minister, the urbane former university lecturer Peter Caulfield, personally relayed the daunting news.

The Prime Minister's private secretary took the call and relayed the communiqué:

Argentinian troops have invaded the Falkland Islands. The British garrison fell shortly before ten p.m. GMT. Port Stanley occupied by Argentinian Marines. HMS Leeds Castle **destroyed. Governor Manton under arrest. The**

national flag of Argentina flies over the islands.

The color drained from the PM's face. He actually thought he might throw up. Twice in the previous month he had been alerted to the obvious unrest in Buenos Aires. He had been informed by his own Ambassador of the shouted words of the Argentinian President from the palace balcony on New Year's Eve.

There had even been reports from the military attaché in Buenos Aires of troop movements, and more important, aircraft movement at the Argentinian bases in the south of the country. He also recalled ignoring reports of Argentinian anger at the oil situation on East Falkland.

He had three times spoken to the Foreign Minister in Cabinet, mildly inquiring whether there was any need to sit up and take notice. Each time he had been told, "We've been listening to this stuff for over twenty years. Yes, the Argentinians are less than happy. But they've been less than happy for the biggest part of one hundred eighty years. In point of fact we've had exceptionally agreeable relations with Buenos Aires for a very long time. They won't make a move. They wouldn't want another humiliation."

The Prime Minister had accepted that. But the decisions in the end were his, and so was the glory, and so was the blame. And this was a Prime

Minister who was allergic to blame, at least if it was pointed at him.

He excused himself from the crowded dinner table and walked with his secretary through the central hall, past the huge log fire that permeated this historic place with the faint smell of wood smoke in every room. He entered his study and picked up the telephone, greeting the Minister of Defense curtly.

"Prime Minster," said the voice on the other end. "Not to put too fine a point on it, Argentina just conquered the Falkland Islands. Our troops defended as well as they could, but we have at least one hundred fifty dead, and HMS **Leeds Castle** is still on fire, with her keel resting on the bottom of Mare Harbor."

"God almighty," said the PM, his thoughts flashing, as they always did in moments of crisis, on to the front pages of tomorrow's newspapers, not to mention tonight's television news.

"I'm sure you realize, sir," continued the Minister, "we have no adequate military response for thousands of miles. I regret to say you are in an identical situation to Margaret Thatcher in 1982. We either negotiate a truce, with some kind of sharing of authority, or we go to war. I firmly recommend the former."

"But what about the media?" he replied. "They'll instantly compare me with Margaret Thatcher. They'll find out about the warnings we received from Buenos Aires, then blame me, and to a lesser extent you, for ignoring them. The Foreign Secretary will have to resign, as Mrs. Thatcher's did. And then they'll ask what we're made of."

"Prime Minister, I do of course understand your concerns. But right now we have one hundred fifty dead British soldiers, sailors, and airmen on East Falkland. Arrangements have to be made. Someone has to speak to the President of Argentina. I am happy to open the talks—but I think you are going to have to speak to him personally.

"Meanwhile, I think the Foreign Office should start by making the strongest possible protest to the United Nations. I'm suggesting an emergency Cabinet meeting in Downing Street tonight, perhaps attended by the military Chiefs of Staff."

"But what about the media?" repeated the Prime Minister. "Can we stall them? Can we somehow slow it all down? Call in the press officers and our political advisers? See how best to handle it?"

"It's a bit late for that, Prime Minister. The Argentinians will have the full story on the news wires, probably as I speak—**Heroic forces of Argentina recapture the Malvinas—British defeated after fierce fighting—the flag of Argentina flies at last over the islands...Viva las Malvinas!!** We can't stop that."

"Will the press blame me?"

"Undoubtedly, sir. I am afraid they will."

"Will it bring down my government?"

"The Falklands nearly brought down Mrs. Thatcher. Except she instantly went to war, with the cheers of the damned populace ringing in her ears, and the military loved her."

"They don't love me."

"No, sir. Nor me."

"Downing Street. Midnight, then."

"I'll see you there, sir."

The British Prime Minister walked back across the central hall of Chequers with a chill in his heart. He was not the first PM to feel that emotion since first Lord Lee of Fareham gifted the great house to the nation in 1917, during the premiership of David Lloyd George.

And he probably would not be the last. But this was a situation in which there was no room for maneuver. And it was a situation that would require him to address the nation, immediately after the Cabinet meeting. He knew instinctively the press would give him a very, very rough ride...

Surely, Prime Minister, you were aware of the unrest in Buenos Aires...? Surely, you must have been told by your diplomatic advisers that all was not well in the South Atlantic...? Stuff like this never happens without considerable preparation by the ag-

gressors...surely someone must have known something was going on?

But the one he really dreaded was...**Prime Minister, you and your government have spent years making heavy cuts to the defense budget, especially to the Navy...do you now regret that?**

He would take no questions at that first announcement, that was for certain. He needed time to think, time to confer with his media advisers (spin doctors), time to arrange his party line, time to deflect the blame onto either Whitehall or the military. But time. He must buy himself some time.

Meanwhile, he must not display panic. He must return to his guests. And he thanked God he had not invited anyone for this Sunday night dinner who was connected in any way with the military.

Seated around the table were the kind of people a modern progressive Britain admired. There was one hugely successful homosexual pop singer, Honeyford Jones, who was reputed to be a billionaire. There was the international football striker Freddie Leeson and his gorgeous wife, Madelle, who once worked in a nightclub. There was the aging film star Darien Farr and his wife, Loretta, a former television weather forecaster. Plus the celebrity London restaurateur Freddie Ivanov

Windsor, who sported a somewhat unusual name for an English lout.

These were the kinds of high achievers a contemporary Prime Minister needed around him, real people, successful in the modern world. Not those dreadful old establishment politicians, businessmen, diplomats, and military commanders so favored by Margaret Thatcher.

These were people who were proud to be his acquaintances. They were people who hung on his every word, and did not ask a lot of unnecessary questions. And when he sat down he decided to tell them what had happened.

"I'm afraid our armed forces have had a bit of a setback in the South Atlantic," he said gravely. "The Argentinians have just attacked the Falkland Islands."

"Where's that?" said Loretta.

"Oh, it's in the South Atlantic—just a tiny British protectorate going way back to the nineteenth century," he replied. "Of course we knew there was a lot of unrest in the area, but I don't think my Foreign Office realized quite how volatile the situation was."

"Jesus. I remember the last time that happened," said Darien. "I was in my, like, dressing room on the set...and they announced on the television we'd been attacked...I was...you know...like, wow!"

"Oh, that must have been, like, awful for you...in the middle of a movie and everything," said Madelle.

"Well, we all knew it was very uncool," he replied. "You know, like really, really bad, getting attacked by a South American country...but I mean everyone was totally, like, wow!"

"So what's it with these fuckin' Argeneeros then?" asked Freddie. "I mean, what are they on about? First up, they got a bloody big country, ain't they? Second, do I look as if I care there's a war or whatever in the Falktons, I mean, like who gives?"

The Prime Minister, for the first time in his premiership, suddenly wished he had chosen different friends for tonight's dinner. He stood up and said, "I'm sorry. But I'm sure you all understand I have to return to London."

Everyone nodded, and Loretta called out, "Get on your mobile, babe. The Army will get down there. Best in the world, right? Sort them Argeneeros out, no pressure."

The PM shuddered as he made his way back across the central hall to the government limousine waiting outside. He had staff to sort out the details of his return to Downing Street. He just climbed in the rear seat of the Jaguar and sighed the sigh of the deeply troubled.

Like all Prime Ministers, he loved the grandeur of this seven-hundred-acre country retreat.

And he was aware of the immense decisions that had been reached down the years within its walls. He also knew, and the knowledge caused his soul a slight quiver, that Margaret Thatcher had sat in her study at Chequers to compose her perfectly brilliant personal account of the mighty British victory in the Falklands nearly thirty years ago.

He was assailed by doubts, the kind of doubts that cascade in upon a self-seeking career politician who does not possess the guiding light of goodness and purpose that always gripped Margaret Thatcher. Gloomily, he doubted his manhood, and he gazed out at the Chequers estate, which was frosty in the pale moonlit night.

He truly did not know if he would pass this way again, given the Brits' unnerving habit of unloading a Prime Minister before you can say knife. Out of Downing Street in under twenty-four hours; glorious weekends at Chequers...well...those became instant history. Pack your stuff and make a fast exit.

Traffic returning to London was light, and the PM had only an hour or so to ruminate on his recent exchange with Sir Jock Ferguson, the Chairman of the hugely influential Joint Intelligence Committee. In two very private phone calls, Sir Jock had tipped him off there was trouble brewing in Buenos Aires over the Falkland Islands.

This had been precisely the news no government wanted to hear with a general election coming up in less than seven months. No PM wants to be seen to take his nation to war, and then ask for everyone's vote. Even Winston Churchill was unable to pull that one off after World War II in 1945.

And if they could throw the Great One out, they could sure as hell throw him out. "Jock," the Prime Minister had said, "let me have a nice little memorandum, would you? One that mentions there are popular rumblings in Argentina about renewed military action over Las Malvinas. But in your opinion there is not one shred of hard evidence on any of the diplomatic grapevines to suggest any such thing has a basis in reality."

"Well," replied Sir Jock, "that is more or less true."

"Absolutely," replied the PM. "But it gives me a bit of cover if everything blows up and we're caught unaware. You will not regret this, I assure you."

From this Prime Minister, that last statement meant one thing: **Sir Jock, old boy, stand by for an elevation to the peerage in the next Honor List.**

Lord Ferguson of Fife, that's got a fine ring to it, thought the JIC Chairman. That memorandum, the one that would partly exonerate the Prime Minister, was tucked away in a desk drawer in Downing Street, in readiness for the day when it might be needed.

Driving swiftly through the suburbs of West London, the chauffeur had the head of the British government home in his official residence before 11:30 p.m. And when he arrived, there were three further shocks awaiting him.

First, the Argentine Marines had pressed on to both of the major oil-drilling rigs on East Falkland, to the north of Darwin Harbor, and to the south of Fitzroy. According to the message from ExxonMobil in Rio, they had arrested every last one of the British and American oil personnel and flown them out in an Air Force C-130 to Rio Gallegos. No one thought they would be returning any time soon.

Just as malevolent was news of a further Argentinian Marine landing on the island of South Georgia, another purely British protectorate 1,100 miles southeast of the Falklands. South Georgia was the Alps of the South Atlantic, a far-flung remnant of the British Empire, a forbidding land of glaciers and towering mountains, the last resting place of the legendary British explorer Sir Ernest Shackleton.

None of the above, however, prevented the Argentinians from raising their national flag above the islands, when they landed there in 1982, and it took a very determined group of Great Britain's finest to recapture it.

The British Prime Minister was right now staring at a message from government house in

Buenos Aires informing him the Argentinians had not only done it again, they had arrested all U.S. and UK oil personnel working on the gigantic new South Georgia natural gas strike zone, which ExxonMobil and BP had been organizing for the past eight months.

To make matters infinitely worse, there was a disgruntled message from the President of the United States, requesting a call-back to discuss what Great Britain planned to do in order to rectify this disgraceful military aggression against the citizens of both countries.

The Prime Minister retreated immediately to his private office and put in a call to the President of the United States. And, as communications between the two allies went, this one was not encouraging.

The President recommended immediate negotiations with Argentina. He did not recommend a war, but he wanted a deal done over the oil. In the event the Westminster Parliament felt they needed to declare some kind of war against the military occupiers of this British colony, the U.S. President stated his country would help and assist all they could, but they would not send in troops.

"The Falklands are British islands. And if you guys really want them back, that's up to you. As friends we're here to help. But I will not take my country into someone else's war in someone else's country unless the reasons are overriding, as they were in Iraq.

"If you want 'em back you'll have to go get 'em on your own," said Paul Bedford. "We'll do what we can. But we do want a deal over that oil, hear me? You better speak to Pedro whatsisname in Buenos Aires and see what you can agree."

The British Prime Minister was highly skeptical about Pedro whatsisname. Like most of his Cabinet, the PM had never had a proper job in the private sector, where money and results count. He was essentially a politician, a bureaucrat, paid for from the public purse, and used to spending enormous amounts of government money, living high on the hog, surrounded by spin doctors who tried to manipulate the press in his favor, day after day.

A down-and-dirty powwow with a South American President, ex-military, ex–cattle rancher, and horse trader from way back—well, that was not really the PM's game. He knew nothing of the cut and thrust of big business, preferring obscure, abstract speeches about saving the starving children of Africa, and AIDS, and democracy. Stuff where you can't get caught out.

This was different. This was a one-on-one with a military hard man, some fucking Napoleonic figure from the pampas who'd just conquered 300 British islands in about ten minutes.

Jesus. What the hell did Bedford want from him? And what if he took the country to war? And what if the British lost? What then? This was probably the worst day of his life. He'd always wanted a place in someone's history book. But not like this.

And where the hell was South Georgia? He remembered, vaguely, from back when he was a student, that a group of Argentinians had somehow landed there in 1982 and raised their flag. He could not remember whether they were civilians or military, or whether they had finally fled or been forcibly removed. But it all seemed much more difficult now.

The memorandum from Buenos Aires suggested today's raiders were trained professional troops, and that like the assault on the Falklands, the operation had been planned in great detail and carried out with absolute ruthless efficiency. The PM did not like it. And the prospect of all these damn Argentinian flags being raised all over the place quite frankly gave him the creeps.

A further note on his desk reminded him that a few weeks ago an angry crowd in Plaza de Mayo had carried in a huge cardboard banner showing him, with a black patch over his eye, and scrawled across it the words...**Bandito de las Malvinas.**

The PM did not speak Spanish but he got the drift of that one, and he had been none too pleased to hear the crowd had set fire to it, chanting whatever was Spanish for "Public Enemy Number One." The crowd, of course, had no idea whatsoever that he was actually their best friend, and it was his swinging cuts to the British military and Royal Navy that would make the reconquest of Las Malvinas darned near impossible.

And now what? Every member of his government knew what they had done. Though they would all duck and dive out of harm's way when the blame began to be hurled at them. Damn cowards. He'd see about that. He was not prepared to take the rap for this. No. He most definitely was not.

And in the back of his mind, there was one most terrible dread. What happens when the media nails some high-ranking military officer who says flatly, "We warned this damn government dozens of times, it was emasculating the Army and the Navy, and now for the first time in four hundred years we are unable to answer a bullying foreign aggressor, some common garden dictator, with a military response of our own."

At that point the Prime Minister of Great Britain understood very clearly the roof would fall in. The right-wing section of the press, which had been gunning for him for years, would finally have the ammunition they craved. And they would be utterly merciless. The prospect of the headlines that would appear in the next forty-eight hours filled him with ice-cold horror.

And the trouble was, everything was way out of his control. The world news was breaking from

Buenos Aires, and the global media system would be consumed with the devastating victory of the Argentinians. He, Great Britain's Prime Minister, was a bit player at the scene of his own potential destruction.

The press would want to know exactly two things from him. Should someone have known this was about to happen? What was he going to do about it?

To the former, the answer was plainly yes; and the most junior reporter would take about fifteen minutes to prove it. To the second, the answer was a plain, simple, unequivocal God knows.

By ten minutes to midnight, his colleagues were arriving. The Foreign Secretary, Roger Eltringham, was first, followed by the Minister of Defense, Peter Caulfield. He had taken the time to call in the First Sea Lord, Admiral Sir Rodney Jeffries, and the Chief of the Defense Staff, General Sir Robin Brenchley. The Home Secretary was there, plus the Transport Secretary.

Peter Caulfield, however, had considered it a waste of time to invite people like the Education Secretary and the Minister of Health. But he did request the presence of the Lord Chancellor and the Chancellor of the Exchequer, both of whom could be counted on to have a joint heart attack at the very mention of war with its attendant expenditure.

The Prime Minister mentioned to Peter Caulfield that he may have gone beyond his brief to summon the Navy and military. But the Defense Minister replied, "Sir, we're talking war here. We have been attacked. And we may be obliged to hit back. We need the military for advice and assessment."

"Very well," replied the PM, who had himself invited one press secretary and three of his personal political advisers. He called the meeting to order and opened by stating, "As you all now know, Argentina has attacked the Falkland Islands, apparently with some success, and now declares the islands, **las Malvinas,** free of British rule for the first time in one hundred eighty years."

Roger Eltringham immediately informed the Cabinet members he had sent the strongest possible protest to the United Nations, demanding the Security Council take action of censure against the Argentinian Republic. It had been nothing short of a pre-emptive and brutal military strike at a peace-loving sovereign people, loyal to the British Crown, who now stood under the jackboot of a South American dictator.

The Prime Minister nodded his thanks and turned to Peter Caulfield, who said, "I think you should perhaps decide whether or not you wish to retain the possibility of a military response, in which case I think we should first hear from Admiral Sir Rodney, and General Sir Robin. I say this because they may consider a military response is impossible, in which case your options are very narrowed."

The Prime Minister visibly winced at being asked to consider the possibility of going to war, and at the prospect of being lectured first by the General and then by some bloody battle-hardened Admiral.

Slowly, he turned over the pages of the notes in front of him and then said, in a statesmanlike way, "No country with our traditions and position in the hierarchy of the world's nations can afford to dismiss the possibility of a military response to an attack on its people. But before I make any decisions, I think Roger should enlighten us to the likely reactions of the rest of the world."

Foreign Secretary Eltringham looked doubtful. "So far as I can see," he said, "most of the world will be damn glad not to be involved. Our nearest neighbor, France, has, of course, sold the Argentinians practically every piece of military hardware they own, particularly their Mirage fighter jets, the Super-Etendards, and the Exocet missiles. And they will mostly hope to sell them more. They probably hope we will be defeated."

"I thought we already had," interjected Admiral Jeffries.

"And just to conclude," added Roger Eltringham, "the only other nation with any real interest in this conflict is the United States. I can state right now they will not want to fight alongside us. But neither will they want to lose that oil situation down there. Like last time, they'll help. But they won't join us in a ground or even a naval war."

"I spoke to President Bedford a short while ago," said the Prime Minister, "and he said more or less what you just outlined...I suppose the question I must ask is, do we have the capacity to fight a war in the South Atlantic, eight thousand miles from home?"

"Rather more pertinent, Prime Minister," said General Brenchley, "is whether or not you have the courage to stand up in the House of Commons and tell them we don't."

The Prime Minister bridled. "General," he said, "you are here to offer military and naval advice, perhaps you would restrict yourself to those areas. And perhaps you would answer my question. Do we have that capacity?"

"No, Prime Minister," said the General gruffly, glaring at the professional politician he utterly despised. "We don't. And if we went, we couldn't win."

The Cabinet room went silent. "Surely there's some course of action open to us?" said the PM.

"How about surrender?" grunted the General.

Admiral Jeffries chuckled, at the perfectly hideous but ultimately inevitable way all of their chickens had come home to roost; the defense cuts year after year, the reductions in recruits, equipment, ships, aircraft, regiments, and in the end morale.

Like General Brenchley, he sensed the onrushing feeling of power. If the military chiefs said no, there could be no armed response to the Argentinian assault. They both knew that. So did the Prime Minister and his Cabinet colleagues.

In the end, it was General Brenchley who stood up, towering over the table of professional politicians, not one of whom had ever served in the military, not one of whom had ever had a proper job, outside of political parties, trade unions, or general public rabble-rousing. Maybe a couple of lawyers, specializing in human rights, or some such bloody nonsense. All of them, in the opinion of the military, were, generally speaking, either beneath contempt or hard on the border line.

And right now the military held sway. General Brenchley said coldly, "Prime Minister, I feel I owe you an explanation. And I'm going to give it. You and your Chancellor, over the past several years, have made the following increases in government spending budgets: sixty-one percent for the International Development Department, whatever the hell that is. Sixty percent for the Home Office, that's several million more civil servants; fifty-one percent for Education, mostly trying to teach the unreachable; and fifty percent more for Health.

"Alternately, the Defense budget has been increased by three percent, which represents of course a massive net loss to us who try to serve in it. It used to be one civil servant for every eleven soldiers, it's now one and a half civil servants for every one soldier, which is, of course, bloody ridiculous."

The words of the General absolutely stunned everyone around the table. But Robin Brenchley had the beleaguered Prime Minister on the run. And they both knew it. Right now, General Brenchley, Chief of Great Britain's Defense Staff, was unsackable, and he intended to make the most of it.

"Because you and your Chancellor for some reason regard us, disdainfully, as spenders of the nation's wealth, you have systematically undermined every branch of the armed services, all in the cause of your constant desire to seek savings. Your disdain for us has reached all ranks—their morale, their sense of self-worth, and their concerns for their future careers.

"Defense expenditure in this country has declined by thirty-five percent. One-third of our personnel has vanished. Our conventional submarine force has gone from thirty-five to twelve. The destroyer and frigate force is down from forty-eight to twenty-eight, our infantry battalions are down from fifty-five to thirty-eight. Our tank strength has fallen by forty-five percent. The number of effective fighter aircraft in the Royal Air Force remains at zero, where it has been ever since the Phantom was taken out of service.

"Prime Minister, five years ago, you and your Chancellor scrapped the only decent fighter-bomber the country possessed. Not only was it a highly effective all-weather interceptor, it could also operate as a ground attack fighter, a recce and probe aircraft, and as a ship strike aircraft. Furthermore, it could operate from the steel deck of an aircraft carrier anywhere in the world.

"I must tell you, Prime Minister, the loss of the Sea Harrier FA2 capability represents the loss of our fleet's ability to defend itself. This applies also to its associated land forces and their ability to defend against any form of sophisticated air attack.

"We have no new carriers in sight. Which means we are left with **Ark Royal**, which is small, twenty-five years old, with only ground attack aircraft and helicopters on its deck. And the **Illustrious** at three months' notice, and even older.

"We do not even have the air defense capability of Sea Harrier FA1, which we had in 1982. Today we face a greatly improved Argentinian Air Force. The FA2, which you so carelessly discarded, was, I must remind you, armed with a fully integrated missile system that could engage four aircraft, or even sea-skimming missiles, simultaneously, at ranges out to thirty-five miles, at speeds up to Mach 3.

"That little Sea Harrier effectively won the war for us in the Falklands in 1982.

"As you know, you and your financial ministers forced this brilliant little warhorse out of service, well before the planned date, purely because of cost. And with a statement we all regarded as madness, your Defense Minister—" Barely pausing, the General rasped, "Not you, Caulfield"— and then continued, "Your Defense Minister announced the Harrier's replacement would be the Harrier GR7 or 9. Understandable. That's the only fixed-wing aircraft we have left, which will operate from the deck of a small carrier.

"**But,** the GR7/9 is a small STOVL ground attack aircraft with no radar. It can carry two advanced short-range air-to-air missiles—AS-RAAM—for strictly visual launch. That means daylight and good visibility only. And the damn thing flies for only one and a half miles. By the way, it was called advanced more than thirty years ago. Now the bloody thing belongs in the Victoria and Albert Museum.

"And you may require me to order the Navy into battle—with **that**? And I should remind you, we don't have even one fighter attack aircraft on the Mount Pleasant Airfield. And if we did, it would sure as hell be destroyed by now. So much for your economies. I suggest you stand up in the House of Commons later today and tell them what you have done."

For the second time in just a very few hours, the Prime Minister of Great Britain thought it entirely possible that he might throw up. He felt as though he had been hit by a truck, and this bombastic damn General was walking all over him. **Christ**, he thought, **if this man ever gets loose in the newspapers, he'll finish me. He could actually bring down the government**.

But it was the newspapers and the television that really bothered him, and it was clear there was no sense arguing with the military. "General," he said, in his most conciliatory manner, "I am certain that all of my colleagues understand your point of view..."

"Not a point of view, Prime Minister," interjected the General. "Just a few plain, simple, irrefutable facts."

"Of course—nothing you say is in dispute. It's just that this has all been so damned sudden, it came at us all like a bolt from the blue..."

"Did it?" said General Brenchley. "Did it indeed, Prime Minister?" His voice dripped with irony.

"Well, certainly it has tonight. And I think it would be wise for us to fight the battle we're in, rather than several battles that have been fought, won, and lost in the past. I mean that, of course, metaphorically."

Peter Caulfield stepped in to save his boss. "General," he said, "I think the Prime Minister is actually looking at a worst-case scenario. What happens if Parliament demands we go and retake the Falkland Islands with military force? We cannot just tell them it's impossible."

"Well, it is."

"General, I realize there are substantial difficulties. Of course, we all do, and most of them certainly not your doing. But if Parliament demands we act, is there any hope we could pull something out of the bag like last time, in 1982?"

"We have two old aircraft carriers and four active squadrons of the Harrier GR7/9. I suppose we could muster a naval force at least to go down there. The GR9 can fly off a carrier, but without the Harrier FA2 we have no Combat Air Patrols, CAPs...only last-ditch air defense for the fleet.

"By that I mean we have nothing to stop all incoming Argentine bombers, and some are bound to get through. I'm only talking about aircraft carrying two thousand-pound iron bombs, any one of which is capable of sinking a ship. They will explode this time too, like they did in HMS **Coventry** in 1982. She sank in twenty minutes.

"Our missile system has no time to do anything about it, except shoot down the A4, **after** it's delivered its bombs and is on its way home. By which time it's a bit bloody late."

The General offered hardly a ray of hope. "If we had the new aircraft carrier the government promised, and just a dozen of those Harriers, we'd probably beat them...high CAPs swooping down on the A4s before they could attack. If we had both the aircraft carriers, as promised, and two dozen Harriers, we'd wipe them out. But we don't."

"Any chance of the new Eurofighter being advanced in time?"

"None. The bloody thing will be two years late, never mind one year early."

"Will the Army have a view?"

"Yes, a very simple one...they will refuse to make a landing without air cover...and the only air cover they have is the GR9, which can't see anything in bad weather and carries a missile that flies only a mile and a half."

"And we cannot provide anything else?" asked Eltringham.

"Not against those French Mirage IIIs. But Foreign Minister, in answer to the original question...yes, I suppose we could mount some sort of a show, although the soldiers don't even have decent boots, unless they bought them themselves.

"And there is one thing I want to make absolutely clear. If you propose to send several thousand of my troops and the crews of Royal Navy ships to what I regard as certain death, you'd better make up your minds which of you will stand up before the British people and accept responsibility, as Members of Parliament who were acting against military advice."

No one in the Cabinet room was anxious to step into that role. And the Prime Minister himself looked positively ashen.

"How good a story can we draft to make it seem we are not too worried?" asked the PM. "That there have been many months of negotiations with a view to Argentina taking over the islands...you know, makes geographic sense and all that. Could we make it seem the Argentinians just got a bit overexcited and jumped the gun...but we were always in agreement with them really?"

Admiral Jeffries looked up sharply. "With a warship and an air defense system blasted to hell, and one hundred fifty British servicemen lying dead on that godforsaken island...I don't think so."

"Well, gentlemen," said the PM, "with the military situation as it is, we appear to have no options, except to negotiate, and perhaps ring some kind of apology and maybe even reparations out of the Argentinians, just to save face for us..."

"First of all, I do not think you will even have that option by the time you've read the morning papers," said Peter Caulfield. "The tabloids will be baying for blood. And this ridiculous nation, which is essentially a football crowd, is going to be baying for revenge. By the time it all gets into the House of Commons tomorrow you'll have demands for war, just like last time, from every possible corner of the British Isles."

And Roger Eltringham, a renowned mimic, said solemnly, "And here is an e-mail from 'Irate' of Thames Ditton."

At which point he put on his most exaggerated working-class English accent and said, "I've just about 'ad enough of this—bloody politicians sitting on their arses fiddling their expenses, while the rest of the world tramples all over us. Where's the Dunkirk spirit, that's what I wanna know? Let's get down there and sort 'em out."

"Jesus Christ," said the Prime Minister of Great Britain.

THE FOLLOWING MORNING, LONDON

The **Times** was swiftly into its stride, with a front-page headline treatment that read:

Here we go again...150 servicemen dead
ARGENTINA SLAMS BRITISH GARRISON TO
CONQUER THE FALKLAND ISLANDS
Royal Navy on 24-Hour Alert to Head South

The **Sun** went for

MASSACRE AT MOUNT PLEASANT

The **Mirror**:

SURRENDER! THE FALKLANDS
FALL TO ARGENTINA AGAIN

The **Telegraph**:

ARGENTINA RECAPTURES FALKLANDS
British Garrison Surrenders
HMS Leeds Castle **Destroyed**
150 dead in fierce fighting

By 7:30 a.m. there were 172 journalists, photographers, and TV cameramen camped outside the main door of the Ministry of Defense in Whitehall. Forty-two political correspondents were practically laying siege to the gates of Downing Street.

The Prime Minister had already announced he would broadcast to the nation at 9:00 a.m. The Minister of Defense would speak at a press conference in the briefing room in Whitehall at 10:00. And there was something close to a riot meeting taking place outside the Argentinian embassy around the corner from Harrods in Knightsbridge, where traffic was now at a complete standstill.

Pictures were scarce, and likely to remain so, since no foreign aircraft were currently permitted to land at Mount Pleasant Airfield. The Argentine military had made it clear that any flight, for whatever purpose, attempting a landing would meet precisely the same fate as HMS **Leeds Castle**. And that included any invasion of Argentinian air space anywhere around Islas Malvinas.

The only communiqué the Foreign Office had received from Buenos Aires was a polite memorandum suggesting that the British military dead be buried with the full honors of war in a hillside cemetery at Goose Green, alongside the fallen Argentinian warriors of both 1982 and 2011.

The President hoped that in less troubled times there could be a British ceremony of remembrance there, in which the Argentinian military would very much like to participate. The President further wanted to assure the Westminster government that everything possible was being done for the British wounded, and that if necessary they would be flown to the highly regarded British Hospital in Buenos Aires. A list of their names, ranks, and numbers was enclosed, as was the list of the dead.

In victory, grace and humility. And, boy, was this ever a victory.

The British government did not have the slightest idea what to do. Although everyone was keenly aware they had to do something. An emergency debate was called in the House of Commons that afternoon, starting at noon, and the

Prime Minister's entire front bench of ministers was, to a man, dreading it.

The Prime Minister himself quite frankly loathed the House of Commons, and attended it as rarely as possible, much preferring to run the country from his private office in Downing Street.

He did, however, rejoice in one possible outcome of the debate: if Parliament voted to send a battle fleet to the South Atlantic, and he personally voted against it, nothing would be his fault, no matter what the outcome. Nonetheless, the thunderous possibility of being regarded as the most cowardly Prime Minister in the entire history of the nation was not terribly appealing.

Throughout his entire tenure in Number 10 Downing Street, this Prime Minister had one dominant modus operandi. He loved the flowery speech, particularly the ones with the big, bold new ideas, what he called the "great initiatives."

His game plan was to stand up there, wearing his most concerned look, and promise damn near anything: extra cash, extra committees, better police, more for the poor, better armed forces, a prosperous Africa—the kind of stuff that takes a long time to come to fruition.

Right now he was at that point in his premiership when only the very stupid, or very needy, believed a word he said. And today's problem required him to step right up to the plate, make a decision, and have it carried out, on the double. None of the above three points of action represented his strong suits.

By twelve noon the chamber in the House of Commons was packed. Almost every one of the 635 Members of Parliament were in their seats. To the Speaker's right were the government benches, Her Majesty's loyal opposition to the left. The government whips had informed the Speaker's office the PM would open the proceedings personally, and at three minutes after noon the Speaker called the House to order with the words "Silence for the Prime Minister."

In the grand tradition of the Mother of Parliaments, he rose from the front bench, where he was flanked by his Defense Minister and his Foreign Secretary. And standing in front of the ancient dispatch box on the huge table, he outlined the events of the last twenty-four hours to the best of his knowledge.

Details were no more available now than they had been the previous evening. Sergeant Alan Peattie had been permitted to make calls back to Army headquarters in Wilton, and it was clear that he and his men had fought a gallant but losing battle against an Argentine force that outnumbered them four to one.

The position had been untenable from the first ten minutes, during which the assault force had knocked out Britain's entire sea and air defensive cover system without a shot being fired. Just a couple of bombs.

The House listened in silence for fifteen minutes as the Prime Minister outlined the options, many of them optimistic. But he ended on a grave note. "Honorable Members have been called this afternoon to debate this outrage by an armed aggressor. Ultimately this House must decide— do we negotiate a peace with the Argentinians? Or, do we do what we did last time, and sail a Royal Navy Task Force to the South Atlantic and defeat them in battle on the high seas, in the air and on the land?"

He sat down with the jingoistic cheers of the Members almost raising the roof of the House, as the Speaker rose from his chair and requested silence for the Leader of the Opposition, the somewhat colorful former Oxford University 400-meter champion, Adrian Archer.

And it was clear from his opening sentence where he stood, in the shadow of Margaret Thatcher. He railed against the "pitifully weak" response of the Prime Minister, and he castigated the Labour government for its endless defense cuts, its inability to see what England stands for.

And he concluded by asserting, "Honorable Members, we belong to a tried and tested society, and it's a society to which other weaker, poorer countries turn to, in times of need. Great Britain has always stood for a sense of fair play, and above all it stands in favor of the rule of law. It does not and could not ever condone some damn quasi-Nazi rampaging over two thousand of our citizens down in the South Atlantic.

"Honorable gentlemen, I think you know our history, our traditions of standing up for what is right—even if that has meant standing alone. We are so often the one nation to whom others turn when international crime is committed.

"I should like, if I may, to quote more or less accurately the great First Sea Lord of the 1980s Admiral Sir Henry Leach. On the night the Argentinians invaded the Falklands in 1982, he told Margaret Thatcher that if we funked this, if we backed down now and did nothing—'Then tomorrow morning, Prime Minister, we shall both be awakening in a very, very different place.'

"Honorable gentlemen, I think those words apply to each and every one of us here in the chamber today."

He sat down amidst thunderous applause from both sides of the divide, and the Speaker of the House motioned for Peter Caulfield, the Defense Minister, to be heard.

He stood and faced the opposition across the dispatch box. And, reading from notes, he outlined the somber situation in which the government found itself. He pointed out that Argentina, with its national, near-maniacal passion for the Islas Malvinas, had been smarting ever since the

1982 defeat. He stated that forces within the Argentinian military, which has so often ruled the country, had been building their arms and scheming for this coup d'etat for several years.

He said, "The recapture of those islands means everything to them. They feel it's a birthright, and almost the entire nation is prepared to rise up and take them back. On the other hand, at least until they found oil down there, we were there purely out of a sense of honor.

"The Falkland Islands have always been nothing short of a monumental nuisance to us. An expensive one at that. Our presence in any form on East Falkland is merely because we may one day have to protect the locals from attack. There's nothing in it for us, except expenditure, irritation, and possibly blood and tears.

"It is no wonder we are not so militarily prepared as the Argentinians are. They live less than four hundred miles away. From us it's eight thousand miles. A war down there would just about double our national debt. It is not worth it for us to fight, it could not be worth it in terms of money and lives, and anyway, from my standpoint we'd have a very good chance of losing it."

At this point the Conservative MP for Portsmouth, ex–Naval Commander Alan Knell, waved his order paper in a request for Mr. Caulfield to accept an interruption. And, in the established ritual of courtesy in the House, the Defense Minister said: "I give way to the Honorable gentle-man," and sat down.

"I appreciate the position of the Minister," he said, "and of course I realize he is in fact defending an extremely weak Prime Minister. But my constituency on the south coast has many naval officers, and for years I've been hearing how appalled they were at the cuts to the Royal Navy budget. Would it be fair to say these idiotic Defense policies have finally exposed this government for what it is? Perhaps the word **useless** might spring to mind?"

The Tory benches erupted in a burst of laughter and cheers, with Members waving their order papers. On the government side, Mr. Caulfield climbed again to his feet, and continued, man-fully, "The Honorable gentleman knows as well as I do that sudden, unexpected military actions by a hostile and passionate nation can cast the very best planning into total confusion.

"And I would remind him, when the Conservatives were in power during the 1982 Argentinian attack, there were as many people shouting 'Retreat!' including the Defense Minister, as there were shouting 'Forward!'"

Commander Knell, above the rising din, yelled angrily, "Yes, but we had a leader then!"

At which point the Tory benches erupted with yells of support, while from the Labour benches a shrill cry of protest at this obvious rudeness echoed to the rafters.

"Order! Order!" bellowed the Speaker, amid the uproar. "I insist on **Order**. The Defense Minister must be allowed to continue."

Peter Caulfield nodded to the Chair, and said deliberately, "Thank you, Mr. Speaker. I was not attempting to make a long speech, but I do intend to point out the futility of such a lunatic military adventure, which has almost no upside to recommend it, and an enormous downside, like defeat on the high seas for the Royal Navy."

By now, three more Tory MPs were on their feet, and the Speaker chose Robert Macmillan, a distant cousin of the former Prime Minister Harold Macmillan. He was a tall man in his middle forties, and he seemed to have inherited all the Macmillan respect for tradition, plus some extremely gung-ho attitudes of his own.

"Mr. Speaker," he said, "I never thought I would stand here in the cradle of the British Commonwealth and hear a government Minister suggesting it was somehow beyond our capacity to send a fleet down to the South Atlantic and reclaim our own territory from a foreign gangster. I mean, what's the point of having a Navy if you can't use it? What's the point of having an Army if it can't fight?

"So far as I know the Defense budget of the United Kingdom, despite all the cuts, is still substantial. And I see no point in having even a Defense Minister if the best he and his Prime Minister can do is stand up and point out we can't do anything against a country that by any standards is essentially Third World.

"I wonder if either of them understands what it means to be British? How other countries see us? How we are viewed in the international community? Are we spineless or are we an upright force for good, which will brook no nonsense from tin-pot South American dictators?

"Do we have beliefs? Do we recognize the great mantra of Margaret Thatcher, the Rule of Law Is Everything? Or are we just nothing, a small island that once meant something? And now can't be bothered to go and help two thousand of our citizens, currently being held in captivity by a foreign power?

"Mr. Speaker, I must ask, Who are we? What do we stand for? Are we totally unmoved by a shocking crime perpetrated against us and our people? Plainly the old Empire should strike back at the aggressor. We should go down there and blast them off our island. We should take all the force at our disposal and let 'em have it."

Mr. Macmillan's voice rose as he concluded, "Margaret Thatcher once wrote of the morning we landed our troops in San Carlos Water. An officer of the Parachute Regiment went and banged on the nearest farmhouse door. And, with the backdrop of the Royal Navy warships behind him, he said to the farmer, 'I expect you're surprised to see us?'

"The farmer replied. 'No, not a bit. We all knew Maggie would come.' And as Lady Thatcher wrote, 'He said Maggie, but he meant all of us. He knew we would not abandon them.'

"And that dogged, very British quality is what we are now discussing. The question perhaps the House will be called upon to answer is, **Do we still have the guts for it?** Or has this weak, passive, utterly dishonest, left-wing government stripped us even of that?"

Roars of **"Hear, hear!"**—that traditional parliamentary shorthand for "I agree"—rang out from the Tory side of the House. But there was little response from the government benches. There was no need for the speaker to call for order. He just stood up and called out the name of Derek Blenkinsop, the Labour Member for East Lancashire, who rose from his seat.

"Mr. Speaker, I have several people in my constituency who lost sons, brothers, and fathers in the last Falklands conflict. None of them would wish the same fate that befell them, to now be suffered by others. The 1982 war in the South Atlantic was absolutely ridiculous.

"We had ships sunk, sailors and their officers burned to death as our warships were bombed, we lost our bravest soldiers on the battlefield fighting for a barren, desolate bunch of rocks that mean nothing to anyone.

"And for what? If we had not gone down there, we would have negotiated a truce with the Argentine government, the language would gradually have changed to Spanish, and after a period of shared rule we would have quietly and calmly handed the islands over to the big country that is situated close to them. And close to two thousand fine young men from Great Britain and Argentina would not have died.

"Was that reasonable? I mean their deaths. Were they sacrificed for a just cause? Perhaps. But was it fair to them and their families? Of course not. How could that possibly be fair?

"Mr. Speaker, I have heard talk of fair play in this chamber today. I have even been told that we, perhaps above all nations, stand for that very quality. But was it fair to all of those families, devastated in the cause of a gung-ho, senseless war that my opponents on the opposite benches seem more than happy to start all over again?"

The Speaker now pointed to Richard Cawley, a former chief executive of a high-tech surveillance corporation, and now Conservative Member for Barrow-in-Furness, home of Britain's submarine builders. "Mr. Speaker," he said, "I imagine most of the Honorable Members realize the Royal Navy's conventional-weapon submarine fleet has been cut from almost thirty to only ten. It is perfectly obvious that the new aircraft carriers may not show up until 2016.

"We have no Harrier FA2 strike force. That was scrapped four years ago and does not exist. When it was withdrawn from service, that little fighter jet was generally regarded as the most capable, most respected All-Weather, Beyond-Visual-Range fighter in the entire European inventory. Its look-down, shoot-down, state-of-the-art Blue Vixen radar provided the capability to detect and destroy four targets simultaneously.

"Its AMRAAM weapons system was designed to detect and engage high-threat, small, fast targets like sea-skimming missiles. It was the **only** UK weapons system capable of defending the fleet against the new generation of antiship weapons, including the Krypton and the Moskit supersonic missile. And now it's gone. And it was of course the first major step taken by this government toward British military impotence.

"I have no doubt that today you will be told we still have four squadrons of GR7/9 aircraft. They do fly off an aircraft carrier, but their radar and missiles are not in the same league as the Harrier FA2, and less capable than the Harrier FA1 of 1982.

"This also applies to the new Typhoon, which for years has failed to come up to scratch in any of its trials. Aside from being grotesquely late in its production, when it does arrive it will be touch and go whether the damn thing hits the enemy or a friend.

"Is the government finally admitting we cannot go to war with the equipment the Ministry of Defense has provided? If not, what is the reason the Prime Minister seems so reluctant to go to the South Atlantic?"

The enormity of Great Britain's scandalous lack of naval air capacity was very steadily becoming obvious to the House. And MP after MP stood and regaled the House with assessments of the sheer humiliation Great Britain would suffer in the world community.

These patriotic pleas for the Government to show some resolution were interspersed by other Honorable Members railing against the deprivations of the military under this Prime Minister.

One MP stood up and revealed the scale of the cuts to the military budgets, which have resulted in mass reductions in training exercises, especially overseas; huge fuel reductions; reduced track mileage for tanks and other armored vehicles; reduced amounts of training ammunition; and less money for overseas training.

He explained how instant financial savings are made by delaying recruitment of trainees for six months of the year, and then attempting a recruiting drive for the second six months, thus avoiding paying salaries for maybe 6,000 recruits for a six-month period. Of course that doesn't work because too many of them get fed up waiting.

One Member of Parliament pointed out that six British military policemen who were killed in the 2003/4 conflict north of Basra, surrounded by a rioting mob of five hundred Iraqis, had only radios that did not work in an urban environment. One mile away, he said, the paras fought it out for four hours with terrorists, but had satellite comms and were able to call in reinforcements for their decisive victory.

"The new British forces' radio system is years late," he added. "The soldiers' clothing is moderate, especially their waterproofs, and their boots are a disgrace, often splitting in half in the first couple of weeks. Almost all British troops heading for a theater of war buy their own.

"I am unsurprised," he said, "this government is not anxious to go south and fight for the Falkland Islands."

The debate wore on into the late afternoon, and finally a motion was agreed: **That the government should instruct the British Army to prepare to retake the Falkland Islands by military force from the Argentinians. And that the Ministry of Defense be ordered to show good cause within forty-eight hours if for any reason they considered the task untenable.**

The motion was carried by a majority of 159 votes. Barring a major objection by the Royal

Navy, Great Britain was going to war against the Republic of Argentina.

The Prime Minister looked as if he had seen a ghost. Exposed finally in the House of Commons for his folly in listening to his Chancellor and ignoring his Generals and Admirals, he found himself heading for the forefront of an ensuing battle, which, if lost, would surely see him removed in disgrace from Number 10 Downing Street.

He was the man who may have penny pinched his way to a military humiliation for Great Britain. What a total indignity for a politician as ambitious as the British Premier. As Darien Farr and his lovely wife, Loretta, might have put it at the Chequers dining table, I mean, this was like, wow!

0800, FEBRUARY 15,
OFFICE OF THE C-IN-C
HOME FLEET,
PORTSMOUTH DOCKYARD
SOUTHERN ENGLAND

The ministerial limousine was cooling its wheels outside the official home of Admiral Mark Palmer, the Royal Navy's Commander in Chief, Home Fleet. This was a grand, imposing Queen Anne house hard by the jetties toward the end of the dockyard. Admiral Palmer's formal office was in fact on board the nearby HMS **Victory**, Admiral Nelson's magnificently restored flagship at the Battle of Trafalgar.

But much of the C-in-C's work was carried out in naval offices here in his residence, with its views out to the waters of Great Britain's still-feared fighting ships.

It was a place steeped in naval history. Portraits of legendary battle commanders and their ships adorned the walls. The whole building felt like an elegant ops room from the nineteenth century. If an admiral could not plan strategy in here, he probably couldn't plan it anywhere.

Quite frankly, it gave Peter Caulfield the creeps. He never felt at home here, faced with the hard-eyed men who ran the Royal Navy, despite the obvious truth that he was their lord and master, as head of the Ministry of Defense.

He appreciated their courteous treatment of him, and their impeccable manners. But when he mentioned any government course of action of which they did not approve, their silent, penetrating stares made him feel, unaccountably, as if he was ripping the very heart out of England.

And this morning he dreaded the meeting more than usual. He was shown into Admiral Palmer's drawing room and introduced to a heavily built, uniformed naval officer, the four stripes on his sleeve indicating the rank of Captain.

"Minister, I'd like you to meet Captain David Reader, commanding officer of our one serviceable aircraft carrier, HMS **Ark Royal**.

"She's over there at the minute," he added, pointing through the window. "As usual David's brought her home safe and sound, with about a half million pounds' worth of repairs to complete in the next couple of weeks."

Captain Reader stepped forward and offered his hand, nodding coolly. "Good morning, Secretary of State," he said. "Rather a rough ride you chaps endured in the House yesterday?"

Peter Caulfield stared across the Captain's shoulder, out through the window toward the 20,000-ton, 685-foot-long **Ark Royal**, the modern successor to the first **Ark Royal**, which carried fifty-five guns as the flagship of Lord Howard of Effingham against the Spanish Armada in 1588.

Somehow, even without one shred of knowledge of naval history, the Defense Minister felt like a little boy in the presence of the man who operated that towering modern fortress at sea, moored on the other side of the harbor.

"Yes, it was a rather difficult time for the government," replied Peter Caulfield. "You see, strange as it may seem, we are incredibly concerned about loss of life in our armed forces, particularly in a potential war zone such as this in the South Atlantic, which holds just about nothing for us."

"Oh, I don't know," interrupted Admiral Palmer, amiably. "I think there's something to be said for honor. The Navy's built on it, you know."

Slightly embarrassed, feeling rebuked, Britain's Minister of Defense said quickly, "Of course I understand that, Admiral. But even with our honor at stake, do you really wish to see perhaps two or three hundred of our best troops killed or wounded, essentially for nothing?"

"My dear Minister," replied the Admiral, "we do not enter any conflict counting our dead before anything happens. We expect to enter a conflict and win; to misquote General Patton, we don't intend to die for our country. We anticipate making the other poor dumb bastard die for **his** country."

"Yes, yes. Quite," said Peter Caulfield. "That's the way you must think…"

At that moment an orderly came into the room bearing hot coffee in a silver pot on a silver tray. There were three china cups and a plate of cookies.

"I'll pour," volunteered the Admiral. "Thank you, Charlie."

"This is very kind," said Peter Caulfield. "And I shall do my level best to have this over in a very short time, so you won't have me for lunch…"

"Come now, Minister, we're all on the same side in the end. I would be most hurt if you were not here for lunch…"

"Well, we'll see how things turn out. But, as you know, I have a very specific purpose here. I am compelled to ask you whether the Royal Navy believes it possible to sail to the South Atlantic, fight off the Argentinian Navy and their quite formidable Air Force, and then put a sizeable land force on the beaches somewhere on the Falklands, and fight yard by yard for the territory? That's my question."

"Do you want my personal opinion or my official response?"

"Let's start with the official response."

"Very well, Minister. I, and all my officers, are loyal servants of the Crown. If the Parliament of Great Britain decides we must go and fight for those islands, we'll go. It's not our place to argue the toss whether it's worth it, even whether it's right. We have all taken the Queen's shilling, as it were, for most of our service lives. If we are asked to go out and earn it, possibly the hard way, then so be it."

"Captain Reader?"

"Same."

"And your personal view, Admiral?"

"We have a rather greater chance of defeat now than we had in 1982, and even that was a bit of a close-run thing."

"And your principal reason for that view?"

"Oh, definitely the loss of the Harrier FA2, Minister. With that, we always had a chance in the air. Now we do not even have a fighter aircraft."

Peter Caulfield nodded. "And may I ask the commanding officer of our aircraft carrier the same question?"

"Again, much the same, sir. Except to add that **Ark Royal** is a quarter of a century old. She's tired, she's feeling her age. Every time we go out we return with some operational defect. This time it's her starboard driveshaft. May need a new one.

"It's a very distant war for an old lady. Eight thousand miles down there, and if she goes wrong, we'd be in shocking trouble, thousands of miles from a garage, in bad weather and under constant enemy attack."

"But you'd still go if you were asked?"

"Yessir."

Admiral Palmer stood up. He poured himself a little more coffee, and said, "Minister, it's how we were all brought up. It's what I call the **Jervis Bay** syndrome. That was an old fourteen-thousand-ton passenger ship converted into an armed merchant cruiser for convoy escort in the North Atlantic in World War Two. They mounted seven old six-inch guns on her deck.

"She was commanded by Captain E. S. Fogarty Fegen RN. And one morning they came in sight of the German pocket battleship **Admiral Scheer**. Instantly Captain Fegen ordered the seventeen-ship supply convoy to scatter, and, in an action he must have known was suicidal, he turned his ship to engage the enemy.

"It took the **Scheer** about thirty minutes to lambaste and sink the **Jervis Bay**, by which time the convoy had vanished, far and wide, over the horizon. When rescuers turned up that evening to pick up survivors, Captain Fegen was not among them. They gave him a posthumous Victoria Cross for that.

"It was the same with Lt. Commander Roope VC, of the **Glow-worm**, also in World War Two. In desperation, with his ship on fire and sinking beneath him, he turned and rammed the big German cruiser **Hipper**. Took her with him.

"That's what we do, Minister. We'll fight, if necessary to the death, just as our predecessors did, just as we've been taught. And should, one day, our luck run out, and we should be required to face a superior enemy, we'll still go forward, fighting until our ship is lost."

Peter Caulfield took a few moments to compose himself after that. He stood up and walked to the sideboard to refresh his coffee cup, and he did not turn to face the two commanders because he did not wish to seem so affected.

But he was. And all he could manage was, "Then you will not declare the Royal Navy unable to sail to the South Atlantic to fight for the Falkland Islands?"

"No, Minister, I will not say that. Not on any account. And neither would any other Admiral who has occupied this office during the last two or three hundred years."

"However bad it may look? However the odds are stacked against you?"

"No, Minister. The Royal Navy will not refuse to go. **Jervis Bay** sacrificed herself to save the convoy. If, of necessity, we must do the same, to save you and your boss, we will not refuse to go."

CHAPTER FIVE

Peter Caulfield vacated Portsmouth Dockyard shortly before noon and headed straight back to Downing Street. Which was significant only because he missed lunch with the Chief of the Defense Staff, Sir Robin Brenchley, and the First Sea Lord, Admiral Sir Rodney Jeffries, who arrived in Portsmouth in a staff car directly from Whitehall.

Peter Caulfield had made a sensible move in leaving before lunch. Because the following two hours would be as grave and depressing as the late afternoon of October 21, 1805, when Admiral Nelson died on the lower deck of HMS **Victory** at Trafalgar.

The two Admirals, one Captain, and one General were after all discussing the total demise of the Royal Navy, and the likelihood of possibly the worst defeat in the history of Britain's Senior Service.

"We don't have much," said Admiral Palmer. "So, do we take everything down there, and leave just sufficient here to fight another day? Or do we just say the hell with it and take the lot?"

"We have so little, I'm afraid we'll have to take the lot, the whole Navy," said the First Sea Lord. "If it's anybody, it's everybody. We don't have fifty destroyers and frigates anymore, we have only eighteen, and three of them are in refit. We hardly have enough to provide a proper escort for the carrier."

"You say carrier in the singular," said General Brenchley. "I thought we had two?"

"One of them, **Illustrious,** is more than thirty years old. We can't take her, she'd probably never make the journey, never mind a battle."

"Can **Ark Royal** make it?"

"Just about," said Captain Reader, "but not for long. The wear and tear on any warship in a sea-battle environment, and that weather, is very high. I'd give her six weeks maximum, and that's only if our luck holds."

"If anything," said Admiral Palmer, "the aircraft situation is even more serious. I suppose we could rustle up a couple of dozen GR9s, but they cannot fly at night, and in bad weather they can't see a bloody thing.

"Robin," he added, "we have no air defense. None. And the quicker everyone accepts that the better. This damn government has dug a bloody great hole for itself and jumped into it."

General Brenchley, a powerfully built son of a Kentish pub owner, had fought his way up the ranks of the British Army to the very pinnacle of the service. He would have made it big anywhere. He was tough, inclined not to panic, inhumanly decisive, and had commanded his paras in both Iraqi wars. Also, he had been a close friend of Admiral Jeffries since childhood, both having attended Maidstone Grammar School, in Kent.

Never in their fifty-year friendship had Admiral Jeffries seen the bullnecked Army chief so utterly distraught. General Brenchley was pacing the room, shaking his head, torn between obedience to Her Majesty's government, which he had sworn to serve, and the shocking possibility of casualties beyond the call of duty.

"Rodney, old boy, I suppose we have to decide," he murmured. "Will we allow X thousand men to die, or do we all resign and let this witless Prime Minister and his shoddy little group of ex-communist friends get on with it?"

An appalled silence enveloped the room. "It seems to me," said the First Sea Lord, "the PM is finished either way. If we, and our principal staff, quit, he'd have to resign because of the uproar. No politician could weather that storm. If we agreed to go and fight for the islands, and were defeated by a greater enemy, he'd also have to quit. Either way, he's done. But in the first instance we'd save many thousands of lives."

"Not to mention what's left of the Royal Navy," said the General.

"And yet," said Admiral Jeffries, "we are sworn to duty, in an unbroken tradition of obedience to the government or the Head of State that goes back centuries. You and I are sworn to serve the Crown, and its elected government. And we ought not to be blind to the fact that we would both face lifelong disgrace if we quit and our successors somehow went down there and pulled the bloody thing off."

"Rodney, despite this somewhat cathartic conversation, you and I are not going to quit. And we both know it. We're going to dig in and go fight for the Falkland Islands as our Parliament has requested. We may think it's a lunatic request, we may seethe with anger at the criminal destruction of the services, but we're still going..."

"And if our enemy should be too strong, and our ship should be sinking, we'll bring her about, and if she still has propulsion, we'll ram them, correct?"

"Correct," said General Brenchley, gravely. "We'll both, in the end, do our duty."

0900, TUESDAY, FEBRUARY 15
NATIONAL SECURITY AGENCY
MARYLAND

Lt. Commander Ramshawe had spent twenty-eight of the last thirty-six hours pondering the military brilliance of Argentina's whiplash strike against the British defenses on the Falkland Islands. The operation had been carefully planned. No doubt of that. And anyone with a lick of sense must have seen it coming.

Certainly the U.S. Ambassador in Buenos Aires had seen it coming. His communique just before Christmas had stated he would be surprised if something didn't shake loose in a couple of months. And Admiral Morgan had told him, Jimmy, that the observations of old Ryan Holland should always be regarded.

But here we are again. The ole Brits caught with their strides down (that's Australian for pants). **And everyone in a bloody uproar about who's going to do what to whom. Are the Brits going to fight for their islands, or will they leave well enough alone?**

"I've got a bloody powerful feeling the Brits are gonna fight," he muttered to the empty room. "And then the shit will hit the fan, because we'll be caught in the middle of it, and President Bedford will have the same problem as Ronnie Reagan—do we help our closest ally, or do we refuse because of our friendship with the Argentinians?"

Admiral Morris, Jimmy's boss, was again working on the West Coast for the week, and Admiral Morgan had taken Kathy to Antigua in the eastern Caribbean for twelve days. Which left Jimmy bereft of wise counsel. So far as he could tell the United States must protest to the United Nations today about the seizure of the American oil and gas complexes in both the Falkland Islands and South Georgia.

"You can't have U.S. citizens being frog-marched off the islands at bloody gunpoint, their equipment seized," he muttered. "I mean Christ, that's like the Wild West—Bedford is not going to have that. But that military strike was about oil. Buenos Aires thinks it belongs to Argentina and they won't easily give it up. That damn newspaper the **Herald** laid it out pretty firmly."

He took a sip of coffee and keyed in his computer to the section on the Falklands he had saved a couple of months ago. "Well," he said, "Exxon-Mobil and British Petroleum have sunk a ton of money into those oil and gas fields. The question is, will we go to war for it? Bedford won't, but Admiral Morgan might tell him to. And the Brits might think they have no choice. Streuth!"

Three hours later, the U.S. State Department formally complained to the United Nations about the willful, illegal seizure of the Falkland Islands by the Republic of Argentina. And two hours after that, Ryan Holland requested an official audience with the President of Argentina in Buenos Aires. Thirty minutes later the British Ambassador, Sir Miles Morland, requested the same thing. Neither embassy received a response.

In London, the Argentinian Ambassador was summoned to 10 Downing Street, and in Washington the Argentinian Ambassador was summoned to the White House. The former was instantly expelled and given twenty-four hours to vacate the building in Knightsbridge, or face deportation.

In Washington, the President gave the ambassador forty-eight hours to allow ExxonMobil execs to restart the oil industry in both East Falkland and South Georgia, or else the U.S. government would begin seizing Argentinian assets in the United States. In particular, the United States would take the grandiose embassy building on New Hampshire Avenue, Washington, plus the consulate properties in New York, Miami, Chicago, Los Angeles, Houston, New Orleans, and Atlanta.

President Bedford also put in a call to the St. James's Club in Antigua and requested Arnold Morgan to return to Washington as soon as possible, since the prospect of a war without the former National Security Adviser's advice was more or less unthinkable.

Admiral Morgan agreed to come home a couple of days early, so long as the President sent **Air Force One** to collect him.

Meanwhile, back in Westminster, the English Parliament gathered to hear the Prime Minister speak at two p.m. on Wednesday afternoon. It was the first time in living memory he had attended the House two days out of three.

And he was not doing it out of a sense of duty. He and his spin doctors were desperately trying to halt the onrushing tide of editorials and features, which by now had convinced most of the country that he and his left-wing ministers had ruined the great tradition of British armed forces and that the UK might not have the military capability to fight for the Falkland Islands.

Defense correspondents, political commentators, editors, and newspaper proprietors were finally expressing the simple truth: if you want to live in strength and peace, you'd (A) better listen to your Generals and Admirals, and (B) be prepared for war at all times. It had taken the media a long time, but this second Falklands crisis had rammed it home, even to them.

The **London Times** had produced a scorching front-page headline that morning:

YEARS OF NEGLECT DISARMS BRITAIN'S MILITAR
**Labour Ministers Stunned
at Navy's Accusations**

The **London Telegraph**, a Tory and military stronghold, had talked to General Robin Brenchley:

TOP ARMY GENERAL LAMBASTES
GOVERNMENT "STUPIDITY"
Brenchley's Warnings in New Falklands War

The following interview had nothing to do with the ability of the soldiers or their commanders. It had to do with equipment, air cover, missile defenses, and ordnance. What he called the "criminal neglect of our requirements." Without fear for his own career, General Brenchley described this British Prime Minister and this British government as "the worst I have ever known, and, hopefully, the worst I ever will know."

And his views were echoed over and over, in all the newspapers, and in all the television news programs, as if toadying up to Labour politicians was a thing of the past. It was as if the government had become a meaningless impediment to the gallant fighting men who would soon be sailing south to fight for the honor of Great Britain.

It was as if every chicken in the coop had somehow come home to roost. The media gloated, slamming into a Labour government that had thought it might somehow be able to wing it, feigning financial competence by increasing taxes and capping military budgets at well below required levels.

They had then handed over all of the saved money to state hospital bureaucrats, social security, disadvantaged gays, lesbians, the homeless, single-parent families, the unemployed, the unemployable, the weak, the impotent, the helpless, and the hopeless. Not until this day had they truly realized the stark naïveté of those policies.

And now the Prime Minister's cronies sat packed into a tightly grouped little enclave of nervousness, while their leader stood before the House and tried to explain how Great Britain's naval and military powers were not in any way weakened. And how the armed forces were absolutely ready to obey the will of the House, and head south to fight the jackbooted aggressors from the land of the pampas.

"I tell you now," he said in his customary, shallow, cocksure way, "in our many years in government we have prepared the Navy and the rest of the military to fight a modern war. We have reduced numbers of personnel, but today we are more prepared for the kind of war we now face in the twenty-first century. Our professionalism is greater, our commanders have been given free rein to train our people to the highest standards.

"Our warships have state-of-the art weapons systems, and no one would dispute our aircrew are the finest in the world. I have spoken personally to all of our service leaders. I have explained the will of the House of Commons, expressed in this place on Monday afternoon, must prevail.

"And, Honorable Members, I can say with enormous optimism they were completely in agreement with our decision. Indeed, several of them thanked both me and my government for the farsighted changes we had made to the Navy—by that I mean the two new, state-of-the-art aircraft carriers, and the superb new Typhoon fighter jets, which will soon be developed to launch from their flight decks.

"I received nothing but gratitude from the Army for the new streamlining of the regiments, the foresight of our Secretary of State for Defense, Peter Caulfield, and the new twenty-first-century professionalism that we now enjoy.

"Honorable Members, the forthcoming conflict in the South Atlantic will be hard, as all wars are hard. But I have the utmost confidence in our commanders, and feel quite certain they will return victorious.

"We are at war with Argentina over the Falkland Islands. And at this stage I see no reason to extend that state of war to the Argentinian mainland. If, however, that day should come, then I am assured by all of our commanders that we are ready, capable, and certain that we shall prevail.

"But, like another Prime Minister, a lady from the opposite benches, who stood in this very place twenty-eight years ago, I say again to the House, we in government cannot tolerate a brutish, unprovoked attack on our islands. We cannot and will not put up with it.

"As in 1982, the Royal Navy will sail to the South Atlantic. The Admirals have told me personally of their total optimism. And they will bear with them a mighty Task Force. And either the Argentinians will surrender, or we will blast them asunder on the land, in the air, and on the waters that surround the islands. But they will not get away with this..."

At this point, the entire House erupted with a roar that must have been heard outside in Parliament Square. Members stood up, waving their order papers, cheering lustily, in perfect imitation of the football crowd, baying for revenge, as described by Peter Caulfield in Downing Street on Sunday night.

There was absolutely no political advantage for any Member to stand up and challenge the validity of the Prime Minister's words. No one wished to hear them. This was an afternoon of the highest emotion, the hours of doubt were long gone. Britain's naval and military commanders had told the government they would go and win back the Falkland Islands. **Rule Britannia**.

So far as the MPs were concerned, this was Super Bowl II in the South Atlantic. Older Members could somehow recall only the triumph, as Admiral Woodward's flagship **Hermes** came steaming home to Portsmouth. There was the memory of the big Argentinian cruiser **General Belgrano** listing, sinking, in her death throes.

There were the pictures of the Argentinian surrender, thousands of troops lining up, laying down their arms. And of course the timeless vision of the men of Britain's 2 Para, marching behind their bloodstained banner, into Port Stanley, their commanding officer, Colonel Jones, slain, but their victory complete.

Who could forget those distant days of pride and conquest? And who could resist a faint tremor of anticipation as once more the sprawling, historic Portsmouth Dockyard revved up for another conflict?

Not the veteran MPs of the House of Commons. Because the onset of battle seemed somehow to give them stature, to add to their sense of self-importance, if that was possible. But they left the great chamber that afternoon with their heads high, chins jutting defiantly, upper lips already stiffening. They were men involved with a war, a real war. They were men involved in life-or-death decisions.

But if the military were to be believed, it would be mostly death. After all, none of the MPs had sailed with Admiral Woodward into a gusting, squally Levanter off the Gibraltar Straits in the spring of 1982. None of them saw the entire ship's company of a home-going British warship lining the port-side rails to salute the warriors heading south. None of them heard the singing, as Woodward's armada sailed by…the achingly prophetic notes of the hymn that morning, "Abide With Me."

None of them witnessed the paras, raked by machine-gun fire, fighting and dying on the flat plain of Goose Green. They never heard the cries and whispers of the injured and dying in shattered, burning warships. And they surely never saw the shocked faces of the doctors and nurses in the hospital on board **Hermes** as the horribly burned seamen and officers were carried in.

They didn't. But Admiral Mark Palmer did, and the memory of lost friends stood stark before him as he stared at the television, listening to the hollow words of the Prime Minister. The Admiral winced at the sight of the ludicrous, complacent grins on the faces of the government ministers, nodding earnestly as their leader spun and distorted the naval and military picture to the House of Commons.

Admiral Palmer was sixty years old. He had served in the first Falklands War as a twenty-two-year-old Sub-Lieutenant in HMS **Coventry** before she was hit and sunk just north of the islands in the late afternoon of May 25, 1982. He recalled the helplessness, the desperation, as they tried to maneuver the ship, with its long-range radar on the blink, not knowing from which way the Argentinian bombers would come.

Twenty-eight years later, he still awakened in the night, trembling, his heart pounding when he heard again, in his dreams, the blasts of the bombs smashing into his ship, the screams of the injured. And he felt again the searing pain in his own burned face as the bomb blast hit him while he tried to supervise the 20mm gun on the upper deck.

Admiral Palmer was not afraid. His grandfather had fought at the Battle of Jutland in World War I. In truth Mark Palmer was a modern-day Roope VC. He'd have rammed an opponent when all was lost; he would most certainly have died for his convoy; and if required, he would have died to save this benighted British government, which, like all of his colleagues, he secretly loathed.

It was not a lack of courage, skill, or daring that in his mind doomed this new operation in the South Atlantic. It was the hideous truth that his men had been denied the correct resources to fight a new war by their own government. And Admiral Palmer turned his back on the television, and walked, coatless, out into the chill of the dockyard, appalled that somehow the very best of British people were being led by some of the very worst. The brave and the honorable, sent to the plate by a group of self-seeking opportunists with their limousines, chauffeurs, and bloated expense accounts.

"Christ," he muttered, alone in the cold dockyard, "what a tragedy."

He signaled for a driver, but first ran inside to collect his greatcoat. Five minutes later he was on the jetty where HMS **Arc Royal** had suddenly become the center of the universe. At least, the 20,000-ton light aircraft carrier was now the center of his own particular universe, twenty-six years old or not.

A team of engineers was still at work deep inside the propulsion area, checking and servicing those four hardworking Olympus gas turbines, and examining the two massive driveshafts that transfer more than 97,000 horsepower to the huge propellers.

The good news was neither shaft needed replacing. The bad news was the spare part to replace a cracked mounting had to be flown from Scotland, but not until tomorrow. And that meant the repair crew, and the servicing engineers, were still operational while the gigantic task of storing the ship took place.

There was already an old-fashioned "humping party" passing boxes hand over hand up the starboard forward gangway. Alongside them was a mobile conveyer belt, with another crew loading enormous boxes of food—frozen, canned, dried, and fresh. And already the debris was mounting as the seamen ripped stuff out of the big outside containers, all of which were superfluous to the journey south.

In the middle of all this, the Fleet Maintenance Group and the carrier's own staff were at work all over the starboard hull rectifying any defects, removing rust, repainting, checking every inch of the Battle Group's flagship, which, within days, would be heading to a theater of war.

From all over the country, thousands and thousands of stores were arriving from various depots, by train, by the Ministry of Defense's own transportation, and by commercial vehicles. And they were not just there for the **Arc Royal**. All over the dockyard there were ships lining up for the journey south. And all of them needed food, clothes, ordnance, ammunition, shells, and missiles.

Massive amounts of fuel were arriving, diesel for the gas turbines, Avcat for the aircraft. And it was not only the warships being fueled, it was also the huge replenishment ships of the Royal Fleet Auxiliary oilers, which would keep them topped up on the journey south and in the battle zone itself.

Personnel from every branch of the Navy were being drafted into Portsmouth, every available section of manpower was heading for the jetties, trying to clear the debris, helping with the loading, assisting the Supply Officers who paced the loading areas, checking off their "shopping lists" on big clipboards, calling out commands and instructions to the toiling, twenty-four-hours-a-day workforce.

Captain Reader came down to meet the C-in-C, and together they paced the wide jetty where the **Ark Royal** was moored. It was already noticeable that new stores were arriving with such regularity that team after team was being seconded to join in the loading process, and the pile of debris was beginning to look like the European grain mountain.

But the services are expert at priorities. What mattered was loading the ships, not clearing up the rubbish. Only when the piles of empty cartons became a serious detriment to the process was action taken to reduce the problem.

By now the great arc lights along the waterfront were being switched on. Captain Reader and Admiral Palmer went aboard and took the elevator to the quarters of the commanding officer, while some swift refurbishment took place above them, in readiness for the arrival of Rear Admiral Alan Holbrook, who, as Task Force Commander, would fly his flag from the **Ark Royal** throughout the operation.

His ops room, where he and his staff would plan the war, was located right above Captain Reader's quarters, and of course their duties would be entirely separate. The Captain's task was to steer the 685-feet-long carrier safely around the South Atlantic, taking overall command of the 550-foot-long flight deck, the 680-man crew and 80 officers.

Admiral Holbrook would plan the deployment of the ships, the air and sea assault on the Argentinian islands, plus the landing of the military force, in consultation with COMAW, Commander Amphibious Warfare, Commodore Keith Birchell.

The GR9 ground attack aircraft were due to begin arriving, straight onto the deck of the **Ark**

Royal, from Yeovilton Naval Air Station. Altogether there would be twenty-one of them, the full complement for a small carrier like the **Ark Royal**, as opposed to the eighty-four that a big U.S. Nimitz-class carrier can accommodate.

Of course, the nonarrival of the two new Royal Navy carriers, both 60,000-tonners, was widely considered to be a national disgrace. Despite the Prime Minister's somewhat glib, self-congratulatory remarks about the new ships, the fact remained there had been government delay, delay, and delay, and the earliest they were likely to arrive was sometime in late 2015.

Every senior officer in the Royal Navy recalled the chilling words of the First Sea Lord, Admiral Alan West, six years earlier when he had stated with quiet certainty that recent defense cuts "have left the Navy with too few ships to sustain even moderate losses in a maritime conflict."

With only a dozen destroyers and frigates ready for battle at any one time, the First Sea Lord considered the situation untenable, simply not enough warships. At the time he had suggested, modestly, that after forty years in the Navy he knew something of what he spoke, since his own ship, the **Ardent**, was sunk in Falkland Sound in 1982.

One way and another this was a somewhat modest recounting of the events of May 21, 1982, when a formation of Argentine bombers launched nine five-hundred-pounders at the battle-hardened

Ardent in which the Seacat missile launcher suddenly jammed. Three of the bombs smashed into the Type-22 frigate, blasting the stern hangar asunder and blowing the Seacat launcher into the air. It crashed down, killing the Supply Officer Richard Banfield, and the helicopter pilot Lt. Commander John Sephton, who was manning a machine gun in company with his observer, Brian Murphy.

Almost the entire stern section of the ship was on fire, a huge plume of smoke lifting high above the Sound. Minutes later another formation of Argentine Skyhawks came screaming in over West Falkland and instantly spotted the burning furnace of the **Ardent**. Commander West ordered his helmsmen to turn their just-repaired 4.5-inch gun to face the enemy, and they opened fire with everything they had.

Commander West had cleared one of the ship's cooks to man one of the big machine guns, and he had actually downed one of the raiders. But nothing could save the **Ardent** from this bombardment. Seven bombs slammed into her, almost lifting the ship out of the water.

The blasts and the fires had killed or wounded one-third of all the ship's company—the same number as in HMS **Victory** at this same time in the afternoon at the Battle of Trafalgar. Unlike Admiral Nelson, Commander West survived, and with the fires blazing all around him, he once more ordered his gunners to turn and face the enemy.

But she could no longer steer, and the fires were roaring toward the missile magazines. Men had been blown overboard, and she was shipping ice-cold seawater by the ton. The **Ardent** was sinking, and Alan West ordered his crew to abandon ship. Not until the last man was taken off by HMS **Yarmouth** did Commander West, tears of rage and frustration streaming down his face, finally leave HMS **Ardent**. She sank early the next morning.

He knew of what he spoke.

And when Admiral Holbrook arrived shortly before 1900, he shook hands warmly with the commanding officer and with his Fleet C-in-C, just stating solemnly, "We haven't got enough, have we?"

"No, I'm afraid not," replied Admiral Palmer. "What we have, we take. But the GR9s are blind at night and in bad weather. If we need ship replacements…well…I'm afraid there won't be any."

"Hmmmmm," replied Admiral Holbrook. "We'd better move pretty sharply if that's the case. There's nothing quite so bleak as attrition you can't afford, eh?"

He gazed out onto the flight deck, scanning the area. "It's a clear night," he said. "Are we expecting the GR9s soon?" he asked.

"Starting around 2100," said Captain Reader.

"Helicopters?"

"Tomorrow morning."

"How about marines? Will we have them on board the **Arc Royal?**"

"Probably around six hundred."

Admiral Holbrook nodded. He was a slender, rather handsome man with well-combed wavy brown hair. As a Commander he had served a previous Captain of the **Arc Royal** as Executive Officer, and had subsequently jumped a few slightly more senior officers to make Rear Admiral. The Navy High Command wanted a new flotilla Commander with firsthand experience of the only aircraft carrier likely to be operational for a long-range war.

Captain Reader told him his quarters would likely be ready right after dinner, and meanwhile perhaps they should have some cocoa, and take a look at the available warships that would accompany the **Arc Royal** on the long ride down the Atlantic. As with the previous Falklands conflict, the Americans would make Ascension Island available as a halfway house for re-storing and refueling.

Eight warships from the Fourth Frigate Squadron would form the backbone of the Task Force, all of them Type-23 Duke-class ships built between 1991 and 2002. These are 4,200-ton gas turbines, all based at Portsmouth, and right now undergoing similar storing as their flagship, **Arc Royal**.

In fact, HMS **Lancaster** and HMS **Marlborough**, both twenty years old, were unlikely to be out of refit to sail with the Task Force, but the

Royal Navy was attempting to have every available warship in battle order.

This left the following six-frigate lineup, all of them carrying a new(ish) upgraded version of the old Seawolf guided-missile system:

HMS **Kent**—commissioned in the year 2000, and commanded by Captain Mike Fawkes, a forty-one-year-old ex–Fleet Air Arm pilot who had transferred to surface ships and impressed everyone with his handling of the ship during the second Gulf War. Married, with two boys aged twelve and fourteen, Mike Fawkes would assume command of the naval force, under Admiral Holbrook, if the **Ark Royal** should be lost.

HMS **Grafton**, commissioned in 1997, commanded by the urbane, smoothly attired Captain John Towner, whose dandyish appearance, complete with knotted white silk cravat, belied his expertise with the Plessey 996 search radar system. At forty-five, he was probably the best guided-missile officer in the Royal Navy. Known locally as Hawkeye.

HMS **St. Albans**, commissioned in 2002, was the newest of the class, commanded by Captain Colin Ashby, at forty-nine the former Commander of one of the old Type-42 destroyers, and a veteran of the last Falklands War, where he served as a Sub-Lieutenant on the flight deck of HMS **Hermes**. Captain Ashby's father, a World War II battleship gunnery officer, had long had ambitions for his only son to join the Navy. But after the eighteen-year-old Colin managed to slam the family river cruiser into Rochester Bridge, on the Medway River, breaking every cup and plate in the galley…well, after that Ashby Senior insisted. And he lived to see his son become the first Commander of the brand-new HMS **St. Albans**.

HMS **Iron Duke** was now seventeen years old. Her captain was Commander Keith Kemsley, at thirty-seven the youngest of the frigate COs, and tipped by many to make it straight to the top of the Royal Navy ladder. An outstanding exponent of guided-missile warfare and an expert in both ASW and gunnery, Commander Kemsley was by nature an aggressive war fighter and, privately, Admiral Holbrook thought it entirely likely he might end up with a Victoria Cross, or else die in the attempt. A young Fogarty Fegen was Kemsley.

HMS **Westminster**, one year younger than **Iron Duke**, was a very-well-maintained ship under Commander Tom Betts, who ran his ship with considerable discipline and limited laughter. But it was highly efficient, particularly in the field of ASW. Commander Betts was himself a former torpedo officer with an expert's grasp of the complicated operational procedures with the Marconi Stingray weapons carried by **Westminster**.

HMS **Richmond** was commanded by Captain David Neave, former Executive Officer in the Type-45 destroyer **Dauntless**. At forty-six, he had always longed for a full command but had not considered the possibility of going to war within three months of his first appointment. Today he stood on the jetty watching stores being loaded into his ship, awaiting the new Westland Lynx helicopter that would arrive on his aft deck within the next hour.

And that, essentially, was it for the Royal Navy's guided-missile frigate force, which would face the Argentinian air assault less than five weeks from now.

Two bigger, 7,350-ton Type-45 destroyers were definitely in the group heading south. HMS **Daring** would sail from Devonport under the command of Captain Rowdy Yates, from Sussex, a barrel-chested former center-three-quarter for England Schoolboys, and then the Navy.

The brand-new HMS **Dauntless** was going, despite still conducting her sea trials. She would sail under the command of Commander Norman Hall, a former able seaman on HMS **Broadsword**, who had come up through the ranks and was enormously popular with his 187-strong crew.

The twenty-five-year-old HMS **Gloucester**, commanded by Captain Colin Day, would also go, and all three of these destroyers were taking on board stores and ammunition on the jetties near the **Ark Royal**. The shore crews were attempting to have HMS **Dragon** and HMS **Defender** ready to join them. Failing that, two of the old Type-42s would go, probably HMS **Edinburgh** and possibly HMS **York**, which were smaller, 4,675 tons, and equipped with the old Sea Dart missile system.

Sea Dart was a medium-range missile, best used against high-level aircraft, but pretty useless against an incoming sea-skimming missile. Also, its radar was suspect when aimed across the water and over the land. It was neither as modern nor as efficient as the new Harpoons on the Type-45s, which also carried the new European PAAMS surface-to-air system as their principal antiair missile defense.

HMS **Ocean**, the Royal Navy's 22,000-ton helicopter carrier and assault ship, was also going. The **Ocean**, under the command of Captain John Farmer, would carry six Apache attack helicopters, a half dozen big Chinooks, plus vehicles, arms, and ammunition for a full Marine Commando Assault. It could transport more than 1,000 troops comfortably, 1,350 at a pinch. For this trip it would take the full 1,350.

A second specialist assault vessel, the 19,000-ton HMS **Albion**, would transport a thousand troops, sixty-seven support vehicles, plus a couple of helicopters. She would sail under the command of Captain Jonathon Jempson, whose legendary Royal Navy lawn tennis partnership with Captain Farmer of the **Ocean** had once seen them reach the second round of the men's doubles at Wimbledon.

The final significant ship was the almost new 16,000-ton Landing Ship (Logistics) **Largs Bay**, built at the great Swan Hunter Yards on Tyneside, and intended as the lynchpin of a second wave of an amphibious assault. The ship held, if necessary, 36 Challenger tanks, 150 light trucks, 200 tons of ammunitions, and 356 troops. Its reinforced flight deck could cope easily with heavy Chinook helicopters. It would sail under the command of Captain Bill Hywood.

Portsmouth Dockyard now resembled an industrial city, with transporters arriving by the dozen twenty-four hours a day. Of course, the government's idea of a "rapid deployment force" was a mere euphemism for cutting back on everything. What politicians never understand—among several other things—is you cannot have rapid deployment when you don't have enough of anything.

For military commanders it is a constant struggle to put together any kind of force when the entire operation is beset with shortages—not enough artillery, not enough warships, not enough tanks, not enough top-class combat clothing, not enough spare parts, everything scattered thinly, and worst of all, not enough people.

There remains a mind-set in the Parliaments of the United Kingdom, based on hundreds of years of history, that the armed services can pull together a fighting force at the drop of a hat that will beat any other armed force in the world.

It's been a very long time since that was true, and with each passing year of leftward-inclining governments, it has become less and less feasible. Certainly the British troops and Royal Navy performed heroically well in the two conflicts in the Gulf. And there was much to recommend the operations in Bosnia. But they were all comparatively low-tech campaigns.

But by the year 2011, Great Britain had not gone into battle alone for almost thirty years, when they last fought for the Falkland Islands. And that was a close-run thing. A look at Admiral Woodward's private diary revealed a somewhat disturbing sentence. **"On the night of June 13, 1982,"** he wrote, **"I do not have one ship without a major operational defect. I am afraid if the Argentinians breathe on us tomorrow, we might be finished."**

As it happened, the Argentinians surrendered the next day, and Britain celebrated a hard-won victory. But it may prove to have been her last, unless Westminster governments began to rectify the problems they have created.

In any event, assailed by problems, the Task Force struggling to take shape in Portsmouth in the freezing winter of 2011 was the antithesis of rapid deployment. The shortages made everything take twice as long.

And two more weeks went by until the troops were able to show up in significant numbers. The first to arrive were members of the Royal Marine Brigade, plus their artillery support, the engineer squadron, their Logistic Support Regiment and the Air Squadron. Altogether 5,000 men from Forty Commando, Forty-two Commando, and Forty-five Commando began to embark the ships.

They were followed by a second 5,000-strong formation, the Sixteenth Air Assault Brigade, including 1 and 2 Para, and a battalion from the Royal Green Jackets. This was part of the Army's rapid-response force, equipped with Chinooks and Apache attack helicopters. It was a specialist force, trained specifically for this type of mobile operation.

They personally supervised the loading of their beloved Apache helicopters, which bristled with guns and rockets, and would provide valuable air support against Argentinian armor and ground troops.

The Artillery Regiment had their eighteen light field guns, which hopefully could be deployed all over the combat area...**If** they could make a landing.

On March 4, a declaration signed by the Prime Minister informed Buenos Aires if the Argentinian armed forces had not vacated the Falkland Islands completely in five days, the British Task Force would sail from Portsmouth to the South

Atlantic, where they would wage war upon the Republic of Argentina until the islands were cleared of this foreign invasion.

Suitably warned, the Argentinians made no response, despite much urging from the American State Department, which was doing everything in its power to persuade Buenos Aires to back down and then negotiate. The U.S. government even offered to broker the talks, which could be held in Washington, until some satisfactory agreement was reached.

But Argentina was not about to negotiate. And the British Prime Minister was essentially in the hands of his own Navy and military High Command. All the Admirals and Generals were making it clear that once the Task Force sailed, it had either to fight or return home. They simply were not sufficiently strong to reach the South Atlantic and then hang around indefinitely while politicians and diplomats argued.

The problems of food, fuel, and supply lines were colossal, and many of the ships were old and likely to have serious malfunctions. They could fight perhaps once, fiercely, for maybe a month, but they could not waste time. Britain's naval and military leaders made it clear... **You may not leave us down there in bad weather and high seas, falling apart in the middle of the ocean: once we arrive, we either fight or leave. There's no halfway ground.**

General Sir Robin Brenchley in person told the Prime Minister an 8,000-mile journey down the Atlantic, and perhaps a four-week battle for the islands, was the maximum stress this Task Force could take.

"Prime Minister," he said, "to leave us down there for several weeks, fighting the weather, waiting for your clearance for battle, would be suicide for us, and perfect for our land-based opponents. So you'd better get used to it. When we clear Portsmouth Dockyard we're going to fight, and if you can't cope with that, you'd better call the whole thing off. Because if we get there and you put us in a holding pattern, we'll probably lose half of this aging fleet before we even start.

"Try to remember," he added, as if talking to a child, "all engineering problems, great and small, which would normally be carried out in a dockyard, will have to be completed at sea. I cannot condone any delay.

"And if you try to achieve one, you'll have the immediate resignations of both myself and the First Sea Lord, plus a dozen of the highest ranked commanders. Our reasons will be unanimous: **the total incompetence of your government**."

The Prime Minister was beaten and he knew it. "Very well, General," he said. "I must agree. When the Task Force sails there will be no further delay. Your rules of engagement will be set out and not subject to change."

Which essentially boxed everyone into an even tighter corner. The days were running out, the American diplomats were making no progress whatsoever, and Argentina had nothing to say to anyone.

At 0800, March 17, 2011, the Task Force sailed. The dockyard was packed with well-wishers. Families of the men on board the Royal Navy flotilla lined the jetties, many of them in tears. The band of the Royal Marines played "Rule Britannia" over and over as the warships cast their lines and headed out into the Solent, line astern.

Great crowds lined the seafront at Southsea, watching the ships sail slowly out into the English Channel and then toward great waters, where devastating battles had been fought and won for centuries.

Admiral Alan Holbrook's flag flew from the mast of the **Ark Royal**, and the route they took was close to the shore, enabling the carrier to pass close to the naval stations along the south coast, Lee-on-Solent, Devonport, and Culdrose. And as they passed, a constant stream of helicopter deliveries were made from the shore. There were also stores and ammunitions being unloaded for other ships that had not been prepared in Portsmouth itself, but which were heading out later in the day.

And all along the historic coastline the crowds were out watching the warships on their way, clapping and cheering them in the gusty offshore breeze that carried their hopes and best wishes out into the Channel.

In the sprawling naval base in Devonport, where HMS **Daring** was preparing to depart, a naval chaplain was present to conduct a short service of hope and prayer for relatives of the ship's company. And as the big Type-45 destroyer pushed out through the harbor, a Navy band played, poignantly, the hymn "Abide With Me," a fragile shard from the past, the last sounds of England heard by Admiral Woodward off Gibraltar all those years ago.

0900, MARCH 17, 71.00N 28.47E
DEPTH 300, COURSE 225, SPEED 22

She slipped swiftly through the cold deep waters off the most northerly coast of Norway: **Viper K-157**, the 7,500-ton pride of Russia's ever-dwindling attack submarine fleet. The old Soviet Navy was probably in terminal decline, but no expense had been spared in building this sleek, black underwater warrior, completed a dozen years earlier, lightly used and now "worked up" to its maximum efficiency.

They built her right across the wide estuary of the Severnaya Dvina, opposite the port of Archangel, on the often hard-frozen shores of the near-landlocked White Sea. This is the location of that cradle of Russian maritime engineering, the shipyards of Severodvinsk, where even the attack submarines built in faraway Nizhniy Novgorod on the Volga are transported for their nuclear engineering.

The **Viper** took four years to build, constructed with the meticulous care of the Severodvinsk nuclear engineers, many from the same families as the men who had built the enormous old Soviet Typhoon-class 26,000-ton ballistic missile submarines back in the 1980s.

By general consensus **Viper K-157** was the finest submarine ever built in Severodvinsk. She was nuclear-powered by a VM5 Pressurized Water Reactor, which thrust 47,600 horsepower into her two GT3A turbines. A member of the excellent Akula-class ships, she was 14 feet longer than the old Akula Is, and, at 360 feet overall, was the first of a new class of Akula IIs. The standard of engineering around her extra-long fin was unprecedented in Russian submarine building. She was comfortable dived to a remarkable 1,500 feet, where she would make a good twenty-five knots.

Every possible radiated noise level had been notably reduced. She was virtually silent at seven knots and under. Her sonar system was the latest improved Shark Gill (SKAT MGK 53) passive/active search and attack. It functioned on low-medium frequency, hull-mounted.

And she packed a serious wallop, with her batteries of submerged-launch cruise missiles, the Raduga SS-N-21s, which were also surface-to-surface weapons. She also carried Sampson (GRANAT) missiles, also fired from twenty-one-inch tubes, making Mach 0.7 for 1,600 miles, flying two hundred meters above the ground, carrying a 220-kiloton nuclear warhead, if required.

She carried forty torpedoes, the twenty-five-foot-long TEST-7IME fired from tubes fifty-three centimeters wide. This is a Russian ship-killer that travels through the water at forty knots, up to thirteen miles, packing a 220-kilogram warhead—nearly five hundred pounds of pure dynamite. Two of these would probably level the principal buildings of the Smithsonian Institution.

Viper had slipped her moorings in the Russian submarine base of Ara Guba shortly after midnight. Aside from the shore crew, just one lone Russian Navy Admiral stood on the north jetty to see them off. And a substantial figure it was, that of the giant greatcoated figure of Admiral Vitaly Rankov, who had been personally briefing the Captain and his senior officers for two days.

Free of her lines, **Viper** ran north up the long bay, which by some geophysical freak was not frozen solid, and headed up the channel into the icy depths of the Bering Sea. She dived in twenty-five fathoms, turning west toward the North Atlantic, on a voyage during which her crew would not see daylight for possibly three months.

The opening few hundred miles would see her running down the endless narrow coast of Norway, which sweeps 1,100 miles, from the southern city of Stavanger, straight past the western frontiers of Finland, Lapland, and Sweden to the Kola Peninsula, way up on the Russian border. It's six hundred miles down to the Arctic Circle, and five hundred more south to Stavanger.

Generally speaking, **Viper** could move pretty briskly during the first part of the journey, but would need to slow down measurably as she approached the narrowest point of the North Atlantic, the eight-hundred-mile wide electrically trembling waters of the GIUK Gap.

This is the most sensitive submarine country in the world, the stark line that runs from Greenland, bisecting the island of Iceland, dead straight to the northern coast of Scotland. The waters between Iceland and Greenland, the Denmark Strait, are often used by submarines, despite the danger of ice floes, the trawl nets of local fishermen, and generally shocking weather.

But it's the stretch between Iceland and Scotland that matters. These are the waters through which every Russian submarine from the Northern Fleet must pass if they wish to join the rest of the world. These are the waters still patrolled assiduously by submarines from the United States Navy and the Royal Navy.

During the Cold War, the U.S./UK patrols were even more intense than they are today. It would not be stretching a point to claim, as the U.S. Navy does, that no Soviet submarine traversed those waters, running either south or north, between the 1960s and the 1980s, without being detected.

In addition there is installed all through the GIUK the U.S. Navy's ultrasecret Sound Surveillance System, a fixed undersea acoustic network of passive hydrophone arrays, sensitive listening equipment connected to operational shore sites, which collect, analyze, display, and report acoustic data, relayed back from the strings of hydrophones laid in the deep sound channels.

These systems are laid in all of the key areas of the Pacific and North Atlantic, crisscrossed over the seabed, forming a giant underworld grid. Nowhere, repeat nowhere, is the system more vibrantly sensitive than in the waters of the GIUK Gap. They say if a whale farts, fifty American hearts skip a beat as the undersea sound waves ripple the SOSUS wires.

It would be prudent, of course, to say this was a slight exaggeration. Except that it's not. Little imagination is required to picture the total, steely eyed reaction in the U.S. Navy listening stations when the steady engine lines of a possibly hostile submarine are detected.

The commanding officer of **Viper K-157**, Captain Gregor Vanislav, one of Russia's most senior submariners, knew that once he ran south across the Arctic Circle he would be treading on eggshells. Like all Russian COs, he was highly nervous of being picked up electronically by the Americans.

He also knew no one would ever know precisely what had happened if his ship were sunk. Because the chances of a submarine being found in water two miles deep, somewhere in an area of several thousand square miles, was remote. It usually takes a couple of days for any command HQ even to realize one of their underwater ships has vanished, by which time it could be anywhere. Also, no one ever wants to admit the loss of a big nuclear ship, and certainly no one wishes to admit they destroyed it. Submarine losses are thus apt to remain very, very secret.

Captain Vanislav would run underwater some fifty miles off the Norwegian coast, past the fabled Lofoten Isles, a windswept, hundred-mile-long cluster of islands that jut out from the mainland, forcing submarines out into the 4,000-feet-deep Voring Plateau.

All through these waters, which were not particularly sensitive and were the regular exercise grounds for Russian ships, **Viper** would make almost five hundred miles a day. They would make a course change off the port of Namsos, swinging more westerly out into the Norwegian Sea, before running down to the Iceland–Faeroe Rise and the unseen line that marks the waters of the GIUK Gap.

Making only seven knots, they reached this relatively shallow water, only 850 feet deep, on the morning of March 22. And now they really were moving on tiptoes above the electronic lines on the ocean floor, as lethal as cobras, just waiting to detect any significant underwater movement, before raising all hell in the American listening station.

Captain Vanislav ordered their speed cut to five knots, and oh so slowly the most deadly attack submarine in the Russian Navy eased her way forward, her great turbines just a tad above idling speed as she slipped south into the Atlantic, with just three commands from Admiral Rankov in the mind of her commanding officer:

1. **Do not under any circumstances be detected anywhere along the route to the Falkland Islands.**
2. **Locate the Royal Navy Task Force and hold your position until hostilities begin.**
3. **Sink the** Ark Royal.

1130 (LOCAL), TUESDAY, MARCH 22
NATIONAL SECURITY AGENCY
MARYLAND

Lt. Commander Ramshawe was staring at the front covers of the major U.S. news magazines. Without exception they carried large photographs of the Royal Navy Task Force sailing for the South Atlantic. Most of them had shots from helicopters showing the decks of the aircraft carrier and the big assault ships, lined with the GR9s and helicopters.

The British military's ultimatum, that they would be unable to hang around in bad weather beating up the ships if not permitted to fight, had not been made public. However, the U.S. ambassador to London was in receipt of that knowledge and had informed President Bedford of the situation.

The Pentagon had been alerted, as had the NSA and the CIA. Jimmy Ramshawe was among those who knew that when the Royal Navy Fleet cleared the English Channel, it was going to war with the Republic of Argentina.

He poured himself a fresh cup of coffee and continued to look at the U.S. coverage of the crisis. "Jeez," he muttered. "These bastards are actually going to fight for those islands all over again."

And he realized that this time there was a lot more involved than was immediately apparent.

For a start, the U.S. President was under enormous pressure from ExxonMobil to do something about the Falkland Islands oil fields, for which they had paid an arm and a leg to the British government for drilling rights, and for the massive investment in drilling-rig equipment, miles of pipeline, enormous pumps and transportation.

ExxonMobil had $2 billion tied up in that operation, and all of their guys had been frog-marched, at gunpoint, off the island by Argentinian troops. The oil giant wanted action. In fact, the oil giant wanted President Bedford to get down there with a U.S. Carrier Battle Group and "roust these bastards back to where they came from... doesn't seem right to let the Brits go it alone."

But President Bedford did not want to take his country into another war, especially with Argentina, which had always extended the hand of friendship to the USA. The problem was that when Uncle Sam picked up his musket, any ensuing war had to be won, and the High Command in the Pentagon knew how thoroughly the Argentinians were prepared for this conflict.

The political ramifications of American boys fighting and dying in that godforsaken group of rocks, which anyway belonged to someone else, filled the President with horror, never mind the oil. And the Pentagon chiefs themselves were not mad about such an adventure either.

The U.S. military was willing to assist Great Britain, willing to run the base at Ascension Island in a way that would make life much, much easier for the Task Force in terms of supplies and fueling, even assistance with missiles. But President Bedford, like President Reagan before him, would not commit American troops, and he would not commit U.S. Navy ships, and he would not commit any U.S. fighter attack aircraft.

After two or three weeks of hard negotiating, he accepted that the Brits needed help, but it would need to be arm's-length help, which did not entail one single death of an American serviceman.

In truth, President Bedford felt somewhat guilty about the whole operation, because ExxonMobil was ultimately the biggest player in the Falklands oil business and would thus be the biggest benefactor of any victory achieved by the forces of Great Britain.

And there was also the question of the massive natural gas strike on the island of South Georgia. President Bedford understood that the Task Force could only attend to that after recapturing the Falklands themselves. And he had a disturbing vision of the Union Flag once more fluttering above Port Stanley, with the battered remnants of the Royal Navy Fleet, with all of its burned and wounded sailors. Then turning southeast to South Georgia in order to save 10,000 British national penguins and to wrest 400 billion cubic feet of ExxonMobil's natural gas holdings from the hands of Argentinian brigands.

It was not at all fair. He knew that. But then nothing was, and the prospect of a couple of hundred body bags arriving back in the United States was more than he could risk. Because in the end it would cost him his Presidency. And, good guy or no, Paul Bedford was a politician, and ensuring his own survival came as natural to him as breathing.

He would do damn near anything to help the Brits, except take his country to war, which would be tantamount to throwing himself on his sword.

Jimmy Ramshawe understood the high stakes. He had read, over and over, the carefully constructed assessments of the forthcoming war by Ambassador Ryan Holland. He knew the heavy strength of the Argentinian fighter aircraft, the Mirage jets, the Skyhawks, and the Super-Etendards stationed at the newly active Rio Grande base.

And he knew that when battle commenced, the Argentinians would launch everything at the Royal Navy Fleet. It would be an overwhelming aerial armada, and yes, the Brits would down several of them. But they would not down them all, and many bombers would get through and probably blast the British Task Force out of the game. Because the Brits had insufficient air power.

And no one understood the real issues here more thoroughly than Admiral Arnold Morgan. Recalled from his winter vacation on the Caribbean island of Antigua he had arrived back in the States, on board **Air Force One**, and flatly refused to see the President until he had read the assessments by Ryan Holland and the summaries from the Pentagon.

"There's quite enough political assholes briefing you on subjects they do not understand," he grated, "without me joining them. Gimme two days and we'll talk."

That had been Friday, February 18, and since then the President and the former National Security Adviser had been in constant communication. And as ever, Arnold Morgan had brought a clarity to the situation, which the President simply could not ignore.

"I understand you do not want to take the United States to war," said the Admiral. "But that is only the simple part of your problem. The difficult issue is that the Brits are plainly going to get beat. There's no ifs, ands, or buts, they cannot win.

"I know they pulled it off last time. But they had infinitely bigger resources then. Many more ships, fifty percent more fighter aircraft, all of them Harriers, which were vastly superior to these no-radar GR9s they're fucking about with. And above all they had replacements. Sandy Woodward lost two of his major Type-42 destroyers, but they brought out more.

"They cannot do so this time. They're too small a fleet, too thinly stretched, and they cannot defend themselves against iron bombs. Quite frankly I'm astounded the Royal Navy agreed to go. As for the Army, God knows what's going to happen to them. If they manage to land on the Falklands, to form an enclave preparing to march on the Argentinian positions, and the weather's bad, they'll get blasted out of sight, because those GR9s can't stop an incoming enemy air assault.

"In my view we're looking at the most shocking military defeat for Great Britain since Dunkirk."

President Bedford walked across the Oval Office. He said nothing, but his concern was obvious. "Can we ignore it, if that happens?"

"Christ, no," replied Arnold. "Refuse to help our best friends in the international community? A nation that stood shoulder to shoulder with us, twice, in the Gulf? Our one completely trustworthy ally in Europe? Hell, no. We can't just leave them to it. It would be construed as something close to treachery. No one would ever count on us again.

"And, of course, the lion's share of the oil and gas fields in the Falklands and South Georgia is held by ExxonMobil. That's about as American as it gets.

"Mr. President, I obviously appreciate your problems with taking this nation into a war. But it might be a whole lot easier to join the Brits right off the bat, in the hope we may frighten the shit out of the Args and they'll withdraw from the islands in the face of American fury."

"Something tells me, Arnold, they're not budging from that pile of rocks," replied the President. "And I don't think the oil and the wealth under the land is the true issue. I think they're all nuts, and feel they are fighting some kind of a pampas jihad, battling for the birthright of every Argentinian. They've been simmering over their defeat in the Malvinas for nearly thirty years.

"They have said, plainly, they would have fought for the islands even if the oil had never been there. In my view the oil and gas are merely the casus belli. Sooner or later the Argentinians would have attacked the pathetically weak British defenses in the Falklands. And then battled 'til the last drop of blood to hold on to their conquest. I agree with you. The Brits, and in a sense us as well, have our backs to the goddamned wall trying to fight these fucking fanatics."

Admiral Morgan nodded, in a clearly somber mood. He leaned back in his chair and suggested another pot of hot coffee. The President pressed a bell, then leaned forward to hear what the Admiral was about to say.

When he finally spoke, it was more like a father to a son than an ex–submarine commander to a President. "Paul," he said, "you and I have known each other for a while. We both served in the United States Navy. And I want to ask you one question..."

"Shoot," said the President.

"What would you do if you were in command of the Argentinian military and wanted to win this forthcoming war in the fastest possible time?"

"I'd take out the Royal Navy carrier, the one with the entire air force embarked on board."

"Correct. So would I. In fact I'd aim to hit the **Ark Royal** and about a half dozen other warships. I'd launch a hundred fighter-bombers and send half of 'em after the **Ark Royal**. That way I'd put her on the bottom of the Atlantic about four hours after the start of the war."

"Well, I guess they knew that last time, but they either could not or would not do it."

"Last time," replied Arnold, "they had only five Exocet air-to-surface missiles. And Admiral Woodward kept the **Hermes** well out of range during the daylight hours. This time it's all different. The Arg Air Force is much bigger, much more efficient.

"They probably have two hundred Exocet missiles, because they've been stockpiling for this very day. However, the Brits have improved their antimissile systems and they might actually stop most of the Exocets, but they won't stop the bombs from the A4s. They cannot stop them.

"The Args will take their losses and in the end break through, and smash the carrier. And that, ladies and gentlemen, will be the end of the game."

"Christ," said President Bedford. "Then what?"

"Then what, indeed?" said the Admiral. "But in my view that's where we're likely to stand four weeks from now. So we better start thinking about it."

"You staying for lunch?"

"Depends what you're offering. Tuna sandwiches, forget it. Decent steak and salad, count me in. Tell you what, I'll even go for a roast beef on rye, so long as you run to mayonnaise and mustard. But we better start thinking. This Falklands bullshit gets to be more of a goddamned problem by the day."

"If my wife catches me eating roast beef sandwiches with mayonnaise she'll have a heart attack," grinned the President.

"Then I guess we'd better be good boys, and have two nice little grilled steaks with grass and fucking dandelions," confirmed Arnold.

"But what we really need to do is think. Because the day's not far away when some comedian walks through that door and says the Brits just conceded defeat and left the Falkland Islands, which remain in Argentinian hands. The Chairman of the

Joint Chiefs wants to know where we stand, and the Chairman of ExxonMobil is fit to be tied."

"That," added Admiral Morgan, "would be a darned awkward moment."

"You said that right," said the President. "Let's take a stroll along to the dining room, clear our heads and make a few decisions."

"We may as well," replied the Admiral. "Because when this happens, it'll happen real quick and the lines will be very clearly drawn. Do we or do we not help the Brits? And the answer to that one must always be yes. The question is, what do we do?"

The two men stood up and pulled on their jackets. They left the Oval Office and walked along the West Wing corridor to the President's small private dining room. The butler met them, and poured them each a glass of sparkling water, knowing that neither man ever touched alcohol during the day.

"Well, Oh Great Oracle," said the President, "what will we do?"

"Dunno," said Arnold, unhelpfully.

"You mean I sent the most expensive jet aircraft in the country halfway across the world to some goddamned Caribbean paradise to drag you off the beach with that goddess who married you, and at the end of it I get 'Dunno.' Jesus Christ."

Arnold chuckled. "And the really bad news is I've just spent three weeks thinking about nothing else, night and day, and it's still 'Dunno.'

"However," he added, uttering the one single word the President was waiting to hear, "I know what we **cannot** do, under any circumstances. And that's rustle up fifty thousand troops and somehow storm the place, with all guns firing, air, sea, and land."

"Why not?" said the President, with synthetic innocence.

"Because we don't even own the goddamned islands, and we would be universally accused of going to war over that oil and gas, which is a charge we've heard quite enough of for one century."

"True," said the President. "Well, what's left?"

"Dunno," said Arnold.

"Jesus Christ," added the President.

"Tell you the truth," replied the Admiral, "I'd really like time to think about this, and I'd like to have a talk with some of the Pentagon guys, in particular the Special Forces officers.

"Meanwhile, there is something that concerns me. And I've been trying not to dwell on it…but in the last few months we have been exercised by two substantial events.

"The first was the murder in the White House of old Mikhallo whatsisname, the Siberian. And that was also a part of what the CIA believes was a massacre of Siberian oilmen and politicians in Yekaterinburg.

"From that we must deduce that somehow Moscow is hugely concerned to the point of neurosis about developments in Siberia, and the possibility that in the end they may prefer to sell their oil not to Moscow but to their good and wealthy southern neighbors in China.

"The second great event was the Argentine invasion of the Falkland Islands, conducted with scarcely a warning, with massive confidence, and total disregard for the possibility of a vicious counterattack by the Brits.

"Both of those drastic scenarios were conducted within weeks of each other. They were brutal, ruthless, and betrayed no apparent fear of consequences. And both of them were about oil and gas—the West Siberian reserves, which Moscow wants but may not keep. And the Falkland and South Georgia reserves, which Argentina has grabbed.

"I'd sure hate to think that somehow those two events were in any way connected. Because that would sure as hell be bigger trouble than either you or I, or anyone else, could ever have imagined."

The Admiral's global view invariably astounded President Bedford. And the two naturally garrulous men slowly ate their steaks and "fucking dandelions" in somber, uncharacteristic contemplation.

CHAPTER SIX

HMS **Ark Royal** crossed the fifty-degree line of latitude in the western reaches of the English Channel, twenty miles south of the ancient Royal Navy city of Plymouth. The weather was foul, blowing a force-eight gale, and the carrier pitched through ten-foot waves, the crests of which were beginning to topple, with dense streaks of foam marking the direction of the wind.

Rain that had swept up the Atlantic in the approaching depression was light but squally, sweeping across the deck in lashing bursts against the base of the carrier's island. The two Type-45s **Daring** and **Dauntless** ran a half mile off the carrier's port and starboard bow.

Two miles astern of the **Ark Royal** there were three of the frigate squadron, **Grafton**, **Iron Duke**, and **Richmond**, in company with a massive fleet oiler. Captain Farmer had the **Ocean** positioned three miles off the carrier's port quarter, with Jonathon Jempson's **Albion** a mile astern, all of them making twenty knots.

Several hundred miles out in front were two 6,500-ton nuclear submarines, **Astute** and

Ambush, both recently built in Barrow-in-Furness, as the newest, state-of-the-art improvements on the old Trafalgar class.

Single-shafters with two turbines apiece, they each carried submerged-launch Tomahawk cruise missiles and thirty Spearfish torpedoes. They were equipped with the outstanding Thompson Marconi 2076 sonars, with towed array, and were probably the quietest attack submarines in the deep, quieter even than **Viper K-157**, which right now was still fighting its way down the coast of Norway.

The **Astute** was commanded by Captain Simon Compton, and the **Ambush** by Commander Robert Hacking, both men experts in navigation and weaponry.

The surface Battle Group pushed on down the English Channel toward the Atlantic, through the now driving rain and plainly worsening weather. It was not yet storm force, but up ahead to the southwest the skies were darker, and the clouds seemed lower, and the warships seemed to brace for the rough seas before them.

Admiral Holbrook had planned to visit the ships one by one and address the crews, but he elected to wait until the weather improved before making a succession of windswept helicopter landings on the flight decks of his various escorts.

They were in open water now, and the waves were beginning to break over the bows of the frigates, but the forecast was pretty good, and the Admiral reckoned they'd be clear of the stormy conditions within twelve hours.

With the coast of England finally slipping away behind them, the little fleet suffered its first equipment problem. Captain Yates's destroyer, the **Daring**, developed a minor rattle in her gear-box, which was disconcerting though not life-threatening.

The **Daring**'s engineering team thought it was minor, and they elected to keep going until they reached calmer waters, where they were certain they could conduct the repair. All of the ships carried some spare parts for the routine running of a warship in rough seas at moderate to high speeds. The engineers would not, however, wish to cope with anything much worse while so far from a dockyard.

One day later, on Saturday morning, March 19, they steamed out of the rain and gloom into much calmer waters and blue skies that would, with luck, hold fair for the thousand-mile run down to the Azores, which rise up from the sea-bed only just short of the thirty-degree line of longitude, the halfway point across the North Atlantic.

Admiral Holbrook decided to visit the **Dauntless** and the **Daring** in the morning, and then fly back to the **Iron Duke** and the **Richmond** in the afternoon. And to each of those four groups of highly apprehensive sailors he delivered the same somewhat brutal message:

"Gentlemen, there's no point beating about the bush. We are going to war, and it is likely that some of us may not be returning. I expect to lose ships, and people. And I am obliged to remind you that for several years now you have been paid by the Royal Navy to prepare for events such as this.

"I realize this is all something of a shock, but I am afraid you are all now required to front up, and earn it, perhaps the hard way. You may not have realized it before, but this is what you joined the Navy for.

"To fight one day a battle on behalf of your country. Royal Navy seamen have long had a phrase for it—**you shouldn't have joined if you can't take a joke.**

"With regard to our enemy, the Args have two twenty-six-year-old diesel electric submarines, both somewhat tired and slow. We ought to detect them far away, and deal with them accordingly. They also have an even older, even slower submarine that one of their commanders ran aground in the River Plate at the end of last year. I do not regard the Argentinians as a major subsurface threat."

This raised a tentative laugh, but Admiral Holbrook's words had already had a sobering effect. "Their surface fleet is more of a problem," he said, but added, more encouragingly, "although I expect our SSNs to have dealt with it before we get there.

"I refer to their four German-built destroyers, all of them equipped with Aerospatiale MM 40 Exocet surface-to-surface missiles, which is not good news.

"They have another couple of elderly destroyers, one of them a British-built Type-42 with Exocets. The other one, **Santisima Trinidad**, is probably out of commission.

"They have nine frigates, mostly carrying an Exocet missile system. Two of them only ten years old. We must be on our guard at all times, absolutely on top of our game. And if we stay at our best we'll defeat them."

Admiral Holbrook saw no point in dwelling upon the awful discrepancy in the air war, Argentina with perhaps two hundred fighter-bombers, God knows how many Super-Etendards, all land-based, against the Royal Navy's twenty-one GR9s with no radar, unable to find each other in bad visibility, never mind the enemy. All of them bobbing about in the South Atlantic with no second deck, should the **Ark Royal** be damaged.

And each day the Admiral flew to address a different ship's company, and to confer with his Captains. And they continued to make passage south, mostly in good weather, covering hundreds of miles every twenty-four hours.

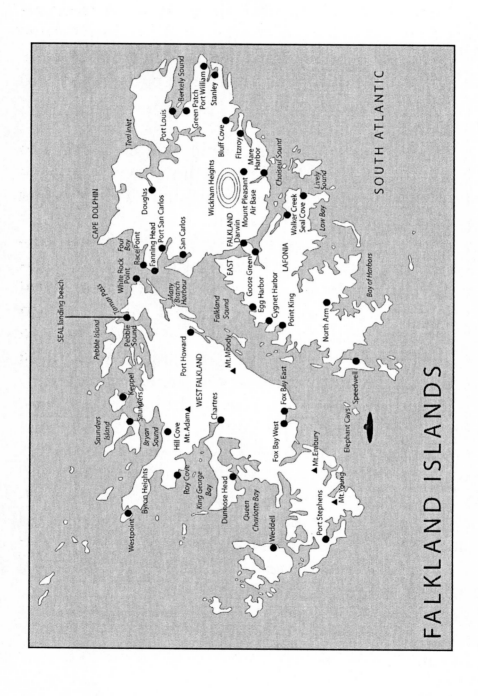

FALKLAND ISLANDS

The aircrews continued to work up their attack force, with takeoffs and landings being conducted all day and into the evening. They were rarely interrupted, except, on several occasions, by Russian Long-Range Maritime Patrol Craft, known locally as Bears. Every time they visited, they just flew along the horizon watching the British ships, and every time they came, the Task Force Commander hoped to hell they were not talking to the Argentinians.

However, they never came south of the Spanish coast, and eventually the Bears vanished altogether. Nonetheless, the deep frown on Admiral Holbrook's brow never eased as he and Captain Reader discussed the appalling task that lay ahead of them, both men understanding this could be the last battle a Royal Navy Fleet would ever fight.

231440MAR11 50.47N 15.00W
NORTH ATLANTIC
SPEED 7, DEPTH 500, COURSE 195

Captain Vanislav had thus far conducted his long voyage with exemplary caution. He had run **Viper K-157** swiftly for two days down the Norwegian coast, then cut his speed dramatically as he angled more westerly out into the Norwegian Sea, and delicately over the SOSUS wires of the United States Navy.

They'd crept down through the GIUK Gap, making only seven knots as they moved over the Iceland–Faeroe Rise in only 850 feet of water, straight along the ten-degree westerly line of longitude. They had pressed on over the Iceland Basin, where the Atlantic suddenly shelves down to a depth of nearly two miles.

And then they had run on five hundred miles southwest, now down the fifteen-degree line of longitude until they approached the Porcupine Abyssal Plain 120 miles west of the Irish trough. And right here they ran into one of those deep-ocean phenomena, a school of whales out in front, showing up on the sonar like an oncoming Battle Group.

In fact, no one was concerned, since such events are fairly commonplace in the deep waters of the North Atlantic. And the whales swerved away. Almost simultaneously, however, something else, much more serious took place. One of **Viper**'s "indicator buoys" broke loose and made the most frightful racket on the hull for two minutes until its mooring wire broke.

They were directly over a deepwater SOSUS wire, and two operators in the secret U.S. Navy listening station on the craggy coast of County Kerry in southwest Ireland detected them instantly. Huddled over their screens deep in the cliff side of the Iveragh Peninsula, south of Dingle Bay, the Americans picked up the signal from a distance of more than two hundred miles.

Almost immediately, with the loose buoy transmitting on the international submarine distress frequency, **Viper**'s comms room sent in a short-burst 1.5-second transmission to a satellite just to let home base know right away they had not in fact sunk.

The Americans heard all three bursts of noise.

Sounds like a submarine in trouble, sir. It's plainly Russian. Nothing else correlates. I'm checking, it's a Russian nuclear—probability area small.

Degree of certainty on that?

Eighty percent, sir. Still checking. She runs at the northern line of a ten-mile-by-ten-mile square. But right now the contact's disappeared.

Keep watching...

Everyone knew, of course, the Russians were perfectly entitled to be running a Navy submarine down the middle of the Atlantic south of the GIUK Gap. Just as the Americans or the British were.

But this particular submarine had not been detected for several hundred miles as it crossed that unseen line in the North Atlantic. Which suggested it did not want to be detected. Had it been making an aboveboard voyage at probably twenty knots, the Americans would have picked it up a dozen times.

But it had been moving very slowly, and remained undetected except for the very minor two-minute uproar when the buoy broke loose, and it all suddenly popped up on the U.S. Navy screens in Ireland.

Then, as suddenly as it appeared, it vanished. Which again suggested it had no intention of being located. Indeed, it suggested, strongly, that its commanding officer was operating clandestinely, on a mission that was plainly classified.

Of course everyone in the U.S. listening station knew there were several possibilities. The Russian ship could easily have been on a training run, or testing new equipment on a long-distance voyage. Maybe the U.S. operators had picked her up at the end of the training run, and located her as she made her turn. But if so, why was she not making proper speed north, when everyone could locate her?

The U.S. Navy Lt. Commander did not like it. Any of it. And he put an immediate signal on the satellite to Fort Meade:

231610MAR11 Southwest Ireland facility picked up a two-minute transient contact on a quiet submarine. Data suggests Russian heading south. Abrupt stop. Nothing on friendly networks correlates. Fifty-square-mile maximum area. Still checking longitude 15, 200 miles off west coast Ireland.

The Navy's Atlantic desk in the National Surveillance Office drafted a request to Moscow to clarify the matter. But no reply was forthcoming.

And none of the Americans, of course, understood the depth of the fury within Admiral Vitaly Rankov, who paced his office in the Kremlin and spent fifteen minutes roundly cursing the errant carelessness of **Viper**'s crew.

Thirty-six hours later, on the morning of March 25, Lt. Commander Jimmy Ramshawe set a half hour aside to scroll through the pages on the NSA's Internet system. Twenty minutes later he was staring at the message from County Kerry. And the fifth line stopped him dead, because it contained the word **submarine**—and the teaching of Arnold Morgan cascaded into his mind:

> **Ramshawe, my boy, when you see the word** submarine, **think only one thing...sneaking conniving little sonsobitches, hear me? When you see the words** Russian submarine, **take that to the tenth power, and throw in the words** devious, furtive, shifty, underhanded, **and** villainous. **Because they are always up to no good.**

He logged in to his Classified Intelligence CD-ROM and accessed the section on Russia. He hit the keys and ran through the classes of submarines that might be on the loose. Most likely, he thought, were the Akula-class boats, and there were ten of them, with three laid up. Four of the old Akula Is were confirmed in the Pacific Fleet, which left three, all in the Northern Fleet either in the base at Ara Guba or operational in the Barents Sea to the north of Murmansk. These were the newest, the improved Akula IIs—**Gepard**, commissioned in 2001, **Cougar**, commissioned in 2005, and **Viper**, commissioned in 1996.

"Well," muttered Jimmy, "our operator in Ireland reckoned it was a Russian nuclear, so it probably was. Still, I wonder what the little sonofabitch was doing heading south down the Atlantic."

The word **Atlantic** of course triggered in his mind the thought of the Royal Navy Task Force heading for the Falklands. And he immediately checked its whereabouts...**800 miles north of Ascension...that's bloody miles from the Russian submarine, damn nearly 3,000. Can't see a connection there...**

He called his boss, the Director, Admiral George Morris, whose antennae rose instantly. "Come along and see me, James," he said. "And bring hard copy of that signal from Ireland, will you?"

Three minutes later they were both standing in front of a large wall computer screen, staring at a map of the Atlantic, straight at the area where the Russian ship had been detected.

"Strange place to be suddenly heard, then just as suddenly disappear," mused the Director. "He obviously did not want to be located—and when he was, it was a pure accident."

"Can't tell if the bugger turned around or kept on going," said Jimmy.

"No," replied the Admiral. "No one can tell that. And no one's heard a squeak from the damn thing since? Guess we just have to wait 'til he makes another mistake. Because it sure as hell was a mistake. That was one creepy little sonofabitch, and he did not wish to be detected…let me know if Moscow offers an explanation."

"You want to touch base with the Big Man, sir?"

"Jimmy, I'm real tied up this afternoon. But maybe you could have a quick word with him— you know how he is about submarines…"

"Okay, Chief. I'll give him a call."

Twenty minutes later Admiral Morgan, in a cheerful mood, answered the phone in Chevy Chase. "Don't tell me," he said, "the Russian secret police just committed murder in Buckingham Palace."

Jimmy chuckled. "Not quite, sir. But I just received a signal from our listening station in southwest Ireland, where they think they picked up a Russian nuclear submarine running south a couple of days ago."

"What submarine?" snapped the Admiral, all traces of bonhomie suddenly absent.

"Well, the most likely was one of their Akula-class boats. Not the Akula Is, which are in the Pacific. But one of three operational Akula IIs, much newer, all based in the Northern Fleet—either **Gepard, Cougar,** or **Viper**…"

"Are they accounted for?"

"Not really. Just before I called we located **Gepard** on an exercise sixty miles north of Murmansk, and we have a record of **Cougar** in workup after a refit just outside Ara Guba ten days ago. Nothing on **Viper**. But they have those big covered docks up there, so I guess it could have been either of 'em."

"Where did the guys in Ireland detect the ship?"

"Coupla hundred miles west of County Kerry. In deep water…they heard a lot of clattering, then there was an international distress signal. Then they picked up a satellite signal, short burst in Russian. Surveillance say it confirmed they were not sinking. Then it went quiet. I checked with the station, they record no other ships within a hundred miles."

"Wonder what the hell scared her?"

"Can't help. I talked to the operator. He said they picked something up right out of the blue. From nowhere. And it vanished just as sharply. Never came back."

"Hmmmmmm," said Arnold. "Sneaky little sonofabitch, right?"

"Yessir."

"Tell you what, Jimmy. It's eleven thirty—you want to come over for lunch? I'm fooling with a theory that just might fit right into this. But it's so goddamned outlandish I'm kinda nervous about mentioning it. It's not something I want you to act on, it's something I want you to have in your mind…in the back of your mind, right? Just for that moment when something pops out at you, when some tiny bit of data seems to shed some light."

"Okay, I'll just tell Admiral Morris. I'll be there by twelve thirty, and I gotta be back by sixteen hundred."

"Don't get excited. You'll be back before then. This isn't a goddamned banquet, it's a quick sandwich and a cup of coffee. Don't be late…" Bang. Down phone. The Admiral, even in retirement, still didn't have time for "good-bye." Not even for the young naval officer he treated like a son.

Jimmy's elderly, but perfectly tuned, black Jaguar, top down, came squealing into the Admiral's drive three minutes before 12:30, nearly mowing down a couple of Secret Service agents in the process.

"Christ, sir, you'll kill someone in that damned thing," one of them observed. "Hopefully, not me."

"Don't you worry about me, Jerry," called Jimmy, "I've got eyes like a bloody dingo, and reactions to match."

"What the hell's a dingo?"

"Australian prairie dog, a right little killer, stealthy, like me."

"Stealthy! You're about as stealthy as a train crash," replied the agent, laughing. "Go straight in. The Admiral's waiting."

Inside the house, sitting quietly by the log fire in his book-lined study, was the most feared Military Intelligence expert in the world. A man whose high office had once caused world leaders to shudder, and who, even now, was capable of causing great consternation among governments not entirely in step with the United States.

Admiral Morgan looked up from the editorial page of the **New York Times** with a scowl on his face. "The sad and lamentable left," he growled. "Still fighting for the same tired old causes, years out of date, discredited, long dismissed. But only in the biggest newspaper in the entire goddamned country...hi, young Ramshawe, siddown."

"Morning, Admiral," said Jimmy, brightly.

"Morning! Morning!" snapped the old tyrant of the West Wing. "Right now we're nearly a half hour into the afternoon watch. Eight bells before this coffee arrived—want some?"

"Thank you, sir," said Jimmy. "I mean Arnie. It's just damn near impossible to believe you've retired."

"Don't you start off—you sound like Kathy."

"It's just that everyone senses you're still in charge. George Morris says that's what the President thinks."

"Well, I'll have to whip him into line next week," said the Admiral, "because we're taking a short vacation in Scotland, kinda make up for my heavily interrupted rest on a Caribbean beach last month."

Jimmy poured himself a cup of coffee from the heated glass pot on the sideboard, automatically freshened Arnold's cup, and fired out a couple of "bullets" from the blue plastic container that held the sweeteners.

The Admiral flicked them into his steaming coffee, told Jimmy to shove another log on the fire, and to pay attention. He would of course have told the President of the United States, or Russia, or China, to do precisely the same thing. It was part of his charm.

"Now listen, Jimmy, with the exception of George, I don't want you to repeat this conversation to anyone. I have mentioned it to the President, who was having his lunch at the time and damn nearly choked on it. And I'm going to tell you, because I know you will store the information and be watchful for correlating facts."

"Right, sir. I'm listening."

"Okay. I want to mention the biggest thing that's happened in the last few months, which was of course the murder of the Siberian politician in the White House. Never solved, and followed up a few weeks later by what we suspect, but cannot prove, was some kind of a massacre by the Russian secret service of all the big players in the Siberian oil industry. No bodies, damn shaky explanation, no one really believes the Kremlin, right?"

"Right. Certainly not Lenny Suchov."

"Now what does that tell you?"

"Not much. Except the Russians are extremely worried about their Siberian oil, on which the entire economy is based."

"Correct. And sufficiently worried to commit a couple of crimes, one of which was unthinkable, and the other just short of insane."

"Right. Those crimes sure as hell add up to a lot of worry."

"Well, let's consider the political problems in Siberia. On the one hand they have Moscow buying Siberian oil for an extremely low price, and taxing them, and on the other they have their neighbors to the south, China, offering a much better deal, and even arguing about the direction of the new Far Eastern pipeline.

"Now we don't know what triggered this general panic in the Kremlin. But something did. They thought if they took out old Mikhallo Masorin, the most powerful politician in Siberia, that would put out the fire. Well, it didn't. And whatever the hell was going on, they thought it required further, drastic action."

"Drastic is right. We're talking mass murder."

"Precisely, James, precisely. The old tried and trusted methods of the Soviets. Remove the men, you remove the problem. But this Russian President is damned smart, and he's a long-range thinker.

"And if he dwelled on the Siberian problem for long enough, he probably concluded it was an ongoing pain in the ass. And if he took it to its logical conclusion, he probably foresaw the day when Russia might be face-to-face with the Siberians, who wanted independence and wanted their oil on the open market, to China."

"I guess so. And I doubt it's escaped him that China is scouring the entire bloody planet in search of oil supplies."

"No, Jimmy, that will not have escaped him. And now, I'm going to ask you a very serious question...where is the biggest oil and natural gas strike in the world in the last twenty-four months?"

"Not sure, sir."

"I'll tell you. It's in the Falkland Islands. And what happened last month?"

"The Argentinians invaded, conquered, and grabbed the oil."

"From right out of nowhere, Jimmy. From right out of nowhere. For the first time in twenty-eight years there was a sudden rise in the political temperature in Buenos Aires. Just four weeks after the massacre in Yekaterinburg, thousands of crazy fucking gauchos were sounding off about the Malvinas, right in front of the Presidential Palace.

"And only fourteen weeks later, in the middle of February, the Argentinians attack the Falkland Islands, with no apparent thought as to whether the Brits will be prepared to go to war over their territory. It was politically nuts, because it would make too many enemies for Argentina. And militarily reckless, because the British are famously capable of immense beadiness if anyone fucks around with their property."

"Okay, Arnie. Why did they do it?"

"I don't know. But how about Russia told them to do it. How about Russia said they'd take care of the oil, drill for it, market it, build the pipelines, and cut Argentina in for a very generous piece of the deal. In return for which, they would make certain that any Royal Navy Task Force was eliminated, and the islands would remain sovereign Argentinian territory."

"Jesus Christ. Are you basing this on real knowledge, sir?"

"Certainly not. I'm basing it on a series of wild deductions, hunches, guesses, and blind political bias."

Jimmy laughed. "Of course, sir. Stupid of me not to have realized."

Arnold, however, did not smile. He stared at Jimmy darkly, and said, "But it might explain that fucking Russian nuclear submarine of yours, apparently making a beeline south down the Atlantic toward the Falklands."

"Fuck me," said Jimmy, momentarily lost for words. At least, normal words..."You're telling me that nuclear ship might be going to help Argentina defend the Falklands. Maybe attack the British. Christ. That's World War III."

"James," said Arnold, paternally, "you don't have to do much to cripple the Royal Navy's Task Force. A couple of well-aimed torpedoes, straight into the guts of HMS **Ark Royal**, steaming in massively deep water, and that little conflict is over. She'll hit the bottom of the Atlantic with all the British fighter planes, and half the helicopters.

"If the British Army is already ashore, they'll be massacred from the air and then taken prisoner. The fleet, with no air cover, will be hammered sideways and the survivors will be forced to return home...and no one will ever know what happened to the **Ark Royal**. At least no one who matters. The Russian SSN will never surface. She'll just turn north and creep quietly home. And the world will believe the Brits lost a fair fight against Argentina, a fight she should never have entered."

"Fuck me," said Jimmy, shaking his head, and then, hesitating, "You know the big trouble with that little scenario? It doesn't have any weak points!"

Arnold guffawed. "Except there's not one shred of evidence that makes all those little facts and circumstances hang together."

"What is it you always say, Arnie? You do not accept incompatible facts, right? I'd say the lineup you just gave me is one highly compatible group of facts. I'd say those little bastards are harmonious."

"Jimmy, they are so far-reaching I hesitate to continue. But they have been on my mind. And they were on my mind in the days before you mentioned the submarine we picked up west of Ireland. I suppose no one from the Russian Navy has offered confirmation or even denial about the whereabouts of the Akula II submarines?"

"Not a word, so far as I know."

"And there won't be a word. Which of course makes me think I may be right. Because if they'd sent a nuclear boat on a training exercise down the Atlantic, they'd have told us. You know, the Cold War's over. We're supposed to be buddy-buddy with Moscow. But when the Kremlin starts clamming up, on any subject, you **know** there's something going on."

"I guess there is," said Jimmy. "But if you're right, this is a huge development. I mean what if the Brits catch 'em, and sink the boat. I mean, where the hell does that put us?"

"Jimmy, I'll just have our sandwiches sent in—Kathy's out, which means we get roast beef with mayonnaise and mustard. Our housekeeper is on pain of death if she mentions it…I'll be right back…get some more coffee…and then I'll tell you where we stand."

Jimmy took off his jacket, tossed it over a chair in the hall, and sat down again in the warm study. He glanced at the third lead story on the front page of the **Times**, its headline set in italicized type, which signified it contained nothing new.

No Political Solution Yet— Argentina Occupies the Falkland Islands

At that moment the Admiral returned. "Ignore that rubbish," he said. "Kipper knows more about it than they do."

"Who the hell's Kipper?"

"Kathy's new dog. A King Charles spaniel. I think he's as silly as a sheep. But he might learn, which is more than they will at the **NYT**."

"Where is he?"

"Gone out with Kathy. Virginia somewhere."

Arnold sat down, and said quietly, "This damn Russia connection could cause more trouble than anyone realizes, mostly because in the end we can't leave the Brits to suffer defeat at the hands of an armed aggressor.

"I know Argentina will blather on about the Malvinas belonging to them. But that's just horseshit. The Falkland Islands are a legal British protectorate, full of British citizens, and they are ruled and financed by Westminster. The Argentine action, whether they like it or not, is that of a gangster.

"And we cannot support that. Neither will the United Nations. Neither will the EU. The trouble is, we'll be expected to do something about it, if the Brits are defeated. And we'll have to do something about it, though I'm not sure what. Because Paul Bedford will not take this nation into someone else's war, whatever the UN says."

"So what happens?"

"I'm toying with the idea of forcing an Argentine surrender on the islands with Special Forces only."

"But they'll need air cover, just like the Brits, won't they? And now you're talking aircraft carriers, fighter-bombers, and F-16s all over the place. That's war, real war."

"Jimmy, I was actually wondering whether in this modern, high-tech age, we could not eliminate the Argentine Air Force and retake the island with just a force of landed U.S. Navy SEALs working with the British SAS."

"Where will the SAS come from?"

"I'd be surprised if they were not already in there, or at least well on their way."

"You mean the SAS, in place, on the islands?"

"I do. Plus the Brits' other Special Forces. That's the Special Boat Service, kinda SAS with flippers."

For five more days, the Royal Navy Task Force steamed south, running into relatively calm waters north of Ascension on March 28. At this point, **Viper** was still more than 2,000 miles behind. However, with SOSUS inactive in the southern half of the Atlantic, the submarine was now moving swiftly, often at twenty knots, five hundred feet below the surface, hugging the eastern edge of the Mid-Atlantic Ridge.

Captain Vanislav had no intention of going anywhere near Ascension, and would pass its line of latitude, eight degrees south of the equator, some thousand miles to the west, off the jutting, most easterly headland of Brazil.

Meanwhile, the Task Force was moving into the anchorage at Ascension Island, which had been rapidly transformed from a U.S. communications and satellite tracking station into a forward fleet and air base. President Bedford had been as good as his word...**all the help they need, except actually going to war with them.**

There were literally piles of extra stores flown out from the UK, and within a few days the Royal Navy's understrength Task Force would at least be equipped with everything they would need for the forthcoming conflict.

The two nuclear submarines, however, **Astute** and **Ambush**, did not stop off at Ascension. They pressed on south for very good reason. **Astute** was carrying sixteen members of 22 SAS, and **Ambush** had sixteen members of the SBS on board. These were the iron men of the British armed forces, the force that would go into the islands alone under cover of darkness, equipped with radios, computers, and satellite communication systems.

And for possibly two weeks, they would communicate back to the Task Force the troop placements of the Argentinians. They would work in conditions of extreme danger, perhaps the most lethal part of the operation being the night entry onto the Falklands.

Because it would have to be by boat, fast, hard-deck rubberized Zodiac outboards, launched off the decks of the submarines, and driven in, from four miles offshore, possibly under Argentine radar.

The SAS would certainly make a landing on the craggy coastline beneath the eight-hundred-foot-high Fanning Head at the northeastern end of Falkland Sound. They would work from there, moving around the island only after dark.

The Special Boat Service troops were scheduled to go in somewhere on the coast of Lafonia, probably in Low Bay, which is situated to the south of Mount Pleasant Airfield across Choiseul Sound. Their task was to scout out the territory for the British military landing, perhaps 10,000 men. The land they would investigate was not hospitable; it was flat, with little cover, and rock-strewn, but a place from which the land forces could at least locate their enemy by air, sea, and land.

The military chiefs in Whitehall had of course discussed the possibility of an entry by parachute drop. But the risk was simply too great, because no one knew quite what the Argentine troops could see and what they could not.

Things were quite sufficiently tough without risking some of the best men in the entire landing force being shot to pieces immediately after they landed. The solution was obvious. If the advance Special Forces were going in at all, they were going in by sea.

The embarked SAS troop was commanded by thirty-year-old Captain Douglas Jarvis, a member of a venerable racehorse-breeding family from Newmarket in Suffolk. He had considered becoming a bloodstock agent, but his elder brother had inherited the racing yard, and his elder sister, Diana, had insisted on selling the family stud farm, of which she owned 50 percent.

Which left young Douglas with a bit of money from his quarter share of the stud farm, a diminished family, and not much career choice. Anyway, he was "fed up to the teeth with bloody racehorses," and managed to pass selection for entry into the Royal Military Academy at Sandhurst.

He was commissioned into the Second Battalion Parachute Regiment, and five years after that he was accepted into the SAS, from an intake of only 6 out of 107 applicants. Douglas Jarvis was generally considered one of the toughest young officers who ever wore the beige beret of 22 SAS.

A lifelong foxhunter, steeplechase rider, and amateur boxer, he once made the front page of England's horseracing daily, the **Racing Post**, when, at the age of eighteen, he had forged his entry to the annual Stablelads Boxing Championship and flattened four stable-staff hard men from desperate inner-city council estates, to win the heavyweight championship.

That was only a 138-pound weight class among the race of relatively small men who form England's jockey population, but the committee took a poor view of the well-born son of a stable proprietor plundering the championship, which traditionally belonged to horse racing's other ranks.

Douglas was disqualified, and he somewhat grudgingly handed back his silver trophy. The authorities were not able, however, to take away his steam-hammer right hook, and years later he was narrowly defeated on points in the Sandhurst Middleweight Final, but won the trophy for the Royal Military Academy's bravest loser.

The lean, wide-shouldered Douglas somehow remained a legend in his native Newmarket, especially when he won a coveted Military Cross for leading his paras, fearlessly, in a pitched battle against insurgents in Basra during the 2003 Iraqi war. He shared the front page of the local paper with a sixteen-hand dark bay colt named Rakti, who had won Newmarket's prestigious Champion Stakes, and was trained locally by his cousin Michael Jarvis. THREE HEROES FROM NEWMARKET proclaimed the newspaper, presumably referring to the trainer, the horse, and Douglas.

"Jesus Christ," said one of 2 Para's best young commanders.

The beautiful Diana Jarvis adored her kid brother. But in recent years she had become something of a socialite, foxhunting in Ireland, and occasionally assisting a French trainer with the purchase of expensive thoroughbred yearlings at the major sales in Saratoga and Kentucky. She and Douglas saw each other whenever possible, but stayed in touch mostly by e-mail.

Neither of them married in their twenties, but then, suddenly, last year, Diana finally packed her bags, in order to emigrate to Kentucky and marry an American who owned a huge breeding farm in the heart of the Blue Grass. They had been meeting for a couple of years at the Keeneland Sales.

When she left Newmarket, she rather carelessly told a reporter her **only** regret about leaving England was how much she would miss Douglas. This did not go down especially well with the rest of the family, which included about 7,000 uncles, aunts, and cousins.

NEVER MIND 200 YEARS OF THOROUGHBRED
TRADITION—
DIANA JARVIS WILL MISS ONLY THE BOXER

That was really great. Especially typeset over a double-page spread with photographs of the great Jarvis trainers and breeders of the past. And by that time, she was glad to board the aircraft to the USA.

Six weeks later she became Mrs. Rick Hunter of Hunter Valley Farms, at a mutually agreed upon small ceremony in the Lexington registry office, and a reception for thirty or forty friends and neighbors. Douglas was unable to attend, and it took Diana five more months to realize her new husband, like her brother, had also been a member of his country's Special Forces.

The towering, superbly fit Rick had willingly told her he had been a Commander in the United States Navy, but only reluctantly admitted he had served a short tour in the Navy SEALs...**just a small Special Forces group, kinda like your brother's SAS guys**.

The enormity of that particular sin of omission was of course lost on the new Diana Hunter. But from time to time she picked up a few wry references to bygone conflicts, particularly when Rick's Vice President of Thoroughbred Operations, Dan Headley, came to dinner. Apparently, he also had once been in the U.S. Navy.

Anyway, that was the modern pedigree of Captain Douglas Jarvis, who right now was five hundred feet underwater, speeding south down the Atlantic, 1,500 miles off the coast of Brazil, locked in conversation with the **Astute**'s commanding officer, Captain Simon Compton.

They were in the ops area of the Navigation Officer, Lt. Commander Bill Bannister. Spread before them was a large Navy chart of the waters around East Falkland, and they were all looking at the northernmost points along the giant headland that guards the entrance to Falkland Sound.

This is a great craggy coastline, with high cliffs forming a seaward crescent facing to the northwest. The outermost top end of the crescent is Cape Dolphin, which sits on the end of a barren peninsula some two miles long. "Militarily worthless," in the judgment of Douglas Jarvis.

The other end of the crescent is formed by Fanning Head, which really does guard the entrance to the Sound. It used to be 800 feet high with sensational views over the water. Today it still had sensational views, but stood only 787 feet high, its summit having been blown away by the guns of the Royal Navy frigate HMS **Antrim** during the first Falklands conflict.

"You think the Args might be up there again?" asked Captain Compton.

"They might," said Captain Jarvis. "But only if they think we might do precisely what Admiral

Woodward did last time—send the fleet straight under their Fanning Head garrison at the dead of night. All lights out."

"Hell, they can't believe we're that bloody dreary, can they?" said the CO. "They must think we'd try something new."

"You would think so," replied Jarvis. "But all of our satellite interceptions suggest they know a lot about us. They don't have much satellite observation themselves, if any, and we know the Americans are not helping them. But someone is, God knows who. And it would not be surprising if they closed Falkland Sound to us completely. They may have mined it, of course, but they did not do so last time, and all they need now is a powerful missile and gun position up on Fanning Head with modern radar."

"Yes, I suppose so. And where does that put us?" The CO had quickly grown to respect the SAS Captain, as had everyone on board.

"Essentially we have to appreciate the logic of their position. An Argentine stronghold on top of that headland closes the north end of the Sound to us. It means we have to go right around the back of West Falkland or swing way south down the Atlantic and come at them from the southeast. If we want to make a landing, that is.

"For very little time, trouble, and cost, they can establish a powerful position on Fanning

Head, which would plague us throughout this conflict. Simon, we have to land at the base of that cliff and take the bastard out, not exactly by storm, but somehow to blow the fucker up."

"Christ, who's going to do that?"

"I am," said Captain Jarvis. "With seven of my best troopers."

"You're going to climb that rock face?"

"In the absence of a chairlift, I suppose so. Where do you think we are, Courcheval!"

They returned to the chart. And Captain Compton began talking the SAS boss through their route into Falklands waters...

"We come in from the northwest, dived in about two hundred feet of water, all the way to this light blue area where the ocean starts to shelve up...see these numbers here in meters... the ocean floor rises up to only a hundred twenty feet, then stays at around a hundred all the way in to Fanning Head...

"This narrow seaway into the Sound is only seventy feet deep, so we can stay underwater only until we're about a mile offshore...so long as we watch out for this fucking great rock marked here...only fifty feet below the surface with no warning light or even a buoy.

"Right here we're in the shadow of the cliff. And at 0200, it'll be as black as your hat. I'd prefer to launch the boats in here, just behind

Race Point…you'll have a mile longer to walk, but that's probably better than having your bollocks blown off by a radar-guided Argentine missile."

Douglas Jarvis grinned. "I assure you, Captain Simon, if anyone's going to have their bollocks blown off, it will not be me. You think I could call my sister in Kentucky and tell her the Args have gelded me? That'd be a family disgrace where I come from."

"Well, I suppose you would have to be scratched from the Derby," laughed the CO. "No geldings, right?"

"Simon, could we change the subject from my bollocks to this load of cobblers you're giving me about ocean depths."

"Certainly, Douglas. This submarine is seventy feet high, keel to mast. We need a hundred feet minimum depth. If it's less than that, we surface, since I do not wish to see either you or your bollocks scraping along the seabed, 'specially if it's rocky."

Both officers laughed, and even Lt. Commander Bannister, who'd been trying not to, joined in the nervous merriment.

"Let's get some coffee," said Captain Compton finally. "And then you can tell me where you want the second half of your troops to be landed."

The Lt. Commander vanished in search of coffee, and Captain Jarvis continued looking at the chart of the jagged coastline. "Simon," he said, "the second part of the SAS recce entails a thorough look at the Argentine defenses around Mount Pleasant Airfield.

"I've eight men detailed to carry it out, and I cannot see any other way to get there except to walk. From this landing beach it's about forty-five miles through the mountains, and they'll need three days in these conditions.

"They'll be hauling a lot of weight on their backs and they can only move at night. So I think we may as well land on Fanning Head more or less together, separated by just a couple of miles. I want to avoid having all our eggs in one basket, right? If one group gets caught the other's still on the loose.

"We'll take the Zodiacs in together, so you can make the fastest possible getaway. My guys are priceless, but I think the Navy values a five-hundred-million-dollar nuclear submarine even higher."

"We don't have many," said Captain Compton, but just then they were interrupted by a seaman handing over a satellite signal from the comms room, hard copy.

311300MAR11. Argentine warships heading for battle stations around the Falkland Islands. Two destroyers and three frigates cleared Puerto Belgrano 0500 today. Satellite intercept confirms destination East Falkland. All warships carry modern missile

radar systems. Anticipate wide Falklands surveillance by Args, surface and air. Holbrook.

"Very timely," said Captain Compton sharply. "We stay deep, all the way in."

The same signal was also received by Captain Robert Hacking on the **Ambush**. And, curiously, he was in conference with the SBS Team Leader, Lt. Jim Perry, dealing with exactly the same subject: where to land the sixteen Special Forces in Team Three, the guys who would hit the beach on the rough coast of Lafonia, and work under cover of darkness for the next couple of weeks.

As on the **Astute**, the **Ambush** team was in the navigation area, poring over the chart, wondering where the nearest Argentinian defenses would be situated along this truly desolate part of the island, south of the airfield.

The deep inlet of Choiseul Sound was seventeen miles long and in places three miles wide. And it was this inlet that separated the "business part" of East Falkland, where the oil fields and the airport and the military garrison were located. Indeed, Choiseul Sound very nearly bisected East Falkland altogether. Only the narrow causeway at Goose Green prevented this freezing east-west seaway from cutting the big eastern island clean in half.

Much more pertinent, however, was the fact that it was so damned shallow. There was a kind of navigation channel along the northern edge passing the entrance to Mare Harbor, to which at least one Argentine warship was plainly headed.

But even in this channel there was never as much as a hundred feet of depth, and the rest of the seaway was nearer thirty feet, in some places only ten. It was strewn with uninhabited small islands, submerged rocks, kelp beds, and God knows what. It was a submariner's nightmare. No go. No even think about.

And somewhere in these treacherous waters Lt. Jim Perry had to find a place to drive the Zodiacs up the beach. He preferred to prevent his team getting wet, since there was nowhere for them to dry out. And the weather, according to local forecasters, was already rain, with squalls out of the south, despite late March being only the equivalent of late September in the Northern Hemisphere.

Lt. Perry's team had a formidable task. After the landing they had to establish a hide about a quarter mile behind the beach, from where they could move out and watch, log, and record all Argentinian activity...the times and strength of shore patrols, if any; the proximity of the nearest Argentine military garrison; the regularity of sea patrols moving along the shore, if any; the times and depths of high and low tide for the incoming British landing craft; sites for missile batteries; helicopter landing areas; sites for shore radar systems that would scan across the flatlands to the north.

And all of this without being caught. When Lt. Perry's Zodiacs came in for the landing, one of them would be dragged up the beach and hidden, just in case a fast getaway was required. These big rubberized boats would hold twelve comfortably, but one of them would have to take sixteen if they were required to evacuate.

Privately, Lt. Perry thought there would be no need for an evacuation, and in the end he might not bother with the getaway Zodiac, which was very heavy, cumbersome, and an all-around nuisance for mobile troops. For now it was on the probable list. But if the men of the SBS were caught, they would expect to eliminate their enemy and carry on with their tasks. Running away was not in their training manual.

Both Royal Navy submarines continued their run south for seven more days. At noon on Friday, April 8, they were one hundred miles northwest of the islands. Captain Vanislav's **Viper** was still three days behind, and the Task Force, which had cleared Ascension on April 3, five.

New intelligence from the U.S. Navy in Ascension confirmed an Argentinian destroyer, an old Type-42, was moored on the jetties in Mare Harbor, while two guided missile frigates now patrolled two miles off Mengeary Point and Cape Pembroke, the two headlands that guard the entrance to the harbor and main town of Port Stanley.

The newest Argentine destroyer was currently making passage north, about three miles offshore. At the time the signal was sent, she was moving quickly, around twenty knots right off McBride Head, thirty miles east of the entrance to Teal Inlet. At the north end of Falkland Sound, another Argentinian guided-missile frigate appeared to be almost stationary.

According to the satellite signal, this ship had come in from the northwest and had entered the Sound through the narrows below Fanning Head. When Simon Compton showed the signal to Douglas Jarvis, they agreed it suggested the Argentinians planned to guard the Sound by sea, without building a missile launcher at the top of the cliff.

But the SAS leader could not take that chance. And his plan remained unaltered during the final miles of their long journey to the South Atlantic. Perhaps the more disturbing aspect of the signal from Ascension was news of the departure of three more Argentine warships from Puerto Belgrano, all making direct course for the Falkland Islands.

Any chance the Royal Navy once had of the Task Force making a covert entry into these waters was plainly shot. The Argentines seemed to be aware of every move the Royal Navy made on the voyage from Ascension. And they assumed, of course, the imminent arrival of probably two Royal Navy nuclear submarines. However, neither **Astute** nor **Ambush** knew of the existence of **Viper K-157**. Yet.

In the normal course of a Royal Navy commanding officer's duties, he would have received the information about the enemy destroyer off McBride Head and the frigate at the north end of the Sound, then moved in and put both of them on the floor of the South Atlantic.

However, this was different. The submarines were obliged to do anything rather than get caught. The one massive secret that could not be revealed was the insertion of the Special Forces.

The slightest indication of a British attacking presence was likely to double and treble Argentinian awareness, and defensive positions. Right now the less they knew the better. And Captains Compton and Hacking moved stealthily, cutting their speed, reducing their engine lines on any probing sonar that might be transmitting on the north side of East Falkland.

The course of the two submarines diverted thirty miles north of Fanning Head, where the fifty-ninth line of longitude bisects the fifty-first degree line of latitude. **Astute** steamed on south making only five knots, and **Ambush** made course 120, for her longer hundred-mile journey around the east side of the island to Choiseul Sound.

The water was still almost four hundred feet deep and would remain so for **Ambush** almost all the way. However, the Atlantic began to shelve up here for **Astute**, and for most of her journey inshore the depth would be around two hundred feet, growing shallower every mile.

For the final run across Foul Bay, **Astute** would come to periscope depth in a hundred feet of water, protected on three sides by huge cliffs, and protected from the Argentine frigate by Fanning Head itself.

Captain Compton ordered the ship to PD at 1826, by which time the SAS team was preparing to exit the submarine. Each man was dressed in full combat gear, including the windproof, rainproof Gore-Tex light smock that covered their regular thermal clothes. SAS combat teams always wear the best waterproof boots money can buy, and they carry in their bergans light thermal weatherproof sleeping bags, plus a quilted combat jacket in case the weather turns especially bad.

Each man carried his own automatic rifle and ammunition, with a couple of hand grenades clipped to his belt. There was "sticky" explosive for the possible attack on an Arg garrison at the top of Fanning Head. And there was plenty of concentrated processed food, water, and medical supplies. The transmitter, laptop computers, cameras, and radios were shared among the troops. Strangely, for the SAS, they would not bring a heavy machine gun, since their mission was supremely clandestine, and the object was not to get caught, rather than mow down the enemy.

Upon their efforts of observation, assessment, and transmission of facts, the success or failure of the entire British operation might depend. Every member of the submarine's crew knew the critical nature of the SAS operation, and every member of Captain Jarvis's team knew how high the stakes were.

At 1930, Captain Compton ordered the submarine to the surface, about one mile east of Race Point, tucked right behind the granite fortress of Fanning Head. They were still in a hundred feet of calm water, and the moonless night was already pitch-black. But this remained the most dangerous part of the operation.

Astute's deck crews were instantly into action, hauling the half-inflated Zodiacs out of the entrance at the base of the fin. A jury-rigged davit was raised above the companionway to haul up the four 250-horsepower outboard motors. The engineers were already out on the casing, ready to fit the engines onto the sterns of the two boats.

No SAS operation of this importance ever takes to enemy waters with only a single engine, just in case one of them cuts out. However, these particular engines had been given the best servicing any Royal Navy engine has ever had. Nothing was going to cut out.

Deck crews were loading the boats even as the electric pumps drove the final pressure pounds of air into the hull. A thick boarding net and two rope ladders were rolled down the submarine's starboard-side casing for Captain Jarvis and his men to embark.

They trooped out of the fin, carrying their bergans and weapons, which were loaded into the boats at the last minute before they were lowered gently into the water. Unrecognizable now, because of the camouflage cream that coated their faces, they waited in the cold still of the night until Captain Compton gave the order to embark the Zodiacs. And then they moved swiftly down into the boats, just as they had practiced so many times during their week's training at Faslane.

No one spoke during the deafening silence of the night exit, and the boats would run without lights, guided only by the big, softly lit Navy compass on the small dashboard around the wheel. The course was 185, almost due south, and the water would not be much deeper than ten feet all the way in, but the Zodiacs, at any speed, drew no more than eighteen inches.

The first two away were those of Captain Jarvis's group, heading in toward Fanning Head. The second two, which would leave four minutes later, were for the group that had to walk forty-five miles across the mountains to the airfield. Sergeant Jack Clifton, twenty-nine, who was about eight months off promotion to Staff Sergeant, would lead the mission. Tonight, he hoped to be ashore by 2030 and knock off the first fifteen miles before dawn.

The navy helmsman ran the Zodiac slowly toward shore at around five knots. The big Yamaha outboard, which would cheerfully have shoved her along at forty knots, was barely idling at this slow speed, and the noise was negligible. Essentially you needed to trip over the Zodiacs in order to locate them.

The journey took less than fifteen minutes, but gradually as they approached the shore they made a slight increase in speed, hauled up the engines on the automatic lift, and came scudding into the shallows and up the shingle beach.

The Navy seaman on the pointed bow thus jumped onto dry land, holding the thick painter and hauling against the very slight waves that lapped the stern of the boat. One by one the SAS men leapt ashore, with their big bergans now strapped onto their backs and holding their automatic rifles.

It was an awkward maneuver in the pitch dark, but they all hit the beach at a full run. And, more important, they all had dry feet for the two-week-long operation that lay before them.

The seaman holding the painter now shoved his full weight against the bow of the boat and, assisted by a rising tide, heaved the Zodiac until she floated. Then he clambered back onto the bow, his sea boots still dry on the inside, and cleared the small windshield to land back inboard.

"Good job, Charlie," said the helmsman, increasing the revs. "Now let's get the hell out of here."

Douglas Jarvis heard them go, just a faint engine beat on the wind, but then he was trained to hear engine beats on the wind. A normal person would never have noticed.

He counted his seven companions, made sure everyone was ashore and ready to go, then checked his compass and began to move west, leading his team over the rocky, already rising ground in the foothills of the eastern side of Fanning Head, which jutted skyward some two and a half miles away.

Captain Jarvis considered it possible that an Argentine battery was already in place on the top of the mountain, and that the area was being patrolled from a small base established on the peak. The guns of HMS **Antrim**, commanded by Brian Young in 1982, had made the new Argentine operation easier, since the shells of 1982 had blasted a hollow on the summit that formed a natural area of cover.

Douglas planned to climb five hundred feet up the east face tonight and establish a hide around a hundred yards from the top, mostly downward, on ground that was nearly impossible for the Argentinians to patrol.

From there they could observe all troop and artillery movements, and, far below, any patrolling warships. The trick was to not get caught, and when the British fleet arrived, Douglas Jarvis and his men would eliminate the entire Argentinian operation at the top of the mountain. When the island finally fell, as they were assured it must, the SAS team would wait to be airlifted off by helicopter back to one of the ships.

And so they half walked and half climbed up through the darkness that enveloped the silent mountain. And as they walked the terrain grew steeper, and even with their new night sight, established after thirty minutes in the pitch black, it was still difficult to see between the rocks, boulders, and crags that formed these lower reaches of the escarpment.

A huge cloud bank hung over the Falkland Islands. There was not a sliver of moon, and the stars were invisible. Also it was raining lightly, with a chill southerly wind. But they kept going, climbing steadily, until, just before 2230, they reached an unmistakable rock face, not quite sheer, but close.

Douglas, a former Team Leader with the Sandhurst Mountaineering Club, had once climbed Mont Blanc in the French Alps, and he knew about these matters. He worked his way along the rock face looking for a gully or an outcrop he could go for.

That took him about a half hour, and then he set off with his bodyguard, using crampons when necessary, hammering the little steel footholds into the rock as quietly as he could. It took him another forty minutes to reach a point some eighty feet above his team.

The bodyguard, carrying two hundred-foot climbing ropes, made them both fast to a jutting rock. One rope was for safety; each man would tie it around his waist and shoulders and would be hauled up by the Captain as he climbed.

The ropes dropped silently down the cliff face, and the operation took an hour, at the end of which Douglas Jarvis and his seven-man team were established on this thirty-five-yard-long, deep ledge, which at one point seemed to burrow back ten feet into the cliff.

The ledge faced the wind, which was bad, but it looked a lot easier to climb onward and upward, which was good. They would not need the ropes on the three-hundred-foot ascent to the summit. And Captain Jarvis whispered carefully that everyone should eat something, have some water, and rest until 0200, when four of them would continue up to the peak and check the place out.

By 0300 their guesswork was confirmed. There were four Argentine military tents inside the hollow, but, so far as Douglas could see, no one was awake. He and his men were facedown behind a clump of windswept bracken peering through night glasses. There were signs of a fire, but the place was quiet.

The SAS men strained their ears, listening for a sound, any sound, from a guard, a lookout, anyone. But there was nothing. The Argentine troops had decided, not unreasonably, their chances of being disturbed up here were zero. It had taken, after all, two helicopters to get up here in the first place, and it would take at least two more to airlift the guns, missile batteries, and radar installations into position later today.

There was, of course, no earthly point in Captain Jarvis and his men taking the place out at this stage. That would have caused an island-wide manhunt, which might have seen everyone shot or captured. And anyway, the men and missiles would immediately have been replaced, just as soon as the Argentinians had blasted to oblivion the SAS aerie on the cliff...probably with a couple of missiles from that frigate that patrolled the northern part of Falkland Sound.

No. Captain Jarvis and his boys had to sit tight and observe, and they already had critical information. The Argentine troops had established a position at the top of Fanning Head. And they would transmit that information one hour from now, direct to the **Ark Royal**, encrypted, from right here on their secret rain-swept ledge below the summit.

Meanwhile, Sergeant Clifton's team was walking, with extreme caution. They carefully tramped away from the shoreline and down the valley behind Port San Carlos. Two hours after they had disembarked the Zodiac, they reached the narrow river that rushed from its source on the 2,000-foot-high Mount Usborne and was still rushing when they arrived on its banks.

Jack Clifton's map showed a bridge a half mile downstream, and they crossed there, preferring the detour to getting soaked and frozen. They continued along the valley toward the distant peaks of Usborne and the Wickham Heights, the last of which they would have to cross, probably two days from now, in order to advance downward toward the Mount Pleasant Airfield. That way they could establish a hide from which they could see everything happening at this newest Argentinian air base.

For the same reasons that restricted Captain Jarvis, they were not allowed to blow it up. Which to any member of the Special Forces is tantamount to telling him breathing had just been forbidden.

Around the same time Sergeant Clifton and his troops crossed the river, Captain Hacking had concluded a long sweep around East Falkland and was feeling his way through thirty-five fathoms of rock-strewn inshore waters on the way in to Lafonia. There was a southern branch of the ninety-foot-deep channel that ran up to Choiseul

Sound, and this would drive **Ambush** to the surface, since no submarine CO likes to have less than ten feet below the keel.

The third group, who would prepare the landing beaches, had selected a tiny inlet on the east side of Lively Sound, named presumably for the crashing waves that thundered in from the South Atlantic in winter.

Well, it was not quite winter yet, and the sheltered waters of Seal Cove looked inviting to the men of the Special Boat Service. The submarine came to the surface south of the headland, and the two Zodiacs proceeded to make a two-mile run around the shoreline and dropped the men off on the north shore of the cove. This avoided the problem of crossing the river.

It was very dark on the beach, and raining, and there was a large amount of equipment to unload. In addition, three inflatable dinghies had been towed behind, and a pile of heavy wooden paddles. Lt. Perry, who led the group, had determined back in England they would almost certainly have to cross Choiseul Sound alone, since it would be madness to land on the "Argentinian side" in the dead of night, possibly running into an armed patrol.

"We need light rowing boats to cross that channel in the dark," he had said. "Because if we land blind, and run into a patrol, we may as well have not bothered."

Thus they arrived in Seal Cove in the dead of night, certain in their minds they were safe here, and that recces to the far shore two and a half miles away should be carried out in light rowing boats. Just so long as the weather remained merely awful instead of highly dangerous.

They hauled the dinghies up on to the beach and dragged their equipment with them. The boats were light but made heavier by their firm wooden decking. However, they had no engines, and four canvas handles. Teams of four each carried one boat across the hard rocky ground, searching for a sheltered spot for their hide, which must be established by dawn.

Twice during the first twenty minutes of their short journey they saw military aircraft coming in low over Lafonia heading northeast, which gave everyone a precise idea of the location of the airfield. Maps and charts are good. The real thing is always, somehow, better.

The land was flat here and there was little vegetation, but there were various outcrops of rocks at the landward end of the beach. One of these was not quite a cave, but there were four huge boulders that formed only a very narrow opening to the sky, eight feet above the ground.

It was not perfect because it was not big enough for the men and the boats, but it was a lot better than open ground. So they moved in with a couple of shovels, hauled out various scattered rocks and pebbles, unloaded waterproof ground sheets and sleeping bags, stacking the boats at the entrance with the third one turned upside down on top of the other two.

The dinghy's gray underside blended in with the boulders. At least in Lt. Perry's narrow-beam torchlight it did. And the young Team Leader decided they would risk lighting the Primus, brew some tea and soup, and conduct a patrol at 0100, to ensure their first ops area was deserted.

Their biggest problem was they had to operate in both directions, because they had to establish the first landing beach on the southern side of the five-mile-wide Lafonia Peninsula, somewhere in Low Bay, remote from Argentine defenses. And then establish a second beachhead across Choiseul Sound, much closer to the action, from where the British troops could launch their main attack on the airfield, Argentine garrison, and the harbor.

The launching point for this principal assault could not be the landing place for the amphibians, which had to arrive in secrecy, on an obscure stretch of coastline. But Lt. Perry and his men knew what was required, and they knew the dimensions of the various terrains they were looking for.

As Admiral Arnold Morgan had thoughtfully forecast in faraway Washington the previous week,

Britain's Special Forces were in. And not one member of the now-massive Argentinian invading force had the slightest idea they were there.

CHAPTER SEVEN

The three British Special Forces recce teams were not merely surprised by the level of Argentina's naval and military buildup on the Falkland Islands. They were uniquely stunned. None of them had ever seen anything quite like this.

Veterans of two wars, in the Persian Gulf and Iraq, they thought they'd seen it all. But this was incredible. Clinging to the cold, wet rock face of Fanning Head, Captain Jarvis's men had watched the Argentinians airlift not only multiple-launch missile systems but heavy 155mm howitzers.

All of them were ferried from the supply ships coming in at night to Mare Harbor, and then transported by helicopter across the mountains to the summit of the towering headland where Douglas Jarvis and his men lay hidden.

Any ships trying to make passage through the narrows into Falkland Sound were on a suicide mission once this lot was in place at the top of the cliff.

Sergeant Clifton and his boys arrived in the southern foothills of Wickham Heights shortly after midnight on Sunday night. They completed their forty-five-mile trek in a total of twenty-five walking hours. Below them, Mount Pleasant Airfield was well lit and extremely busy. All through the night they had both seen and heard military aircraft arriving and taking off.

Of course, no one knew yet what was actually incoming, nor indeed outgoing, but whatever it was, it was big. This was one of the busiest airports Jack Clifton had ever seen, and through the night glasses he could make out several parked military helicopters and a line of fighter aircraft, as well as several Army and Air Force trucks parked near the terminals. There seemed to be people everywhere.

Down on the south shore of Choiseul Sound, Jim Perry's team had crossed the channel for the second time, rowing the little boats hard across the tide, hardly daring to take a rest in case they were swept off course.

It was a tough pull, but they had discovered a lonely, uninhabited little island right on their route, and it made a useful stopping point just after the first mile, a place to get their breath back after pulling hard for twenty minutes.

The final stretch lasted for around a half hour; they could of course have made it in one shot, but everyone agreed the stop-off, for just ten minutes, made an enormous difference. In fact, Jim Perry calculated it probably made no difference in terms of time spent rowing. The first half mile after the break was always the fastest.

On the far shore they had a carefully selected landing point, a thousand-yard spit of rock and sand jutting out to the east, about four miles west of Mare Harbor, and 150 yards from the actual mainland. They made this their forward base, mostly because it seemed to have plant life, some high bracken and a few scattered gorse bushes. A cluster of thick tussock grass grew over some hefty boulders, and inside the thicket there was a place to hide the boats.

Lt. Perry had personally hacked out a pathway into this unlikely undergrowth, and last night, Saturday, they had left four men out there with sleeping bags and ground sheets, to continue through the day monitoring Argentinian aircraft, both coming into and leaving Mount Pleasant Airfield. They had taken it in turns, two on duty, two off. And there was hardly a moment for twenty-four hours when they were not writing and recording. The verdict of trooper Fred Morton: **the Args must have more fighter aircraft than the fucking Luftwaffe in 1941.**

As an assessment, that was a tad wild. But it revealed one thing of critical importance. The Argentinians really did have a formidable air attack capability, and they were most definitely planning to launch opening strikes against the Royal Navy from this stronghold on East Falkland.

Worse yet, at first light Lt. Perry's spotters had made positive identification of three incoming Argentinian Skyhawk A4s, which can deliver thousand-pound bombs at very high speed. Once launched, nothing could stop the bombs, but everyone in the Navy and Royal Marines knew the now discontinued Harrier FA2 **could** have stopped the Skyhawks before they had a chance to launch their bombs.

The SBS men were Marines, and in the back of their minds, every one of them knew they had somehow been let down by their government. Lt. Perry knew precisely why, but he never, of course, discussed it. Not in a theater of war. Especially when they were so isolated from the main force.

0400, MONDAY, APRIL 11, 51.45S 56.40W SPEED 15, DEPTH 300, COURSE 180

Viper K-157 was still in more than two hundred fathoms when she arrived on station fifty miles off the northern coast of East Falkland, her mighty nuclear-powered turbines still running sweetly after her 11,000-mile voyage from the frozen north.

Captain Vanislav's orders, delivered from Admiral Rankov in person, were to patrol the waters east of the islands awaiting the arrival of the Royal Navy Task Force. He was then to track the carrier from a distance, and with the utmost stealth, stay in satellite communication with the Rio Grande air base, and sink the **Ark Royal** with torpedoes one hour after the Argentine air assault was launched.

This of course would all have been much more difficult had the Task Force already arrived on station, but Captain Vanislav had given himself all the advantages of being in place first, in position, quietly awaiting the arrival of the enemy, transmitting nothing, moving slowly, betraying no sound, no radar paints in the dark underwater caverns of the South Atlantic.

The Royal Navy Fleet would be on high alert and extremely sensitive, not to mention trigger-happy. The slightest mistake from the crew of **Viper** would probably cause the roof to fall in, and not just metaphorically. The Royal Navy antisubmarine capability was legendary.

But now, in the small hours of this Monday morning, the Russian nuclear boat was in place, precisely where she wanted to be—in an area through which the British Task Force must pass if they were to fight this war.

Admiral Rankov had been specific... **The British will not go west of the islands because that brings them within a much closer range of the Argentine air attack. They will stay east, as Admiral Woodward did last time. Position yourself in those eastern waters, stay quiet, and the Royal Navy will come to you. At the**

correct time, in the pandemonium of the air-sea battle, you will sink the Ark Royal. **Then come home.**

Captain Vanislav knew what to do. What he did not know, however, was the precise position of Captain Simon Compton's **Astute,** now patrolling some fifteen miles out to the west. He assumed at least one Royal Navy SSN was quietly patrolling these waters somewhere. And he guessed correctly it would be moving very slowly, virtually silent.

Astute's towed array was operational and she was listening for engine lines from an Argentinian submarine, as she had been for the past two days, and would continue to do until the Task Force arrived. Captain Hacking had **Ambush** doing precisely the same thing.

But there were no Argentinian warships anywhere outside the close-in coastal waters around the Falklands, and out here, where the seas were mostly deserted, there was no trace of any intruder.

At 0438, however, a decision was made in **Viper** that in retrospect might be judged as careless. Almost everyone on board knew there was still a slight noise in the indicator buoy stowage area, suggesting something was still loose, and had been all the way from the North Atlantic, where the buoy had broken loose.

Captain Vanislav, in the middle of this dark, overcast night, elected to surface and have it fixed or removed. And **Viper K-157** blew her ballast and came sliding up out of the deep. It looked smooth, it was smooth, but in the underwater caverns of the South Atlantic, the sound of the high-pressure air expelling the ballast was loud, extremely loud to a patrolling Royal Navy SSN.

In HMS **Astute**, there was a glimmer of activity in the sonar room. Chief Petty Officer Roddy Matthews suddenly thought he may have heard a slight rise in the background noise..."Only a small increase in the level," he murmured. "Wait...it might have been rain, swishing on the surface. But I thought I heard something...give me a few minutes."

The sonar operators froze. No one spoke, hearts momentarily paused. And three minutes later, at 0441, Chief Matthews spoke again..."I have a definite rise in the level...**Christ! It sounds like a submarine blowing ballast...**"

At 0451 a lightning bolt went through the sonar room...there was now a note of urgency in Chief Matthews's voice...**Captain—sonar...I have definite sounds of a submarine surfacing...several miles away.**

Sonar—captain...I'll be right there.

The CO literally ran into the room to be told immediately, "It's not very close, sir. But no one could miss it. That was a submarine surfacing."

Three minutes later the trail went cold, and the sounds of the Russian submarine slipped away. It was the last time she would be detected in these waters, because in the next couple of hours Captain Vanislav would slow down to five or six knots, as instructed by Admiral Rankov. And then she would be as silent as **Astute** and **Ambush**. Or very nearly so.

Captain Compton put a satellite signal on the net to the advancing Royal Navy fleet, directed to the Admiral's ops room in the **Ark Royal**. It read: **110458APR11: SSN** Astute **picked up unidentified submarine surfacing app. 51.50S 56.40W 0451 today. Estimate forty-five miles offshore. Request orders should possible Russian prowler stray again into Falklands battle zone. Compton, CO** Astute.

Admiral Holbrook relayed it on to the UK, Fleet Headquarters, Northwood. Admiral Palmer was in the situation room in conference with the First Sea Lord, Admiral Sir Rodney Jeffries, and the two men both gazed somewhat quizzically at the signal from the depths of the South Atlantic.

"Possible Russian SSN? Christ, what's that about?" Admiral Palmer looked extremely disconcerted.

"Well, before we give it serious thought, I think we should alert the Americans. They may know more than we do about a Russian prowler, and they may have an immediate answer."

Sir Rodney nodded and handed the signal to a young Lieutenant and requested it go immediately to U.S. Naval Intelligence, Washington. Five minutes later it was circulated to Fort Meade, and four minutes after that, at 0430, the NSA duty officer called Lt. Commander Ramshawe at home.

Jimmy was just out of the shower, intending to leave almost immediately for the office. With the Royal Navy about forty-eight hours from a head-on armed confrontation with the armed forces of Argentina, he and Admiral Morris were regularly meeting in the Director's office shortly after 0530.

He listened carefully to the signal that had come from Royal Navy HQ, Northwood, and snapped, "Get it on my desk and on Admiral Morris's desk right now. We'll both be there inside an hour."

In fact he was there inside forty-five minutes, and having read it carefully could think only one thought...**I have to tell the Big Man. He'll probably have a fit if I wake him at 0530, but not as big as the one he'll have if I don't.**

"This better be fucking critical," growled Arnold Morgan down the telephone, not caring one way or another who was on the end of the line.

"It is, Arnie," said Jimmy, all business. "That possible Russian submarine, the one we almost concluded was an Akula-class boat, **Gepard, Cougar,** or **Viper,** just showed up in the middle of the battle zone, forty-five miles off the eastern side of East Falkland. Royal Navy SSN picked it up on sonar, surfacing, couple of hours ago."

"Tell me you're kidding."

"Nossir."

"Is George in yet?"

"No, but he'll be here in ten."

"I'm coming over right now." Bang. Down phone.

For some obscure reason, the Admiral's flat refusal to utter the word **good-bye**, or even **thanks for calling**, always took Jimmy by surprise.

He was not, however, as deeply startled as Mrs. Kathy Morgan, who very nearly fell out of bed when her husband actually bellowed at the top of his lungs, one hour before the sun rose over the Potomac, **"Ch-a-a-a-a-rlie!!! Quarter deck ten minutes with the car!"**

"God Almighty," she said. "Did you have to yell like that?"

"Oh, don't worry," replied the Admiral. "Charlie's used to it...gotta go."

Downstairs, Charlie did indeed hear the Admiral's bellow. The people who lived three houses away probably heard the Admiral's bellow.

Fully dressed, in readiness for just such a call, the chauffeur rushed outside, pulled the car up to the door, engine running, and was waiting patiently when the Admiral came piling out into the dawn, nine minutes later, dressed immaculately in a dark gray suit, white shirt, Annapolis tie, and highly polished shoes. Since his days as a midshipman, he always shaved right before he went to bed, just in case there was an emergency. As this most definitely was.

Forty minutes later, he was in Fort Meade, being escorted up to the Director's office on the eighth floor. When he arrived, Jimmy and Admiral Morris were standing in front of the illuminated computer screen on the wall, staring down the 56.40W line of longitude.

"George...Jimmy," said Arnold, nodding curtly, heading straight for the big chair he once occupied, and shooting a laser glance at the coffeepot. "Two bullets, Lieutenant Commander, one calculator, and your full attention." To Admiral Morris, "You got him under control, George?"

"Absolutely."

"Excellent. Date of the Akula detection off the coast of Ireland?"

"March twenty-third, sir."

"Time?"

"Sixteen ten, sir."

"Latitude?"

"Fifty-one thirty north, sir."

"Date and time of detection in the South Atlantic?"

"Today, sir. April eleventh, 0500."

"Latitude?"

"Fifty-one fifty south, sir."

Arnold hit the calculator buttons. "Over six thousand miles running south," he muttered. "You got an accurate mileage, Jimmy—taking in the distance west?"

"Yessir. Seven thousand two hundred and eighty-two point nine five."

"Vague, Ramshawe, vague. Try to be more precise, would you?"

"Yessir." Lt. Commander Ramshawe was well up to this game.

"Nineteen days, eh?" said Admiral Morgan, again hitting the buttons. "He must have been making an average of fifteen, sixteen knots all the way."

"Sixteen point four, sir. It was only eighteen and a half days."

"Shut up, James."

"Yessir."

Arnold chuckled and sipped his coffee. "I guess it's gotta be the same boat. And it's gotta be Russian since nothing else could possibly have been anywhere near. And there's no point trying to call the Russians. Rankov would never return this call. He'd guess right away the Brits had picked up his fucking submarine."

"And anyway, we may not want to alert them we know something's going on," replied Admiral Morris.

"No. I suppose not. Unless we want to try and frighten them off. I could get the President to make the call, and feign absolute fury, demanding the Akula be removed instantly from the Falklands battle zone."

"Yes. We could try that. But you know, Arnie, I'm not sure it would work. The Russian President would just say he had no knowledge of any submarine in the South Atlantic, and then Rankov would tell everyone to be even more careful. We may never see the damn thing again."

"But what if the damn thing took out the Royal Navy carrier?"

"If that's his plan, there's not a whole lot we can do about it. Short of going down there and hunting it down."

"We don't have time," replied Arnold Morgan. "The Task Force arrives on Wednesday, and the Brits cannot afford to waste their own time. That's a very weak fleet they have down there, and they've no replacements. If I were Holbrook I'd start firing as soon as I was in range before it all starts falling apart."

"It's kinda frustrating, isn't it?" said Admiral Morris. "We ought to have been able to stop this, but we can't. We ought to be able to defend American oil interests, but somehow we can't. And we ought to be able to sink this Russian intruder, but we can't. It's been that way right from the start."

"Nonetheless," said Admiral Morgan, somewhat grandly, "I think in the end, like the Russians, we're gonna be in this thing up to our fucking jockstraps."

0320, WEDNESDAY, APRIL 13
100 MILES WEST OF EAST FALKLAND

HMS **Ark Royal** steamed into the old Falkland Islands Total Exclusion Zone, which had served Admiral Woodward so wretchedly in 1982, with its absurd **don't shoot 'til they shoot** doctrine.

Today, however, there was no Total Exclusion Zone. The Royal Navy had informed the Prime Minister and his politicians they had so many disadvantages, they would shoot at anyone they damn pleased whenever they damn pleased, so get used to it.

By this time, the Prime Minister was so nerve-wracked about his own career, he would have agreed to anything put forward by the men who were going to try to rescue his government.

Mercifully, a thick blanket of fog covered the ocean, which at least provided some cover from air attack, but it also rendered all flying impossible. The GR9s, remember, can't see.

Admiral Holbrook and his staff knew there may be a Russian submarine in the area, and everyone was also worried about minor repairs that had to be carried out on at least three of the escorts before battle commenced. And with this in mind, they made course south, across the old TEZ straight for the Burdwood Bank.

This is a large area of fairly shallow water on the edge of the South American continental shelf. It's two hundred miles long, east to west, by about sixty miles wide, north to south. It sits one hundred miles south of East Falkland.

On its southern side the bank slopes steeply down into waters two miles deep. To the north, around the islands, it's only around 300 to 400 feet deep. But on the bank itself the seabed is only 150 feet from the surface, and no submarine can run across it at speed without leaving a considerable wake on the surface.

Deep in the fog of the Burdwood Bank, Admiral Holbrook's Task Force would conduct their repairs, refuel, and make ready for battle. Both the Royal Navy submarines were headed inshore to patrol the coast and, if possible, sink any Argentine warships, since none of them had yet been seen by the Task Force.

When the fog lifted, the Royal Navy would turn to the north, and come out fighting. In the broadest terms, they would immediately launch missiles at any Argentine warship that came within range. They would get the GR9s away in an attempt to slam the airfield and the harbor, and pray to God they could hit the incoming Argentine air attack. And hit it early.

In the dark hours before that, the **Ocean, Albion**, and **Largs Bay,** which carried 2,700 troops, helicopters, light trucks, and ammunition, would already have headed north for the rough, craggy southeastern shores of East Falkland. There they would begin the amphibious assault, the drastically difficult task of landing a 10,000-strong army on the quiet, deserted beaches of Lafonia, as selected by Jim Perry and his team.

But for two days and two nights the fog bank never moved; the winds were light, and sometimes it rained, but visibility was constantly poor. The CO of **Viper** had picked up distant sonar traces of warships in the area, and ascertained he himself may just have been detected.

Nothing was definite, either way, but Captain Vanislav stayed in deep water, very slow and very quiet, waiting for the satellite signal that would tell him the time and day of Argentina's aerial onslaught from Rio Grande and Mount Pleasant.

When the Royal Navy ships moved, he was confident he would pick them up. Right now in the fog he could only wait twenty miles north of the Burdwood Bank, where he suspected they were. But he was not about to venture into those shallow waters, where he would most certainly be detected.

Back in Washington there was no feedback whatsoever from Buenos Aires. President Bedford had carried out his threat and closed down the

Argentine consulates all over the country. London also had no communique from Argentina, even after the Ambassador and all the diplomats had been expelled.

At 1530 on Friday afternoon, April 15, with the repairs completed, the wind got up, and so did the sea. But the skies became clear, and the sun fought its way through the dank and rainy clouds of the South Atlantic.

Admiral Holbrook, by now regretting the loss of the fog cover, placed the **Ocean**, **Albion**, and **Largs Bay** on immediate notice to begin their journey into the landing beaches on the coast of Lafonia. The two Type-45s, plus HMS **Gloucester**, were ordered to prepare to move forward at midnight to form the Task Force's first picket line to the west of the fleet. This is the first line of defense, well up-threat from the main force, and one of the loneliest places in all the ocean.

A clear and moonlit night followed the temporary departure of the fog, and at 1950 the assault force steamed away from the warships that would ultimately fight the battle. Captain John Farmer, on the bridge of the **Ocean**, had the **Albion** and the **Largs Bay** line astern as they moved north through the dark, making twenty knots in a long rising sea, a cold southwesterly gusting in off their port quarter.

The guided-missile frigate **Richmond**, under the command of Captain David Neave, accompanied them, acting as goalkeeper out to the left, just in case they were spotted at first light and needed missile cover against incoming Argentinian Super-Etendards.

The voyage itself was uneventful. The ships traveled with very few lights, and within four hours were within reach of the landing beaches, where Lt. Jim Perry and his men awaited them. The **Ocean**'s comms room had been in contact for the previous half hour and details of the landing area were now with the amphibious commanders.

By midnight the three ships were in position to unload their cargoes, while Captain Neave stood guard, facing westward in the ops room of the **Richmond**. The frigate, its missile radar on high alert, was steaming at only three knots in approximately six fathoms of water, in the middle of Low Bay, which is fourteen miles wide at its seaward end.

At five minutes past midnight, the huge stern doors of the **Largs Bay** were lowered and the first of the landing craft, packed with Marines, began to float out. And one by one they made their way to the bay on the south shore of the desolate Lafonia Peninsula, where Jim Perry's SBS men were waiting to signal them in through the shallows.

Back on the Burdwood Bank, at precisely this time, the picket ships were lining up to leave on their four-hour journey to their lonely outpost. And none of their commanding officers were especially looking forward to the experience. They were, they knew, the chosen few, because in the Royal Navy, you're not really grown-up until you have commanded a picket ship, out there on your own, not really covered by the weapons system of the rest of the force.

In fact, with a Battle Group stretched as tightly as this one, you were principally covered by your fellow picket ships.

By definition, the picket ship operates in solitary waters, and it's always quiet, and it seems peaceful. But no one really enjoys it because, historically, the picket ships are the very first to get sunk by the enemy. The simple truth is, they are deliberately placed in harm's way, a strategy of which the opposition is well aware.

For the attacking force, the idea is to take one of the pickets out, thus punching a gaping hole in the defenses through which to drive a main attack.

Both British Type-45 commanding officers knew this perfectly well. And it was an extremely thoughtful Captain Rowdy Yates who had HMS **Daring** under way first on that moonlit night, in the somber hours that would almost certainly herald the dawn of the second Battle for the Falkland Islands.

He would continue to position his ship way out to the right, more than twenty miles up-threat from the aircraft carrier. HMS **Gloucester**, commanded by Captain Colin Day, would occupy waters a similar distance but far out to the left. Commander Norman Hall's **Dauntless** would occupy the center.

They made their way off the bank line astern, all three commanding officers on the bridge, staying busy, trying to fight to the back of their minds any fears inspired by the brutal reality of this particular Friday night. In all three of the ships, the long-range air-warning radars were already on high alert.

Three decks below in the ops room, everyone was already at battle stations, dressed in full antiflash gear, the yellowish cotton head masks and gloves designed to prevent skin from instant burning from the sudden flash-fire explosion caused by an incoming bomb, shell, or missile.

In grim contrast to the bright starlit night outside on the water, the ops room was a sinister place, a half-lit scene from a sci-fi movie, the amber lights from the computer consoles casting an eerie glow, the quiet watch keepers making terse comments into pencil-slim microphones, the keyboards chattering in the background.

The Principal Warfare Officers, so highly trained, so utterly certain of their tasks, were always standing, moving, quietly watching everything and everyone. The supervisors were walking softly behind the young operators, checking, double-checking, ready with a word of encouragement.

And every time the ship hit a wave, with that dull, majestic thump it always makes on the hull of a warship, many, many hearts beat just that fraction faster.

No sooner had the three destroyers cleared the Burdwood Bank than Admiral Holbrook's second line of defense was also under way. Two newer Type-42 destroyers, the Batch Threes, **York** and **Edinburgh**, had arrived in the middle of the foggy night on Thursday. And now they would continue their long-held defensive formation in the center of the second line, flanked by the frigates from the Fourth Duke-class squadron, **Kent**, **Grafton**, **St. Albans**, and **Iron Duke**, some five miles up-threat from the **Ark Royal**.

Between the carrier and the frigates, Admiral Holbrook placed three ships from the Royal Fleet Auxiliary, principally to add confusion to the enemy radar. The **Ark Royal** would be positioned astern of these, accompanied by her goalkeeper, **Westminster**, the no-nonsense missile frigate commanded by the austere and able Commander Tom Betts.

By some miracle, the Navy had completed the work on both the **Lancaster** and **Marlborough** in Portsmouth, and both of them arrived in one piece on Friday afternoon. They would operate around the coast to the north, specifically trying to get rid of any Argentine warships in the area and launch naval missile and shell attacks on any new Argentinian positions at that end of the island.

The most impressive arrival of all, however, was that of P and O's huge ocean cruise liner the **Adelaide**, which had been ordered to abandon her next journey to the Caribbean and get to Portsmouth for instant conversion into a troop carrier. She had arrived on Thursday, from out of the eastern Atlantic, bearing 7,000 troops, her decks shored up to stand the enormous weight of men, equipment, and ordnance. Her galleys were now filled with rather more basic fare than the rich **gourmet de luxe** to which her cooks and steward were accustomed.

As colossally useful as she was, the **Adelaide** was a bit of a problem. She had totally inadequate damage-control and firefighting arrangements, and she was essentially, just as her sister ship the **Canberra** had been in 1982, in the words of Admiral Woodward, "a bloody great bonfire awaiting a light."

Admiral Holbrook intended to unload her massive cargo of men and materiel, hopefully into other ships, as soon as it was humanly possible to undertake such a formidable cross-decking operation.

Meanwhile, the warships were on their way to the Admiral's designated position four hundred miles east of Burdwood, well out of Argentinian air range. The **Ark Royal** brought up the rear with her goalkeeper, **Westminster**. Both ships were largely dependent on the accuracy of the new improved Seawolf missile system carried by the frigate. Commander Betts described it as "amply competent to knock any Argentine fighter-bomber clean out of the sky, just so long as the chaps are paying proper attention." That was Betts. No nonsense.

0300, SATURDAY, APRIL 16
RIO GRAND AIR BASE
TIERRA DEL FUEGO

Argentina's Aviation Force Two, the Second Naval Air Wing, in concert with the Second Naval Attack Squadron, had virtually evacuated from Bahia Blanca, the sprawling air station that sits at the head of a deep bay 350 miles southwest of Buenos Aires, sharing its geographic prominence with Puerto Belgrano, the largest naval base in the country.

These two bastions of Argentina's air and sea power are situated exactly where the South American coastline swings inward, and begins to narrow down, running south-southwest, 1,200 miles all the way to the great hook of its granite southerly point of Cape Horn.

The fighter aircraft from Bahia Blanca had been flown a thousand miles south to Rio Grande, the mainland base from which Argentina would conduct its defense of its newest territory, Islas Malvinas, which lay 440 miles to the east.

Admiral Oscar Moreno, Commander in Chief of Argentina's naval fleet, a devoted, lifelong **Malvinista**, had been instrumental in planning the entire naval attack strategy. And now he had his substantial squadron of fourteen Super-Etendards, with their Exocet missiles, in position on the huge airfield.

It was curious, but in the last conflict against the British, the success of this missile had taken some people by surprise. Today Admiral Moreno was not quite so sure. He knew the Royal Navy had spent years perfecting an antimissile shield against the Exocet.

And he was well aware the British ships carried an excellent chaff system and top-class decoys, all designed to seduce an incoming missile through a large cloud of iron filings, which the stupid missile recognized as bigger than the warship and therefore representing a more desirable target.

But the Argentine Navy had a very large Exocet inventory and they were obliged to use them, unless it became obvious they were a total waste of time against Admiral Holbrook's ships.

Nonetheless, Oscar Moreno considered if you hurled enough Exocets at the Royal Navy, some may get through, and when one did, the damage would be colossal, as it had been in 1982.

With this in mind, he had flown four Super-Es into Mount Pleasant Airfield, hoping that an assault that began on land would initially confuse the British warships' radars, as they scanned the horizon and ran into the customary difficulties all search radars encounter while looking across the water to a coastline.

Admiral Moreno understood these matters. And he understood he was facing the possible failure of his Exocet attack. Which was principally why he had removed the entire Third Naval Air Wing down the coast from their east coast base of Trelew, a distance of 650 miles, to the new operations center at Rio Grande.

With them the Third Wing brought their entire squadron of twelve Dagger fighter aircraft, an Israeli-built, cheap and cheerful, no-radar copy of the magnificent French Mirage jet. With a few minor adjustments, the Dagger was capable of carrying two thousand-pound iron bombs, slung underneath in place of the 1,300-liter centerline fuel tank.

To compensate for this shorter range, Admiral Moreno had stationed six of them on the airfield at Mount Pleasant. At H-hour he would send them in, flying low-level, against the British ships, which were, he knew, totally vulnerable to bomb attack. This time there were no high-altitude Harrier Combat Air Patrols, with their medium-range radars, always ready to hit and down the Daggers. The most the ships' missiles could achieve would be to slam the aircraft **after** the bombs were away. And even that was pretty tenuous.

The remaining six would take off from Rio Grande, rendezvous with one of the Hercules tankers and refuel in midair, before pressing on with their bomb attacks on the British ships.

The Argentine Air Force was also working closely with Admiral Moreno, who, as the most fanatical of all the military **Malvinistas**, was rapidly acquiring Homeric stature in Buenos Aires.

At his request, the Air Force removed its Fifth Air Brigade, based at Villa Reynolds, down to Rio Grande. This included its formidable force of fighter-bombers—two squadrons of Lockheed Skyhawk A4Ms and one squadron of A4Ps, a total of more than thirty-six aircraft.

The bigger Sixth Air Brigade had left its inland home HQ southwest of Buenos Aires at Tandil air base, and moved south to Rio Gallegos, which lies to the north of Rio Grande on the coast, a 496-mile flight from the Malvinas. The Sixth Attack Group flew seven Mirage Interceptors, thirteen Mirage 111 E fighter/attack aircraft, and a squadron of twenty Daggers, all bombers. The Mirage jets would mostly be used for high-escort cover for the Israeli-built antishipping specialists—the

Daggers, the ones with the thousand-pound iron bombs.

Admiral Moreno requested ten Skyhawks from the Fifth Brigade and six Daggers from the Sixth, to fly to Mount Pleasant in readiness for the attack at first light on the opening morning of the battle. For many weeks, of course, he had no idea when this would be.

But he did know on the previous afternoon, the fog around the islands and on the Burdwood Bank had cleared, and the Royal Navy ships were on the move, in the dark. He also guessed they would come out fighting at dawn. His task was to hit them first, hit them hard, hopefully with the ships silhouetted against the eastern horizon.

A few hours earlier, at midnight, he had been driven to the Roman Catholic church on Avenue San Martin, in the nearby town of Rio Grande. There, on his knees, he had prayed devoutly for the success of Captain Gregor Vanislav's torpedo attack on the **Ark Royal...that we may restore once more these ancient Argentinian territories of the Islas Malvinas to Thy Holy Will**.

Presumably Admiral Moreno considered Great Britain's grand brick-and-stone edifice of Christ Church Cathedral on Ross Road, Port Stanley, complete with its superb stained-glass windows, made no contribution whatsoever toward His Holy Will.

However, Moreno was now back from his prayer interlude, working as ever on the split-second timing required for his dawn assault on the Royal Navy. As he worked, massive refueling operations were going on, both at Rio Gallegos, on the airfield beyond his office in Rio Grande, and on Mount Pleasant Airfield itself.

The KC-130 Hercules refueling tankers were ready to take off from both the southern air bases and would rendezvous with the fighter-bombers 150 miles offshore. Both the Daggers and the Mirage fighters had new flight refueling receiving gear that they did not enjoy in 1982. That was the one shining fact to comfort Admiral Moreno: the extended range of his aircraft. There were no longer the endless concerns of the pilots running out of fuel before they made it home from the Malvinas.

By 0500 Admiral Moreno's Navy and Air Force command HQ in Rio Grande had received an encrypted satellite signal from Moscow that the Royal Navy Task force was currently positioned 140 miles east of Port Stanley.

The signal made no mention of the landing operation taking place on the south coast of the Lafonia Peninsula, and contained no details of the deployment of the British fleet. That would all have to wait until dawn finally broke over the South Atlantic.

There was, however, one commanding officer operating on the Argentinian side of the equation who did know the whereabouts of HMS **Ark Royal.** Captain Gregor Vanislav's sonar room had picked up the sounds of the British warships on the move as they came off the shallow waters of the Burdwood Bank, and by the small hours of that Saturday morning had closed in.

Viper K-157 now ran slowly, ten miles to the southeast of Admiral Holbrook's Battle Group. The submarine was transmitting nothing active three hundred feet below the surface. Vanislav was just tracking the warships, listening to the pings of the sonar, waiting for the dawn, when they could come to periscope depth for a seven-second visual sighting.

At 0515, shortly before the first light began to illuminate the horizon, Admiral Moreno ordered the four Super-Etendards on the runway at Rio Grande to take off on their 440-mile race to the Malvinas. They would rendezvous with the tanker, refuel, and come hurtling over East Falkland heading east at six hundred knots, flying below the radar of the British ships.

At 0614 they came streaking over Weddell Island, crossed Queen Charlotte Bay, and the narrowest part of West Falkland, before flying low over the Sound and straight across Lafonia. All four Argentinian pilots saw the three Royal Navy ships still anchored in Low Bay, and their own Air

Force radar at Mount Pleasant Airfield picked the Etendards up as they flew over.

Making eleven miles every minute, the French-built guided-missile jets, flying in two pairs eight miles apart, rocketed out over the Atlantic, flying very low now, only fifty feet above the water, gaining the protection of the curvature of the earth from the line-of-sight sweep of the forward radars of the three British picket ships.

They held their speed and course for the next nine minutes, at which time the second pair swung farther left. The first two prepared to pop up to take a radar fix on whatever lay up ahead. None of the four Etendard pilots dared to turn on a radio, and the concentration required to stay that low without flying into the ocean was so intense they were each virtually alone.

And now, forty miles out from Admiral Holbrook's picket ships, they climbed to 120 feet, leveled out, and hit the radar scans. Immediately both pilots saw two blips on the screens, and simultaneously they both reached down to the Exocet activate button.

Deep in the heart of Captain Rowdy Yates's **Daring**, the ops room was on high alert. Everyone was wearing their antiflash masks, the Air Warfare Officers were murmuring into their headsets, the supervisors were pacing, all eyes were glued to the screens. They all knew dawn was breaking. They all knew an attack might be imminent.

It was 0632 when Able Seaman Price called the words that sent chills through the hearts of every experienced officer and Petty Officer in either ops room...young Price blew his whistle short and hard and snapped: **"Agave radar!"**

Daring's AWO, Lt. Commander Harley, shot across the room and demanded, **"Confidence level?"**

"Certain," snapped Price. "I have three sweeps, followed by a short lock-on—bearing two-eight-four. Search mode."

Captain Yates and Harley swung around to stare at the big UAA 1 console, and they could both see the bearing line on Price's screen correlated precisely with two Long-Range Early-Warning radar contacts forty miles out.

"Transmission ceased," reported Price.

Harley called into the Command Open Line, **"AWO to Officer of the Watch...go to action stations...!!"**

And he switched to the UHF radio, announcing to all ships, **"Flash!** This is **Daring**...Agave bearing two-eight-four...correlates..."

And Price called again, **"Agave regained!!**...bearing two-eight-four."

The ship's radar officers confirmed the contacts, range now only thirty miles.

"That's two Super-Es just popped up," called Captain Yates crisply.

"**Chaff!!**" roared Harley. And across the room the hooded figure of a Chief Petty Officer slammed his closed fists into the big chaff fire buttons.

Harley again broadcast on the circuit to the whole Battle Group..."**This is** Daring...**Agave radar bearing two-eight-four**..." But the picket ships were all up to speed, Commander Hall's ops room in **Dauntless** was instantly on the case, and Captain Day was only fifteen seconds behind as HMS **Gloucester** prepared to tackle the second pair of Etendards heading to their right, straight toward him.

For the next five minutes **Daring** had to place herself carefully between the four clouds of chaff that were blooming around her, taking account of the wind and the natural drift of the giant clouds of iron filings, which Harley hoped to Christ were confusing the life out of the radar in the nose cones of the incoming missiles.

Captain Yates called to the Officer of the Watch on the bridge, "Come hard left to zero-eight-four...adjust speed for zero relative wind."

At 0638, the Argentine pilots unleashed their missiles and banked right, not knowing for certain at what they had fired. Their Exocets fell away, locked on to their targets, and the two Etendards headed for home, flying once more low over the water, but this time heading west.

And in the ops room of **Daring**, the familiar cry of a modern warship under attack was heard…**"Zippo One! Bruisers!** Incoming. Bearing two-eight-four. Range fourteen miles." But the two amber dots flickering across **Daring**'s screen were so small they could scarcely be seen.

"Take them with Sea Dart," snapped Captain Yates, knowing his fire-control radar would have trouble locking on to the tiny sea-skimming targets at this range, but hoping against hope the missile gun director could get the weapons away.

Eventually he did, but only one of them struck home, blasting the Exocet out of the sky. The second one was completely baffled by the chaff and swerved high and left, crashing harmlessly into the sea six miles astern.

Commander Hall's **Dauntless** never did get her Sea Dart missiles into action, but the chaff did its work and both missiles aimed at the destroyer passed down the port side.

Captain Day's **Gloucester**, out to the left of the **Ark Royal**, found herself facing four incoming Exocets, and her Sea Dart missiles, given more choice, slammed two of them into oblivion. Again the priceless chaff did its work and the remaining two Exocets swerved right into a huge cloud of iron filings and careened into the ocean with a mighty blast, two miles away, off the destroyer's starboard quarter, prompting a roar of delight from the seamen working on the upper decks. Argentina 0, Royal Navy 8.

But not for long. Two formations of four Skyhawks and four Daggers were on their way off the runway at Mount Pleasant. The British frigates, armed with only Harpoons as a medium-range missile, were still seventy miles too far east to attack the airport, and the GR9s were only just ready to fly off the carrier, thanks to an early morning fog bank.

The returning Etendard pilots, flying slower now, had already been in contact with Mount Pleasant and had passed on the range and positions of the three British ships they assumed they had located. They also alerted the base to the possible location of three, possibly four, other large Royal Navy ships anchored in Low Bay.

And meanwhile the Daggers and the Skyhawks continued their fast, low journey, flying fifty feet above the waves, well below the radar, straight at the Royal Navy picket ships, the Type-45 destroyers, **Daring**, **Dauntless**, and the older **Gloucester**.

They lifted above the horizon and into range of the ships' missile systems at a distance of around ten miles. But the visibility was poor, and within sixty seconds they would have overflown the entire picket line.

All eight of the Argentine aircraft had their bombs away before the Sea Darts could lock on. Desperately the three commanding officers ordered their missiles away, and with mounting horror the observers on the upper decks saw the big thousand-pounders streaking in, low over the ocean.

That's the way a modern iron bomb arrives. It travels too fast to drop. It comes scything in at a low trajectory, its retardation chute out behind it, slowing it down. The bombs are primed to blast on impact.

All Royal Navy Commanders know the best defense is to swing the ship around, presenting not its sharp bow to the incoming attack but its beam. That way there's a fighting chance the damn thing may fly straight over the top, as such bombs frequently do.

But there is so often no time. And there was no time right now on Admiral Holbrook's picket line. As the Skyhawks and the Daggers screamed away, making their tightest turns back to the west, eight miles from the destroyers, the lethal Sea Dart missiles came whipping in. The first one from **Daring** slammed into a Dagger and blew it to smithereens. The second smashed the wing off a fleeing Skyhawk and sent it cartwheeling into the ocean at five hundred knots.

Three more missed completely, but Colin Day's first salvo downed another Dagger and blew a Skyhawk into two quite separate pieces. This was the very most they could do. They had no other defense, because, high above, they had no Harrier FA2 Combat Air Patrol, which would probably have downed all eight of the Argentine bombers twenty miles back.

Meanwhile the first two bombs from the lead Skyhawk slammed into HMS **Daring** with colossal force, one crashing through the starboard side of the hull and detonating in the middle of the ship, killing instantly everyone in the ops room and twenty-seven others. It split the engine room asunder, and a gigantic explosion seemed to detonate the entire ship.

The second bomb, meeting the ship on the rise, crashed through the upperworks, blasting the huge, pyramid-shaped electronic surveillance tower straight down onto the bridge. Everyone inside was killed either by the explosion or was crushed, which brought the death toll to fifty-eight, with another sixty-eight wounded. There were huge fires, the water mains were blown apart, and HMS **Daring**, shipping seawater at a ferocious rate, was little more than a hulk on her way to the bottom.

HMS **Dauntless** was hit by three bombs, two of them in the same spot, which just about broke her back, one single explosion destroying the engine room and causing an upward blast that literally caved in the entire upperworks. More than a hundred men were dead, and almost everyone else was wounded. The destroyer would sink into the freezing ocean in under fifteen minutes.

Captain Day's **Gloucester** fared best. She took only one bomb, fine on her starboard bow. But it was a big thousand-pounder from one of the Daggers, and it smashed deep inside the ship before exploding with a blast that obliterated her foredeck, ripped apart her missile-launch systems, and blasted overboard the forward Vickers 4.5-inch gun. She, too, instantly began to ship water from the gaping hole on the waterline on her starboard side, and there was a terrible fire raging dangerously close to the missile magazine.

At this point hardly anyone, aside from the ships' companies in the pickets, knew what had happened. There was no communication from either the **Daring** or **Dauntless**, but Captain Day sent a signal back to the flag reporting his own fairly drastic damage, which might yet cause the **Gloucester** to sink.

However, the loss of life on his ship was negligible compared to the others, just twelve men killed and fifteen wounded. It took only another minute for the lookouts on the frigate line positioned just a few miles behind them, to see three plumes of thick black smoke and flame on the horizon.

Captain Day, who was closest, now reported the **Dauntless** was sinking. He was out of contact with the **Daring**, and two of the frigates, the **Kent** and **Grafton**, were nearer. The CO of the **Gloucester** knew the fire was raging toward his missiles, which would blow the entire ship into oblivion.

His firefighting teams were down there trying to work in incinerating heat, but they were fighting a losing battle. At 0642 Captain Day gave the order to abandon ship. And Admiral Holbrook ordered his frigates forward to assist with the rescue of the wounded.

The trouble was, information was very limited. And he was not to know that eight more Skyhawks were already in the air from Rio Grande, refueled and heading east at maximum speed. The Admiral, of course, understood the likelihood of further attack, but without a Harrier CAP, he was reliant on his downrange helos, and then the medium-range radar of his destroyers' missile systems, and the Argentinian pilots were flying below that.

There was, however, quite sufficient information for one commanding officer. Captain Gregor Vanislav, still moving at minimum speed out to the east of the **Ark Royal**, had already picked up on his sonar the savage iron bomb detonations that had decimated the British picket line.

And now, shortly after 0700, he came quietly to periscope depth for a visual sighting of his quarry. He could see the **Ark Royal** out on the horizon through the telescopic lens, and there was no doubt in his mind. This was the Royal Navy's only active aircraft carrier. He'd come a long way for this, and now he intended to carry out the instruction issued to him with such firmness and clarity by Admiral Vitaly Rankov in person.

The carrier had in fact moved three miles farther east and was now well astern of the other warships, in readiness for its lower deck hospital to begin receiving the wounded from the burning destroyers. Right now this was the only hospital the Task Force had since the other main medical facilities were on the **Ocean** and **Largs Bay**.

Captain Vanislav, now almost stationary, was no more than three miles to her southeast. His plan was to circle the carrier, staying deep and slow, five hundred feet below the surface, a depth at which his Akula was more than comfortable. He intended to launch his attack from two miles off the **Ark Royal** 's starboard beam, and it would be made easier by the fact that the carrier was scarcely moving, and that there would, he knew, be a great deal of diversionary action taking place. His last satellite communication, relayed from Moscow, had made that absolutely clear.

Down periscope...helmsman, steer course three-zero-five, speed four...bow down ten... three hundred...

At this speed, the **Viper** was absolutely silent, undetectable, as it crept through the water, slowly drawing a bead on the 20,000-ton Royal Navy carrier. The submarine was transmitting nothing, her Captain relying on a visual fix when his ship was in position.

At 0708 **Viper K-157** was precisely where he wanted her. They came to PD and he took one final look. Even then, for the fleeting seconds his periscope was jutting eighteen inches out of the water like a telegraph pole, he was not detected.

Admiral Holbrook had already signaled for two escorts, the Batch Three Type-42s **York** and **Edinburgh**, to position themselves on his port and starboard quarters and use intermittent active sonar, since they were all alerted to the bizarre outside possibility of a submarine threat, from Russia! But there was plainly no point having both destroyers passive, eight miles up-threat from the bombs and missiles.

But the destroyers were still a couple of miles short of this new station, and the British Admiral had so much on his mind after the destruction of his picket line that he was giving scant regard to the very real danger of a torpedo attack on his own flagship.

Right now there was something close to havoc in his ops room. Everyone was handing out advice, how best to deal with the crisis on the picket line, the urgency of getting the GR9s into the air and launching a major bomb and missile attack on the airfield from whence, it was assumed, the Skyhawks had come.

No thought was being given to the classic evasive maneuvers a big warship might take to avoid a submarine attack—moving in a zigzag pattern, varying speed drastically from twenty-five knots to six, forcing any tracking submarine to show its hand by forcing it to increase speed.

Captain Vanislav intended to fire three torpedoes at his massive target from a range of 5,000 yards. Right now they were a little over five miles away, and ready for the final approach. **Viper**'s CO ordered her closer.

Meanwhile, the two flights of Skyhawks were clear of the Falkland Islands and headed at wave-top height toward the Battle Group, making in excess of six hundred knots. The frigates **Kent** and **Grafton** were still about two miles short of the disaster area, with the **St. Albans** and **Iron Duke** farther to the left, and about three miles astern of the other two.

The four lead Skyhawks cleared the horizon and could now see the blazing destroyers, but their targets were two miles back, and all four of the Argentinian fighters unleashed their thousand-pound bombs straight at the **Kent** and **Grafton**.

Both frigates acquired and opened fire with their Seawolf missile systems. They hit the first two Skyhawks, missed the others, and attempted to swing around to the right.

The **Grafton** was not in time and took two bombs hard on her port beam, both of which smashed into the interior of the ship, detonated, and blew apart the ops room, the comms room, and the engine room, killing thirty-two men and wounding forty. The ship was crippled. In fact she would never sail again. Like the **Daring**, like the **Dauntless**, she was on her way to the bottom.

Much luckier was Captain Mike Fawkes's **Kent.** She swung around fractionally faster, and while two of the bombs sailed right past, two of them came screaming over the top, fifty feet above the upperworks.

The second four Skyhawks now cleared the horizon, and the first ships they saw were the two frigates in the rear, Captain Colin Ashby's **St. Albans** and Commander Keith Kemsley's **Iron Duke.**

The very sharp, short-range Seawolf systems in both frigates locked on immediately, and both ops rooms had the missiles away in a matter of seconds. But again not before the iron bombs were released. And there was absolutely nothing the Royal Navy Commanders could do. The first two smashed into the **St. Albans**, one through the port-side bow, one amidships. The second two, on the rise, slammed down the communications tower and blasted the radar away from the **Iron Duke.**

The carnage in the **St. Albans** was truly shocking. Forty-seven men were killed instantly. Somehow the Captain survived, perhaps protected from the blast by his own high, television-style screen. But the ops room was on fire and three other survivors helped Captain Ashby to get out, leaving behind them a scene from hell as the bodies of the computer and missile operators burned.

The missiles from the two ships knocked down two more Skyhawks. The trouble was, without a squadron of Harriers, there was no early air defense from a high CAP, and no early warnings from the Harrier pilots. As General Sir Robin Brenchley had warned the Prime Minister not so very long ago in the small hours of a February morning in Downing Street, the loss of the Harrier FA2s represented the loss of the Royal Navy Fleet's ability to defend itself.

And with a total of six warships ablaze in the south Atlantic—four of them sinking—and at least 250 men killed and even more wounded, many of them badly burned...well, this was a catastrophe that had, perhaps, been very well foreseen by the Navy, but totally ignored by their political masters.

Eight miles astern of the wrecked warships, Captain Vanislav came to PD for his final visual. HMS **Ark Royal** was less than four miles away, moving slowly, her starboard beam exposed to the submarine's line of sight.

The CO prepared to fire. He would launch his big TEST torpedoes quietly at thirty knots, running in toward the carrier, staying passive all the way.

0725: **"Stand by, one!"**
"Last bearing check."
"Shoot!"
The Russian torpedo came powering out of the tube, seemed to pause for a split-second as her engine fired, and then went whining off into the dark waters.

"Weapon under guidance."

"Arm the weapon."

"Weapon armed, sir."

Ninety seconds to go. "Weapon now one thousand meters from target, sir."

"Weapon has passive contact."

At that moment **Viper K-157** fired her second torpedo, and within seconds it too was streaking straight at the massive starboard hull of the carrier.

With the lead weapon only eight hundred yards out, **Viper**'s third torpedo was under way, and at this precise time the sonar men inside the **Ark Royal** picked up the incoming ship-killers. At least they picked up one of them...

Admiral—sonar...Torpedo!Torpedo!Torpedo! Bearing green zero-zero-four...Really close, sir, really close!

That meant about five hundred yards, which put the lead torpedo about thirty seconds from impact, directly off the beam. It was out of the question to fire back—the old 20,000-ton carrier was simply not built for close combat of this type.

Someone bellowed, **"Decoys!"** But that was at least two minutes too late. The Combat Systems Officer alerted all Task Force ships still floating that the flag was under attack, along with everyone else. But he never even had time to yell, **"Unknown submarine!"** before the big TEST-7IME Russian torpedo slammed into the hull amidships and blew up with stupendous force.

The second torpedo struck home farther forward, and the last one almost blew off the entire stern area, fracturing both shafts, rupturing the flight deck, blasting four helicopters over the side. It was a classic submarine attack, conducted with the utmost stealth, and executed with total brutality. When Captain Vanislav came to PD for the last time, what he saw in those seven seconds would remain with him for however long he lived.

Gregor Vanislav could see the aircraft carrier was ripped almost in two, her back broken by the blast of the first torpedo, the entire stern of the ship sagging back into the water. And even as he watched, a huge fire suddenly broke out right below the island, the big chunky superstructure on one side of the flight deck.

The immediate inferno was almost certainly caused by a ruptured aircraft fuel line, and now Captain Vanislav could see British seamen jumping from the flight deck into the ocean, their clothes on fire. It reminded him of the gruesome pictures from the World Trade Center disaster in

New York ten years ago. Surely none of the one-thousand-strong crew, save those working high in the tower, could possibly have survived.

The huge warship was swiftly ablaze from end to end, but the fires would not be long lasting, since the ship was also sinking. For the moment, however, the only part not burning was the upper floor of the island, where presumably the Admiral and the Captain were still alive. The **Ark Royal**, now with thousands of gallons of jet fuel blazing, was an inferno, and Captain Vanislav, a very senior Russian career naval officer, almost went into shock at the catastrophe he had caused.

The only thought in his mind was a feeling of profound regret, and a realization that if he could live the last ten minutes over again, he would not have done it. Because, knowing the reality as he now did, he would have been incapable of committing this act upon a British ship that, so far as he knew, wished him no harm. Captain Vanislav ordered his ship deep again, and with a surprisingly heavy heart, accepted that his grotesque mission was accomplished. He turned north for Mother Russia.

Meanwhile, on board the carrier, Admiral Holbrook was still alive, but the heat was becoming too intense. He and Captain Reader were together until the last, knowing, as the flames leapt toward their quarters high above the flight deck, their only chance was to jump, before they were burned to death.

That was like leaping from the George Washington Bridge. But others had done it. There was no other way down, except to walk down the companionway into the flames, and there was no time to wait for helicopter rescue, even if that were possible.

The two senior officers walked outside and climbed to the platform area above the Admiral's ops room. They were both still wearing their life jackets and antiflash gear, hoods and gloves, and they stood there in the stifling smoke as the great ship, now in her death throes, suddenly lurched violently, thirty degrees to starboard. This reduced the distance down to the water, but confirmed the inevitability that the **Ark Royal** was sinking. The GR9s, mostly in flames, were slewing across the flight deck and falling overboard.

So far as the two officers could tell, there was no enemy in sight. And the rails were growing hot, almost too hot to hold, and they just stood there, until Captain Reader said quietly, "We never had a chance, did we?"

"No, David, we never did. And I'm not sure we'll ever know what hit us."

Ten seconds later, as the ship listed even farther, they both jumped, and hit the water, now forty-five feet below, feetfirst. Both men miraculously survived the fall, but not the almost-freezing water.

When the destroyers moved in to pick up survivors two hours later, both senior officers were found floating, but no longer alive.

Anyone in water that cold has approximately two minutes to live, which meant there were no survivors from the crew of the Royal Navy carrier. Historians would in future regard it as the greatest single Royal Naval disaster since the old 41,000-ton battle cruiser HMS **Hood** was sunk by the **Bismarck** in the Denmark Strait seventy years earlier. Fourteen hundred and twenty men were lost that day, but even the **Hood** had three survivors.

It rapidly became apparent to all the British officers the flagship had been hit and almost certainly destroyed. Captain Mike Fawkes, on the bridge of the amazingly lucky frigate HMS **Kent**, now assumed command of the remnants of the fleet.

But there was not much left, and the rescue operation was by now the most colossal task. No one knew what was happening on the landing beaches. It was obvious the Army must now be devoid of any air cover whatsoever, and their situation, exposed on the shores of Lafonia, must be critical.

In fact, during the final moments before **Viper** fired her salvo, two of the GR9s did get off the deck and were making their way toward Lafonia, when the ops room in the frigate **Kent** informed them of the disaster to the carrier. This, of course, left the British pilots stranded with nowhere to land.

They both made a swing around the southeastern coast of East Falkland and came in over the landing beaches, where they ejected, sending their aircraft forward to ditch in the Atlantic. This avoided the possibility of Argentina claiming them as the spoils of war, which would most certainly have happened if the aircrew had requested permission to land at Mount Pleasant.

Both pilots survived the landing, right behind the beach, but they quickly understood this was no place to be. Four minutes after their arrival, two Argentine bombers came in low and hit the assault ship **Albion**, which had mercifully unloaded its Marines.

Then two more fighter attack aircraft came in low and strafed the beach, firing four rockets in among the parked Apache attack helicopters. Then another bomber came in and hit the **Largs Bay** with a thousand-pound bomb. The British Army, like the Navy, was a sitting duck before the onslaught of Argentine bombs. And there was no Harrier CAP to protect them from air attack.

The success of those opening raids on the Lafonia enclave was entirely due to the brilliance of Admiral Oscar Moreno and his Army counterpart, General Eduardo Kampf. They had guessed, correctly, that the marine battalions that had landed during the night would immediately set up a missile shield against attack from the Argentine joint force land base at Mount Pleasant, fifteen miles to the north, across Choiseul Sound.

And this they had already accomplished. The big Chinooks, landed from HMS **Ocean**, had been ferrying the Rapier batteries into the rolling hills to the west of Seal Cove. From there they were well placed to down any incoming Argentine jet fighter or attack helicopter flying in low from the north after takeoff from Mount Pleasant. It had taken them several hours to install, and the 2,700 landed troops all felt considerably safer.

But both Admiral Moreno and General Kampf had fought and lost in the 1982 conflict. And both of them clung, in their own minds, to the rare Argentine successes against the invading Brits.

One of these had been conducted by three Skyhawks, bombing the British landing ships **Sir Tristam** and **Sir Galahad** as they lay at anchor in Port Pleasant Bay. The key to this successful attack was that the Skyhawks came in from the open ocean, and then streaked straight up the bay and unleashed their bombs, which killed fifty still embarked soldiers, and decimated the First Battalion Welsh Guards.

Admiral Moreno understood this monstrous chess game, and he knew the answer was to come in from out of the Atlantic from the southeast, away from the British Rapier missile defense. He was accurate in his assessment, and once again the British landing ships, stationary in calm waters, were sitting ducks.

Admiral Moreno planned to go on launching his air attacks from Rio Grande all day, if necessary, with Skyhawk and Dagger bombers, and Super-Etendard guided-missile aircraft. All day, until the British flew the white flag. As he knew they must, sooner or later.

On the beaches, the troops tried to dig in, tried to find cover, manned their machine guns, strived to get Rapier batteries into position to fire out over the sea. But time was short. Indeed, time was running out.

One hundred miles offshore, the aircraft carrier had sunk. Captain Mike Fawkes, now effectively an acting Admiral, assessed the carnage inflicted upon the fleet, assessed the weapons with which he could still fight, and the inevitability of the Argentine bombing attacks, against which he had no defense.

At 0800 on that Saturday morning, after just two hours of ferocious battle, Captain Fawkes, with tears of sorrow and anger streaming down his face, sent the following signal to Britain's Joint Force Command Headquarters in Northwood, to the West of London:

160800APR11. From Captain Mike Fawkes, HMS Kent. **Flagship** Ark Royal **hit and sunk. Type-45 destroyers** Daring **and** Dauntless **hit**

and sunk. **HMS** Gloucester **burning and abandoned. The frigates** Grafton, St. Albans **and** Iron Duke **all destroyed. More than 900 men believed to be dead in** Ark Royal**, 250 in the other ships. Medical facilities now nonexistent. We are defenseless against Argentine bombing. The land forces ashore are without protection. None of us can survive another two hours. Can see no alternative but to surrender.**

CHAPTER EIGHT

Captain Fawkes copied his Northwood signal to the Marine Brigade Commander on the beach at Lafonia, where his HQ had just been established. Things were bad: five fully fueled Apache helicopters were on fire and forty-seven men had been killed in the rocket and strafing attacks.

The scale of the damage to the assault ships **Albion** and **Largs Bay** was as yet unclear. But there were two huge plumes of black smoke rising to the south, and Brigadier Viv Brogden was uncertain whether the **Ocean** could possibly now survive another attack from the Argentine bombing force.

The signal from Captain Fawkes added another, near-impossible dimension to the myriad of problems. With the Navy out of action, the fact was, the British landing force was now effectively stranded, 8,000 miles from home with no cover from the air or even the sea. Evacuation was out of the question, and their fate was effectively sealed—surrender, or perish under Argentine bombing, here on this godforsaken beach, essentially fighting for what?

Never, in a long and distinguished career, had Brigadier Brogden, a decorated Iraq War veteran, faced such an insoluble conundrum. It was plain the remainder of his 10,000-strong force, currently marooned in the cruise liner **Adelaide,** could not possibly make a landing. Not without naval escort or air cover. The Army Commanders would never permit that, and the **Adelaide** had no defenses of her own.

Brigadier Brogden ordered his satellite communication team to open the line for transmission. His signal, also to Joint Force Command, Northwood, read: **160816APR11, Brigadier V. Brogden RM. Lafonia, Falkland Islands. Helicopter attack force destroyed. Forty-seven dead. Fifty wounded. Believe two assault ships also hit and burning six miles south. Like Captain Fawkes, we have no defense against bomb and rocket attacks. Landed force of 2,700 men now faces unacceptable losses. Agree with Captain Fawkes. Surrender our only option.**

The signals from the South Atlantic landed within fifteen minutes of each other in the headquarters of the Joint Force Command. General Sir Robin Brenchley, Chief of the Defense Staff, was in the war room when the duty officer brought in the first signal and handed it to the C-in-C Fleet, Admiral Palmer. He read it, and passed it to General Brenchley, who stared at it with undisguised horror. He had, in his soldier's soul, expected something like this would occur in the next three or four days. However, he had not expected anything quite so stunning as recommendations for total surrender after just two hours of battle.

He looked up and said quietly, "Gentlemen, you are about to bear witness to possibly the most humiliating surrender in the history of the British armed services, certainly since General Cornwallis asked for terms from the Americans at Yorktown in October 1781. General Cornwallis, however, had the excuse of running out of appropriate ammunition and artillery. I am afraid we never had either, even before we went."

He passed the signal back to Admiral Mark Palmer, who stared again at the sheet of paper that heralded the destruction of his beloved Royal Navy. "My God!" he kept saying, over and over, "This is beyond my comprehension."

General Brenchley, part of whose job was to keep the Minister of Defense, Peter Caulfield, informed, seemed to be transfixed by the signal. He just stared at it, knowing the words had somehow made him a prophet, but nonetheless hating the experience, knowing he must now inform the Defense Secretary that all was lost.

"Anyone know the correct procedures here?" asked General Brenchley. "No one ever really taught me what to do in the event of a national surrender of our deployed forces."

"Well," said Admiral Palmer. "I suppose we inform first the Ministry, and then the Prime Minister. I think he must be told of the necessity of informing the Argentine government that Great Britain is no longer able to pursue the war, and would like to sue for peace and a swift cessation of hostilities."

At that moment, the duty officer returned with the signal, just in, from Brigadier Brogden on the beaches in Lafonia. He once more handed it to Admiral Palmer, who just stared, and passed it to the General.

"Good God!" he breathed. "There's no braver chap than Brogden, but the damned landing force is marooned with no air cover and no sea cover. They'll be bombed to hell. Someone better get this on a fast track. We could lose two thousand men in the next two hours."

He picked up the nearest telephone and looked around the room, growling, "You deal with the Ministry, I'll talk to the PM..." And then to the operator, "Downing Street, fast."

Twenty seconds later, everyone heard him say, "Operator, this is General Brenchley, Chief of the Defense Staff. Please connect me to the Prime Minister immediately, whatever he may be doing."

It took four minutes, which seemed a lot longer in the operations room in Northwood. Finally the Prime Minister came on the line and said calmly, "General Brenchley?"

"Prime Minister," he replied, "it is my unhappy duty to inform you that the Royal Navy has been badly defeated in the South Atlantic. Also the land forces that landed on East Falkland early this morning are now stranded, and taking quite heavy casualties. Both battle commanders are defenseless against the bombing, and are recommending an immediate surrender."

"A what!?" exclaimed the PM. "What do you mean surrender?"

"Sir," said the General, patronizingly, "it is the course of action battle commanders usually take when victory is out of the question, and casualties are becoming totally unacceptable. It applies mostly to forces that are not actually carrying out a defense of their own country. That of course requires a different mind-set."

"But surely, General, our casualties cannot be that unacceptable. I mean, my God! Do you have any idea what the media would do to my government if we suddenly ordered our forces to surrender?"

"Yessir. I imagine they would probably crucify the lot of you. And for that they would receive the inordinate thanks of every single man who has been obliged to fight this war for you—all of them were improperly equipped, insufficiently armed, and inadequately protected."

"General, for the moment I will ignore your insolence, and remind you that I have been elected by the people of this country to look after their interests. I am the elected head of government, and I imagine the final decision on any surrender will be mine alone?"

"Absolutely, Prime Minister," replied the General, "but if you do not, you will have the resignations of all your Chiefs of Staff on your desk in a matter of hours. Which would make us free to explain to the media precisely why we had done so.

"My advice is thus to signal to the Argentinians, formally, that the armed forces of Great Britain no longer wish to pursue the war."

The Prime Minister gulped. Before him he saw his worst ever nightmare—driven from office by the public, and the military, for failing in his duty to protect the country. Disgrace piled upon disgrace.

Nonetheless he elected to remain on the attack. "After all, General," he said, "professional soldiers and sailors are paid to run these risks, and possibly face death. Are you quite certain they have done their absolute best? I mean, it must be centuries since a British Prime Minister was obliged to report the surrender of our armed forces to any enemy."

"Would you care to know the state of the battle down there?" asked the General.

"Most certainly, I would," replied the PM, a tad pompously. "Tell me how it is, as we speak. And I warn you, I may judge the situation rather more harshly than you do. These men owe a debt of honor and duty to the country they serve."

General Brenchley wasted no time. "The Navy's flagship, the aircraft carrier **Ark Royal**, has been hit, burned, and sunk—no survivors among their thousand-strong crew. All three of our picket line destroyers are on fire, two of them sinking.

"The frigates **Grafton, St. Albans**, and **Iron Duke** have been bombed and destroyed. Admiral Holbrook and Captain Reader perished in the carrier. Altogether the Navy estimates twelve hundred fifty dead and possibly two hundred more wounded, many of them badly burned, many of them dying in the water. That's as we speak, by the way."

The Prime Minister of Great Britain, the color literally draining from his face, put down the telephone, rushed from the room, and somewhat spectacularly threw up in the sink of the second-floor staff washroom, leaning there for fully five minutes, trembling with fear at what he now faced.

Back in Northwood, General Brenchley said, "Something's happened. The line's gone dead."

"Fucking little creep's probably fainted," murmured Admiral Jeffries, not realizing how astonishingly close to the truth he was.

General Brenchley demanded to be reconnected, and when the Downing Street operator came on the line, he just said, "General Brenchley here. Please put me back to the Prime Minister, will you?"

It took five minutes to locate the PM, who was now using the other washroom sink to wash his mouth out and his face down. And three minutes later, he once more picked up the telephone. "I apologize, General," he said. "Been having trouble with these phones all morning."

"Of course," replied Brenchley. "Now, let me inform you about the first-wave assault troop landing. In the hours of darkness we put twenty-seven hundred troops ashore, plus helicopters, vehicles, and a couple of JCBs.

"The Argentine bombers came in shortly after dawn and hit two of the big landing ships. We have no casualty reports yet, but both ships are burning. Right afterward the Arg fighter-bombers hit the beachhead with bombs and machine-gun fire, killing forty-seven men, injuring another fifty, and wiping out five of our six attack helicopters.

"We have no defense against their bombs. And if we continue to fight, I suspect there will be no survivors on that beach within two or three hours. They have no naval support, no air support, no possibility of reinforcements, and no means of evacuating a fortified island on which they are outnumbered by around seven to one.

"Prime Minister, we're looking at a massacre, and I will have no part of it. I'm a soldier, not a butcher. I am suggesting you contact the Argentinian government and request terms for the surrender of the British armed forces in the South Atlantic. And I suggest you do so in the next ten minutes."

"But what about Caulfield? What does he have to say about it? What about my ministers? I must have a Cabinet meeting."

"Very well, Prime Minister. You have thirty minutes. But, if by then we have taken significantly more casualties, we shall again advise most strongly that you contact Buenos Aires, and sue for peace on behalf of my troops, who should be ordered to raise the white flag. Any other course of action on your part will cause me to offer, publicly, my resignation. And perhaps you can talk your way out of that."

"Don't do that, General. I implore you. Think of the government...think of the national disgrace..."

"Prime Minister, at this precise moment my thoughts are entirely with burned and dying seamen in the ice-cold Atlantic, and with mortally wounded young men dying on the beaches of Lafonia. I am afraid that at this time, I have no room in my heart for anything else."

"I understand, General, I understand. But right here we're talking about the total humiliation of the government of Great Britain. And I must remind you of your troops' debt of honor to the nation, and of the courage our armed services have shown in conflicts of the past."

"Prime Minister, I wonder how your beloved tabloids will treat those fifteen hundred heartbroken, devastated families, up and down the country, whose sons, fathers, husbands, and uncles were killed in the South Atlantic because we sent them to fight with inadequate air cover? Good afternoon, Prime Minister."

In fact, the PM thought he might throw up all over again, right in the middle of the vast Cabinet table. But he braced himself and asked to be connected to the Ministry of Defense.

Back in Northwood, his eyes suffused with tears, General Sir Robin Brenchley put down the telephone and turned away from his colleagues, wiping his sleeve across his eyes. Everyone saw it and no one cared. He was by no means the only man in the war room so personally and overwhelmingly affected by this morning's events in the South Atlantic.

There was more information beginning to trickle through now from HMS **Kent**, the acting flagship for the remnants of the fleet. It seemed the warships' missile directors had downed six Skyhawks and two Daggers. But war of this type is about attrition. Argentina's big land-based air assault force, both Navy and Air Force, could afford the loss of eight fighter aircraft and their pilots.

It looked now as if Great Britain had lost its entire flight of GR9s, two ditched in the Atlantic and nineteen lost in the carrier; her two best destroyers, the Type-45s, were gone, plus the **Gloucester**; three guided-missile frigates were destroyed; two 20,000-ton assault ships, one of them brand-new, were ablaze; almost every attack helicopter was either on fire or lost in the assault ships; and the flagship, **Ark Royal**, which represented the only British airfield for 4,000 miles, was sunk in six hundred fathoms. Total casualties: 1,300 and rising by the hour. Great Britain could not afford that.

Perhaps in all the world, the only nation that could have absorbed that kind of punishment and still come back fighting was the United States of America. And right now she was not playing. The shocking news, flashing around the globe from the Falkland Islands, was that British resistance must be at an end. Which indeed it was. Almost.

Four hours earlier, three hundred feet from the summit of Fanning Head, Captain Douglas Jarvis and his seven-man SAS team were in their granite cave making satellite contact with the SAS Commander on board the carrier. They had been forbidden to attack anything until hostilities formally commenced. And, in the opinion of Major Tom Hills, currently masterminding the SAS reconnaissance operation, this was likely to happen in the next hour.

When news of the opening attack by the Super-Es was first transmitted on the fleet network, Major Hills unleashed his tigers. **"Attack and destroy the Argentinian position at the summit of Fanning Head,"** he ordered.

And Captain Jarvis needed no further encouragement. His team was ready. Two of them would remain in the cave manning the communications, trying as they had been for the past two hours to make contact with the British landed assault forces on the beach at Lafonia.

The other six would climb stealthily upward to the stronghold on the top of the mountain, which effectively controlled the gateway to Falkland Sound. At least it did for approximately the next twenty minutes.

At which point, Douglas Jarvis located the tent with the radio and satellite aerials erected outside, hurled a hand grenade straight through the opening, and dived behind a rock for cover as the blast killed all three occupants, and blew to pieces the entire Argentine communications system on Fanning Head.

The noise was shattering in the early morning light, high above the ocean, and it seemed to echo from peak to peak among the not-too-distant mountains. From four other tents, the Argentinian troops came running out, fumbling to get ahold of their rifles. They never had a chance. The men of 22 SAS cut them down in their tracks, all sixteen of them, the complete staff of Argentina's Fanning Head operation.

Immediately Captain Jarvis set about his real task of the night. He hurled a hand grenade into the big Chinook helicopter that was parked on flat ground right behind the tents, presumably for lifting heavy artillery pieces and missile batteries to and from Mare Harbor.

He and his five explosives experts attached sticky bombs to the missile launchers, dynamite to the howitzers and gun barrels, and high explosive to the missiles themselves. Fifteen minutes later, the explosion that ripped across the summit of Fanning Head was every bit the equal of those that were currently sinking the Royal Navy's destroyers.

The shallow cave in which Douglas and his boys sat cheerfully eating chocolate bars and drinking water literally shook from the violence of the impact.

"Okay, chaps," said the Captain. "Fire up the comms and let's tell Major Hills what we just did."

The trouble was, his young comms man, Trooper Syd Ferry, was having no luck reaching anyone. All night long he had been trying to touch base with Lafonia, and the last time he spoke to

SAS HQ in the **Ark Royal** the bloody line had suddenly gone dead.

"Fuck," said Syd. "There's more electronics in that damn ship than they have in Cape Kennedy. And we can't even make a phone call."

"Keep trying," said Douglas. "If we have a link problem, try the destroyer **Daring**, we've got a secondary unit in there, Lieutenant Carey. Do your best, Syd, we need orders and we need an escape route. We can't hang around up here. The Args must have heard or seen something, and the bastards will hunt us down like rats…"

Syd's best, however, was not nearly good enough. Because no one was ever again going through on the military link to either the **Ark Royal** or the **Daring**. Syd kept sending his signal and the result was always silence.

Ten minutes later Captain Jarvis decided they had to pull out of the Fanning Head area, fast, before someone decided to come looking for whoever just blew up the top of the mountain.

"Christ," said Syd, "we're not climbing down that rock face, are we?"

"No," replied the CO. "We don't want to end up on an exposed beach. We'll go up and west, down the other side of the headland. According to this map it's still pretty steep, but not like that cliff face. We'll walk for maybe five miles, just get out of the immediate search area. Then we'll sleep for the day, and make our move at night."

"Any idea where to?" asked someone.

"Absolutely none," said the Captain. "But we can't stay here…come on, let's get our stuff… that's everything…and get moving. We can get rid of things when we're a few miles away."

"You thinking of making for the coast again, sir?"

"In the end, yes. Because if we can't whistle up a helicopter rescue, we'll have to leave by sea."

"But we can't tell anyone where we are," said Trooper Syd. "The comms are down. And we definitely don't have a boat."

"We can get one," replied Douglas. "I mean steal one."

"Well, what happens if the Argentine coast guard catches up and wants to know who we are?"

"Well, we just eliminate them in the normal way."

"Oh, yes," said Syd. "Silly of me to ask."

"We are at war, Trooper. And the enemy's the enemy."

What neither of them knew was that Great Britain and Argentina were no longer at war, as of about a half hour ago. The British Prime Minister was obliged to accept the advice of his military and end the one-sided debacle before more military and naval personnel were killed.

The PM asked Peter Caulfield to contact his opposite number in Buenos Aires and offer the immediate surrender of the armed forces of Great Britain, on the land, the sea, and in the air.

The Argentine Defense Minister, Rear Admiral Juan Jose de Rozas, was courteous in the extreme, and made no further demands, save for the raising of a significant white flag over the beach at Lafonia and a formal e-mail signed by the Prime Minister that the Falkland Islands were no longer under British rule, and that henceforth they would be known as Islas Malvinas, a sovereign state of Argentina, governed and administered entirely by that nation.

A complete cessation of all hostilities was formally agreed for ten a.m. on the morning of Saturday, April 16, 2011. Admiral Oscar Moreno, surely the next President of Argentina, was given the news on the direct line between Buenos Aires and Rio Grande.

He instantly ordered all of his pilots back to the base at Mount Pleasant, and he instructed two warships to make all speed to the battle area where HMS **Gloucester** was still burning, and to assist with rescue operations and evacuation to Argentinian hospitals by air from Mount Pleasant as soon as possible.

Sergeant Clifton's SAS team above the airfield was informed by the Royal Marines' commanding Brigadier on the beach at Lafonia that all was lost, and that they should surrender immediately. Fortunately this line had been established in the moments before the first rocket attack on the Apache helicopters.

Not so the line to Captain Jarvis and his men, who had been working directly with the SAS ops room in the carrier, in readiness for their task as a gunnery guidance team when the ships' bombardment began.

The fact was, no one knew quite where SAS Team One was located, especially the Argentinians, who were hopping mad about the destruction of their highly expensive stronghold on the top of Fanning Head, in particular about the cold-blooded killing of every one of their missile personnel who were serving on the heights.

General Eduardo Kampf was extremely upset about the incident and had ordered an inquiry, informing the commander on the ground at Mount Pleasant he wanted a search conducted in the area. He added that he was certain a British Special Forces team had been involved, and his orders were simple: hunt them down and execute them.

This had taken place in the twenty minutes before the surrender, and attack helicopters were in the air, on their way to Fanning Head, none of which was especially good news for Douglas Jarvis and his boys.

They went to ground, as only a camouflaged SAS team can, swiftly becoming invisible in the sparse vegetation found on these bleak high hills of the Falkland Islands. But they saw the Argentine helicopters moving into the area, and kept their heads well down.

The Air Brigade, which manned the Bell UH-1H attack helicopters landed on Fanning Head, were relatively shocked at what they found, the bodies of nineteen men, most of them half dressed, and the remnants of the missile systems and artillery pieces. So far as they could see, it was a classic predawn sneak attack by Special Forces, and they reported back to base those precise findings.

When General Kampf heard what had happened he was even more furious, and told the commander at the Mount Pleasant base, "Treat the British with courtesy. Make maximum effort with the wounded and dying. Try to assist the ships if possible and prepare to receive prisoners of war.

"The only exception to the regular guidance of the Geneva Convention is that Special Force, probably SAS, which sneaked up there and murdered some of our top missile men. Find them, and show no mercy. Because I do not regard them as prisoners of war. I regard them as thieves in the night, murderers. Whatever you deem necessary please carry out as you wish, in the utmost secrecy, of course."

Again, none of this was especially good news for Douglas Jarvis and his boys.

Trapped in the western foothills of Fanning Head, out of contact with their headquarters, they were forbidden to use a mobile phone, because it could so easily be traced. And now they had not the slightest idea what was happening, on the islands, at sea with the Battle Group, or on the landing beaches of Lafonia.

Douglas had few options except to make his way furtively out of the Fanning Head area, and try to select a seaport with some kind of a fishing trawler and attempt a getaway. Trouble was, he'd have to take the crew with him, otherwise the boat would be missed and they might end up being strafed by the Argentine coast guard. Right now there was a lot of bad news for Douglas Jarvis and his boys.

1130 (LOCAL), BUENOS AIRES

The Argentinians lost no time in announcing their victory. Agence Argentina Presse released the government's statement to the world's media as it stood, no comments, no interviews, and no follow-up. It read simply:

> **At 0930 this morning, Saturday, April 16, at the request of the Prime Minister of Great Britain, Argentina accepted the unconditional surrender of the British armed forces in the Battle for the Islas Malvinas.**
>
> **Argentina suffered relatively minor losses of just eight downed fighter-**

bombers, while Great Britain's losses were enormous. The heroic pilots of Argentina hit and sank a total of nine Royal Navy warships, including the flagship aircraft carrier the Ark Royal.

Great Britain's entire force of fighter jets, the GR9s, were all destroyed. More than 1,250 Royal Navy personnel are believed dead, with many more injured. The gallant commanding officers of the Argentinian Navy are currently in the area of the sea battle, assisting the Royal Navy with the wounded.

In the early hours of this morning, British forces, numbering almost 3,000, made a landing on the beaches of Lafonia. They brought with them attack helicopters, heavy-lift troop transport helicopters and missile installations. At 0945, after fierce fighting, this force surrendered to the armies of Argentina.

A white flag of surrender still flies over those landing beaches and we are currently in talks with London as to the immediate future of the prisoners of war. We have been asked to be merciful, and your government will comply with this British request.

A communiqué has been received from the British Prime Minister confirming that their former colony, described as the Falkland Islands, has now and shall be in future known as the Islas Malvinas and shall constitute a sovereign state of Argentina, under Argentine law, and Argentine administration. The national language shall henceforth be Spanish.

All islanders who wish to remain after the change in national structure will be welcomed to do so, and the government of Argentina will work closely with the former administrators to ensure the most peaceful transfer of power.

The important oil and gas fields, seized by the Argentine Army in February, shall remain the property of the Republic of Argentina, and there will be future announcements as to its administration.

The statement was signed by the President of Argentina. And countersigned by Admiral Oscar Moreno, Commander in Chief (Fleet), and General Eduardo Kampf, Commander of Five Corps, which had secured the island and was deployed to face the British in the Battle for Mount Pleasant Airfield, had that been required.

No statement ever flashed around the world faster. It has been said that King George III fell back in a chair and almost fainted when he heard of the loss of his American colonies six months after the surrender at Yorktown.

Several dozen of the world's news editors very nearly did the same thing, out of sheer excitement, when news of the British surrender reached them about an hour and a half after it happened.

There were several military experts in London, Washington, and Moscow who had long considered the outcome to be inevitable. But to other nations, especially journalists with their mostly superficial knowledge, the news came as a snowstorm might present itself to residents of Tahiti Beach.

Shock. Horror. And Panic. Brits pounded by the Argentinians. The Third World Strikes Back. Headline writers hauled out their big guns and turned them to face the public. Then, in a hundred different versions, they let fly.

BRITS BLASTED IN BATTLE FOR THE FALKLANDS
—New York Post

PAMPAS PILOTS PULVERIZE BRITS
—Boston Herald

GALLANT GAUCHOS SLAM THE ROYAL NAVY
—Washington Times

MASSACRE IN THE MALVINAS AS BRITS SURRENDER
—Clarin Buenos Aires

VIVA LAS MALVINAS—IT'S OFFICIAL!!
—Buenos Aires Herald

In Spain it was VIVA LAS MALVINAS. In France it was FRENCH JETS HELP ARGENTINA WIN THE FALKLANDS (never mind their European Union partners in London). Russia's **Izvestya** was subdued, SHORT NAVAL BATTLE FOR THE FALKLANDS ENDS IN ARGENTINE VICTORY. In Iran and Syria, the theme was BRITAIN'S LAST COLONY FALLS TO ARGENTINA. South China's **Morning News** announced, THE END OF THE EMPIRE—MALVINAS RETURN TO ARGENTINA.

Great Britain's Prime Minister instructed the Ministry of Defense to break the news of the calamity in the South Atlantic to a stunned nation—a nation that in the past 230 years had known setbacks in war, had withstood bombs and attack, suffered and retreated in the Crimea, Gallipoli, and Dunkirk; but never decisive, overwhelming defeat and unconditional surrender to a foreign enemy.

Two hours after that news bulletin, the Premier himself broadcast to the people on all television and radio channels. Six spin doctors had worked ceaselessly in a bold but futile attempt to distance their man from the disaster.

He made a rambling speech, referring to "unending courage," and "gallantry beyond the call," about meeting "an enemy that had secretly been preparing for several years." **Let down by his Admirals and Generals, not kept fully informed by the Intelligence services, unaware of the limitations of the fleet.** Blah, blah, blah.

"No Prime Minister can make decisions when the information is not thorough…no one regrets this catastrophe more than I…no one could have foreseen these consequences…I do expect some very major military resignations." (Not his own, of course.) And… **"I shall personally be taking charge of the evacuation back to Britain of our wounded, and also of the reparations that I have already insisted will be paid to families who have lost their loved ones."**

Right after that he recalled every Member of Parliament to Westminster to begin an emergency sitting at midnight.

1200 (LOCAL), SAME DAY
CHEVY CHASE, MARYLAND

Admiral Morgan was not surprised at the outcome of the war, but he was slightly surprised at the speed with which it had been accomplished. He first heard the news shortly after eleven a.m.

on Fox News, but the updated version of the bulletin at noon contained another surprise. According to the best naval sources available, it seemed the aircraft carrier **Ark Royal** had been sunk in less than fifteen minutes.

This was extremely fast for a big ship hit by either bombs or missiles. There were few examples of the time taken for a major warship to sink finally beneath the waves after a hit by an Exocet. But certainly in 1982 it took Britain's HMS **Sheffield** three days, and in that same war the **Atlantic Conveyor** burned for twenty-four hours before she blew apart and sank. Both ships took an Exocet above the waterline.

The **Ark Royal**, however, appeared to have gone down in a quarter of an hour. And her comms room had time to broadcast to the fleet she had been hit, three explosions reported. However, the flagship went off the air immediately, and another CO positioned within three miles reported fire broke out "at least six minutes after the ship began to list."

"I'd be surprised," muttered Arnold, "if she was hit by bombs or missiles. That ship went down too damn quick, like she was holed below the waterline, or somehow had her back broken... or both. I'd guess the fires broke out in the engine room and then spread fast. Those damn carriers are full of fuel."

He wandered outside, absentmindedly inspecting his daffodil beds. In his hand he carried a recent message from Jimmy Ramshawe informing him that the two Russian submarines, **Gepard** and **Cougar**, had been sighted in the Murmansk area in the past two or three days.

"I wonder," he murmured, turning back toward the house, "whether our old friend, the elusive Mr. Viper, was in attendance when the Royal Navy carrier was sunk. I'd sure as hell like to ask Vitaly Rankov, but there's no point seeking the truth from a lying Soviet bastard, right?"

Thoughtfully he answered his own question, "Right, no point at all," and continued walking back to the house, his mind once more in the dark cold depths of the South Atlantic, where he guessed **Viper K-157** would now be running slowly north, away from the datum, her work done.

No sooner was he back inside than the telephone rang in his study. He checked the call identity and recognized the private number of Lt. Commander Ramshawe.

"Hi, Jimmy, told you it wouldn't take long."

"You sure did. Two hours flat. Game, set, and match. Everyone back in the bloody pavilion."

Arnie chuckled. "I got a few thoughts for you to work on. First, thanks for the information on the **Gepard** and the **Cougar**. That leaves **Viper K-157**, right? The **only** nuclear submarine that could possibly have been in the South Atlantic, right? And twice picked up on her way there—once by our guys in Ireland, and again by the Royal Navy CO east of the Falkland Islands coupla days ago, correct?"

"That's what we have, Arnie. You hear anything more?"

"Only from my own highly suspicious mind, kid. That aircraft carrier went down awful quick. Fifteen minutes. And eyewitnesses are saying the fires started about six minutes after she began to list.

"The fires didn't sink her. What sank her was a damned big hole below the waterline. Nothing else puts a warship on the bottom that fast. And it must have been a very big hole...sounds to me like something broke her back. And there's only one thing coulda done that...a wire-guided torpedo from a submarine. And I'd guess she was hit by more than one."

"We got a report of huge fires," said Jimmy. "Spread fast. Started below the island."

"Fires don't sink warships," said Arnold. "They burn 'em. And if they burn 'em for long enough they'll probably reach the bomb and missile areas, which will blow the ship in half. But that usually takes hours and hours. This baby was on the bottom in fifteen minutes. That's not a fire, that's a hole."

"So who fired the torpedo, Sherlock?"

"I'd guess Comrade Moriartovich, sneaky little sonofabitchovich. Straight out of the tubes of the Akula-class hunter-killer **Viper**, which had been watching, for several days, waiting for that fog to clear...just lurking, silent and villainous. That's who."

"I didn't realize you spoke fluent Russian," said Jimmy. "But I'm with you. That bastard just slammed a couple of big ones straight into the Royal Navy's **Ark Royal**."

"Well, the Argentinians could not have done it, kid. They don't have a good enough submarine for that. But someone did, and someone did it for them. And if you want to know who, just watch to see who gets the biggest oil contract in the world in the next few months. The one less than a dozen miles from the airport on East Falkland."

"Excuse me, sir. A matter of protocol. I believe they just became the Islas Malvinas."

"But perhaps, young James, only temporarily."

"How do you mean? The Brits have turned it up, right?"

"Yes. But we are still left with a very clear situation. Those islands have been British since 1833, everyone who lives on them is British. They have been a legal protectorate of Great Britain for darn near two hundred years. Argentina has been griping and moaning about it for a long time, but Argentina has **never** owned the islands. Spain did, and the Brits threw 'em out a long time ago.

"So what happens? Argentina suddenly decides to grab 'em, lands a military force, blows up the British defenses, kills a hundred troops and takes over. They kick out the legal oil companies, two of the biggest, most respected corporations on earth, both of whom have paid fortunes to be there, and then marches them out at gunpoint.

"Then they effectively say, **you want us out, come try it.** At which point they blast and kill another thousand or more troops and accept a surrender. That worked fine in the nineteenth century. Doesn't work now. There's the UN and Christ knows whom else to answer to.

"It would be as if Paul Bedford and I decided we'd very much like to own Monaco, went over there in a couple of warships, kicked Prince Whatsisname in the ass, and took his fucking principality. Accepting the surrender of that poncey Palace Guard that prances around in fancy dress. It'd probably take us about an hour and a half. And no one could do a thing about it.

"But, Jimmy, you just can't pull that pre-nineteenth-century shit anymore. Not in the modern world. And I gotta talk to the President later this afternoon. And ExxonMobil are fucking furious. They want their goddamned oil and gas back, and I don't blame them. And they wanna know whether the God Almighty United States is going to just stand around while some fucking lunatic in a poncho rampages around all over their god-damned possessions.

"And the President is not going to like it. And a thousand fucking disaffected sonsobitches are going to be asking him what he plans to do about it. And he's not going to know, and frankly neither do I. That's why I'm going to talk to him later. But someone's sure as hell going to need to do something. We simply cannot condone it."

Jimmy Ramshawe was very thoughtful, and there was a momentary silence between the senior world Intelligence maestro and one of the sharpest young minds in the National Security Agency.

Eventually, it was Jimmy who spoke. "Arnie," he said, "I forgot to tell you why I called. You scanned through the Business Section in the **Times** today?"

"Not yet."

"There was an item there I thought was significant. One of the biggest international agricultural deals in recent years..."

"If you tell me it's Argentina and Russia I'll probably stand on my head..."

"Upside down, sir. You got it first time. Beef cattle. Millions of 'em."

"You know what that is, Jimmy? That's the start of a new cooperation between those two countries. And it's going to end with oil and gas in the Falklands and South Georgia...if, that is, the Argentinians are permitted to get away with what they have done."

"You decided what to advise the President yet?"

"No. Because I want to hear what the British Ambassador has to say this afternoon. I've met him a couple of times, and he's coming in to the White House. Just the three of us. A lot will depend on what he says.

"And then of course we've got the complication of the goddamned United Nations. They've got a meeting of the Security Council tonight. I think the Chairman's from someplace west of the Blue Nile...probably dressed in a bedspread... Mgumboo Nkurruption or someone...so that's gotta be real significant."

Jimmy burst out laughing. Arnold Morgan's opinion of African dictators who lived liked pashas in impoverished countries, which collected millions of dollars of foreign aid every year—well, that opinion was on the withering side of discourteous.

"I suppose you never considered the Diplomatic Service, did you?" asked Jimmy.

"Not this week, kid. Keep me posted." Crash. Down phone.

Three hours later Admiral Morgan drove himself to the White House, where Sir Patrick Jardine, Great Britain's Ambassador to the United States, was already in the Oval Office chatting with the President.

Sir Patrick was a tall, somewhat gaunt figure, wearing an immaculately tailored Savile Row suit. A scion of the great Hong Kong financial empire, he was a career diplomat despite having inherited 4,000 acres of prime farmland in Norfolk.

The fifty-six-year-old diplomat had only one customer, and that was one of the biggest brewers in England. Sir Patrick was what the Brits refer to as a Barley Baron, with his large swath of relatively rare, flinty land that grows malting barley, the prime ingredient for beer. Whichever way the market fluctuated, it kept Sir Patrick very handily in Savile Row suits at $3,000 a pop.

In his youth, he had trained to be a barrister, passed his exams, and then quit. "I simply can't imagine spending the rest of my life defending scruffy, spotty, mostly guilty young thugs who should probably be locked up on sight," he had told his father.

"Yes, I do see that's rather disagreeable," said Jardine Senior. "I think you better go and work in the Foreign Office. Won't make you rich, but you'll have a pleasant enough time, unless you get mixed up in some bloody war."

Anyway, thirty years later, the dread of the late Sir Arthur Jardine had come full circle. His son was not taking cover under the bed while gunfire rained plaster and furniture down on him in some besieged British embassy. But he was right in the thick of it, and, for the moment, he was Great Britain's last frontier in the struggle to persuade the USA to remove the Argentine Army from the Falkland Isles.

Sir Patrick, however, realized there was only one reason he was currently sitting in this chair, facing the President of the United States. And that was the stolen oil and gas that belonged to ExxonMobil.

He stood up to greet Admiral Morgan, who made his usual entry, without knocking, and held out his hand to the Ambassador. "Patrick," he said, "I'm afraid we meet again in rather trying circumstances."

President Bedford was clearly very concerned by the entire issue of the South Atlantic, and its myriad of ramifications.

"Arnie," he said, "I've been talking to the Ambassador for twenty minutes and I must say we have so far clarified nothing. But I think you'll be interested in the position the Brits are taking…Sir Patrick, why don't you outline the situation for Admiral Morgan?"

"Of course, and I'll be as quick as I can," replied the Barley Baron. "I'm sure you know the history. The Falklands have been British since 1833. Argentina has always wanted them, went to war for them in 1982, has been negotiating for them ever since, and a couple of months ago seized them by military force."

"Yup," said Arnold, nodding. "A regular coup d'etat, no bullshit."

"Well, you probably also know we went through the usual channels of protest, and the United Nations practically ordered the Argentinians to vacate the islands. However, a Security Council motion to censure them and even expel them from the United Nations was vetoed by Russia. So it didn't go through.

"Buenos Aires refused to discuss the matter with anyone, save to announce the Malvinas had always been theirs and that was an end to it."

"So Great Britain understandably decided to take matters into their own hands as they did in 1982?" said Arnold. "And drive the Argentinians off with military force."

"Not quite," said Sir Patrick. "Under very firm advice from the Foreign Office, my government made no threat to the Argentinians. We did not announce the formation of a Battle Group, even though Parliament had voted for such an action. We just got ready and set sail.

"Our fleet arrived in the area. In international waters, at least a hundred miles off the east coast of the Falkland Islands. We launched no attack, we opened fire on no one. But at first light, flying from both the mainland and the islands, Argentina launched an unprovoked airborne assault on our ships, and very nearly wiped us out. You might say it was their second great crime of the year 2011."

"I suppose they'll say the presence of the Royal Navy Fleet was in itself a major provocation and indeed a threat to their own troops," suggested Arnold Morgan.

"I suppose they may," replied Sir Patrick. "However, we were not in Argentinian waters, and despite their act of banditry in February, those islands belong to the Crown. They are packed with British institutions and people.

"Argentina had no right to have an army occupying the territory. No right at all. Under any law, local, national, or international, their occupation was illegal. And the fact that the Royal Navy attempted to defend itself against a very sustained attack is highly irrelevant. This was not a formal war. It was one country whose possessions had been ravaged by another, contrary to every known international charter and treaty of the last hundred years."

"Yes, I see that," replied Admiral Morgan. "But I suppose there was also the issue of the twenty-seven hundred troops that landed on Lafonia."

"Well, that ought not to be an issue. We are surely entitled to land anyone we wish on our own islands."

Arnold grinned. "Yes, I suppose you are."

And the President interjected, "Yes, but the Args are so damned convinced of the righteousness of their claim, it makes things very difficult. And of course the pure damned geography of the place is kinda on their side. Almost like China owned Nantucket."

Sir Patrick smiled. "Mr. President, I sometimes think people do not understand how very British the Falklands are, aside from the fact the natives are to a man British citizens, mostly living in harmony around a damned great Church of England cathedral in Stanley.

"There's Departments of Mineral Resources, Fisheries, Treasury. There's an Attorney General, an immigration officer, a Chief Executive, a Customs office, government offices. There's a Chamber of Commerce, a Development Corporation, a Met Office. There's even a Falkland Islands Company with offices in Stanley and Hertfordshire, England. It's all connected to London."

"But not, on this occasion, protected by London," said Arnold wryly.

The President ordered tea, Lapsang Souchong from China, which was both his own and the Ambassador's favorite. Paul Bedford made a habit of checking out all visiting Ambassadors' preferences, just in case Colombian coffee or something sparked an unexpected suicide attempt by an appalled Ecuadorian diplomat.

Sir Patrick informed the Americans that Great Britain would return to the United Nations and once more request some strong, decisive action, which Arnold Morgan remarked had never been their strong suit.

But what Sir Patrick really wanted was for the USA to make a stand, to growl that the actions of

Argentina had been nothing short of international piracy, and if Buenos Aires did not come to heel forthwith, Uncle Sam would surely make life very, very difficult for them. The Rule of Law must surely, in the end, in a civilized world, take precedence.

Just before the Ambassador left, Admiral Morgan reminded him that it was sometimes necessary to take draconian measures to uphold that Rule of Law. And that he for one was not averse to implementing them if required.

Sir Patrick, as he walked from the Oval Office, said he took great comfort in that closing statement from the Admiral. And he hoped to hear favorably from them in the next few days. Admiral Morgan decided, in this instance at least, not to raise the possibility of the **Ark Royal** having been sunk by the Russians.

But when Sir Patrick left, the President and his most trusted friend had much to discuss. Because deep in their hearts both men realized that regardless of Argentinian passion, the South Americans had nonetheless committed acts of international mayhem.

"Ask yourself, Paul," said Arnold. "How would it be if everyone rampaged around like that? If France suddenly turned its power on Morocco and told Marrakesh, **we've always owned your country**. What if the Brits did it to Jamaica? If we did it to Japan? If Portugal did it to the eastern part of Brazil? There's no difference. What Argentina did was wrong. And all their pious territorial claims are still wrong, and still unlawful.

"For us, this is one giant pain in the ass. But it's still wrong. And we still have to face the goddamned oil corporation. And, of course, there's still the Russian connection...another vicious act of international barbarism that may have killed more than a thousand people."

President Bedford frowned. "Can we take this step by step? I'll ask the questions, you give the answers, okay?"

"Fine."

"Right. Are you proposing we come straight out and say publicly we do not approve of this in any way? And Argentina must retreat behind her lawful borders?"

"I think we come straight out and say it. But not publicly. I think we send a private communique to the President of Argentina. It must be signed by your good self, saying exactly that, and citing it as the formal opinion of the Pentagon chiefs. Because that's gonna wake 'em up for sure."

"Okay, Arnie. So they either don't answer or they tell us to mind our own business. What then?"

"Well, I guess we have to be prepared to give them an ultimatum..."

"Like what? Nuke Buenos Aires? Because I got a feeling that's what it's likely to take to get 'em to change their minds."

"So have I. And no, not that. No nukes."

"Well, what?"

"I know this is not traditionally my instinct, but how about we do something subtle, something that will leave them scared and uncertain."

"You mean like some Mafia don, some sinister threat…the kind of thing gangsters pull?"

"Yes."

"You mean tell 'em we'll knock down the Presidential Palace if they don't give us back our oil and gas?"

"Not quite. But how about we tell them we are proposing to make it our business to have them vacate the Falkland Islands. And if they have not begun to evacuate by next week, they will surely feel the hot breath of Uncle Sam breathing down their necks. But we will tell them nothing."

"Okay. Then what?"

"We do nothing publicly. We say nothing to anyone. But we very quietly move our Special Forces into the area. And we have the Navy SEALs link up with the British SAS, and we begin to exact a very serious revenge."

"Like what?"

"Well, the Argentinians have a reasonable Navy, don't they? How about we sink a few warships, and maybe knock out a few aircraft. The Special Forces could do that without any trouble. And we admit to nothing. The Argentines may guess we're at the bottom of it, but they'll never know for sure. And they'll never find a way to prove anything."

"Arnie, you think we could inflict so much damage on their military they'd throw up their hands?"

"They might. But in any event, they'd never admit to their people what was happening to them. And we could certainly make it impossible for them to retain their army of occupation in the Falkland Islands. We could make it possible for the remnants of the Royal Navy to retake the territory, and in return to hand over the oil and gas to ExxonMobil and BP. And we sure as hell could throw the Argentinians out of South Georgia."

"I do see the merit of it all, Arnie. But do you think we could really keep the whole thing secret?"

"We'd need two things to help us. We'd want the total cooperation and support of Admiral John Bergstrom, who's in the final six months of his command as head of SPECWARCOM. And we'd need some silent support from Chile, as the Brits had in 1982. That would make a huge difference. Give us a forward base, way down there in South America."

"Do you see a lot of people dying?"

"Not really, Mr. President. I see a lot of very expensive equipment getting trashed. And I see a very angry Argentina demanding to know what's going on. And I see us saying we know nothing about it. It must be the Brits, and that's just their tough luck. Shouldn't have taken their islands in the first place."

"And how, great genius of my life, do you see it all ending?"

"Mr. President, we make the Brits hand over the Falkland Islands to Argentina, peacefully over a period of two years. With cooperation and a certain amount of chivalry.

"We make Argentina thrilled to get the hell out of this highly destructive row they're having with us, or at least with someone. And we make the Brits delighted to get out of the goddamned islands, and somehow save face. That way everyone's happy, or at least happier.

"Of course, part of our price is the restoration of the oil and gas to their rightful owners, ExxonMobil and BP. But we make the Argentinians signatories on the contract for fifty years, and then cut them in for a decent royalty, which begins twenty-four months from restoration. That way we've got the oil companies off your back, Argentina has a piece of the pie, and everyone can go back to work."

"The weakest part of the equation, Arnie, is the Brits, who basically get little from it."

"True. But they get oil money for two years. And compared to the very obvious mess they're in right now, that will be fine. And they will quietly claim ultimate victory, in what the press will call the Secret War. Which will suit us very well.

"And British Petroleum will have its oil and gas back. We'll probably throw in a few further sweeteners that Argentina will have to agree to. But they'll agree to anything, just so long as they can see the time two years from now when the Islas Malvinas formally become a sovereign territory of Argentina…without endless grief from us and the United Nations."

"Very neat, but I'm going to throw one final monkey wrench into the works before we send for John Bergstrom. What about Russia? What about that damned submarine that you think whacked the **Ark Royal**?"

"Russia will slink quietly away if Argentina does not end up owning the oil free and clear. You can trust me on that. It's what they came for."

"And the goddamned nuclear submarine?"

"Well, Mr. President. Since no one ever announces the loss of a nuclear ship that has hit the bottom of a vast, open ocean two miles deep…I actually thought we might sink that."

The President came about as close as he had ever done to shooting a hot jet of Lapsang Souchong down his nose. He groped for his handkerchief, and looked up with a conspiratorial grin.

"Why, yes, Arnie. What a remarkably good idea. That was a very wicked thing it did, killing a thousand men. I think there should be a price for that. Do we tell the Brits?"

"Absolutely not. We tell no one. Ever. And if anyone inquires, we deny it. Just so long as the comrades suspect we know and disapprove of their goddamned antics. 'Specially that lying so-nofabitch who runs their Navy."

MIDNIGHT (LOCAL), SAME DAY LONDON

Like most of the Western world's newspapers, the British press has few, if any, morals. As in the USA, all of their newspapers and almost all of their television channels are thoroughly commer-cial operations, unconcerned with the public or national good, only with the sale of their product. And, generally speaking, the best way to take care of that is to frighten the living daylights out of the population whenever possible. Fear sells, right?

The only operation in the British media that is not, formally, a profit-seeking corporation is the BBC. But that is a fat, government-funded mono-lith stuffed with executives and journalists earn-ing absurd salaries for what they really are, and running up mighty annual expense accounts.

Between them they represent an even more self-interested commercially minded block than those outside the Corporation, and like all gov-

ernment employees they don't have the problem
of their parent operation losing money.

When a big story breaks, the BBC often leads
the way and cheerfully wades into the fray, em-
barrassing the government, humiliating the nation, or the military, as it thinks fit.

The day the Falkland Islands fell, Britain's media collectively went bananas. Headlines unknown
for decades leapt into the minds of the editors.
Words like **Defeat**, **Humiliation**, **Catastrophe**,
and **Disaster** crowded onto front pages and news-
casts, all mixed in with **Royal Navy**, **warships**,
and **surrender**.

And through it all, the press smelled an even
bigger story—had the fleet put to sea inadequately
armed, because of government cuts to the armed
services?

The top brass of the Ministry of Defense
and indeed the Army and Navy were of course
sworn to silence. But an issue as topical as this
could scarcely be held in check. It seemed that
all through that early evening in England, every
retired officer in either service was quite prepared
to bring up the matter of the retired Harrier FA2
fighter jets.

The BBC's first words in their 10:00 p.m.
newscast were: "Was this the war that should never have been fought?"

The early editions of the Sunday newspapers,
traditionally on sale in London's Leicester Square

at 10:30 p.m., were absolutely lethal to the Prime Minister and his Cabinet.

The Sunday **Times** splashed over eight columns on its front page:

ROYAL NAVY BLAMES THE GOVERNMENT
FOR DISASTER IN THE SOUTH ATLANTIC
Falkland Islands fall to Argentina—
British warships "defenseless"

The source, or sources, for this scything statement of fact was in truth a succession of off-the-record conversations with a half dozen retired Admirals and Captains, three of whom had commanded ships in the first Falklands conflict.

Like everyone in a senior position in the Navy, they knew of the reductions in the Senior Service, the cuts to the fleet, the closures of dockyards, the lateness in the arrival of the new aircraft carriers, and above all the four-year gap in the production of a top-class guided-missile fighter jet to fly from the carrier's decks.

And every last one of those sources had instantly said the same thing...**You can't fight a state-of-the-art war at sea facing any threat against aircraft or missiles without fixed-wing air defense aircraft armed with a state-of-the-art medium-range air-to-air missiles system. Hit the archer, not the arrow.**

Great Britain had gone to war 8,000 miles from home without the proper kit—and the British media sensed blood, and they were going to ride this "story" to the bitter end.

ROYAL NAVY SURRENDERS FALKLANDS
Can't shoot, can't fight, Government Cuts Blamed
—Sunday Mirror

Falkland Islands fall in two-hour massacre at sea
ARGENTINA WIPES OUT "DEFENSELESS" NAVY
—Sunday Telegraph

ARK ROYAL SUNK—

ROYAL NAVY

SURRENDERS

FALKLANDS
—News of the World

(This narrow headline ran alongside a huge picture of the British aircraft carrier in her death throes.)

The newspapers devoted pages and pages to interviews with Whitehall Press Officers, and were currently engaged in a relentless, ghoulish search for photographs of the dead. By midnight reporters were besieging naval towns like Portsmouth and Devonport, trying to contact families whose sons and husbands may have gone down with the **Ark Royal**.

By first light the press would have done its work, sowing the seeds of doubt and suspicion in the minds of the British people. Was this government as bad as many people think? Was it just a self-seeking bunch of incompetents, concerned only with their own jobs, and careless of their duty to the armed services?

That's what it looked like as dawn broke over London. And, prophetically, an enormous black rain cloud hovered over Westminster and the Houses of Parliament. At least that's how it seemed. But inside the debating chamber, that cloud seemed to hang over the Prime Minister alone.

He had taken his seat on the government front bench as, high above, Big Ben chimed midnight. He arrived, predictably in this Parliament, to thunderous roars from the Tory benches of, **"Resign!! Resign!! Resign!!"**

And, at the invitation of the Speaker, he had begun the proceedings with a frequently interrupted speech, in which he had endeavored to explain away the obviously shattering defeat of the Royal Navy in the South Atlantic.

The fact was, no one was listening. The scale of the nightmare, the reverberations of the consequences, were too great for any British government. And, with the aid of the media, the loss of those little islands four hundred miles off the coast of Argentina was rapidly being compared in the minds of MPs to the end of all life as they knew it.

When finally the PM did sit down, the Tory leader of the opposition stood up and demanded, "Well, I'm sure the House would like to join me in thanking you profusely for shedding a glaring light on the obvious...now perhaps you would tell the House what you plan to do about the recapture of the islands and the rebuilding of our armed forces?"

Another storm of derisive cheering broke out, and the Prime Minister's Secretary of Defense, Peter Caulfield, climbed to his feet and revealed that in the opinion of his Ministry, it was far too early to make any such announcements, but that the Cabinet would be considering all of the facts later in the morning.

It may have been too early to ascertain the precise moment-to-moment ebb and flow of the short sea battle. It was not, however, too early to discuss the ramifications of the defeat and the surrender.

And the debate was now open to the floor. The first Member of Parliament on his feet was the Tory Alan Knell, who represented Portsmouth, and stated flatly, "The Right Honorable gentleman was warned a thousand times about the dangers of rendering the Royal Navy impotent by scrapping the Sea Harriers. Indeed he was warned by me on many occasions.

"Now his folly has been exposed, can there be any reason why the Right Honorable gentleman should not immediately offer his resignation to his party and to the House?"

Before Alan Knell had regained his seat on the green leather back benches, the Tory side had once more erupted with howls of "**Resign!! Resign!! Resign!!**"

The Speaker stepped in and demanded "**Order!!...Order!!**" And now the Tory MP for Barrow-in-Furness, the Prime Minister's old nemesis on issues of defense cuts, Richard Cawley, was on his feet, to remind the House of the many warnings he had personally issued about the sheer scale of slashes in the Navy and military budgets.

"I personally warned the Right Honorable gentleman about the loss of the Harriers—and what the lack of a beyond-visual-range fighter jet would mean. I told him over and over that without that look-down shoot-down Blue Vixen radar in the Harriers the Navy was in shocking trouble.

"And now there are twelve hundred and fifty of this country's finest men dead in the South Atlantic. And the blame can be laid at no other door than the one that opens into number ten, Downing Street, his home and that of his benighted government..."

The cheer from the Tory benches ripped into the great vaulted ceiling of the House. And again the Speaker stood up and demanded **Order** from the Members.

And so it went on. And five more times the echoing chimes of Big Ben tolled out the hour. Until eventually the Members staggered out into the morning air, the opposition congratulating themselves on a debate well won. Government ministers were wondering whether indeed their leader would have to resign in clear and obvious disgrace.

Throughout the night, they had been watching the glaring newspaper headlines, reading reports from the twenty-four-hour television news programs. The drift against the Prime Minister was becoming very plain. The outrage of the Admirals and Generals was apparent on every page of every newspaper.

The headline on the leader column of the Tory **Daily Mail** was darkly amusing, parodying one of Churchill's most moving wartime speeches. It quoted the Tory party chairman, the droll and urbane Lord Ashampstead...

IF THIS PARLIAMENT SHOULD LAST
FOR ANOTHER WEEK (GOD FORBID),
MEN WILL STILL SAY, "THIS
WAS THEIR DARKEST HOUR"

In the dying moments of the debate, the Tories had pushed for a vote of no confidence in the PM. And this would take place later in the afternoon, after everyone had taken a couple of hours' sleep. The PM did not enjoy a huge majority in the House, and many people thought it might well be his last day in office, since traditionally a Prime Minister who loses such a vote is obliged to resign.

The fallout from those Argentine bombs had rippled a long way north in a very short time. And as the weary British Members of Parliament walked outside into the reality of the dawn, few of them risked a glance at the eight-foot-high statue of Sir Winston, glowering down with withering gaze from his granite plynth right opposite the outer wall of the chamber.

The gloomy heart of London could scarcely have differed more from the joyous heart of Buenos Aires at exactly that same time, midnight in the city on the wide estuary of the River Plate.

There were almost a half million people crammed into the Plaza de Mayo—eight different tango bands were trying to play in harmony with each other, the entire Boca Juniors soccer team, a symbol of national obsession and sometimes of unity, was assembled on a stage erected in the middle of the celebrating throng.

The President was on the balcony of the palace waving to the crowd in company with Admiral Moreno and General Kampf, whom he announced as the great architects of the Argentinian victory in the islands.

To the north side of the square stood the grand edifice of the Catedral Metropolitana, which houses the tomb of Argentina's thus far greatest warrior hero, General Jose de San Martin, one of the early-nineteenth-century liberators of South America from Spanish rule.

It was as if the great man had suddenly risen up to lead them once more in their joy, as the enormous bells of the cathedral chimed out the midnight hour. And the rising anthem of the victors once more rang out over the square—in part a lament for brave men lost, and yet a ferocious roar of triumph, tuneful and rhythmic in its unanimous delivery…**M-a-a-a-l-v-i-n-a-s!!…M-a-a-a-l-v-i-n-a-s!!…M-a-a-a-l-v-i-n-a-s!!**

CHAPTER NINE

1500 (LOCAL), SUNDAY, APRIL 17
NORTH OF THE SAN CARLOS
   SETTLEMENT
EAST FALKLAND

Under the cover of a cold mountain fog, Captain Douglas Jarvis and his seven troopers had moved almost six miles south of the western slopes of Fanning Head. As this Sunday afternoon grew increasingly gloomy, they found themselves north of the San Carlos River, which snakes across the rough, rock-hewn plain between the Usborne and Simon ranges.

The weather had palpably worsened since their arrival on the island nine days earlier. It was colder, wetter, windier, and the nights were closing in. Three weeks from now it would be winter, a vicious South Atlantic winter, with ice-cold gales and snow squalls sweeping up out of the south, where the Antarctic Peninsula comes lancing out of the Larsen Ice Shelf, only 750 miles from Port Stanley.

We have to get the hell out of here was the only thought in the mind of Douglas Jarvis as they moved through the soaking landscape, the all-weather Gore-Tex smocks fastened tight around their hips, hoods pulled down, gloves and waterproof combat boots firm, heavy rucksacks weighing heavier by the hour.

At 1520, Captain Jarvis raised his right fist in a signal to halt. The troopers, walking carefully in pairs, stared ahead across the rough country. In the far distance, still north of the river, they could see the lights of a farmhouse. At least they hoped it was only a farmhouse.

Out to their left, beyond a line of gray jagged rocks, barely moving, they could just make out a large group of grayish, shadowy figures, woolly shadowy figures. "Thank Christ for that," muttered Douglas. "A decent dinner. We've earned that."

And, not for the first time, he appreciated the long evenings of detailed, meticulous training the SAS instructors instill into every last one of their personnel before anyone leaves on a mission.

Back in Hereford, they had undergone intense practice in survival for the Falkland Islands. And the one good lesson they had been taught was that around seven billion sheep regarded the Falklands as home, and had done so for more than a hundred years.

This was a land of ranchers, with huge flocks of sheep raised by the thousands for their wool. For more than a century sheep had been the principal commerce of the islands; almost all the seaports were founded for the export of wool. In recent years, fishing and then oil had crowded into the economy of the islands.

But there were still a zillion sheep grazing these rough but strangely fertile lands of damp grass and ever-flowing mountain rivers. Douglas Jarvis and his team had stumbled upon one of the historic areas of Falklands farming...north of the settlement on the San Carlos River, where sixth-generation shepherds patrolled the gently sloping land as it rose toward the hills.

In their rucksacks, the SAS men had knives and razor-sharp butcher's axes. They had been given specific lessons on how to skin and swiftly cut the carcass. Douglas himself knew how to sever the two hind legs and cleave out the shoulders. They all knew how to slice out the rack of chops.

"Okay, Peter," said Douglas. "Move up to that boulder over there and take out a couple of small ones. Remember Sergeant Jones told us they always taste best."

All eight men knew how to live off the land. That was a basic requirement for any SAS man. And the total silence from their satellite transmissions now made it clear something had gone drastically wrong with the Royal Navy's attack, and perhaps even the landing.

They therefore understood they might be there for a while before rescue, and it was no bloody good whatsoever being starving hungry in the kingdom of the roast leg of lamb.

Trooper Wiggins shrugged off his bergan and unzipped the SSG 69, the renowned Austrian-built bolt-action SAS sniper rifle, which in trained hands can achieve a shot-grouping of less than forty centimeters at a range of eight hundred meters. Peter Wiggins's hands were well trained, and to quote his mate, Trooper Joe Pearson, he had "an eye like a shit-house rat."

Of the 2,000 sheep quietly grazing in these windswept foothills, there were two that were essentially in real trouble.

Trooper Wiggins moved swiftly through the grass to the boulder, and selected his targets, both of them within fifty meters. Two single shots, fired only seconds apart, cracked out from the rifle, and two good-sized lambs dropped instantly from a 7.62mm-caliber bullet slammed into the center of their tiny brains.

Three more troopers raced out to help gather their quarry, and Douglas Jarvis pointed at a cluster of rocks and a few bushes farther north in the rapidly darkening hills. They moved fast, and no kitchen was ever set up faster.

Using their one shovel, they dug a hole three feet by three feet by two feet deep. The wet earth moved easily, and while Troopers Bob Goddard and Trevor Fermer skinned and butchered the lambs, Trooper Jake Posgate found round stones and dropped them into the hole.

Douglas lit a fire from brushwood, right on top of the stones, and they used their butcher's axes to hack some bigger pieces of brush into slim but burnable logs. The entire operation took almost an hour, and when the fire began to die on top of the almost red-hot stones, they suspended two legs of lamb in the hole and spit-roasted them close to the stones for ninety minutes. The glow from the fire could not of course be seen from anywhere except directly over the hole...SAS survival manual, chapter three.

No group of Special Forces had ever been hungrier, and no leg of lamb ever tasted better, despite being a bit burned on the outside. When they finished their supper, they dumped everything into the hole, including the remains of the carcasses, and the wool, and filled it in, rolling a rock over the fresh earth. Only a very highly trained tracker would ever have suspected they had once been there.

By 2200 they were on their way, pushing through the darkness, heading south, down toward Carlos Water, hoping to locate a boat that would get them to the probably unguarded shores of West Falkland. They still carried all their camping gear, rifles, submachine guns, and, wrapped in clear plastic bags, four shoulders of lamb, two legs, and thirty-two chops. But they no longer had explosives, and there was no need to carry water. The wilds of East Falkland were awash with it.

And every hour they fired up the comms system and tried to raise the command center in the Royal Navy ships and on the landing beaches, but it was only a cry in the night. There never had been a reply, and Douglas Jarvis understood there never would be.

He did not dare attempt a direct communication with command headquarters in Northwood, because that would certainly have been located and monitored by the Argentinians. The last thing they needed was a seriously determined search party trying to hunt them down, and picking up a radio fix.

They understood there was almost certainly a small, mildly serious Argentinian force looking for them already, but that was not a problem to eight of the most dangerous war-fighting soldiers on the planet...men who believed that odds of five to one against them in any combat was probably fair.

0900, MONDAY, APRIL 18
STIRLING LINES HEREFORD, ENGLAND

Lt. Colonel Mike Weston, commanding officer 22 SAS, had been studying the POW lists from the

Falkland Islands for three hours. They contained the names of all eight of the men who had conducted the airfield recce at Mount Pleasant under the command of Sergeant Jack Clifton, and all eight of them were in Argentinian custody, and now traveling by sea to the mainland.

Lt. Colonel Weston had twice spoken to his opposite number at the Royal Marine headquarters south of Plymouth, and it seemed all of the SBS men who had landed at Lafonia under Lt. Jim Perry were also safe, and were also traveling by sea to the mainland with the rest of the landing force. The Argentine military had intimated they did not intend to detain them, although their weapons had been confiscated.

An Argentinian ship would land them one month from now at the great Uruguayan seaport of Montevideo on the north shore of the River Plate estuary. The Royal Navy was welcome to pick them up there, and transport them home. The assault ships **Albion** and **Largs Bay**, which had been hit and burned in Low Bay, were to be scrapped, while the **Ocean** had been confiscated, punishment for the destruction of the eight Argentinian fighter jets in battle. She would be renamed **Admiral Oscar Moreno**. Captain Farmer and his crew would be going to Montevideo.

But what was currently vexing Colonel Weston was the fate of Captain Douglas Jarvis and his assault group, which was last seen blowing the summit off Fanning Head. The Colonel knew that part of the mission had been accomplished, and he understood the impossibility of further contact since both SAS command centers at sea had been removed from the line of battle. He also doubted whether there was any form of communication between the various assault forces in the final hours before the surrender on the Lafonia landing beaches.

Which all left Captain Jarvis and his team in a very uneasy form of isolation. Colonel Weston did not like it. But he understood the danger a long-range communiqué from Hereford via satellite might pose to the men. If the Argentinians picked it up, Captain Jarvis would be in serious trouble.

Even the most highly trained SAS group could scarcely cope alone against a force of a thousand men in vehicles and helicopters, employing infrared search radars. Colonel Weston could not accurately assess the scale of Argentine anger about the destruction of their stronghold on Fanning Head, but he guessed they would not be overjoyed.

Thus he did not dare open up a line of voice-contact communication to young Douglas, but he did enter a coded satellite communication urging Douglas and his team to keep their heads well down, and that a rescue operation would be mounted. He also instructed them to open up their comms for one hour at 1800 each evening.

Which meant that, for the moment at least, the SAS team must survive as well as it possibly could. But this was an outstanding group, and Colonel Weston personally believed if anyone could stay alive in such a hostile environment, it was probably his guys, the ones who just blew up Fanning Head.

The slight problem he had was if the Argentinians caught them, they might very well execute them and say nothing. That way Here ford would never know their fate. Although he did not believe them dead, Colonel Weston nevertheless listed Douglas Jarvis, and Troopers Syd Ferry, Trevor Fermer, Bob Goddard, Joe Pearson, Peter Wiggins, Jake Posgate, and the Welshman Dai Lewellwyn officially missing in action.

There had been several communications from SAS families in the hours after it was announced the British had surrendered to the Argentinians. And the regiment was prepared to confirm those men who were in the custody of the new owners of the Falkland Islands, which brought immense relief to all of those waiting at home for news.

"Missing in Action," was, however, an entirely different problem, and no regiment likes to be drawn into these discussions. Thus the duty officers at Stirling Lines would say very little, except the regiment could confirm the surrender, confirm the SAS had knowledge of POWs, and were working to insure everyone returned home safely. For those for whom there was no information, dead or alive, they would confirm nothing, only stating they had no knowledge of the men losing their lives, and would try to keep everyone informed of future developments.

When Jane Jarvis of Newmarket called to inquire about her second cousin Douglas, they said, with regret, they were unable to confirm anything except to the next of kin. Then she rang Douglas's elder brother Alan, who had heard nothing. So she rang her other cousin, Diana Hunter, out in the lush grassland of Lexington, Kentucky.

1100, MONDAY, APRIL 18
HUNTER VALLEY THOROUGHBRED
FARMS

Mrs. Rick Hunter was reading the latest issue of the **Bloodhorse**, scouring the results pages for winning sons and daughters of the Hunter Valley stallions. Rick himself was in bed upstairs, having been up most of the night helping to foal a colossally expensive broodmare by the champion U.S. sire A.P. Indy.

The mare, who in her day had won five Grade One stakes races at Belmont Park, New York, and

Saratoga, had tolerated a long and arduous labor, but at six a.m. had safely given birth to a dark bay colt by the superb Irish-based sire Choisir, a charging Australian-bred champion sprinter who had once heard the thunder of the crowd at Royal Ascot and Newmarket.

Diana had dressed and cooked Rick's breakfast, taken a long walk through the paddocks inspecting the yearlings, and was now sitting in the high sunlit drawing room of the main house, with its views between the tall white Doric columns and out into the front paddocks, where several million dollars' worth of broodmares and their foals grazed contentedly.

When the telephone rang, the former Diana Jarvis was delighted to hear from her cousin back home, and the two of them chatted companionably for a few minutes before Jane came to the point.

"Diana, I don't want to worry you unnecessarily, but I think you know Douglas was sent to the Falkland Islands several weeks ago. Well, I expect you know all about the British surrender... but I just called SAS headquarters at Hereford and they refused to confirm one way or another whether Douglas was dead or alive.

"In a sense that was good, but in another sense I thought it sounded a bit gloomy. They wouldn't tell me more because I'm not next of kin. But they'd probably tell you...and I was calling with the number."

Diana's heart missed about seven beats. She had seen on the twenty-four-hour Fox news channel that the British had surrendered, and all she could remember was that 1,500 men were dead.

"Jane, is there any suggestion the SAS men may have been killed?" she asked.

"Absolutely not. But I read they have lists of the men who have been taken POW, and from what I can gather, Douglas is not on those lists."

"Well, where do they think he might be?" said Diana, whose voice was rising, panic beginning to well up inside her.

"They won't tell me, Di. But they might tell you. They would not even confirm he was on the stupid islands. But it's pretty obvious he was landed. There's nowhere else to be down there in that awful place. I'm just hoping he was not still in one of the warships. I expect you saw the Royal Navy lost eight ships, including the aircraft carrier."

"Is that where most of the fifteen hundred were—the ones who died?"

"Almost all of them. But I've read a lot of reports and no one mentions there were Special Forces aboard the ships. You know, they're always the first ones off, first ones ashore. But I thought you might want to call and see if you can find out anything."

Diana wrote down the number and sat at the desk to the right of the French doors, her heart pounding, half with fear, half with shock. **Douglas, her beloved Douglas, he couldn't be dead, he couldn't be...nothing could be that cruel**.

The call went through quickly. Diana announced herself as the sister, the nearest relative to Captain Douglas Jarvis, and she would like to speak to the commanding officer.

Two minutes later, Lt. Colonel Mike Weston was on the line. "Diana," he said, "we met a couple of years ago, at Douglas's birthday dinner at the Rutland Hotel in Newmarket..."

No one ever forgot meeting the vivacious whip-slim horsewoman from Suffolk, who rode with the maddest of the Irish foxhunters, and was rumored to have been pursued by at least three of the richest men in England.

"Of course I remember," she half lied, recalling vaguely a couple of very attractive, cool-eyed SAS officers at the dinner, and guessing he must have been one of them.

"I was just inquiring about Douglas. I expect you guessed."

"Well, of course I did. But Diana, you will understand this is a very highly-classified operation, and I am limited in what I can say. And I should state right away we do have an eight-man recce team, led by Captain Jarvis, which is currently listed as 'missing in action.'"

"Oh my God! Does that mean you think he's been killed?"

"No. Most certainly not. It means that team almost certainly went to ground after the surrender was announced. Their names simply do not appear anywhere on the casualty lists. That means dead or wounded. And they're not on the POW lists sent to us by the Argentinian military."

"Is that encouraging?"

"To the extent that none of their names appear anywhere. If they'd been caught, and killed or captured, we would have a report to that effect. We have nothing."

"If they are caught, will you be informed?"

"I cannot say that. It rather depends how badly the enemy wants them. But our soldiers are not usually captured by any enemy."

"It's just that god-awful island, isn't it?" she said. "There's no escape from it. I just can't bear the thought of Douglas dying in such a terrible place without anyone knowing what's happened to him."

"Give me your number, Diana. I'll call you the first moment I hear anything. And please, don't fall apart. Douglas has some of our best men with him, and no one's yet mentioned any of them might be dead."

She gave the number of Hunter Valley Farms to the SAS chief, replaced the telephone, and raced upstairs to the bedroom with tears streaming down her cheeks.

She awakened Rick and blurted out, "Ricky, the most terrible thing's happened. Douglas is trapped on the Falkland Islands. He's the leader of an SAS recce team, and he's listed as missing in action."

Rick, who had never told her any details whatsoever of his own career in the U.S. Navy SEALs, opened one eye, and in his deep Kentucky drawl, murmured, "Well, that's kinda bad luck on the Argentinians. Those SAS guys are tough. Real tough. Glad I'm not looking for those suckers."

Diana, of course, had no idea that five years previous her husband had led one of the most daring, bloody operations ever mounted by U.S. Special Forces when he had smashed his way into a Chinese jail on a remote island off Hainan and liberated an entire U.S. submarine crew. And she certainly had no idea how closely he had worked with the British SAS on that one.

Rick Hunter knew all about the SAS, their skill, their brutal training, and the absolutely ruthless quality of their work. And he smiled up at his wife, hoping to see a ray of humor cross her very beautiful, very worried face. But there was no such reaction. She just collapsed into floods of tears and kept saying over and over, "He can't be dead, he can't be dead. Please, please tell me he can't be dead."

"Oh, I can tell you that okay. If Douglas was dead, Twenty-two SAS would know he was dead. They might not know if Douglas and his guys had killed a couple dozen Argies, which is a lot more likely. But they'd know if one of their commanders was dead. Hot damn, you can't kill those SAS guys, not if you don't have an atomic bomb handy. You can trust me on that."

Diana stopped crying, and said quietly, "I just hate the phrase 'missing in action.' It reminds me of all those poor guys who never came home from the Somme, World War One, just blown to pieces."

Rick raised himself on one elbow and took her hand. "Listen," he said, "you haven't followed this war probably as close as I have. And so far the Brits have not admitted they even had Special Forces in the islands. Which means they had the guys in there real early, checking the place out, especially the enemy defenses.

"Ninety percent of the casualties were in the Royal Navy's warships. The rest on the landing beach. Now we know Douglas was not in those ships. You don't take Special Forces eight thousand miles and then leave 'em on some kind of a cruise. You get 'em in there, into the islands.

"And Douglas would not have been on the beaches. The Brits leave all that amphibious work to the Special Boat Service, not the SAS. So wherever Dougy was, he was not on the beach. It's much more likely he and his guys are on the loose somewhere, and do not want to surrender, despite the political situation.

"But they'll be armed to the teeth, and they're trained to live off the land, and from what I read, there's several million sheep there. If I had to guess, I'd say Captain Jarvis was right now sitting with his feet up, in some cave in the mountains, eating roast lamb and reading the **Penguin News** or whatever the hell they call their local paper."

Diana smiled through her tears. She loved her brother dearly, but this six-feet-three-inch ex–U.S. Navy SEAL had completely taken over her life since the day she first met him, when he was casually leaning on a balustrade watching the yearlings being auctioned at one of the big sales in Kentucky.

At the time she was watching a superbly bred chestnut colt, sired by a local stallion, walking gingerly around the ring, tossing his head, trying to stop, glaring through an unmistakable white-rimmed eye, and displaying front legs which, if they ever got him to a racecourse, would represent an equine Miracle at Lourdes, or at least Charles Town, West Virginia.

After a few minutes, the colt was knocked down to an agent from the East Coast for $154,000. Diana shook her head, and the big man standing next to her muttered laconically, "Sold to the man with the white stick, guide dog, and very dark glasses."

She could not help herself laughing. And she turned to the towering American and offered a cheerful conspiratorial glance, which racehorse people do when they have witnessed another practitioner of their craft make a blunder well on the absurd side of dumb.

"That was hard to believe," said the master of Hunter Valley Farms quietly. "Sonofabitch could hardly walk, never mind run."

"I suppose they thought he might straighten up and run a halfway decent mile for some trainer when he's three or something," said Diana. "He's bred to run."

"Since he won't walk around the goddamned sales ring for his owner, beats me why anyone thinks he might run a mile for someone else. Still, guess he might make up into a useful nine-year-old...pulling a very light plow."

Again, Diana Jarvis burst into laughter. And she stared up into the smiling face of the former Commander Rick Hunter, who grinned his lopsided grin and inquired, "English?"

"Yes," she said, holding out her hand. "Diana Jarvis."

"Any relation to the immortal Sir Jack?"

"He was my great-great-uncle," she said. "But don't think I'm important. I have about two thousand Jarvis relatives in Newmarket alone. We didn't just breed horses, you know."

Rick had chuckled, and said, "I'm just going out to take a look at a filly my dad likes. Well, he likes the pedigree. We had a couple of very nice broodmares from the same family. This filly's by an English-raced stallion standing in Ireland, but the bottom line's all American, same family as Alydar."

"Yes," said Diana, "I'd like to come—where's she stabled...does your dad breed right here in Kentucky?"

"Oh, sorry," he'd replied. "Kinda forgetting my manners...Rick Hunter, we own Hunter Valley Farms out along the Versailles Pike..."

"Hunter Valley! That's your family's place?"

"Sure is. My daddy's really retired now. That's why he's not here. I run the place with my good buddy Dan Headley, third-generation stallion man. We're selling tomorrow, but we're usually on the lookout for one new filly, good pedigree and might make a broodmare later."

"Well, I'm very glad to meet you," said Diana Jarvis. "Might even buy one of your yearlings for my French owner."

"You mean he owns you...or a racehorse operation, or both?"

Diana laughed. "Not me, mostly because he's seventy-six years old and has been married four times. But he has some very nice horses in training in Chantilly. And he'd like to start a breeding farm."

"And he's hired a very beautiful young Jarvis to carry him forward," smiled Rick. "Come on, let's go see that filly..."

And so they had strolled out to see the baby racehorse, and then gone for a cup of coffee, then, later, lunch, then much later, dinner. They talked on the phone and met at the autumn sales in England and Ireland.

They never did announce an engagement. They just decided to get married. Diana was thirty, Rick thirty-eight. And they were both completely in tune with the rhythms and the ebb and the flow of the thoroughbred racing season. They were students of the form book, experts on pedigrees, both with a keen eye for the conformation of both young and mature horses.

Rick Hunter could scarcely have wished for a more perfect wife. Diana was relatively wealthy, very beautiful, and vastly well-connected in Ireland, especially at the world's most important racehorse breeding empire of Coolmore in County Tipperary, where her family had been sending mares for thirty years. In turn, as chatelaine of Hunter Valley Farms, no horsewoman could have filled that role better than Diana Jarvis.

Rick did not often see her upset. And he hated to see it now. But he understood how close she and Douglas had been, and he knew how unnerving it was to be uncertain whether a close relative was dead or alive.

He climbed out of bed, and took her in his arms. "Don't worry," he said. "I'll make a couple of calls and see what I can find out. I'm coming downstairs in a minute. Let's have a cup of coffee…give me ten."

When he reached the kitchen, he could see she was still hugely upset. She poured the coffee and managed to spill some of it on the table, just as Dan Headley poked his head around the door, saying, "Hi, Rick. That Storm Cat mare just foaled, thank Christ. Colt, dark bay, white blaze like his dad. He's standing...hey, Di, what's up? He been beating you up again?"

All three of them laughed at this. Rick, the iron-man gentle giant, who had been known to weep at the death of a favorite Labrador, said, "Di's just a bit upset because her brother's been posted missing in action in the Falklands. But no one's saying he's been killed or wounded, which normally means he hasn't."

"That's Doug, right? The SAS Captain?"

"That's him, Dan. Tell her he's probably okay."

"Well, Di, those Special Forces Regiments keep very strong tabs on their guys. I'd say if anything had happened they'd sure as hell know. How many guys are with him?"

"Seven troopers, all veterans. None of them on the POW lists, or the killed and wounded lists."

"SAS?" said Dan Headley. "They're on the run. And now that the Brits have surrendered, I wouldn't worry yourself. Chances are the Argentinians won't catch 'em anyway. Hey...remember that Special Forces helicopter that crashed on the Magellan Strait in the last Falklands War? There were six or eight SAS guys in there, and they all just vanished. But every one of 'em got back to Hereford. Christ knows how. I just read a book about it."

Diana was marginally consoled, and she felt better speaking to these two former U.S. Navy warriors. But she still asked her husband to make a phone call to anyone who might be able to reach Douglas.

0830, SAME DAY
SPECWARCOM HQ
CORONADO, SAN DIEGO

It was a pressure day for Rear Admiral John Bergstrom, Commander Special War Command—Emperor SEAL, that is—lord of the most feared fighting force in all the U.S. armed services.

His old friend Admiral Arnold Morgan had been on the line at 0700 checking if he was able to fly immediately to Washington. His new wife, Louisa-May, wanted him to attend a performance by the Bolshoi Ballet in Los Angeles this evening, and there was a general buzz around the SEALs' California base that the U.S. government was likely to intervene in the Great Britain–Argentina negotiations over the Falkland Islands.

At 0845, his private line rang again. Arnold Morgan was calling from the White House, where he was ensconced with the President.

"I don't know why the hell they don't just make you President and have done with it," said the SEAL boss.

"Out of the question," replied Arnold. "I'm just helping out. Remember, I'm officially retired."

"Sounds like it," said Admiral Bergstrom. "Peaceful days in your twilight years. This is your second call this morning. I guess you're planning to start a war somewhere."

"Well, only in the most limited possible way."

"Don't tell me. It's the Falklands, right? The U.S. government cannot afford to let this bunch of Argentinian cowboys rampage all over someone else's legal territory."

"Well," said Arnold, disliking the concept of being second-guessed by the suave and shortly-to-retire SEAL chief, "I'll just say you're kinda on the right lines."

"And what would you and the President like me to do? Send in a couple dozen guys and chase 'em back to Buenos Aires or wherever the hell they live?"

"Again, John, I'd say you were on the right lines. But both the President and I would like you to come in and have a private visit with us here in the Oval Office."

"Tomorrow okay?"

"Tomorrow!" roared Arnold. "This afternoon would be pretty damn late..."

"Okay, okay. I'll leave now. Take off in one hour, which will get me into Andrews at 1750."

"Thanks, John. We'll have the helo waiting at Andrews. See you at 1800."

"Bye, Arnold."

"Jesus Christ," said Rear Admiral Bergstrom, picking up the phone to dial his soon-to-be-furious new wife. But before he could do so, his private line rang again, and not many people had that number. So he always answered.

"Admiral, this is a voice from the past, Rick Hunter from Lexington, Kentucky."

"Hey, Commander Hunter!" John Bergstrom was genuinely pleased to be talking to the best Team Leader he ever had, a combat SEAL who had carried out three awe-inspiring demolition missions—one in the heart of Russia, another way behind the lines in Red China, and one in the middle of a brand-new Chinese naval operational base in the steamy jungles of southeastern Burma, or Myanmar, or whatever the damn place was now called.

"Now this is an unexpected pleasure," said Admiral Bergstrom. "I often think about you, Ricky. For a lot of years I believed it would probably be you taking over the helm when I finally vacated this chair."

"Can't say I haven't missed it. Just guess I didn't feel quite the same after they court-martialed Dan Headley."

"No, I understood then, and like a lot of other people, I still understand. It was a source of the greatest regret to me that Lt. Commander Headley was driven out, and you went with him..."

"Sure. But life goes on. Dan's fine now. He and I run my family's thoroughbred farm, Hunter Valley, out in the Blue Grass. We still have some fun."

"Fun like you had when you worked for me?"

"Nossir. Not that much."

John Bergstrom chuckled. "Ever thought about coming back?"

"Not more than about twice a day."

"Well, let me ask you this—if that damned court-martial four years ago had never happened, how long would you have wanted to stay a Navy SEAL?"

"'Bout a thousand years."

Both men were silent as the tragedy of the past seemed to sweep over them. "You were the best, Ricky. The best I ever saw..."

"Thank you, sir."

"Now, perhaps you better tell me what you wanted from me?"

"Sir, a year ago I married an English girl, Diana Jarvis. Her brother Douglas is a Captain in Twenty-two SAS. I've only met him twice, but he's a real good guy, an ex-para, won a Military Cross in Iraq.

"And right now he's somehow trapped on the Falkland Islands with his troop. Listed as missing in action. I was wondering whether you could find out anything for us…Diana was very close to him and she's completely distraught. Thinks he might be dead."

"Jesus, Rick. I'm leaving for Washington in the next five minutes. But I'll do what I can, and I'll get back to you tomorrow…I know the CO at Hereford pretty well…Captain Douglas Jarvis, right? Gimme your number…"

Ten minutes later, with the words of another distraught wife still ringing in his ears, Admiral Bergstrom was on his way out of the office, having escaped the rigors of Tchaikovsky's **Swan Lake**.

Thirty minutes after that he was hurtling down the NAS runway on North Island, San Diego, headed east in a U.S. Navy Lockheed EP-3E Aries, nonstop to Andrews Air Force Base, Maryland. He had dismissed Louisa-May and Pyotr Tchaikovsky temporarily from his mind.

But the memory of Rick Hunter lingered in the mind of the Coronado boss: **he was the toughest, strongest, steadiest SEAL leader I ever knew. Brilliant marksman, deadly, and fearless in both armed and unarmed combat, could probably swim the Pacific, and expert with high explosive. He must be nearly forty now, but I never met one that good in all my years with the SEALs. Shame about his brother-in-law.**

They rustled up a couple of ham-and-cheese sandwiches during the flight, and there was coffee supplied by one of his assistants, Petty Officer Riff "Rattlesnake" Davies, assault team machine gunner by trade, wounded with Commander Hunter on that last mission in Burma.

The five-hour journey dragged by. The Admiral and Rattlesnake swapped yarns, mostly about the newly topical Commander Hunter. "I guess you'll never know how brave he was," said Davies. "Jesus, when we came under fire in that boat from those Chinese helicopters, I thought we'd never get out alive.

"And there was Commander Hunter, almost unconscious in the boat, blood pumping from a major wound in his thigh, still blasting away with a machine gun, yelling orders at the rest of us...I never saw courage like that..."

"I know, Riff. Don't think I don't know."

They landed on time, and the U.S. Marine helicopter flew them directly to the White House lawn. Three minutes later, Admiral Bergstrom entered the Oval Office and shook hands with the President and Admiral Morgan, who glanced at his watch and observed it was two minutes and thirty seconds past 1800, which made the SEAL chief from California very marginally late. Nonetheless, Arnold couldn't understand what was happening around here. Nearly three minutes late for the last dog watch! Jesus, standards were sure as hell slipping.

All three of the men in the Oval Office had served in the U.S. Navy, and Arnold's insistence on charting the time of day in strictly naval warship terms unfailingly made the President laugh. Which was just as well. Right now he did not have a whole lot to laugh about, since the top execs at ExxonMobil were growing angrier by the day that "these goddamned gauchos had somehow run off with about two billion dollars' worth of our oil and gas, and no one seems to be doing a damn thing about it."

President Bedford could see their point. And it was a source of immense relief to him that his two guests were probably the only two men in all of the United States who could do a damn thing about it. And, better yet, they were apparently ready to do so.

"Gentlemen," he said, "I'm glad to see you both. And I should say, right away, that this Falklands problem has been extremely difficult for me, for all the obvious reasons. Arnold is the only person with a really solid plan. And I think he should outline it for us both...I'll send for some coffee..."

"John," Arnold began, "you know the problem we have sending our armed services to fight someone else's war. The President does not want to do it, and I agree with him. However, we have another problem damn nearly as big. ExxonMobil think we have sat back and passively allowed the Argentinians to run off with their very expensive oil and gas."

"Yeah, I've been following it," said Admiral Bergstrom. "And I've been wondering what was going to happen. You want my guys to go in and blow the place up?"

John Bergstrom was a droll man, with a sardonic sense of humor, which is a common virtue in his line of work. Nevertheless, neither Arnold Morgan nor the President of the United States ever quite knew whether he was joking.

This time he was not. "You aren't going to negotiate the Argentinians out of there," he said. "Because they see the place as some kind of birthright. Which kinda brings us back to the ancient mantra of the U.S. Navy SEALs...**there are very few of the world's problems that can't be solved by means of high explosive.**"

The President laughed. Nervously. "Go on, Arnold," he said.

"In a sense, I have to agree with John," he said. "We are not going to persuade Buenos Aires to get out of Great Britain's Falkland Islands. I actually think they would probably fight 'til the last drop of their blood had seeped into the soil of their beloved Malvinas."

"Jesus, we're getting briefed by a poet," said Admiral Bergstrom. "I like that—culture before the mayhem."

Arnold grinned. But he remained extremely serious. "In order to get them to back down, we gotta first frighten them, then move in as the great conciliators. We need to be the voice of reason, and we have to get that oil and gas back on the road.

"In broad terms, we want a deal where the Brits volunteer to give up their sovereignty in twenty-four months, in return for British Petroleum being allowed back in there with ExxonMobil.

"But right now we have reason to believe the Argentinians plan to hand that oil project over to the Russians, and we cannot allow that. So we need to persuade Buenos Aires that unless they come to heel, they will lose everything. And we gotta do that without the world knowing how hard we are putting the arm on them."

"Will the Argentines realize how hard we're putting the arm on them?" asked Admiral Bergstrom.

"Yes, but they will not be able to prove it's us. I am proposing we launch a succession of highly classified assaults on their military hardware—fighter aircraft, warships, missile launchers."

"Lemme have a sip of coffee, Mr. President," said Admiral Bergstrom. "I just realized what I'm doing here, and I'm trying not to go into shock."

"You're here, John," said Arnold, "to tell us whether your guys could go into the islands and take out the very few warships patrolling those waters, and then get rid of all the fighter aircraft stationed at Mount Pleasant and that other airfield of theirs on Pebble Island."

"You mean, presumably, quietly and without getting caught?"

"Correct. I mean to put the Argentinians in a position where they know they are being badly knocked about militarily, but do not wish to admit it, and will finally agree to negotiate—for both the territory and the oil and gas...I have a hunch the Brits will be happy to get out with a little pride, and their share of the oil."

"Anyone given any thought to how my guys get in there?"

"Not really," said Arnold. "But it obviously can't be by air, we can't risk a parachute drop. So that means by sea, and we can't send in a warship, so that means a submarine, I guess."

"Uh-huh," said John Bergstrom. "Any idea how many guys this will take?"

"Not really. Would you think, maybe, two teams of sixteen?"

"That's not many—not to take out all the fighter jets on two airfields, not when you consider the recce."

"No, it's not. But my first question is, John, can it be done?"

"Sure it can be done. My guys are specialists. They can do it, and they won't get caught. I would have just one request, and that's for you to arrange an immediate evacuation by air, if somehow they get cornered. I want to help, and I will conduct the operation, but I'm not sending the guys into the goddamned Malvinas on a suicide mission."

Arnold Morgan knew Admiral Bergstrom was about to retire, and he smirked at the SEAL chief. "I don't want to give you a chapter for your book," he said. "We're seeing the Chilean Ambassador right here early tomorrow morning. We'll have an evacuation plan.

"First sign of serious trouble, the guys are out of there, direct to the Magellan Strait, land at Punta Arenas on the Chilean side."

"Since we can't get a fixed-wing transporter in there, Arnie, guess you're talking helicopters?"

"Just one, John. We'll use one of the Navy's new Sikorsky Super Stallions, the CH-53E, holds fifty-five Marines. We'll bring it in under fighter escort, and immediately out again. She's fast, and she's armed with three heavy machine guns. Flies above eighteen thousand feet. We'll be fine, especially if your guys have achieved even half their objectives."

"Any thoughts how we get the guys in there?"

"The final part of the insert will definitely be by submarine and inflatables. And we do have an L.A.-class boat on the way down there. But we need to move fast. And I know you'll want a few days' training for the SEAL teams. We can't really afford another two-week journey after that—you think we could make a drop landing at sea?"

"The Brits did it last time off South Georgia," replied Admiral Bergstrom. "Which means we could do it. Just don't want to get too near the Falklands coast and wind up on the goddamned Argentine radar."

"No. We definitely don't want to do that," said Arnold. "But we do have a time problem. The longer we leave this, the better organized the Argentinian defenses will be. So we'll leave it to you to move quickly."

"Oh, Arnie. One thing more. To conduct an operation like this we're going to need kit, especially bombs, sticky bombs and C-4, that is. We'll need enough gear and food to let them live off the land, but they can't carry it all—not with a parachute drop into the ocean."

"No. I was talking to the President about that. I think we'll go for HALO and drop some stuff in, soon as they pick a safe landing area."

"Okay. That'll work."

"One other thing, John. Who's gonna lead this thing? We need a very special guy, an experienced veteran commander who won't make mistakes."

"My guys don't make mistakes, Arnie."

"I know they don't. But this operation is very sensitive. It's got to be carried out by ghosts. By a Ghost Force. Ghosts with hammers in their hands."

Admiral Bergstrom turned to the President. "I think I mentioned, sir, we're being briefed by a poet."

"Yes, I'd noticed," chuckled Paul Bedford. "But I'm loving this conversation, so keep going, get me off the hook with the biggest oil company in the country."

"Well, do you have any thoughts about a Team Leader?" asked Arnie.

"I've got one thought, okay? I know who I'd like. But I can't get him. He retired a while ago. But we got a couple of pretty good instructors who've been on missions. I'll probably recall one of them."

"Okay, we'll leave it to you...but can you tell me the name of your first choice?"

"I don't think so. He left the Navy in rather controversial circumstances."

"Oh, did he now?" asked Arnold Morgan, slyly. "Wouldn't be running a racehorse farm, would he? Not the great Commander Rick Hunter?"

"I wish," said Admiral Bergstrom.

1930, TUESDAY, APRIL 19
HUNTER VALLEY FARMS

Rick and Diana were checking the stallion covering lists. There was a busy night ahead for three of the youngest sires, and big horse vans were already lining up in the lower driveway, bringing in wildly expensive blue-blooded mares from local farms.

At the same time there were six mares who had been in residence for several weeks expected to foal tonight. Rick and Diana usually had dinner at around eight o'clock, and then pulled on their jackets to tour what Rick called the Springtime Battleground, where the fortunes of the farm for another year were more or less decided.

The major yearling and foal sales later in the year were, of course, the principal source of income, but the mares had to go in foal first, and reputations of young stallions were on the line long before any of their progeny made it to the racecourse.

Rick, who was once described as the fittest man who ever wore sea boots, had just completed two hours in the gym he had built in the basement of the house. He worked there four evenings a week, and also ran a hard five miles on the other three days. When he left the Navy three and a half years ago, he had vowed to remain at the peak of his fitness for as long as possible. Thus far he had never faltered.

He and Diana often rode out around the farm together, and they were both used to long walks through the paddocks, looking at various yearlings and mares. But today had been trying. Diana was still extremely upset about Douglas, and had not wanted to venture out despite the invention of mobile phones. Her husband had been restraining her from calling Hereford again.

"Leave it," he had told her. "The SAS CO will most certainly call when he hears something. And Admiral Bergstrom will definitely be speaking to them. He promised."

But Diana could not be comforted. Her only thought was of her lovely Douglas somehow dead on some frozen landscape in the South Atlantic, soldier unknown.

And when the phone rang at 1941, she almost jumped out of the chair. The call identifier showed California, and it was indeed Admiral Bergstrom for Rick Hunter.

"Good evening, Admiral," said the ex–SEAL Commander. "Any news?"

"Yes, I've spoken to Mike Weston in Hereford, and he says they are sure that Douglas and his team are still alive. Otherwise the Argentinians would have included them on the lists of the dead. Hereford HQ believes they have declined to surrender, because they apparently did complete a highly destructive part of their mission—according to Colonel Weston, it was the only big hit the Args took on the Falkland mainland."

"Jesus. You mean they really are on the run, through those mountains, trying to get out?"

"I do. And Mike Weston did remind me the Argentinians might very well be after them in a determined way."

"That's less good news," replied Rick.

"It is, but Weston said it would be a helluva good soldier who managed to kill one of that group. Apparently Doug Jarvis has seven trained killers with him. Hereford say they're not worried and expect to hear something positive any day."

"Well, that's a relief, Admiral. I guess the only problem is the sheer weight of numbers the Argentinians can throw into a hunt, right?"

"That, Ricky, is the problem. They are the SAS, and they are reputed to be indestructible. Trouble is, there's not many of them, and they may be against a determined enemy."

"I guess right now there's no plans to go in and try to save them?"

"Well, certainly not from the defeated and battered Brits. But I think we may have to do something to help...the Argentinians after all have stolen all that ExxonMobil oil and gas...by the way, you wouldn't consider giving us a hand, would you?"

"Who, me? What do you mean?"

"Well, Rick, I won't pretend we've ever really replaced you, because we haven't. And everyone was real sorry when you resigned your commission, although we understood. I just wondered if you'd consider helping us save your brother-in-law."

"Jeez. That's one hell of a question."

"Wanna talk about it?"

"Well, I can't see the harm in talking about it. But I can't come out there, not in the foaling season."

"How about I come visit you?"

"Sure, any time."

"How about tomorrow?"

"Okay. What time?

"Guess I could leave around six a.m. Get in there around four hours later, 1300 for you."

"Fine. I'll meet you. Blue Grass Field, Lexington. U.S. Navy jet, right?"

"I'm gonna be there, Rick. See you tomorrow."

Diana, who had been waiting on the other side of the room, said, "Who's coming?"

"Admiral Bergstrom. You'll like him. He's head of the U.S. Navy's Special Forces."

"But he hasn't found Douglas?"

"No, but he's on the trail. The SAS are certain he's not dead. And John Bergstrom is working on a plan to get them all out. The Brits, who've surrendered, can't do much."

"Why does he need to come here?"

"Wants to talk to me about it. He and I worked on several missions together."

"But you've retired from the Navy and all that stuff."

"Kinda hard to replace a top man," grinned Rick.

1300, WEDNESDAY, APRIL 20
BLUE GRASS FIELD
LEXINGTON, KENTUCKY

Rick Hunter was not tired, which was surprising since he had hardly slept all night. Twice he had been up and out to the covering shed, where a young stallion was not only playing hell but, much worse, was refusing to cover a mare, for which the farm was charging $150,000.

A couple of the more youthful stallion men were about to give up when the boss arrived. "I know he's difficult," Rick had told them, "but unlike any of you, that stallion often earns three hundred thousand dollars a night...I don't care if he demands a candlelit dinner, a string quartet, and a bottle of Chateau Latour for him and the mare...**If he does, then go get it for him, hear me!** But get that mare covered."

Somehow they persuaded the stallion it was not that bad an idea, and twenty minutes later he agreed. Rick went back to bed, and spent the remainder of the night thinking about his life as a U.S. Navy SEAL—the training, the stealth, the terrible danger, the attacks, the supreme fitness, the camaraderie. **My God, what days they were... could I still do it?...Just one more time? Was John Bergstrom joking when he asked me? Christ, guess I'll find out before too long**.

And now he could see the Lockheed Aries coming in to land. The airport was quiet, and he watched the U.S. Navy aircraft come screaming out of the west, over some of the most famous thoroughbred racehorse pastures on earth. He watched it flare out when it reached the runway, and touch down gracefully. The pilot had, after all, probably spent a lot of his working life landing on aircraft carriers. Blue Grass Field was a lot more steady.

Five minutes later he was shaking hands with his old boss, Rear Admiral John Bergstrom, the unrecognized head of SPECWARCOM, walking without uniform through the airport, like just a visiting horse breeder.

They exchanged the warmest greetings, and a thousand memories surged over them both. And by the time they had driven back to Hunter Valley, it was clear in Rick's mind the Admiral wanted him to be a part of the mission to bail out the Falklands for the Brits and the oil companies.

He also had the distinct impression the temporary loss of Douglas Jarvis was precisely the impetus the Admiral needed to try and persuade him to join the mission. By the time they pulled through the big stone gates of the farm, Rick only understood John Bergstrom wanted him to be involved, but whether as a mere planner or instructor he was uncertain.

He decided to ask the big question before they entered the house. "Sir," he said, "are you going to ask me to join you in the back room and help plan the assault?"

The Admiral hesitated. "Not quite."

"You mean you want me to join the guys on the mission, and do whatever we need to get those Argentinians into line, and the SAS out of there?"

"Rick, I want you to command it."

"Who, me?" he replied, stunned at the dimension of the request. "But I'm not even in the Navy."

"As an ex–SEAL Commander, you could be back in by this evening. Guys like you have special rules in Coronado. I am perfectly empowered, any time I wish, to re-recruit one of my best men for a specific mission. Particularly someone with a record like yours."

"Sir, you realize I would have to decline this out of hand were it not for the...er...complication of Diana's brother?"

They were still sitting in the car, the Admiral enjoying this rather optimistic chat, Rick Hunter frozen to the spot with apprehension and God knows what else. Every instinct told him this was nuts, that he could not leave the farm at this time of the year, he could not just pack up and go on some diabolically dangerous mission with the SEALs, and perhaps get himself killed.

And yet...and yet...the thrill of combat, the overpowering sensation of working with top guys against an almost certainly inferior enemy. Oh, boy, how often had he dreamed it, tasted it, remembered the desperation, the fear and the triumph, and the friendship and the laughter. **Hell, he thought, once a SEAL always a SEAL**.

He thought of his Trident, his own personal badge of courage, tucked in his shirt drawer, the little badge he still polished when the mood took him. He thought of the work underwater, the rush of adrenaline when he and his boys blew up two warships in Burma. And what about that power station they'd knocked down, and the getaway, under Chinese fire? Jesus Christ, he'd remember that day 'til he died.

John Bergstrom was smiling, as if he knew what his finest ever SEAL was thinking. "Nothing like it, old buddy, is there? Nothing quite like it."

"Nossir. There's not. How long?"

"A few days' training. Then two weeks max, in and out."

"How do we get in?"

"Submarine, then inflatables to the beach, a totally deserted beach."

"Sir, it's gonna take a submarine two weeks to get down there. How come you're saying two weeks start to finish?"

"You'll fly down, and join the submarine."

"Where?"

"In the middle of the ocean. We're planning a drop zone in the Atlantic a hundred miles north of the Falklands."

"Jesus, sir. I've never gone in by parachute."

"I know. That's what the three days' training are for. You know the rest better than I do."

At that point, Diana came out of the house walking toward the dark green four-wheel-drive, off-road vehicle that bore the logo of Hunter Valley Thoroughbreds.

"I'm sure it's very private," she said and smiled. "But you might be more comfortable inside. I've made you some coffee and there's some lunch when you're ready."

She walked toward the passenger's side, looking extraordinarily beautiful in tight jodhpurs and boots, with a white shirt and light blue cashmere sweater.

She held out her hand to Admiral Bergstrom, and cast him one of those half-smiles that had bewitched some of the wealthiest men in England. "Afternoon, Admiral," she said confidently. "I've heard much about you. All good."

"Diana," he replied, "so far, I'd say you make a perfect wife for the best commander I ever served with."

"I'm trying my best," she said, "as a foreigner."

"People from New York are regarded as foreigners around here," Rick chimed in. "Folk from

Newmarket, like Diana, are more or less regarded as natives."

"Where's Newmarket?" asked the Admiral.

"England," he said. "Racehorse capital of Europe. Diana's family has been raising and training thoroughbreds there since before America was invented."

"Then I'm doubly impressed," said the Admiral, smiling. "Beauty and background, the unstoppable combination."

The three of them walked back to the house together, and it was the Admiral who brought up the subject of the missing Douglas Jarvis. "I'm really very sorry to hear about this, Diana," he said. "But at least Hereford has a much clearer picture now.

"It seems Douglas and his team carried out the demolition part of their mission a short while before the Royal Navy and the British landing force surrendered to the Argentinians. He was apparently operating in a remote part of East Falkland and was out of touch with his command center in the aircraft carrier, which was, of course, sunk.

"So while the free world shuddered at this British setback, Douglas and his men were stuck up the side of some mountain, with no idea what just happened. In Hereford's opinion, they are keeping their heads well down, since they were apparently the only group that did inflict serious damage on the enemy. Under those circumstances, no Special Forces Commander wants to surrender."

"So the SAS are more or less certain they're not dead?" asked Diana, her face clouded with worry.

"Oh, no one thinks they're dead. It's just a matter of getting them out."

"But who will get them out now the British have surrendered?"

"I'm afraid that may be us, Diana. The U.S. had some serious oil and gas interests in those islands, and no one's very thrilled the Argentinians have seen fit to grab it all."

"Gosh, you're not talking about a new invasion, are you—by the Americans?"

"Quite the opposite. But we may send a small team of Special Forces down there and take a careful look at what's happening. Since I talked to Rick, I more or less decided we'd hook up with Douglas and his guys and perhaps they could all leave together. U.S. submarine."

"Oh, that would be marvelous. I can't tell you how worried I've been. I've hardly slept since I heard he was posted as missing in action."

"Yeah, it's a kind of sinister phrase," replied John Bergstrom. "And in this case, I consider it unnecessary. There's no evidence whatsoever that Douglas is even missing, never mind in action. But the Brits' principal radio satellite hookup is on the bottom of the Atlantic, so they can't talk to him."

Diana had really warmed to the SEAL chief and his reassuring words. But in the back of her mind she wondered what he could possibly be doing here in the middle of Kentucky, in the middle of the foaling season, having arrived in a private U.S. Navy jet, to speak to her long-retired husband. And a tiny warning bell was ringing in her mind.

Long used to making firm decisions in the purchase of racehorses that cost hundreds of thousands of dollars, Diana Hunter decided on a direct approach. She went into the kitchen and collected a tray bearing a large, engraved silver coffeepot, a breeder's prize Rick's father, Bart, had been awarded after a Hunter Valley–bred colt had won the Travers Stakes at Saratoga.

There was a fine framed oil painting of the colt on the wall behind the Admiral. And out beyond the west-facing portico, in the stallion barns, the same hard-knocking racehorse was trying to make a name for himself in the less strenuous career bestowed only upon those who could **really** run.

"Admiral," she said as she poured the coffee, "why have you come to see us? What do you want Rick to do for you?"

John Bergstrom knew that to hedge or evade would be absolutely fatal. This very smart English girl would pick up those vibes in a split second. "Diana, I want him to come to Coronado with me and help with this mission.

"Rick has a vested interest. He wants success as much as I do. Partly for me, for old times' sake, but mostly for you. He wants to get Douglas out of

there, and my command has the people, the backup, and the necessary power to achieve that."

He smiled at her and added, "By the way, I
have not really asked him yes or no. Perhaps you'd
like to do that for me."

Diana Hunter had to sit down. But before she
could gather herself to speak, John Bergstrom
added, "If Rick accepts, we'll get Douglas out. If
he declines, I hope we'll get Douglas out. That's
the difference.

"You're married to a Special Forces Com-
mander who's one of the best there's ever been.
They didn't give him that Distinguished Service
Cross for nothing."

Lamely, Diana said, "What Distinguished
Service Cross?"

"It's the second-highest decoration in the
United States armed services, right up there with
the Medal of Honor. Rick has it, bestowed upon
him by the President. I don't just want him, Diana, I need him…and so, in a way, do you."

"Rick," said his wife, "do you want to go? Do
you think you ought to go?"

"How can I not go?" said the big ex–SEAL
Team Leader. "How could I live with myself if
somehow Douglas died? I'd always think I could
have saved him. And, strangely, so would you."

"But what about the farm? We're so busy."

"Dad will come back to work for three weeks.
He and Dan could manage. If necessary, Dan's

father would step in. Hunter Valley and its staff would cope, like they always have. And anyway, I'd rather lose a couple of foals than Douglas... wouldn't you?"

Diana did not answer. But she turned again to Admiral Bergstrom. "Do you mind if I call you John?" she said.

"Not a bit."

"Then, John, will you please tell me, how dangerous is this?"

"It's like everything. The better you plan, the more you think about the problems and the solutions, the greater your chances of success. Frankly, I am not too bothered about my guys getting killed by the Argentinians, because it won't happen. They'll have a ton of backup, by air and, if necessary, by sea.

"If it came to a choice between flattening Argentina's Mount Pleasant garrison and everyone in it, or losing my guys in battle, there's only one answer to that. 'Good-bye, Mount Pleasant.' This is a mission where we must be careful, but it's not nearly so dangerous as the last three operations Rick commanded."

"Well, I seem to be in a bit of a spot," said Diana. "If I object, and Douglas dies, it's true, I'll always think it was my fault for stopping Rick going in to save him. But what if I lost them both? What if neither of them came back? Again, I would not forgive myself for letting him go..."

"Di, the issue is Douglas," said Rick. "And we've got to try. I can't just sit here and do nothing when I have the Commander of SPECWARCOM sitting right here damn near begging me to lead this mission. I think all three of us in the room understand that...especially you, Di...now tell me, do I go with your blessing?"

"Yes, Rick, you must go with my blessing. But God help you both."

Commander Hunter then turned to face his CO. "Sir, you must ask me formally."

"I understand," said Admiral Bergstrom. "And I will do so. Will you, Rick Hunter, accept a new commission in the U.S. Navy, and, with all the privileges and responsibilities of your former rank of Commander, lead the U.S. Navy SEALs in the forthcoming operation to the Falkland Islands?"

"Affirmative, sir."

1500, THURSDAY, APRIL 21
SPECWARCOM HQ
CORONADO

"Hello, Admiral Morgan? Hi, John Bergstrom here. Just wanted to tell you Commander Hunter has agreed to return to the Navy for one single mission and lead the operation to the Falkland Islands."

"Has he really? Hey, that's terrific, John. Well done. Silver-tongued bastard."

"Wasn't much trouble, Arnie. He misses it all like hell."

"Don't we all? Where is he now?"

"He's right here, and still as fit as anyone on the station. He slotted right in, just like he never left. Some of the guys who'll go with him still remember him pretty well. Some of 'em are still in awe."

"So am I, John. How the hell he ever got out of that mess in Burma, I guess we'll never know."

"I just felt so much better with him in charge. He has a way with the guys. They always feel that serving under Commander Hunter you got a darned good shot at getting out alive. They'll follow him into hell if they have to."

"I know. By the way, how does he feel about the air drop into the ocean?"

"I'll tell you later, he's just starting a two-day airborne course right now."

"You worked out an assault landing plan yet?"

"Sure have. The guys move out of the submarine and straight into Pebble Island. They fix bombs to every one of the fifteen fighter aircraft on the ground, with six-hour delayed fuses. Then they get out, by boat, back to East Falkland. That way they make the Args concentrate their search forces up there in the wrong place. Go in with a bang. Immediately get 'em off balance."

"Commander Hunter okay with that?"

"It was Commander Hunter's plan."

CHAPTER TEN

1500, THURSDAY, APRIL 21
NAVAL AIR STATION
NORTH ISLAND, SAN DIEGO

Rick Hunter gazed up at the scaffold from which he was, in a few moments, going to jump. It looked high, thirty feet to the platform. He could see the big fan up there and two SEAL instructors reading off a list.

There was a slight knot in the stomach of the veteran Commander. Standing here in this huge aircraft hangar, waiting his turn, was not much short of an ordeal.

Most of his younger colleagues were already experts, having completed the compulsory course at the new SEALs airborne training facility—regarded since 2009 as essential for modern Special Forces. But Rick had never done any parachute course, mostly because, as the most powerful swimmer on the base, he'd been too busy underwater.

And now the instructors were getting ready to begin the first jump.

"Okay, sir, come on up."

Rick walked to the iron ladder and began to climb. At the top he stepped onto the platform and looked over the edge.

"Jesus Christ," he muttered. "It looks damned high."

By now they were buckling the harness around him, checking the line that was attached to the fan. "Okay, sir," snapped the dispatcher. "All set. You're going to do about half a dozen of these, so let's get the first one over. It's dead easy...step to the edge and jump out when I say Go."

Rick stepped. **"Go!"** yelled the instructor, slapping him on the shoulder. And against all his better judgment, Rick leapt into space, falling down dead straight until the fan above whirred, and then slowed him right down, ten feet from the ground. He didn't even fall when he landed.

Another instructor moved over to unbuckle him. "Knees together...feet together for the landing," he snapped. "Remember, sir, that's what we're doing, practicing landings." Rick was so pleased to be on the ground, alive, he actually smiled.

And, by the end of the afternoon, he was more or less perfect. But because of the time pressures, he was scheduled to face the Tower, which was more than twice as tall, thirty minutes from now.

From the bottom, it looked high and flimsy, and Rick stared straight up the iron ladder. The instructor said, "Okay, Commander, up you go.

And don't worry about this, it's a cinch." But halfway up the ladder, Rick made the mistake of looking down. He had to admit he was scared shitless.

"Look up, sir...keep looking up..."

He heard the voice, pressed on, and reached the platform.

"Okay, sir. Harness on, all set...now remember what we're doing. We're practicing the exit from the aircraft, the flight drill, and the ocean landing drill...now get your lead foot firmly on the step, left arm at forty-five degrees...hold on to the scaffold, there, sir. Now, right arm across the reserve chute... that's it."

Rick looked down, and he might as well have been on top of the Empire State Building. People actually looked smaller.

"Right, sir...nice firm step...jump clear... and Go!"

Rick closed his eyes and went, forcing himself once more into space.

"That's good, sir. Nice and strong, then the landing position as we lower you down... that's very nice, sir. Keep looking around, eyes up, then down, don't want you crashing into the guy below you, okay?"

The high fan whirred and bit, slowing the jumper right down. "Looks good...very nice..." called the instructor on the ground, as Rick landed gently. "Three more of those, you'll be ready for the balloon."

That took place at 0700 the following morning, Friday. And Rick found himself staring up at an enormous balloon anchored in the sky, thirty feet above the ground. Way below it, at the bottom of the cable, was a flimsy-looking standing metal cage. It was big enough to hold six people.

Rick, the lone pupil, was guided in by the dispatcher. The single bar that served as a door was slammed across, and, on the signal, the cage began to move upward with the balloon, its cable being slowly released, unwound from a winch truck.

"You'll feel it tilt all the way up there," said the instructor. "When it clicks off at the top, the angle will change and we'll level out at eight hundred feet. That's when we've arrived."

For the first time, Rick debated whether he might right now declare his nerve had gone. He was more or less struck dumb by fear, but he could control that. Through the low metal-grid rails, he could see the ground slipping away beneath him, as the balloon rose to the dropping height.

The master of Hunter Valley was not enjoying this. Up and up they swayed, the rising wind now whining through the bars of the cage. Rick hung on to the section of the wall nearest to him, knuckles milk white in the eerie silence of the ride. He touched his parachute pack, gripped by the unnerving silence.

He could not for the life of him imagine he was going to jump out of this cage, and probably plummet to his death. **No way. No fucking way. I might be crazy, but I'm not fucking nuts.**

Just then the cage swayed back into a level position...**Jesus Christ. This is it. I've got to get out.**

"Okay, sir, check parachute lines on the static line right above your head...that's good...step forward..."

Rick stayed where he was, gazing out around him, aware of the manifest truth that he could see half of California from here.

"Right, Commander, over here, sir..."

Rick came forward, planting his lead left foot on the toe of the cage. The instructor checked the parachute line. Rick placed his left hand on the outside of the doorway. Someone pulled off the bar, the single bar that stood between him and instant death.

"Look up!"

"Now, when I tell you to go, you **go**, right?"

"Yes."

"Go!"

And Rick Hunter hurled himself out of the cage...into thin air...and as he fell, he felt himself leaning back, his feet riding up in front of his face. Never had he experienced such a chill of fear.

Then high above him he heard a crack, and a billowing sound, and he began to swing back, and his feet began to ride downward, and suddenly he was going slower and his body was at the right angle. Staring above him he could see the parachute had miraculously deployed and the canopy was right up there, and he might not die after all.

And now, temporarily safe, he remembered the drills. And he looked about him, to the left and to the right and especially downward. He knew he was supposed to be going forward, slowly, and he pulled down on his forward lift webs, adjusting his feet for the landing.

Down below he could already hear the instructors on the ground barking commands through their megaphones. **All right, Commander...assess your drift...adjust for landing.**

The ground was now coming up to meet him. Rick kept his knees together, shifting the angle of his feet, as he had been taught.

"Let up now!!"

Moments later he hit the ground, not too hard, and went immediately into the roll. But when he stood up the chute began to pull him across the ground, as the wind took it again.

"Pull in lower lift webs...collapse the canopy," someone was yelling.

Rick obeyed, and broke free of the parachute. He packed up calmly and headed back toward the Navy Jeep, a slight swagger in his stride.

"How was it, sir?" asked the driver.

"No trouble," he replied jauntily.

1100, FRIDAY, APRIL 22

With two instructors Rick climbed aboard the aircraft. It was raining lightly, and they took off into the skies above San Diego to make Rick's first airborne parachute jump.

The main objective right now was to become familiar with the noise, the turbulence, and the need to watch the hand signals from the dispatcher and the lights above the door.

Strapped in now, Rick braced himself as the troop transporter roared down the North Island runway, thundering and vibrating upward, through the low rain cloud and up to an operational height of just under 5,000 feet.

Rick felt the pilot bank right, crawling right around to the north of the city of San Diego, the noise of the engines deafening inside the aircraft. Soon he heard the dispatcher announce, "We've come full circle, we're right above the airfield again...coming up to the Drop Zone now...let's go to **action stations...!!**"

Rick stood up, clipped on to the static line that runs along the fuselage of the aircraft, and moved toward the rear. The dispatcher had the door open now, and the scream of the wind made communication almost impossible.

"Stand in the door...!"

Rick came forward, jaw jutting, always the leader in his own mind.

"Okay, sir, you know the drill...you're clipped on...parachute ready...red on..."

Above the door the red light glared. Rick Hunter placed his lead foot on the step, keeping his eyes up, left hand angled out against the doorway.

"Green on!! Go...!"

Rick Hunter, with one of the supreme acts of courage of his life, leapt clear of the aircraft, and tumbled through space, knees together, falling backward waiting for the magic moment when the canopy would crack open above him.

He heard it first, then saw it, then felt it, stabilizing his fall, pulling him upright again. And now he was swinging down in the wind, dropping through the air.

He could see the ground rising to meet him, and he braced for the landing, feet together, angled for the approach, knees together, pulling the back lift webs to slow his forward movement. He hit the ground less than gently, but going the right way, immediately into the forward roll position. The wind was low on the ground and he collapsed the chute without any trouble, packed up, and walked to the waiting instructors.

"Well done, sir. Nice landing."

"Thanks," said Rick. "Thanks very much. No problem."

"No problem," replied the instructor with a knowing wink, remembering of course his own terrifying, ass-gripping, heart-shattering first jump, right here on this very field. "Remember, sir. Next time it'll be the Atlantic instead of the airfield. And it's just as fucking hard, trust me!"

Rick Hunter chuckled as he walked back to the Jeep that had arrived to pick him up. He hadn't much enjoyed his short course in parachute jumping. But at least he knew how to do it.

Admiral Bergstrom had done the decent thing and permitted Rick Hunter a short lunch break, which the commander considered "real sweet of him," since he, Rick, had just spent one and a half days "executing lunatic leaps into space, somehow cheating death on a goddamned hourly basis."

And now the Navy helicopter was bringing the Commander back to his old home, coming in to land inside the barbed wire that surrounded the SEALs' compound behind the beach at Coronado. Although Admiral Bergstrom had organized an excellent lunch for both himself and Rick, he made quite certain it was a working lunch.

He had also invited two VISs (Very Important SEALs), Lt. Commander Dallas MacPherson and Chief Petty Officer Mike Hook, both of whom had served with Rick in the desperate getaway from Burma, three and a half years ago. Both men had manned M60 machine guns in the inflatable boats as they escaped, hammering away at the Chinese helicopters.

And now they met again for the first time since the bloodbath in the Burmese Delta. Commander Hunter walked into the bright, white-painted conference room below Admiral Bergstrom's office and almost died of shock at seeing his old teammates.

He threw his arms around Lt. Commander MacPherson with that joyful affection so often found among men who have fought a terrible battle, shoulder to shoulder, and survived. And he hugged Chief Mike Hook with equal warmth and friendship. Each one of the three had always understood that without the other two, they would surely have all perished.

Admiral Bergstrom thoughtfully left them alone for ten minutes before he joined the group, and when he did so, he began with a very short, dramatic announcement: "Dallas, Mike, I want you to know officially from me that Commander Hunter has rejoined the United States Navy for the purpose of just one highly classified mission."

"You mean he's here to help plan it, or he's actually going on it?" asked Dallas, as if Rick Hunter was not even in the room.

"He's not only here to help me plan it, he's going to lead it. Which should be interesting for you both. You're going with him."

"Me?" said Lt. Commander MacPherson. "I thought I'd done my main mission. I thought I was going to be a senior instructor."

"You are, Dallas. But first you're going to take a short trip to the South Atlantic with your old boss. I should perhaps tell you that I asked Commander Hunter personally if he had any preference for a 2I/C, and he said immediately, 'Dallas MacPherson, if he's available.' You should be very honored."

"I am, sir," replied the Lt. Commander. "It's just a little bit of a shock, that's all. But I'm ready. Where did you say we're going?"

"South Atlantic. Falkland Islands."

Dallas MacPherson, always prepared with a dash of old Southern charm, stepped forward and shook the hand of Commander Hunter. "Death to the gauchos, right, sir? I been reading all about 'em. Battered the Brits and stole the oil, right?"

"That's correct. But we're not going down there to kill 'em all. We're just going to blow a few things up, get their attention, catch 'em off guard."

"Hey, as I remember, you and I are pretty good at that."

"As I remember, Dallas, we're not too bad. Not too bad at all."

Lt. Commander MacPherson was now the principal explosives expert on the base. A wide-shouldered career officer from South Carolina, he had started his military studies at the great Southern academy, the Citadel, but moved after just a couple of semesters to Annapolis. He made gunnery and missile officer in an Arleigh-Burke destroyer before he was twenty-five.

As careers go, that came under the heading of meteoric. But it was nowhere near good enough for Dallas. He immediately requested a transfer to the U.S. Navy SEALs, and finished a sensational third out of around a hundred in the BUD/S indoctrination course.

A lot of people were amazed at such a performance by a very young surface ship missile officer. Dallas, however, remarked that he thought he'd been stitched up. Opinion on his future was fractured into two quite definite camps. One group was convinced he would ultimately take over the chair presently occupied by Admiral Bergstrom. The other believed he was more likely to end up with a posthumous Medal of Honor.

Commander Hunter had always been in the first group, but did not entirely discount the possibility of the second. Dallas MacPherson was as tough as hell and as brave as a lion. But it was his brains that Commander Hunter admired. And after the death-defying mission in Burma, he had developed an unshakeable respect for the wise-cracking, fast-thinking SEAL, whose expertise would, he knew, be critical to the mission in the South Atlantic.

The supremely athletic Chief Petty Officer Mike Hook was also an explosives expert. He came from Kentucky, like Rick, and would act as number two to Lt. Commander MacPherson, in charge of the timing and fuses. They had worked together causing probably the biggest explosion ever seen in the Burmese jungle, petrifying the natives, and shuddering the entire delta of the Bassein River.

Chief Hook stepped forward and offered his hand to his old commanding officer. "Look forward to it," he told the racehorse breeder from his home state. "You got any idea what we're gonna hit?"

"Couple airfields, few fighter-bombers," replied the Commander. "Kids' stuff to guys like us."

"How do we get in?" asked the Chief.

"Submarine, then inflatables."

"How do we get out?"

"Damn fast," interjected Dallas.

Admiral Bergstrom stepped in. "Okay, men," he said, "let's sit down right here and have some lunch, then we'll retire to one of the ops rooms, meet our colleagues, and get down to details. For the purpose of the next hour I'd like to restrict ourselves to basics…the insert…the objectives… the rescue…the mission…and the exit, okay?"

The three SEALs nodded. The Admiral pressed a bell, and an orderly entered the room with plates of salad and warm crusty bread. Then he asked each man how he would like his steak cooked."

"Jeez," said Dallas MacPherson. "I knew that word **rescue** was significant. This has to be real important. Medium rare, please."

"Don't worry, old buddy," replied Commander Hunter. "They're not even captives yet."

"You mean the Brits have left some Special Forces in there, and we gotta get 'em out?" asked Dallas, with truly astonishing perception.

"Now how the hell would you draw such an outlandish conclusion?" asked the Admiral, quietly.

"Well, we're sure as hell not going to rescue any Argentinians," he replied. "The Brits have surrendered the islands. The population is coming to terms with their new rulers, and I guess they're back in their homes and farms. And you said 'rescue,' that means the Brits have left something behind. And that leaves only one option—their recce team, which somehow got stranded, out of the mainstream, and is still in there, out of contact and refusing to surrender with the rest of the troops since no one knows where the hell they are. Probably SAS. Right?"

Bergstrom's chair, no doubt, thought Rick Hunter.

And the Admiral himself, as if by telepathy, smiled, and said "Thank you, Dallas. You don't mind if I keep this chair warm for a few months, do you?"

Lt. Commander MacPherson grinned. He was well used to being a couple of jumps ahead, and he knew he had a long way to go to make Rear Admiral. But he saw himself walking with kings, rather than courtiers, and was accustomed to achieving his objectives.

"No problem, sir," he replied. "Just trying to cast a ray of light on the strategic picture."

"Jesus Christ," said Commander Hunter. "Shut up, Dallas. We all recognize your brilliance."

"You mean we really are going in after a marooned SAS team?"

"Among other things, yes," said Admiral Bergstrom. "But you need to be very careful. For obvious reasons, Hereford dare not risk locating them with a cell phone call. Because if the Args picked it up, Captain Jarvis and his team would be hunted down by sheer weight of numbers. But I have their call sign on satellite radio, and I think that's the way to go when you make contact."

All three of the combat SEALs nodded in agreement. And just then the steaks came in, which kept everyone, even Dallas MacPherson, more or less quiet for a few minutes.

Lunch, as deemed by the Admiral, was restricted to the broad brushstrokes…the final preparations…the ocean drop to the submarine…the arrival of the gear, by parachute, and the number of men who would conduct the opening attack.

In Rick Hunter's view, they should consider the SAS team intact in body, mind, food supplies, and weaponry. "According to your brief, Admiral," he said, "They inserted the Falklands on Friday night, April eighth. They conducted a classified mission in the small hours of Saturday morning, April sixteenth, and according to Hereford were not located, nor even detected.

"The Brits surrendered six hours later that same morning. It's now Friday, April twenty-second, so the guys have been on the run for six days, probably living off the land, hiding out, and eking out their supplies. The place is awash with unpolluted fresh water, and it houses several billion sources of roast lamb. I think we should treat Captain Jarvis and his men as fully operational."

Admiral Bergstrom nodded in agreement. "I think that's a very good point, Rick," he said. "We're not putting sixteen men into that part of the mission to make an evacuation of eight walking wounded. No one's wounded. No one's even been spotted. We're really seconding their eight-man team to ours. And that means Rick's assault group should make contact as soon as they land."

"Sir, if I might refine that," said Rick. "I think we should conduct our first objective as soon as we go in. That airfield in the north. I'd need only eight men, and from there we could link up with

Captain Jarvis, after we find him, and proceed to our next mission, all sixteen of us."

Again the Admiral nodded in agreement, and said, "Okay. I think that's sound. Let's finish lunch right away and move out to an ops room where there's a big computer screen. It's hopeless trying to work out a plan on a pile of remote islands without big accurate charts. Basement situation room. Block D. We can walk."

Twenty minutes later, they filed into the white concrete-walled ops room where Rick Hunter had three times sat before, plotting death, doom, and destruction upon the enemies of the United States.

The four men were the first to arrive, and Commander Hunter automatically fired up the huge wall computer—SEALs never switch on computers, they fire 'em up, just as they wrap dark green scarves around their heads going into combat, like red Indians, and refer to them as their "drive-on rags."

Rick hit a few buttons and a detailed chart of the Falkland Islands illuminated almost the entire wall, in color, with ocean depths, tidal directions and heights, navigation routes, guides, cans, lights, lighthouses and shoals, sandbanks, rocks, wrecks and oil rigs. On land it showed accurate contours of mountains, a few roads, townships, sheep stations, airports, harbors, and government buildings. All updated whenever possible by the Pentagon.

The SEALs gravitated toward it like a flight of homing pigeons...**Christ, it's pretty damn shallow in there...how big's this damn place? Which side are we landing? Anyone know which area the SAS guys are in? Any warships in the north? Is that a garrison on top of this darn great headland?**

The questions came raining in. No SEAL team ever has quite enough information. They wanted to know everything. **Is this a gate? Does it squeak? Who lives in this farmhouse? Will there be a moon? If it rains, what's the ground like in here? Do we have details on Argentinian patrols? Are they out looking for Captain Jarvis?**

"Gentlemen," said Admiral Bergstrom, "I think we should establish our strategy and size of force immediately. Commander Hunter and I are agreed that the submarine will deliver his eight-man team to this area, two miles north of the headland west of Goat Hill...right here...there's a hundred feet depth through here...and the inflatables can run you straight through this gap, the Tamar Pass. You'll launch your attack across the strait and return the same way.

"Team Two is the underwater assault group that will hit the Argentine warships in Mare Harbor. According to our satellites, the Args often have two destroyers plus two frigates in there. They patrol in the day and return at night. That's when we hit 'em, okay? That team will comprise eight swimmers, with four backup...landing right here from inflatables in East Cove...then it's an overland approach, and an underwater, delayed-time hit. Escape from East Cove to the submarine."

"The question I have is this, are we capable of knocking out the Mount Pleasant air base, which is thick with Argentinian troops? And I should record, my instinct is no."

"What's the size of the garrison, sir?"

"There may be up to three thousand troops on the ground, plus maybe fifteen attack helicopter gunships, fifty-plus armored vehicles, and vast supplies of ordnance. They also have some heavy artillery and missile launchers in place, but that will not affect us."

"Jesus," said Rick, "that's not really our game, is it? We can't send a dozen guys in to take down an army, sitting in the middle of an occupied island, with helicopters, rockets, and missiles at their disposal. I guess we might blast a few aircraft out on the perimeter, but I don't think that's a good use of our time and skills."

"I agree with you," replied the Admiral. "I'm just looking for feedback."

"The real problem is," said Dallas, "the first minute they even suspect we're there, we're likely to be real dead real quick. There's too many of them, packing too much firepower. Mount Pleasant sounds like a job for an army, possibly a navy, never mind an air force. It's not really for a dozen wild men with black faces and bowie knives."

"He's right," said Commander Hunter. "Pebble Island is our kind of territory. So is the lightly guarded, unsuspecting Mare Harbor. They're places where we have a real good shot at success. I can't see getting mixed up in the current headquarters of the Argentinian armed forces. Matter of fact, I think the place for us is the Rio Grande air base on the mainland. No one would dream we would turn up there, and it won't be heavily guarded.

"I think we should hit Pebble, locate Jarvis, pick up the SAS, and head straight down to the Magellan Strait, and I'll take an eight-man recce team in to have a good look at the Rio Grande area. Meanwhile, the rest of the guys can land on the Chile side of the border and prepare for the hit on the base.

"We should let Mount Pleasant go about its business, because if we want to bring the Argentinians to heel, victory lies in Rio Grande, where they have more than a hundred aircraft. Hit that lot and they'll agree to anything."

"As ever, Commander Hunter, I agree with your assessment," said John Bergstrom. "And my update from Washington this morning was very encouraging. The President of Chile has agreed to give us every support, from his airfields and military bases, and from his communications network.

"It's funny, the Args and the Chileans are near neighbors with much in common, but there's never been much love lost between them. They helped the Brits last time and they'll help us this time."

"How many guys will you need for the main attack on Rio Grande?" asked Dallas.

"Probably forty."

"But we only have twenty."

"Correct," said Admiral Bergstrom. "But we'll send down another twenty to our forward base in readiness for the attack."

"Forward base?" asked Dallas. "Where's that?"

"Chile. We've been granted takeoff and landing facilities at the Chilean naval airfield in Punta Arenas. Heard that this morning from Admiral Morgan, while your boss was hurling himself into the stratosphere."

"So we all join the submarine," said Commander Hunter. "Then my group leaves for Pebble Island in two inflatables, while the submarine continues on to land the underwater guys on East Cove for the Mare Harbor attack. Then my group finds Douglas Jarvis and his team, and we make our way to a rendezvous with the submarine, and haul the inflatables inboard again…if there's time."

"Correct."

"And what about the East Cove guys? How far away are they? And when do they rejoin the submarine?"

"Mare Harbor is approximately a hundred and thirty-five miles away from the eastern headland of Pebble. But the water's relatively deep and the SSN will make it in a little over five hours.

"The ship will pick up each group as it completes its task. Maybe it'll be yours, maybe the others. Then, with all twenty-eight of you on board, including the SAS, it makes all speed for the Magellan Strait, four hundred and forty miles away, where we rendezvous with a Chilean freighter, which will land you all at Punta Arenas to prepare for Rio Grande. All being well, Rick, you and your guys will leave almost immediately, by helicopter."

"Time frame, sir?"

"Both SEAL teams leave here by air tomorrow afternoon at 1600," said the Admiral. "And that will put you over the drop zone north of the Falklands at 0700 Sunday morning, that's first light. We don't have a problem being seen that far north, and the submarine will have Group One right off Pebble Island by around 1700, just as the light starts to fade.

"The Pentagon has no record of any Argentine patrol up there for the past week after 1400. And anyway, we got depth to stay submerged right up to a couple miles offshore. At midnight, there'll be a HALO drop straight into your landing beach from a United States military aircraft flying higher than thirty thousand feet and transmitting only civilian radar.

"Rick, you've done this before, so you'll carry in the beam to guide the canister down. It'll contain all the explosive and detcord you'll need, timers, fuses, wire cutters, screwdrivers, shovels, extra food, a powerful satellite transmitter, and a big machine gun in case of emergency. You can bury the canister, and load the stuff into the inflatables for the outward journey to East Falkland, where you'll find Captain Jarvis."

"Normally we'd carry a lot of this stuff, right, sir?" asked Dallas. "It's just the ocean drop—can't get too weighed down with the gear?"

"That's correct. None of you have made a drop like this and the planners decided to land the equipment separately. You won't have any trouble. Commander Hunter knows all about it. He did it in darkest Russia, and no one caught him. Anyway, that's the broad game plan, and now we better get down to details.

"First off, there's six A4P Skyhawks parked on Pebble Island with nine of those Israeli Daggers. These are the guys that delivered the big thousand-pound bombs into the Royal Navy Fleet. The air base has a new, extended concrete runway, installed a couple of years ago by a consortium of the oil companies exploring offshore to the north. The new buildings, like the runway, were unused and have now been converted into an Argentinian command headquarters. They were, of course, unharmed during the recent conflict.

"There may be a seventy-five-strong force in there, that's aircrew, ground crew, and guards. It's really the only stronghold Argentina has in the north. But the last thing they'll have on their minds is having the air base assaulted. Remember, their enemy, the Brits, have very publicly left the area, and the Argentinians still hold many prisoners of war."

Rick Hunter nodded. "Sir, there's four eight-man hard-deck inflatables on board this damn great Navy submarine, right? Two for us, two for the others. Now they are going straight into East Cove to do their business and then straight out again to the ship—that's a round trip of less than ten miles.

"On the other hand, according to this chart, our best place to meet the SSN, after we locate Douglas Jarvis, is going to be the south end of Falkland Sound, and that sucker's fifty miles long, all the way down to Fox Bay.

"Now, Captain Jarvis is almost certainly on the west coast of East Falkland, probably trying to find a boat he can commandeer to get the hell out of there. So we are faced with a journey of around sixty miles from our landing beach all the way down the Sound, in a couple of high-powered Zodiacs, which burn gas like a fucking 747. I just want to make certain we've got enough..."

Admiral Bergstrom referred to his notes. "One of those inflatables, running at ten knots without making much noise, uses a gallon every forty-two minutes. You'll hit the beach with full tanks—that's twenty gallons—enough for fourteen hours or a hundred and forty miles. If, for any reason, you have to floor it to make some kind of escape, which is unlikely, both boats carry two full four-and-a-half-gallon spare cans. Basically the boats can make two hundred miles apiece."

"Thank you, sir. Just checking."

"You're welcome, Commander."

"Tell you something," said Dallas. "With full tanks those boats are going to be darned heavy to drag up the beach and conceal while we blow the airfield."

"We thought of that," replied the Admiral. "The boats are each fitted with eight heavy-duty canvas handles. I agree they'd be darn heavy for a four-man team—no trouble for eight of you."

Dallas nodded. "Anyway, sir, I was forgetting. The Commander could probably carry the damn thing by himself." The enormous strength of the SEAL Team Leader was still a well-known standard at Coronado; a standard that, it should be recorded, hardly anyone ever attained.

Right now Rick Hunter was making careful notes. Without looking up, he asked, "We got an accurate GPS on the landing beach where the HALO's coming in?"

"It's 51.21.50 south, 59.27.00 west."

"Midnight, right?"

"Affirmative."

"We got a chart for the phases of the moon?"

"Right here."

"What happens if the sea conditions are very severe and we have to hole up on the landing beach for a day or even two?"

"Not a problem. Just keep the SSN informed on the satellite. And Captain Jarvis, assuming you find him right away, which I think you will."

The meeting had moved from a slightly haphazard beginning into a high-octane military planning session. And it stayed that way, an enclave of the most minute detail and forward thinking, until the five SEALs who would join Rick's team arrived at 1600.

There were two more demolition specialists, both Petty Officers First Class—Don Smith, from Chicago, another great bear of a man like the Commander, and Brian Harrison from Pennsylvania, whose exploits in the Iraq War had gained him a major reputation.

Seamen Ed Segal and Ron Wallace, both from Ohio, had also served in Iraq and were experienced in combat and boat handling. The final man, Chief Petty Officer Bob Bland, from Oklahoma, was inevitably known as "Pigling," but mostly behind his back, since he had won the station heavyweight boxing championship and was apt to react on a very short fuse.

Bob's specialty was breaking and entering. Any fence, wire, wall, door, or gate, old Pigling could get it open, quietly. His task was to silently cut the airfield fence and then move on to attack a metal gate that barred their exit point. He would again move out in front for the final stage of the operation.

Everyone in the room knew of Rick Hunter, but of the five new arrivals, CPO Bland was the only one who had met him before. Admiral Bergstrom motioned them to be seated at the big table and intimated he required only a further twenty minutes, before Commander Hunter would take over and begin a thorough four-hour briefing of his team.

The twelve-man underwater group was in another section going through the same process. They would not meet until the following morning shortly before final preparations for departure.

1400, FRIDAY, APRIL 22
EAST FALKLAND

Douglas Jarvis and his team had walked south for about fifteen miles. It was a frustrating journey, carried out in wet, squally weather down the landward side of Carlos Water. The objective was to reach the coast, but not to become stranded on the western fork, which guards Carlos from the open twelve-mile-wide Sound. The SAS team did not on any account intend to be caught with their backs to the ocean.

And that meant a walk of another few miles south to where the land became less of a peninsula, and where there was the prospect of a fishing boat in a little place called Port Sussex.

They had arrived in wide grazing land within clear sight of Mount Usborne and stared down at the deserted harbor. They could see moorings, possibly four of them, but no boats, which Captain Jarvis remarked was "bloody dull."

It was already growing dark, and there was just a scattering of buildings around the harbor, two of them with lights on. And the problem that faced the young Commander was the same as always—could they bang on the door and announce themselves, running the risk of Argentine soldiers being in residence? Or even the risk of a swift phone call from the occupants to the military HQ at Mount Pleasant?

Of course they could take out the enemy instantly. But what good would that do? The soldiers would be missed, then found, and a manhunt for the outlawed British Special Forces would surely begin. The men from Hereford were, as Douglas put it, buggered. Their options were narrow. There was little they could do, except feast on roast lamb, whenever possible, and try to steal, hire, or borrow a boat to get away at the earliest time.

Tonight was plainly a roast lamb situation.
And they also had to find shelter. It was raining
like hell, and it would be completely dark inside
an hour. Their waterproof clothing and boots had
all held up well, and no one was suffering from
illness or injury. But this was getting depressing,
with no discernible enemy, the constant threat of
an Argentinian manhunt being launched, and no
sign of a proper objective. The only ray of hope
seemed to be the vague, encrypted satellite promise from Hereford several days ago that a rescue
operation was being mounted.

Douglas dispatched Troopers Wiggins and
Pearson to what he called the "local butcher," the
4,000-acre pasture to the east, on which there
were sheep and lambs as far as the eye could
see. And while they were gone, the rest of them
groped around in the sparse undergrowth for a
spot to light the oven. In fact, they were getting
very good at this, wielding the axe, chopping both
the wide bushes and the carcass of the lambs, before lighting the fire in the hole they just dug in
the damp ground.

Douglas toyed with the idea of moving quietly down into one of the empty buildings on the
quayside, but again the risk was too great. What if
a fishing boat pulled in during the night and they
were discovered? What if the fishing boats were
accompanied by Argentinian Marines?

The truth was, the SAS team could cope with anything except discovery, because that might very well mean death from an Arg helicopter gunship combing the area where someone had located them.

No. Tonight looked like another night in the open. And thank God for the excellent waterproof sleeping bags, and may the morrow bring a ship into the hitherto deserted harbor of Port Sussex. Privately, Douglas thought it just a matter of time before some angry shepherd grew irritated by someone stealing his lambs, and reported the matter to the authorities. They'd snatched eight of them by now, and a good detective might easily put two and two together and make four.

He shuddered and checked the lamb, which was beginning to sizzle cheerfully, and once more they made their fast evening communication to their command HQ, and as usual there was only silence. But they left the radio switched on, ready to receive, although no one held out much hope. If they were going to be rescued, they would plainly have to rescue themselves.

Dinner was again very good, and they supplemented the lamb with their own concentrated vegetable bars. But tonight there would be no walking, principally because there was nowhere to go. Captain Jarvis decreed this harbor with its obvious active moorings was as good as any. The

best plan was to sit and wait, through the weekend, and hope to hell a boat came in.

"We might even get a bit of fish," observed
Trooper Wiggins. "Make a change from lamb,
eh?"

And they drifted off to sleep under the bushes,
leaving one man at a time on a one-hour sentry
watch, just in case someone had spotted their fire
deep in its roasting hole.

And at thirteen minutes past one a.m., Trooper Goddard saw a sight that made his hair stand
on end. Winding up the coastal track to the right
of the long sea inlet of Breton Loch was an unmistakable pair of headlights, moving fast. He
grabbed the night binoculars and stared at the
green-hued landscape to the south.

**Jesus Christ! It's an Army Jeep...and if it
stays on that track it's going to pass less than
a half mile from right here.**

Trooper Goddard awakened Captain Jarvis,
who almost leapt out of his sleeping bag in surprise, since long, undisturbed nights were the rule
around here in this desolate southern wilderness.

"What's up, Bob?"

"There's an Army Jeep, sir, moving fast, coming more or less toward us. Right now it's a couple
of miles south of the harbor."

Douglas Jarvis said softly, "Wake everyone, get
into combat gear, weapons primed, and pack up

everything in case we have to move fast. If we have to, we'll take 'em out, but I'd like to avoid that, because if we do, there'll be all hell let loose."

"Okay, sir...binoculars are right there near the sniper rifle."

Swiftly the SAS men slipped into fighting mode, boots tightened, gloves on, hoods fastened, ammunition belts slung into place. The sleeping bags and ground sheets were all packed by two troopers. All of the other six were ready either to repel an attack or launch one of their own.

Douglas Jarvis watched the Jeep pull onto the quayside and stop outside one of the houses that was lit inside. He saw two men jump from the front seats and bang on the front door, which opened immediately, and the light spilled out onto the jetty. One man came out to join them, and moments later a powerful searchlight on the roof of the Jeep began to sweep the hillside, making long lines past the boulders and scrubland below them.

The Captain assessed they were perhaps six hundred yards away, and with every sweep the beam of the light grew nearer their clump of bushes.

Down, guys. Stay well down. We don't want to make this any uglier than it is already...

So far as he could tell, there were only two possibilities. Someone had seen them moving across the foothills of the mountain, or a shepherd had seen a couple of shadowy figures make off with a couple of lambs. He had always recognized this as a danger, because shepherds are inclined to wander around in the twilight.

And he was correct. Luke Milos, a sixth-generation Falkland Islands shepherd, had been darned near certain he saw someone in the pasture running away carrying something. And he knew the main Argentine garrison had issued a warning about wandering intruders who may be armed and dangerous.

And he had placed a call to the small Argentine military compound at Goose Green, which is situated right on the narrow causeway that divides Choiseul Sound.

The duty sentry said he'd have a patrol take a ride up there and maybe stay until first light. There were some British troops, unaccounted for in the battle, who might be about ready to rob and plunder local homesteaders. He'd have someone there inside an hour.

And here they were, combing the hillside with a big mounted flashlight, and right now its beam was slicing into the bushes where Douglas and his men lay facedown, pressed into the ground, gripping their machine guns.

So far as Douglas was concerned, anything was preferable to a fight. But if they had one, they had two tasks, to kill every man in that Jeep, and then make sure no one found it. The first was easy, the second damn near impossible.

And there was a dull ache of anticipation in the stomach of Douglas Jarvis when he heard the Jeep's engine kick over and begin to rumble toward them. Worse yet, he could hear the clatter of machine guns, as the Argentinian patrol raked every bush and rocky outcrop with real live bullets.

"Fuck," hissed Douglas. "Peter, Bob, take the guys on the left side of the vehicle coming toward us. I'll take the driver, Jake takes the backseat on the right."

No one spoke, but each man wriggled and crawled into position, spreading out, ready to open fire in an instant. Suddenly the Argentinians went quiet, then the searchlight went on again, and swept the copse where they had been sleeping, two hundred yards from the edge of the pasture.

The Jeep roared forward again, and a burst of machine-gun fire ripped into the very spot the SAS team had lately vacated.

"Okay, fuck it, that's it," snapped Douglas, "Take 'em **now**!!"

His own Enfield L85A1 assault rifle spat fire at fifty yards' range, the heavy SS109 steel-core rounds ripping through the head and neck of the driver and the front passenger. Troopers Wiggins and Goddard put two savage bursts into the rear seat from the left, Jake Posgate slammed ten rounds into the backseat from the right.

Doug Jarvis ran in, now from the rear of the vehicle, and fired another burst. But there was no movement from inside the Jeep. Four men lay slumped in their seats, dead or very quickly dying.

"Okay, guys," said Douglas. "You see the nearest hillside over there—probably about a mile if this damn flashlight is any good. I'm gonna drive over there, and I'll drop off a trooper every four hundred yards. That way we'll all meet when I find a spot.

"Then we're going to hide this bastard and its passengers. It won't stay hidden forever. But it'll stay hidden for possibly a week 'til someone finds it. By then we'll be long gone. You all know I did not want to do this, but I was just beginning to feel it was us or them, and this way's best."

They manhandled the dead men into the rear seat and then clambered all over the vehicle as it set off toward the distant slopes of Mount Usborne. It took a half hour to find a really secluded gully, and they shoved the Jeep down into it, about six feet below the track they were on. Douglas went in and personally severed the wires that powered the vehicle's radio.

One hour later they had about a half ton of gorse and tall grass piled all over it. You could have walked past it twenty times and never seen the Jeep in the man-made copse.

"That's it for us," said the Captain. "Those guys won't be reported missing for several more hours. Meantime we'll head back to the coast for the next three hours. When it's light, we'll hide up somewhere and try to get past Port Darwin this evening. But we have to stay right next to the seashore. It's our only way out."

1530, SATURDAY, APRIL 23
U.S. NAVAL AIR BASE
NORTH ISLAND

Commander Rick Hunter, in company with Lt. Commander Dallas MacPherson, Chief Mike Hook, and the rest emerged from the final briefing room dressed in full combat gear. Their rucksacks were already loaded. They were armed and ready, and they carried with them the special heavy-duty, hooded wet suits with flippers that would prevent them from sinking and freezing to death in the South Atlantic.

The parachutes and the reserves were already loaded. These would unclip and release the moment the men hit the water. The rest would be up to Captain Hugh Fraser's highly skilled submariners from USS **Toledo** working the inflatable boats in hopefully reasonable seas.

Rick Hunter walked out to the edge of the runway where the Lockheed C-130 stretched Hercules was already fully boarded and running its engines. He walked to the steps of the aircraft, followed by Dallas and Mike Hook. But before he began the climb toward the cabin, he paused for a few moments to chat with Admiral Bergstrom, who had materialized from nowhere.

"Sir, one favor…?"

"Of course."

Rick handed him a piece of paper with a phone number in faraway Kentucky. "Could you please call Di…just tell her I'm fine?"

They all heard the Colonel call out, "I'll do it this morning…and, Rick…good luck."

Dallas stood grinning cheerfully as the officer from the Blue Grass walked firmly up the steps.

Inside the aircraft, the crew was waiting at the door. As Rick walked in, one of them said, "Okay, sir?"

"Let's go," said the Commander, walking back and strapping himself into his reserved seat. And he felt the great aircraft shudder as it made its way to the end of the runway, swerved around and rumbled forward, its speed building, the noise shattering.

No one spoke until the fuel-laden Hercules had fought its way off the ground, hard into the southwest breeze gusting in off the Pacific. They all felt it gain altitude, and then bank left onto its course of 150 degrees, bound for the cold south, and the windswept craggy moonscape of the Falkland Islands.

They climbed into the warm spring skies. The Hercules, always a lumbering giant, seemed noisy this morning thanks to the giant echoey gas tank set in the middle of the main cargo area. Right now they were flying through sunny clear skies. By the early hours of tomorrow morning, they would be close to the Antarctic convergence, flying in temperatures probably eighty below freezing.

No one spoke for a half hour, at which point Dallas turned to Commander Hunter and said, "Sir, do you think we're supposed to be scared?"

"Us? No, not us. We're invincible."

"No, sir. I'm serious. Is this really dangerous, or are we just dealing with a bunch of jokers?"

"I don't think anyone knows that, Dallas. But we have been tasked to find the lost Brits and slam the fighter aircraft."

"Shit, when you think about it, kinda sounds a bit tricky, eh?"

"A bit. Nothing you and I can't deal with."

"Yeah, but hold on a minute, sir. Let's say they send a chopper up after us and start blasting away. What happens then?"

"Dallas, we are about to conduct a standard, classic SEAL operation, infiltration of enemy territory. If they are mad enough to come after us, we'll blow their fucking helicopter right out of the sky with the Stinger, right? Get your mind straight, kid. We're the U.S. Navy SEALs and we're going in. Anyone gets in the way of our mission dies, right?"

"Yessir."

Dallas fell silent, and the Hercules, guzzling fuel by the gallon every few seconds, kept rumbling south at 42,000 feet. They would refuel in Santiago, the capital city of Chile. Tom noticed the veteran Mike Hook was sound asleep. Chief Ed Segal was lying back in his seat, his eyes wide open, his mind on the cold south.

The crew served them coffee at 1900, with hot soup and sandwiches at 2200, and most of them slept through the night until 0330, when they landed in Santiago. The refuel took just thirty minutes, and everyone seemed to awaken, but no one had much to say.

At 0600 Rick Hunter and his team began to change. Their gear and weapons were already secured in the four big waterproof containers they would take with them on the drop. They pulled their heavy-duty, hooded wet suits over the special deepwater Gore-Tex body vests and tight-fitting trousers they would wear for the jump into the freezing South Atlantic. The last task before fitting the parachutes was to pull on their life jackets.

Two hundred and fifty miles farther on, the staff of the submarine USS **Toledo** was preparing for the pickup under still dark skies with intermittent cloud cover. The hard-copy satellite signal was unambiguous. It contained the accurate

GPS rendezvous position, time, and details, plus code word Southern Belle.

Captain Fraser's crew were already lowering two diesel-powered inflatables into the water. It had taken a small crane to haul the deflated boats up onto the casing, and then the engines separately. And even out on the deck it was more trouble than usual because of a heavy Atlantic swell, but Captain Fraser had preferred the boats to a Chilean helicopter, which was apt to be both noisy and slow. And he realized the importance of scooping the SEALs out of the frigid ocean in the fastest possible time.

The Hercules flew on southeast, and 130 miles north of the Falklands the navigator hit the radar button and immediately got a paint on the ocean thirty miles away. He switched the radar off instantly to avoid prying Argentinian eyes, but Captain Fraser's ops room had picked them up... **low flying contact...5,000 feet...speed 250... course three-five-five...range thirty miles... IFF transponder code correlates Southern Belle...**

All four of **Toledo**'s inflatables were now running free, right off the port side of the submarine. The drop was scheduled to happen a thousand yards away, but for the moment the helmsmen kept their distance, just in case one of the SEALs came plummeting down out of a cloud bank and crashed straight into the Zodiac.

Back in the Hercules, Rick Hunter and his men were struggling toward the door carrying the waterproof containers. The dispatcher was shouting out to them, **"Okay, get ready now...we're heading right toward the zone...another couple of minutes..."**

Mike Hook was behind the Commander and Dallas MacPherson, and, generally speaking, Rick sensed they were all very scared. He watched the tremble of his own hands as he hooked on to the static line. Mike's face was white, his mouth dry. Rick called for a bottle of water, mainly because his own mouth was pretty dry as well. Dallas appeared unconcerned, all business, while Ron Wallace was quiet, unsmiling, no jokes, coping with the pressure and his own fear as well as he could. No one looks forward to a mission like this, beginning out on the frontiers of death.

But Rick's adrenaline was running now. He was scared, but the light of battle was in his eyes. Some inherent gene of the Hunter family was driving him forward into the most terrible danger. And in one corner of his soul, he looked forward to it, diving out of that door at the head of a group of hard-trained SEAL assault troops. This was what he had joined for, and it sure beat the hell out of frigging around with baby racehorses.

"One minute!" yelled the dispatcher above the roar of the engines. Rick squeezed his nose and blew hard to clear his ears as the aircraft lost

altitude. He turned back to Mike Hook and told
him not to worry, just to jump, "right after me,
remember the drills and stay cool."

Right then, the aircraft throttled back to a
speed of only 130 knots, and the dispatcher
opened the big aircraft door on the port side.
The screaming rush of ice-cold air was a major
shock, doubling the noise, and tripling the scare
factor. But Rick Hunter was not scared anymore.
Not at all. He experienced only a sense of exhil-
aration. And he gripped the static line, watching
the dispatcher, glancing downward at the deep
blue of the dawn ocean, the big white marks of
the breaking swells. Right now he could not see
the U.S. submarine.

**"We're coming to the Drop Zone now,
right on our nose...Action stations..."**

They could hardly hear the dispatcher above
the howl of the wind, but everyone in the two
groups, all twenty, checked their static lines, and
they moved forward to the area immediately in
front of the opening.

"Stand in the door, number one!!"

Rick came forward, his face grim, shrugging
his shoulders like a heavyweight fighter in his corner preparing for round one. On another man,
this might have been bravado, but it was not so
for Rick Hunter. He was in battle mode, ready for
this fight, ready to go.

"Red on!!"

The Hercules was now running at dropping speed, but the force of the howling wind outside the fuselage formed a wall of freezing air, a curtain of transparent steel. Rick thought he might be forced right back in again. But now he could see the glare of the red light above the door. They were right on the Drop Zone, and he braced himself and stared out.

"Green on…go!"

The dispatcher slapped him on the shoulder, and Rick Hunter plunged out of the aircraft. He swept clear in the slipstream, and then dropped swiftly, sideways. He held his knees together, feeling the familiar sensation of rolling backward, staring upward, waiting for the moment the canopy would billow out. He hoped Dallas, Mike, and the rest were also out. But then his parachute opened and he did not see anyone above him.

Back inside the cockpit the radio operator snapped into the secure VHF encrypted, **Southern Belles go.**

Toledo came back on "cackle"…**Roger. Out.**

All twenty chutes deployed faultlessly, slowing down the headlong flight of the two SEAL teams. In the split seconds of the jump, away to the southwest, Rick glanced below and the sea looked markedly less friendly than it had from a thousand feet. He guessed he was less than 200 feet above the surface, and he could see quite clearly now the outline of the submarine. At 180 feet he could see all four inflatables, still circling close to its port side.

The real difference was the surface of the water, which showed deep troughs and white lacey patterns. The wind was strong, and as he descended Rick could see it whipping the froth off the top of the waves, some of which were breaking, sending a cascade of broiling white water down the leeward side. The sea was running out of the southwest, as was the wind. Long studies of the charts had suggested this was bad news, since the roughest, coldest gales around the Falklands came raging in from the Antarctic shelf.

Rick assessed this was not yet a full-fledged gale, but it was probably building, and he was not real sure how he was going to enjoy the experience of sitting in a submarine in an Antarctic storm. However, he assumed it might be a whole lot better than bobbing around in the Atlantic in a wet suit.

And now, dropping downward to 150 feet, he pulled the harness forward under his backside, so he effectively was sitting in the harness. He quickly banged the release button on his chest, and freed the straps to fall away beneath his feet.

Hanging there now, in a sitting position, holding on to the lift webs above his head, Rick waited the last fleeting seconds, staring down at the shape of the water, which was not good. Twenty feet above the surface, he could no longer see the submarine, or the inflatables. He just felt himself hurtling toward the ocean, as if he had jumped from a diving board. He immediately breathed in deeply, held his breath, gripped the lift webs tighter and thrust his legs downward, underneath him, until he was standing upright.

Ten feet above the surface of the ocean, Rick let go of the parachute and crashed into the Atlantic, submerging perhaps ten feet. He kicked his way to the surface, flippers gripping the water, and felt the freezing cold ocean on his hands and face, but his body remained surprisingly warm.

The parachute was off now, but he was gasping for breath as a massive rogue wave rolled right over the trough in which he wallowed. Rick was a great swimmer, and he had a good lungful of air, but it seemed a hundred feet upward before he broke clear of the water again, and gulped in more air. He stared out toward the next oncoming wall of water and prepared to go under once more, but he need not have worried. Two pairs of brawny seamen's hands clamped on to his shoulders and hauled him out backward, over the broad inflated sides of the Zodiac.

He landed on his back. "Hold it right there, sir..." someone yelled unnecessarily. And he felt the diesel engine accelerate, dragging them around, in the direction of the advancing waves. Before Rick could raise himself up, Mike Hook, gasping and choking seawater, landed on top of him. Then the diesel roared again, as the helmsman somehow got the boat synchronized with the pattern of the surface and with immense skill steered them toward Dallas MacPherson, who was, unsurprisingly, yelling.

The inflatable was now rising up through six feet against the hull of the submarine, and Rick could see a succession of safety lines and harness lines being lowered and grabbed by the seamen. Right now he had no idea what was happening, but he could see the sailors moving and clipping with sure, rapid expertise.

"What happens now?" he said.

"Grab those boarding nets, sir. The guys will haul you on to the casing...don't worry...you can't fall..."

Just then the second boat arrived bearing Don Smith, Brian Harrison, and Ed Segal. Seven minutes later, the first ten SEALs were being greeted by Captain Fraser.

It took another ten minutes for all twenty of them to assemble inside the submarine. The last boat recovered all the gear containers, which had been dropped separately.

This had been a flawless ocean drop—no one lost, no one injured, everyone safe and experiencing a massive sense of relief. This mission might be dangerous, but the part that had concerned them most was over.

0900, SUNDAY, APRIL 24
ARGENTINE MILITARY GARRISON
GOOSE GREEN, EAST FALKLAND

Sir, we're getting no reply on the radio. Nothing. It's dead.

What time did they leave?

Around midnight.

Last contact?

0105.

Position?

Quayside, Port Sussex.

Contacts?

Señor Luke Milos. He reported sheep stealing. I just spoke to him, and he saw our Jeep heading up the mountainside around 0130. He heard machine guns, but they were ours. The men were sweeping the area with a searchlight and rounds of gunfire.

Did he see which way the vehicle went?

Only for around six hundred yards up the hill behind his home. Do you think we should send a search party? Couple of Jeeps?

Well, they may be on their way back. It's very barren up there. I think we should leave it another couple of hours, and then send a helicopter up to Port Sussex. That way we cover more ground ten times as fast.

Yessir.

1100, SAME DAY

Captain Jarvis and his still-intact SAS team had made it to the southern end of Brenton Loch and had gone to ground close to the water at the northern end of the causeway that crosses Choiseul Sound. This rectangle of land is about five miles long and only a little more than a mile wide. The Argentine garrison at Goose Green was in the diametrically opposite southeastern corner, a distance of perhaps five and a half miles from the SAS team. No more.

The land there is flat, but the shoreline is craggy, with a lot of rocks on the landward side of the pebbled beach. Jake Posgate had found an ideal spot, a group of eight huge, flattish boulders that overlapped, two of them resting on the shoulders of three others.

This did not provide much space, but it provided enough for eight hard-trained combat troops to hole up, mount their defensive position, and remain invisible from any direction. The only way anyone could locate them would be to squirm straight into the low tunnel formed by the boulders, and then kiss life on this planet a very sharp good-bye.

The main trouble for Douglas was that there was no possibility of cooking the three joints of lamb they still possessed. At least not until nightfall, and even that was a little risky.

But they had water, and some chocolate, and there was little to do except wait until dark, and then attempt to cross the causeway and head down to the next harbor without being located.

So far the day was passing very slowly and very boringly. But at 1110 they heard the whine of a military helicopter, flying low, maybe a couple of miles to the east. Douglas himself wriggled out of their hide and, lying flat on the pebbles, saw it heading north, making a circular course back toward the coast.

"That's the enemy," he muttered. "They've decided their patrol has gone missing. Guys, we just became the target of an Argentinian manhunt that is likely to get bigger and bigger over the next few hours."

"What do we do?" asked Trooper Wiggins.

"Nothing. We stay right here, and hope to Christ they concentrate their search six miles north of here around Port Sussex. If our luck holds, they may not bother with this stretch of exposed coast 'til tomorrow. Meanwhile, we'll make our move south soon as the light fades."

"How close to the Argentine garrison do we go?"

"Probably within a mile. We'll just keep crawling along the coast and make darned sure no one sees us. In daylight we stay right where we are. Hidden."

And that's precisely where they stayed until, at 1300, they heard another helicopter take off from the south end of the causeway. They then saw what was probably the original one fly back. Then they heard two more helos come in from the south—probably, in Captain Jarvis's view, from Mount Pleasant.

"Jesus, we got 'em worried," said Douglas. "They now believe something happened to their guys. And they're about to scour this fucking island to find out who did it."

"Who's more worried, us or them?" asked Bob Goddard.

"Us. By fucking miles, since you ask," replied the Team Leader. "This is beginning to look very, very hairy."

"If they corner us, do we fight, or surrender?"

"I guess we fight. Because if we surrender they'll shoot us for murdering their colleagues, when the war we came for was plainly over."

"Jesus Christ," said Trooper Wiggins. "Are we dead in the water?"

"Hell, no," said Douglas. "First of all, they're not going to find us; secondly, we know someone is certainly trying to rescue us; and thirdly, we must have a chance of getting a boat out of here. We are British, and any citizen of these islands is effectively a British citizen in captivity. We just need a break, a friendly fisherman with a trawler full of gas that will get us to the Magellan Strait."

"You sure about that rescue stuff?" asked Bob Goddard.

"No," replied Douglas, curtly.

And they all fell silent, trying not to consider themselves trapped in this hellhole, from which right now there was no escape. And for three more hours they lay flat on the ground awaiting the fading of the light.

At 1800 Trooper Joe Pearson switched on the satellite radio communication and put on the headset, same as every night. In the background there was that faint electronic "mushy" sound, but, as usual, no other variation.

Fifteen minutes later, Joe Pearson was almost nodding off to sleep when he heard it...a voice, indistinct, but a voice.

"Jesus Christ, there's someone on the line!" he gasped.

"Careful it's not the fucking Args," snapped Douglas. "Give it to me!"

Joe ripped the headset off and handed it to the boss.

And right away, Douglas heard the voice: **Foxtrot-three-four...Foxtrot-three-four...Sunray SEAL team...Sunray SEAL team...do you copy? Come in, Dougy...this is Sunray SEAL team...do you copy...?**

Foxtrot-three-four...Dougy receiving, Sunray...repeat receiving, Sunray...

Get to free-range dockside ASAP...we're coming in. Good luck. Over and out.

The unseen line of communication from Douglas Jarvis's makeshift cave shut down. And the comms mast of USS **Toledo** slid silently inboard, seconds before the submarine slid below the surface.

And this left Douglas and his boys to work out the details. Sunray is U.S./UK military code for Commander. And the SEALs were plainly on their way. But **free-range dockside? What the hell was that all about?**

As codes go, that one was not trying to fool the entire world. In fact it was not heard by anyone except Douglas Jarvis. And it took about four minutes peering at the coastal map of the western side of East Falkland.

"Right here," said Douglas, spreading out the map. "About fifteen miles east-southeast of this place—tiny little place, sheltered inlet off Falkland Sound...see it? That's where we're going... Egg Harbor."

CHAPTER ELEVEN

2000, SUNDAY, APRIL 24
SOUTH ATLANTIC
NORTH OF WEST FALKLAND

USS **Toledo** ran slowly inshore, 51.16S 59.27W on the GPS, five miles north of the rough and rocky north coast of the island. They came to periscope depth and checked for deserted seas. Captain Fraser ordered the inflatable boats launched in twenty minutes as the submarine came creeping into waters only a hundred feet deep.

Commander Rick Hunter and his team heard the CO order his ship to the surface, and they watched the two Zodiacs being hauled out onto the casing, followed by their four engines, each of which was manhandled up out of the torpedo room on swiftly erected davits set inside the sail.

Commander Hunter and Dallas MacPherson led the other six out onto the casing, and they all stared in awe at some seriously worsening weather, with heavy swells riding up the bow of the submarine. The wind was not yet gale force, but it was almost certainly building, and Captain Fraser advised them to move fast and make the run into the beach with all possible speed.

The embarkation nets and rope ladders were in place on the submarine's hull within two minutes, and the seamen lowered the two boats brilliantly down into the water, each one containing its driver just in case it somehow broke free.

Commander Hunter would be last away, and Dallas MacPherson led the men down the ladders, four in each boat, carrying as much of their gear as possible in extremely difficult circumstances.

At 2030 the helmsman turned the boats south and opened the throttles, driving toward the landing site, the headland jutting out into Pebble Sound, sheltered from the onrushing Atlantic waves, and possibly from a big nor'wester. But it was susceptible to a strong tidal pull through the narrows, which might make things extremely tough for the SEALs.

To the southeast, they could see the 780-foot height of Goat Hill, which would give them some protection from surveillance, if the Argentinians had retained their high garrison on White Rock Point, the western guardian of the entrance to the Sound. But this was ten miles from the landing beach.

The near gale-force wind buffeted the boats in which the SEALs crouched, their loaded rucksacks packed with ammunition, food, waterproof sleeping bags, and the radio. The helmsmen were unable to make much headway in this sea, but they pushed along at ten knots, aware that it would take a very alert surveillance officer to locate them out here in the pitch-black ocean.

Rick Hunter was personally acting as navigator, and he knelt on the wooden deck, staring at the compass, trying to locate the gap in the low hills on the shoreline up ahead, the hills that would identify the Tamar Pass, through which they would find shelter and calmer seas, and the landing beach.

It took ten minutes to spot the flashing buoy on the east side of the gap, and they raced through, much faster now as the water flattened, leaving the warning light a hundred yards to their port side.

The landing beach was slightly more than a mile ahead, dead straight, and they came in at an easy speed, the engines cut and raised forty yards offshore to avoid grounding out on the shingled seabed, while the men paddled in with big wooden oars.

They beached both boats and unloaded them separately, with each man moving to a preplanned task, precise as a tire change by a Grand Prix pit team. The disembarkation took less than forty-five seconds.

Rick Hunter quickly checked his team was all present. And they began the most serious part of the landing, which was to haul the Zodiacs somewhere out of sight. Each of the eight men gripped one of the handles and heaved, generally amazed at how light it was with this much muscle providing coordinated power.

They moved the first boat back around seventy-five yards into the shelter of a few rocks and some sparse-looking bushes and went back for the second. Then they unscrewed the engine bolts and manhandled them flat onto the ground. They turned the boats upside down and placed them over the engines, propping up the bows to give the wheel clearance. It was a major effort, but it removed the problem of metal engine casing glinting in the sun and betraying their position.

Rick asked Don Smith and Bob Bland to cut some gorse to lay over the upturned hulls and to weigh them down with rocks. Within another ten minutes the boats were secure and invisible from the air, ready for the attack, and perhaps more important, ready for the getaway.

Using a flashlight, they discovered they were in a relatively sheltered spot, in an uninhabited area. They pulled out the spade and dug in for the night. It was bitterly cold, but it was dry, and they could stay out of the wind in the lee of a long flat rock.

Commander Hunter ordered Ed Segal and Ron Wallace to stand guard for ninety minutes each, while the rest of them snatched some sleep, and then prepared to receive the HALO drop at midnight. That would keep them up until dawn.

Right now at 2100, the United States B-52H long-range bomber out of Minot Air Force Base, North Dakota, was refueling in Santiago, in readiness for the final 1,300-mile flight down to the Falklands.

This great gun-gray warhorse of the U.S. military was 160 feet long and weighed 220 tons. Its distinctive nose cone made it look like a great white shark with wings, and tonight, with its light load, it would fly high and fast, close to five hundred knots, following the lofty peaks of the Andes. It would stay in Chilean airspace all the way south until it angled east above the Magellan Strait, then straight to the open ocean and the Falkland Islands.

As it skirted Argentinian air space, the B-52 would be cruising at 45,000 feet, too high, but fuel-efficient. It would be transmitting only non-military radar. Civilian aircraft, flying high at night, are not routinely checked out by airline authorities in southern Argentina, nor indeed by Chile. Ryan Holland had been very definite about that.

At 2120 the U.S. Air Force Stratofortress came hurtling off the Santiago runway and set a course due south, which would take it nine hundred miles down the entire Pacific coastal length of Chile. They had flown on an extremely tight schedule from North Dakota, refueling once at North Island, San Diego, where they picked up most of the explosive contents for the HALO canister.

And right now the veteran frontline pilot out of the Fifth Bomb Wing, Lt. Colonel E. J. Jaxtimer, was running approximately seven minutes late. The B-52 would be directly over the SEALs' hide at 0007, though he hoped to pick up time during the high-speed run through the very thin air above the mountains.

Meanwhile, the SEALs slept. And the night hours flashed by. At 2330 everyone was awakened. They ate some concentrated protein, drank fresh water, and prepared for the oncoming arrival of the 250-pound computerized bomb-shaped canister, swinging downward beneath its black parachute, having dropped like a stone for almost 45,000 feet. That was the whole idea of HALO—high altitude, low opening—as untraceable as a falling meteorite for 99 percent of its journey, then too low to be located by anyone's radar.

Rick Hunter was checking the high-tech target marker he would place on the ground, sending a powerful laser beam streaking into the black sky to the east. This was the beam that would flash a pinpoint-accurate GPS reading to Lt. Colonel Jaxtimer and his team—51.21.05S 59.27W. The ops room of the Stratofortress would lock right on to it in the brief minutes before they jettisoned the canister out of the B-52's bomb bay.

The beam in Commander Hunter's target finder was life and death for this mission. If it failed, everything failed. If it functioned, the Argentine Air Force could bid adios to their fighter attack bombers parked on the airfield at Pebble Beach. Parked, incidentally, in this remote, inaccessible spot without even a semblance of a guard.

At 2345, the SEALs took up their positions. Commander Hunter placed the target finder in the precise spot indicated by the GPS system, accurate to within five yards. They made it secure in the shingle and drew out its collapsible aerial pointing to the east. Mike Hook stood with him, and the remaining six spread out in three pairs to form a forty-yard-wide triangle around him.

Rick decided this was such a remote beach he would risk placing three dim chemical light markers with each pair of SEALs in order for everyone to know precisely who was where, a considerable luxury in a pitch-black, moonless night like this. It would also give them the best possible chance of seeing the canister's arrival. They all knew the B-52 would see nothing visually, but would rely totally on the laser beam from the target-finder.

At six minutes before midnight Commander Hunter activated the beam, hitting the switch that would send it flashing up into the dark skies, a lonely beacon in the heavens, ready to guide the precious canister down.

Right now Lt. Colonel Jaxtimer was still thirteen minutes out, which put the Stratofortress a little more than a hundred miles to the east, 61.10 West, flying high and fast toward the jagged headland of Byron Heights, the northwesterly point of West Falkland's mainland.

On the ground, the wind was rising out of the east, gusting a wicked chill across the exposed beach where the team from sunny Coronado was waiting, shivering and hopping around to keep warm.

Rick Hunter knew he would not hear the huge jet arriving eight miles above the earth's surface, but they might catch an echo of the engines as the aircraft rumbled on upwind, and out over the Atlantic.

At four minutes after midnight the laser marker suddenly started painting on the aircraft's receiver. Three minutes to release, and the final seconds were ticking by automatically on the computer.

We're locked on...red light, sir...bomb doors open...looking good...left...left...on track...five-nine-two-seven coming up... still looking good...that's it, sir...the bomb's away.

Beneath the huge bulk of the B-52, the doors of the weapons bay in the central fuselage began to close behind the falling canister, as it hurtled through the darkness, straight down Rick Hunter's laser beam.

On the ground the SEALs were just beginning to gripe and moan about the Air Force lateness, when suddenly they heard the far-distant growl of eight mighty Pratt & Whitney turbofan jet engines.

"It's gotta be them," snapped Rick. "Look up and for Christ's sake keep your eyes open...this thing could kill you."

They all peered into the darkness, and it was Dallas who spotted the flickering ghostly shape of the parachute. "Right here, sir," he yelled. **"Watch your backs...the fucker's down!"**

Twelve feet from where Rick stood the huge canister crashed onto the beach with a shuddering thump. Two SEALs rushed forward to grab the chute and stow it under the boats. The rest of them grabbed the long leather padded lifting bars on either side, and began to carry it back to their hide. It was heavy, but not as heavy as a Zodiac, and they manhandled it with some ease.

Inside was the required explosive for the destruction of the fighter aircraft. That took up two-thirds of the canister, but there were also two extra shovels, eight extra machine pistols, and wet suits for the short ocean crossing to Pebble. There were fuses and timers, plus wire and an extra radio transmitter. Best of all there was canned ham, baked beans, cheese, bread, cold cuts, coffee, and chocolate. Plus two Primus stoves with a couple of containers of fuel.

They immediately dug a large hole in which to bury the canister, which would not be found for a hundred years. And then they lit the Primus stoves and made themselves a midnight feast. The weather was growing worse by the hour, and they all wore their waterproof smocks before turning in for the night, against the rocks, hoping the weather would calm down before tomorrow evening's mission across the water.

The trouble was, the weather deteriorated. And five hours later, when dawn cast a grim light on the gray beach, every member of the SEAL team was shocked by the seascape. Great white-capped waves were rolling through the Tamar Pass and onto the shore. They were whipped by the howling wind. The clouds were high, but the sun was low and hidden. The prospect of pushing an inflatable out into this particular sea was nothing less than daunting. The only sound above the gale was the long sucking noise of shingle, followed by the thumping crash of long rolling waves.

"We could," revealed Mike Hook, "drown our fucking selves before we get five yards. There's no way we're going anywhere in this. Not if they really want that airfield blowing up. My guess is not tonight, guys."

He was right, too. For hour after hour the gale never abated. The sea came raging in through the narrows that separated this rocky outpost of West Falkland from Pebble Island. The tide seemed to turn in the late afternoon, and the wind whipped the water into a frenzy as it surged out between the two headlands.

"Jesus Christ," said Dallas, "if you tried to row across there, you'd get sucked right out through the entrance into the open ocean...I know this mission is supposed to be urgent, but we couldn't survive out there. No way."

The better news was that the entire landscape around them seemed bereft of human habitation. Or any other habitation for that matter. Not as much as a stray sheep or even a goat from the local hill came wandering their way. They had chosen a desolate spot, plainly safe from prying eyes, and in any event, with the machine gun rigged as it now was, they could hold off an army, tight against this rock, protected by solid granite on all sides except the front.

"What d'you think about the radio, Mike?" asked Don Smith. "We safe to use it here?"

"Yeah, I'm sure we can. So long as we restrict ourselves to short bursts. It's darned tricky, tuning into someone else's messages, especially if they only broadcast for a few seconds. Anyway, even if the Args did hear us, it'd be damned near impossible to locate us from that, unless you had really sophisticated equipment, which I doubt they do out here. You wouldn't expect anyone to be here, would you? No one in their right mind anyway."

"No one wants a postponement," said Commander Hunter. "But we'll have to bag it for another twenty-four hours because the journey has to be made at night. And we sure as hell can't do that. No one's gonna thank us for getting drowned."

And so they waited it out for the day, and the sea remained far too dangerous. They fired in a message to Douglas Jarvis on Foxtrot-three-four to stay on hold for forty-eight hours, and once more waited out the night.

Not until noon, however, did the sea begin to die down, along with the wind. It was still very turbulent, even in the relative shelter of Pebble Sound, and the waves still hit the shore with a thumping crash, but it was not like the previous night, nothing like the gale that had been building when the canister first hit the beach.

A blanket of fog closed in over West Falkland by 1300, and it was no longer possible to see across the stretch of water that divided the mainland from Pebble. This was a blessing, because they could relax and use the Primus stoves to make soup and coffee with not the slightest chance of detection by the Argentinians. The South Americans, they hoped, were, anyway, not even looking, with their own enemy long departed.

By 1400, Commander Hunter assessed they could leave when the light began to fail at 1700, and then row as fast as possible across the channel. So far as he could tell, the sea would flow in from their port-side quarter, giving them some assistance, but they would need to keep steering left in order not to drift too far off the headland at which they aimed. The compass bearing would read three-zero-zero all the way. If they were lucky it might be possible to knock it off in two hours, but the wind, calmer now, was still out of the north-west, and it would gust right on their nose.

At 1500, he radioed a satellite signal back to Coronado...**Stormy Petrels seaward 1700. Shingle forecast 1900.**

They began changing into heavy-duty wet suits for the journey, right after 1600. Each man would have flippers and rifle clipped on, the idea being that if either or both inflatables capsized—a fifty-to-one chance at worst—they would be clipped on to the unsinkable hull and able to propel forward with the big flippers.

The engines were of course out of the question because of the noise, and rescue, so far away, ruled out the use of one-time survival suits. If the SEALs went into the sea, they would have to fight their own way back to shore. The waterproof radio was sealed tight and placed in the care of Mike Hook, who anticipated no accidents. The sea looked fierce, but navigable.

At 1700 precisely they carried the two inflatables down the beach and loaded in their equipment and the engines for the getaway.

Hoods up, tight rubber gloves on, Rick gave orders for the four men in the second boat to watch him mastermind the first launch and then follow. His plan was to push the raised bow out into the surf, wait for the wave to thump and pass, then shove, running the boat forward through the frothy shallows. Then they would all leap inboard, and paddle like hell to beat the next breaking wave. "What you wanna avoid, guys, is to get caught under the wave, because it'll swamp the boat and then you'll have to start again."

Rick, forward on starboard, moved into the water, keeping in step with his partner on the port side. They watched the next wave crash twenty feet in front of them, felt it swirl past, knee-deep. Then Rick yelled, **"G-o-o-o-o!"** and all four of them pounded forward, racing through the undertow, watching the rise of the next wave up ahead.

"N-o-w-w-w-w!" roared the Commander, and the three troopers leaped over the side, grabbed the paddles, and straddled the inflated hull as if it were a horse, driving the thick wooden oars into the water and heaving long, deep strokes. They just made it, climbing the breaking wave, paddling with every ounce of their strength, until they broke free at the crest and pushed on into flatter water.

Behind them the second boat was obscured, but as the wave crashed onto the shore they could see Dallas MacPherson and his men charging into the shallows and then diving over the side into the boat. For a minute, Dallas thought the wave had them and would send them tumbling back onto the beach.

But suddenly the boat came barreling off the crest, driven essentially by brute force and ignorance, but staying more or less dry, and now free of the breakers, Dallas and his men rowing with frenzied clumsiness, but moving the boat forward.

"Good job, kid!" yelled Rick across the foggy water. "Now fall in. Get that boat right off our starboard beam where I can keep a good eye on you."

"I'll say one thing, Commander Hunter," the officer from South Carolina shouted back, "even when I'm inches from fucking death in a hellhole like this, you still think I'm as crazy as you!"

Rick's great roar of laughter somehow recalled for both him and Dallas other times when they had cheated death together. And each of the eight men sensed it, and somehow found it comforting as they settled into a steady rhythm, moving the boats forward, through the drifting fog, leaving behind a small bubbling wake on the leaden surface of Pebble Sound.

They stayed close, separated by only fifteen feet. Rick Hunter called out the stroke rate...**And now...and two...and three...and four**...

Occasionally glancing at the tiny light on his compass, he would order a minor course change...**Dallas...follow us...port side easy, and starboard side two hard...now all together...and one...and two...and three...**

They kept going for a half hour, then rested. But Rick was afraid to wallow around for long because he knew the tide would drag them off course. They each had a drink and settled back to row for another thirty minutes, warm in their wet suits but going slower than they had hoped because of the short, choppy sea, which kept shoving the light bows of the boats upward. It was not, however, life-threatening, nor even capsizing, weather. Just roughish water, hard to row through, but ultimately navigable for eight powerful pullers.

By 2030 they were still going in the pitch dark with no sign of land. Rick's GPS was telling him they ought to be on the beach by now, but visibility was so bad he could not know how close they were. Eventually he called the tired rowers to a stop and told them the boats might be somewhere up a bay, with the headlands on either side.

Thus he was proposing to make a right turn and hope to hit a beach.

The weary troopers just nodded and did as they had been told, and Rick's boat scraped up onto a sheltered shingle beach just five minutes later. They had been rowing along this shore for a half hour, about 250 yards from the beach, unable to see **anything.**

They landed in the shallows and dragged the boats out, unloading the equipment and moving toward the low hills behind the shoreline. There was no sign of life, no light, no buildings. Visibility was still only about twenty yards, and they went back for the boats, and then made camp for the night, brewing some more tea, and heating soup, silently preparing themselves for the opening mission at the airfield.

At 2100 Rick Hunter sent in his signal to Coronado...**Petrels nesting on shingle.**

With machine guns cocked and ready, the troopers had tea with bread and cheese at 2200, and for the third time, Rick issued his detailed final briefing..."We cut the wire right here and move forward onto the runway, all together...all the aircraft are parked a hundred yards farther on, to the right...we all move down together... unless there is an emergency or a patrol, in which case Bob and Ron peel off left and right of the concrete and take 'em out. The rest of us hit the deck, in the grass."

"That applies both before and after we fix the aircraft?" asked Dallas.

"No. Only before. Ron and Bob are not explosives guys. During the operation, Bob will man our big machine gun, the one that arrived in the canister...right here...that way he can cover all directions. His relief will be Ed Segal because he'll be leaving early...and, anyway, a patrol can come from only one direction...straight down here from the building. The trick is to stay quiet."

"Okay, sir. Gottit."

"Right," continued Rick. "Only six of you will work on the aircraft. Ed stands guard, while Bob cuts out the new exit.

"Now, the timers are set for sixty minutes after we've finished. That's our getaway window. And we're moving out fast to the west, on a different route back to the beach. There's a gate in the way, which Bob will have dealt with before we reach it. You all know the reason for this...if we are caught on the fucking airfield, we don't want to be restricted by just one way out through the wire, because that's where any Argentinian patrol will be waiting for us, if they find it, and if they've got any sense."

Everyone nodded, and Rick pressed on, lighting the map with his narrow flashlight.

"Okay, guys, we charge through Bob's gate right here...and four hundred yards along here... on this track where we're headed...the guys in planning have marked a very large low building, surrounded by wire, which they think is a huge ammunition dump.

"By the time we arrive there, Bob will have cut an entry gap, and we'll proceed to blow it sky-high with the hand grenades. These places usually have a few minor explosions first, and then it takes about four more minutes for the whole lot to go up, which gives us time to get clear.

"As you all know, the massive blast will attract the Argentine patrols, and hopefully they'll think it was some kind of accident. And hopefully no one will even guess we might blow the aircraft, and that's important. Because until they see that ammo dump go up, they will not even suspect we were there."

"How big a blast is it, taking out one of those aircraft?" asked Bob.

"Not much. Because it's internal," replied Rick. "Our aim is to split the engine in half. This makes a bit of a thump, but it's dull, muted, with hardly any flash. There's a good chance they won't even notice 'til the morning...if the guys at Coronado are correct, that ammunition dump is going to look, and sound, like Hiroshima for about twenty minutes. It's full of fucking bombs and missiles and Christ knows what else..."

The SEALs spent another five minutes staring at the map, and then, gathering up the magnetic bombs and detonating gear, plus their own machine guns, hand grenades, and ammunition, they set off for the airfield, moving low through the elephant grass.

Using just the compass and GPS, they followed the detailed maps, which would lead them to the airfield and the destruction of the entire Argentinian air operation right here on Pebble Island.

It took them a couple of hours to get there, moving well off track, through the pitch-black night. When they arrived, they checked out the small settlement located close to the airstrip, on the south part of a narrow piece of land, about five miles from the landing area.

Each house was marked on the map, but the entire place was dark, no lights, no sentries, probably just the homes of Falkland Islanders, farmers. Anyway, there was not one sign of Argentinian military personnel.

The air base, according to all Coronado intelligence, now contained less than 75 personnel, and Rick's map showed, accurately, he hoped, the position of all fifteen fighter aircraft on the ground parked in lines of three west of the runway. By 2300 they had not seen one guard patrol.

The problem was, as it so often was down here in the fickle, frigid weather systems of the South Atlantic, the wind seemed to be rising again. Rick Hunter could sense it gusting across Pebble Sound, and he imagined it putting whitecaps on the short, low waves through which they must drive the inflatables.

Out in front of the air base where they now stood, he could hear the wind tugging at the beach grass, and the black sky overhead seemed ominous. Rick imagined the dark cloud banks in layers that completely blocked out the moon and the stars.

The getaway would be difficult in these conditions, but the attack on the aircraft would take place in the best possible conditions, out here on the dark western perimeter of the airfield.

Rick could not see a hand in front of his face, and they all crouched against a grass hillock, before Ron Wallace and Bob Bland moved blindly forward to the tall unlit fence where they would silently clip a ten-foot gap in the thick "tennis court" wire netting.

According to Commander Hunter's map, all the aircraft lay dead ahead, down the runway to the right. And by some miracle, Ron and Bob found the fence twenty yards on, right where the map indicated it would be, and all eight SEALs found themselves walking on concrete as soon as they moved forward through the gap.

Rick ordered them onward and they moved slowly down the runway, counting the strides to one hundred, when they guessed the aircraft would be to the right. So far they had not used a flashlight, and they did not do so for another three minutes, when Don Smith walked straight into an A4 Skyhawk and uttered a short sharp cry of **"Fuck!"**

Rick whipped the beam of the flashlight around, and for the first time they could see their targets. The team leader snapped softly, "Okay. Deploy."

The six SEALs with the explosives headed to the first two lines of aircraft. It was 0006, and Brian Harrison climbed the length of the bomber and positioned himself on the wing, as arranged. Ed Segal was crouched low, and Dallas placed his right foot in the middle of his back, pushed upward and grabbed for Brian's hand. Two others seized his legs and pushed up. Dallas MacPherson was on the wing in four seconds flat.

Expertly he moved to the nose-cone panel, where the avionics equipment is located. In there he also found the front undercarriage hydraulics, and he placed a charge right in the middle, setting it for 120 minutes. Then he opened the panel of the port-side engine, the one they use for lubricating, and placed another small magnetic bomb right in there, angled to blow the engine block in half.

At the second Skyhawk, the nose cone was much more securely locked, so Dallas decided to blow both engines clean in half. While he set the charges he ordered a trooper to "Get in the fucking cockpit and cut and rip every wire you can see, and boot out all the dials on the instrument panel on the way out."

Ron Wallace chuckled at the determination of the young SEALs explosives king, but wondered what the point was of wrecking the instruments if the darned plane didn't have any engines. Still, Dallas was a thorough man.

Skyhawk three was tackled in the same way, and so was four, but it was taking too long, and Rick instructed them to take out the next four aircraft with one charge in the cockpit and another in the engine, which was much faster.

"Right now we've got forty minutes for the last seven bombers...Dallas, you and Mike better take the far two...I'll take care of the next two right here. Three men with each aircraft...the timers are all preset for sixty minutes after we leave. Ed's got the chart on the little computer...he'll just hand you the correct timer for the final group, numbered one to seven on the casing."

It took all of the forty minutes to complete the operation, but they made it with three minutes to spare. There had been no sign of a patrol from the air base buildings, and the SEALs gathered up the remains of their equipment, loose wire ends, cutters, screwdrivers, stuffed them in their rucksacks and set off at a jog behind Rick Hunter, making straight for the gate Bob Bland had just rendered useless.

That took only four more minutes, and they ran through it and on down the track, with Commander Hunter using the flashlight every few seconds for the briefest direction check. It took five minutes to reach the big shed, but not until they stood directly in front could they see it, the tall wire gate, inside of which was a large sign. Rick picked it out with the light—a red skull and crossbones, above the word **PELIGRO!**—Danger in Spanish.

"Holy shit!" said Rick. "This is it."

"You're right," said Dallas. "And we plainly have to give it proper attention."

Everyone within range chuckled in the night air. Rick called out softly…"Bob? You in there?"

"Right here," hissed back their resident burglar. "I've severed the gate wire. The lock was too tough to crack in four minutes…but right here, you can get in."

Rick and Dallas climbed through, obliterated a window, and dropped two powerful short-delayed charges inside. Then they climbed back out to the road, hurled four grenades through the broken glass, and ran for their lives, diving into the grass as the smallish explosives went up.

Then they set off fast down the track, putting themselves as far away as possible from the shed, before the real stuff exploded. They were one and a half miles away when the ammunition dump blew with unbelievable force.

The ground literally shuddered. In fact, the whole darned island shook from end to end. The flash from about fifty thousand-pound bombs lit up the night. Three minutes later, staring from the hill on which they had paused, the SEALs could see plainly the raging fires in the shed at the perimeter of the airfield.

They could also see headlights from two or maybe three vehicles speeding toward the area, down the track. Rick stared at his watch and just faintly discerned another shudder in the ground as all fifteen aircraft back down the runway exploded with dull numbing force.

None of them would ever fly again, and Rick doubted if the Argentine military would even have noticed, given their present proximity to perhaps the mightiest blast in the Southern Hemisphere since Krakatoa blew its stack in 1883. Even if they did, they would surely have put it down to yet more detonations in the ammunition store.

"That's it for us, guys," he snapped. "Now, to utilize an old SEAL phrase, let's get the fuck out of here."

He checked the compass, checked the GPS, and led the way. They ran three times as fast as they had on the inward journey. Except for their weapons and ammunition clips they were empty-handed, racing across the biting wind, over the flat, cold, sparse ground, headed straight for the beach.

They covered the final half mile in probably record time and raced into the hide, hurling themselves into the shelter of the rocks, Dallas and Ron Wallace laughing, gazing back at the brightly lit sky to the west, watching the occasional violent explosion.

The time was 0230 and the sea was still pounding.

"We going, sir? In this?" Mike Hook sounded concerned.

"We're going, Mike. In this," replied Rick. "Because at first light someone's going to know we were here, because they'll find the blown aircraft. It'll take 'em about an hour to have a massive search party operational, and they'll be combing this island with helicopters. I don't care where we are six hours from now, just so long as we're not on Pebble Island."

For the next half hour the SEALs ate on the run. Ed Segal made ham-and-cheese sandwiches, while they carried their gear down to the water's edge. Then they upended the boats and carried them both down to the same spot. Separately they hoisted the engines down to the boats, and bolted them on to the stout wooden transom of the inflatables, connected the fuel lines and the electric wires to the oversized batteries. Finally they went back for the extra fuel cans and carried them down to the departure zone.

They were all wearing their heavy-duty wet suits and life jackets, but in this surf there was no question of keeping the boats sufficiently still in the water to load them while they floated. So they piled their gear into the inflatables at the seaward end of the beach. Then came the tricky part.

Once more Rick Hunter lined his four-man team up. In the lead boat he was taking Mike Hook, Bob Bland, and Ron Wallace. Don Smith would provide the heavy muscle at the starboard bow of the second boat with Dallas, the second Team Leader, on the port bow. Brian Harrison and Seaman Segal would work at the stern.

With the inflatables now loaded with all the SEALs' worldly goods, they simply could not afford to capsize, and, standing in the shallows, Commander Hunter went over the drill again.

Wait for the wave to break and roll in, then haul the boat in 'til it floats...then take your positions and shove like hell, straight at the next wave...head-on to the break...

Rick pumped his right fist and added, "The moment you feel the bow riding up **...Get in!!... Up and over the side...Helmsman!! Hit the ignition and open the throttles...The other three get on the bow...Weigh the nose down...and for Christ's sake, hang on to the handles.**"

Commander Hunter did not hear one "**Aye aye, sir**." However, he did hear two "**Fuck mes**," a couple of "**Holy shits!**" and a "**Jesus Christ!**" Personally, he had but one nagging thought in his mind...**If Di could see me now she'd have a heart attack**.

He made one final check, saying quietly, "Everything loaded...no traces left behind?"

"Only the biggest fire since the Brits burned down Washington," muttered Dallas, in his Southern drawl, pronouncing the armies of His Britannic Majesty **Bree-yuts**.

Everyone grinned in the dark, and Rick Hunter said firmly, "Boats to the shallows...we're going together...watch for the wave...and when I shout 'Go,' **move it!!**"

They seized the handles and hauled the boats down the slope and into the inches-deep foaming water. Despite the lightness of the rubberized hulls, the SEALs were appalled at the weight now that the engines were fixed. Rick and Dallas primed the fuel lines and quickly tested the ignition and starter motors. Then they stood, facing the incoming Atlantic, waiting for Commander Hunter to select the right wave.

All seamen know the ninth wave in the succession is often markedly bigger than the previous eight, and Rick waited, counting and watching for the big one. When it came the water came tearing in around the SEALs' knees. And Rick knew the next one would be smaller.

"Okay, guys...into the water and let the next wave suck out...we'll go on the following wave..."

The next wave came in with a crash, but not so heavily as the previous one. The moment it started to suck out, Rick Hunter roared, **"Go!! Go!! Go!!"** And they heaved the boats forward until the water took the weight away, and then they shoved with every ounce of their considerable strength.

The inflatables surged forward for twenty yards as they hammered through the surf in the pitch dark, guided only by the phosphorescence in the ocean. They could see the next roller coming straight at them, maybe eight feet high. And they felt the bow rise, until Rick bellowed above the buffeting wind, **"Now!!...Get in!!...For Christ's sake, get in!!"**

All eight of them grabbed and leaped, floundering inboard with the boat's bow rising upward. Ron Wallace was first. He hit the starter and the big twin Yamahas roared. The other three dived onto the bow and hung on.

In the other boat, Ed Segal hit the starter two seconds behind Ron. Both helmsmen hit the button to lower the engines fully and simultaneously rammed open the throttle. They surged up the face of the wave, but in the rush for the bow, now rising forty-five degrees from the horizontal, Mike Hook slipped and slithered over the side, half in the water, half out, still hanging on, but with only one hand.

With a totally outrageous display of strength, Rick Hunter, lying flat on the short curved bow, grabbed Mike's elbow, left-handed, and hauled him back on board.

And now the wave was breaking, and threatening to turn the boat over backward, but Ed held the throttle open, and suddenly they burst through the crest in a gale of windswept foam and roared forward into the calmer waters beyond the surf.

Rick glanced right and saw Ron Wallace come surging toward him, and the big Zodiacs bumped together.

"Hell, Rick, that was beyond the call of duty," yelled Dallas.

"Duty?" called Mike Hook. "He just saved my fucking life."

"Shut up, Hook," said the Commander, "or I'll have you charged with desertion in the face of the enemy...now fall in, guys, and follow me through the Tamar Pass...it's gonna be a little rougher out there...and we got an eight-mile run along the shore into the Sound...just follow our speed. We're staying real close to the shore."

"We turning in at White Rock Point?" asked Dallas.

"No choice, kid. And anyway, if there's any Args still up there, you can be damn certain they're pretty busy staring at that airfield right now. We'll just creep around slowly, but I'm damn sure that garrison is deserted."

Dallas and his team fell in, line astern, and Rick ordered Ed to make for the flashing light up ahead at flank speed. "This channel's deserted," he said. "We gotta make time while we can. It's 0400 and we need shelter before 0600 when it starts to get light."

The twenty-four-foot Zodiacs made for the pass, making twenty-five knots through the short, choppy sea, slicing through the tops of the waves, riding the stump caused by the howling propellers.

Ed Segal, steering the lead boat, could see the flashing light coming up, on his starboard bow, and arrowed the Zodiac forward, coming off red two degrees, to leave it a hundred yards off his beam. And as he did so, they felt the swell of the open ocean deepen, and the bow rode up alarmingly.

They surged down into the trough, and Ed Segal, with a seaman's instinct, rammed back the throttle just in time, cutting the speed instantly back to five knots, allowing them to ride up the incoming wave rather than plummet headlong into its front wall and take a half ton of green water on board.

"Great job, Eddie!" called Rick above the wind, and he glanced behind to note Ron Wallace had similarly cut his speed. Then the Commander stood and yelled to everyone, **"This won't last...it's just where the tide is rushing through this bottleneck...soon as we break to the right, it'll flatten out a little...but it'll still be rougher than it was in Pebble Sound... Now keep it moving!!"**

In another age, Commander Rick Hunter would surely have stood shoulder to shoulder with Jones in the burning **Bonhomme Richard**.

They chugged through the seething tide for another four hundred yards, then made their ninety-degree hard turn to starboard. Right now they were being pursued by a driving four-knot Atlantic surge on their port quarter. It made steering tough because it threatened to nudge the boat ever inshore, toward the rocks.

But Segal and Hunter were its masters. Rick ordered the helmsman to come off eight degrees from their due east, zero-nine-zero course... **Come left...little more, Ed...this way we'll get a decent shove from the tide without being forced inshore all the time...now make your speed fifteen...no more for the next half hour...that's for seven miles...then we better slow right down.**

Hard astern the sky was still lit up by the burning ammunition store, but right ahead there was a heavy darkness, visibility not twenty feet, even with a bright western horizon. According to the softly lit GPS they were only 350 yards offshore, but the depth gauge showed a hundred feet of water.

This was surely the most dangerous part of the operation—exposed out here right off the north shore of West Falkland, easy prey for any Argentinian warship or helicopter. The slightest suspicion of the SEALs' presence would have put the entire Argentinian Army, Navy, and Air Force into a collective war dance swearing vengeance. Rick Hunter shoved the thought to the back of his mind.

And Ed Segal and Ron Wallace kept going forward into the night, confident of the U.S. military intelligence, sure of their leader, and certain these seas were utterly deserted, as specified by SPECWARCOM in their last satellite communication.

The Argentine military had switched off here in the waters north of the Falkland Islands. Their enemy had gone home, and so far as they could see, nothing else was threatening—except for a band of sheep-stealing brigands who appeared to have kidnapped a four-man patrol somewhere to the landward side of Port Sussex over on East Falkland, twenty miles away from Pebble.

The calm in these northern waters was, of course, a situation that would hold only for per-

haps four or five more hours, until the Air Force
ground staff established incontrovertible evidence that someone had blown the bombers on
the Pebble Island air base. And then all hell might
break loose. Nothing was more important for Rick
Hunter than to get as far away from here as possible, and pray that SEAL Team Two would blow
up Mare Harbor and everything in it sometime
this morning and give his guys a bit of breathing
room.

They pressed on along the coast, gaining
some shelter from the offshore wind, which had
now backed around to the southwest. But it was
still freezing cold, and whoever had insisted the
SEALs wear their wet suits for this entire operation deserved, in Commander Hunter's opinion,
some kind of a medal.

The maximum possible speed, without swamp-
ing the boat and jolting the hell out of everyone,
was still fifteen knots. The Zodiacs were outstanding in a sea, once they were riding the stump of
the Yamahas, driving smoothly along the wave
tops, drawing less than a foot of water. The trick
was to get the speed dead right—thirteen knots
would have been choppier as the boat sagged into
the water, but eighteen knots would have thrown
them out of tune with the quartering sea. On second thought, Rick Hunter decided, both helmsmen, Ed and Ron, deserved medals.

Huddled behind the windshields, trying to keep down out of the cold, the U.S. Navy SEAL team took another half hour to make White Rock Point. They never saw a boat, never heard an aircraft, never even saw a light, neither onshore nor at sea.

They cut back the throttles at the sight of the flashing beacon on the point, and came trundling slowly over the shallow kelp beds with engines slightly raised, and into Falkland Sound. Rick Hunter ordered a course change to one-seven-zero to bring them back into the south-running channel, and at this speed, on much calmer waters, they made hardly a sound, even in the shattering silence of the night.

But they did make some sound, and an alert military surveillance system would have picked it up. Commander Hunter could only ascertain there was no one around, that the Argentinians had abandoned all forms of observation in the remote, scarcely populated northern waters of both West and East Falkland. Coronado, as usual, was correct.

After two miles, running at only eight knots, Commander Hunter ordered another change—"Two-two-five, Eddie...we want to head down the shore of West Falkland, slowly, for about eight miles. That's when we turn away and find shelter..."

"You know where we do that, sir?" asked Ed Segal.

"Sure," said the Commander. "We'll head into Many Branch Harbor...that's to our right, a land-locked bay with only one narrow entrance..."

"Wouldn't want to get caught in there, would we?" said Mike Hook. "Not with only one way out."

"It would be almost impossible to get caught in there," said Rick. "It has probably six narrow bays within the bay, three of them a couple miles long. And there's probably another three just as sheltered. Plus the place is surrounded by mountains, some high, some lower, but protective hills. We could hole up in there for a month and never be found."

"Unless we got spotted by some goddamned shepherd, sir—isn't this place supposed to be covered in sheep?"

"Not in Many Branch Bay, Mike. It doesn't even figure on Coronado's Falklands farming chart—and the words settlement or sheep station do not appear in a fifteen-mile radius of the harbor. These Royal Navy charts are excellent, and this doesn't show even a dock, or a group of moorings."

"Anyway, we land in the dark, and leave in the dark, right?" said Mike. "How long are we in there for?"

"If we get through to Foxtrot-three-four—
we'll be gone by 2030 tonight."

0900, WEDNESDAY, APRIL 27
ARGENTINE MILITARY GARRISON
GOOSE GREEN, EAST FALKLAND

**Goose Green—Mount Pleasant HQ. We have
reports of a massive attack on the airfield at
Pebble Island. All fighter aircraft destroyed,
ammunition dump still blazing, everything
destroyed. No casualties, but Pebble air base
requests assistance for aerial surveillance.
Proceed all three helicopters to Pebble Island immediately, with troops embarked.
Repeat, proceed to Pebble Island. Runways
and landing areas intact.**

**Will extra assistance fly up from Mount
Pleasant?**

**Affirmative. Six helicopters and three
fixed-wing aircraft, containing a detachment
of seventy-five troops.**

Do we have a warship in the area?

**Negative. But destroyer scheduled to de-
part Mare Harbor at 1100 today.**

We're on our way, sir.

The problem with that final piece of Argentinian naval intelligence was that it would never hap-

pen. Even as the radio communications flashed between Mount Pleasant and Goose Green, U.S. Navy SEAL Lt. Commander Chuck Stafford and his underwater team were edging their way back to their base camp meeting point on the shores of East Cove.

They had been holed up for three days, with all their gear and two inflatables in a deep cave right on the shore, which had the inestimable advantage of flooding to a depth of almost two feet at high tide. This meant they kept everything in the boats, and jumped aboard, all twelve of them, when the cave floor started to submerge.

Their getaway was timed for the rising tide at 1900 this evening, when there would be just sufficient water in the cave to escape fast, approximately ninety minutes before the tide peaked at 2030.

More significant, however, was the fact that the veteran explosives expert Stafford and five of his crack underwater crew had attached limpet bombs to all four of the Argentine warships currently moored in Mare Harbor, two old Type-42 destroyers and two guided-missile Exocet frigates.

They were timed to detonate at 2230, which gave the fleeing SEALs ample time to make the three-mile journey back to their cave, over very rough ground, and then get well under cover for the blasting of Mare Harbor.

Right now, Lt. Commander Stafford and his team were cooking hot soup on their Primus. And no one south of Coronado, except for the crew of USS **Toledo**, had the slightest idea they were there.

Forty miles away to the northwest, Commander Hunter's team were hunkered down in the long narrow landlocked bay that runs to a cul-de-sac, southwest out of the main harbor, following the line of the shore.

After a two-hour search they found this utterly desolate spot and chugged into a fifty-foot inlet surrounded by rocky cliffs perhaps fifteen feet high. Rick Hunter had taken one look at it and ordered Brian Harrison to jump out and see what he could see from the cliff top to the east.

The SEAL Petty Officer climbed the easy sloping rock face and was gone for fifteen minutes. When he returned, he told them, "There's a line of low hills about two hundred yards from here. From the top I can see the Sound, way beyond the entrance to the harbor. Aside from that there's nothing, not even a house, not even a shed. And no sheep."

Rick Hunter had already dismissed the idea of any warship coming after them because the water through the harbor entrance was too shallow, maybe eight feet. Even a patrol boat would think twice.

Which essentially meant that the two teams of United States Navy Special Forces, the specialists from SPECWARCOM, were, for the moment, safely in their daytime quarters, unseen, and unknown to their enemy. Which was the way they liked it.

On the other hand, on the far distant shore, Captain Jarvis and his team were slightly the worse for wear. They had made their way to a lonely hillside above Egg Harbor, and positioned themselves in a gully from where they could see down to the waters of Falkland Sound. However, the damn place had little vegetation, and they'd used up much of it on the first night, when they cut the gorse and pulled up grass to give themselves shelter from aerial search.

They'd twice almost been caught moving across the narrow causeway that passes Goose Green, both times by vehicle patrols, but each time they had gone to ground, flattened into the earth, machine guns primed in case they were seen. Both times happened in the late afternoon, and both times the patrols were moving too fast, but the second one passed less than twenty feet from where they were all prostrate, facedown in a ditch.

But the Argentinians did not see them, and when the night grew darker Captain Jarvis steered his men across the barren wasteland of East Falkland to the tiny harbor where he expected the American, Sunray, and his guys to show up.

The silence of Tuesday night, at least it was silent on East Falkland, was a major disappointment to the Captain. No radio communication had been received, and the SAS men were growing tired in their filthy, dirty clothes, totally without any form of washing kit, bereft of razors or shaving soap, no deodorant.

They had maintained fairly high standards of eating, and last night, against his better judgment, when it was clear Sunray had gone missing, Douglas authorized a new sheep raid, and at midnight they had all enjoyed excellent roast lamb and some kind of pressurized bars of spinach that tasted like cow shit. At least according to Trooper Wiggins they did.

But there was no injury or illness. Everyone felt fine, but disheveled. And up here in the hide above Egg Harbor they were nowhere near fresh water, and their supplies were running short. That night Troopers Goddard and Fermer went to sleep in the gully under the bushes with sheep's blood on their hands.

As Jake Posgate had remarked, "It's like a scene from **Dracula's Revenge** up here."

"Just so long as it's not the revenge of Señor Alvarez, the Argentine monster, it's okay with me," said Peter Wiggins.

And so they slept, aware only faintly of the Argentine search going on for them, because it was being conducted in a thoroughly halfhearted way.

Just the occasional helicopter flying north, and nothing overhead along the Egg Harbor shoreline. Douglas guessed, correctly, the Jeep that contained the bodies of the four Argentine soldiers had not yet been found.

But this morning, Wednesday, the skies suddenly resembled World War III. It was now 0930 and three helicopters had taken off in quick succession from Goose Green headed due west, straight over the SAS hide at high speed, not slowing, heading up Falkland Sound.

Three fixed-wing military aircraft had also flown just to the north of them, heading the same way, at no more than 5,000 feet. In the distance they could hear more helicopters clattering, just west of Carlos Water, all apparently heading for the same objective.

"Jesus," said Douglas, "they must have found the bodies." He was as yet unaware of the devastation on Pebble Island, and an hour from now he would be too far away to comprehend the ensuing chaos in Mare Harbor. Right now he was merely counting off the hours to 2000 tonight, when he prayed he would hear again from the elusive Sunray.

Rick Hunter, too, and all of his team, watched the helos thumping through the leaden skies directly overhead. But they were not surprised, only thanking God they had risked the heavy seas and put ten miles between themselves and the Pebble

Island airfield. It was crystal clear to them where all of that Argentinian military hardware was headed.

Rick was very contemplative, as they sat in the lee of the rocky overhang in their tiny bay, within the big long bay, which in turn was within the five-mile-wide Many Branch Harbor. He knew it would be impossible to see them from the air, and even from the south they must surely have been completely hidden.

To find SEAL Assault Team One, an Argentine search helicopter would need to be flying about fifty feet above the ground, very slowly, southwest of them, heading northeast. And even then it would be touch and go. The chances of a pilot finding exactly the right height, speed, and direction were, in Rick's view, negligible. Unless, of course, someone had told him where they were.

At 1030 it was still silent in Many Branch Harbor. No fishing boats. No boats of any kind. Although from the bluff, Brian Harrison reported a couple of trawlers heading north up Falkland South, maybe two or three miles from their little bay.

At 1030 in Mare Harbor, however, things were not silent. Lt. Commander Stafford's twelve limpet bombs, stuck on the warships' hulls, below the waterline, for'ard, midships and aft, all detonated together with a dull underwater **k-e-r-r-u-m-p!!**, which caused the jetties to shudder and the harbor waters to rise up into a boiling maelstrom, which crashed onto the shore, obscuring for a moment the savage destruction of all four ships.

When Argentinian naval personnel looked again, staring through the spray and billowing smoke, they were unable to comprehend what they were most certainly observing. Four warships, calmly moored on the jetties, with no enemy on the horizon, ablaze from end to end. And the skies were completely empty—no one had dropped a bomb, never mind four bombs.

Officers gathered together and quickly leapt to the alarmingly false conclusion that someone's Navy had lambasted the ships with guided missiles, well-aimed guided missiles at that.

But no one had seen anything, no dart-shaped winged killer with a fiery tail hurtling out of the skies. And these ships must have been hit by more than one missile apiece since all of them were ablaze in three different places. Great fires were raging below the foredecks, huge flames and billowing black smoke were surging upward from the engine room area, and one of the frigates looked as though its stern was blown clean off the hull. This was a big multi-hit, carried out by forces who knew precisely what they were doing.

But whose forces? The surrendered Brits, what was left of them, were limping home. **Caramba!** Everyone in Argentina had seen the aerial photographs of the defeated Royal Navy Fleet heading north back up the Atlantic. No, the Brits had not done this. Then who had? There was not a sign of a foreign warship in the waters surrounding the Malvinas within a two-hundred-mile radius. And the skies were clear of military aircraft. Any aircraft, for that matter.

And if it was not bombs or missiles, then what was it? The gathering of Argentinian naval officers, still staring in disbelief at the torrid scene of absolute devastation in the harbor, were totally baffled. Nonetheless, they moved into action, trying to organize stretcher parties to evacuate the wounded, trying to connect fire hoses to aim at the ships, which were growing hotter by the minute.

They were also trying to work out how quickly to evacuate the entire area when the first fire blazed into one of the ships' missile magazines and unleashed the kind of power that could swiftly knock down a town, never mind a few stone buildings in a scarcely used harbor.

As a matter of fact, the scene was much like that which faced the British in February, when their 1,400-ton lightly gunned patrol ship **Leeds Castle** was obliterated by Argentinian missiles. As Saint Matthew mentioned in Chapter XXVI, **Those who take the sword, will perish by the sword.** And, since Matthew was quoting Jesus Christ, those words were presumably equally applicable in both the Roman Catholic church in Rio Grande and in the Protestant Christ Church cathedral in Port Stanley.

And on the subject of death, Lt. Commander Stafford's men had caused a lot more of it than Rick Hunter's team, and they made Douglas Jarvis's skirmish on the mountain look like kids' stuff.

There were crews of at least twenty-two officers and men resident in each of the warships, some on watch, some asleep, some working on maintenance in the engine rooms. A total of only nine survived the savage blasts, the ramifications of which would be heard around the world.

By 1100, there was virtual chaos in the Argentine military headquarters at Mount Pleasant, as commanders tried to make sense of the barbaric unprovoked attacks on their bases by an unknown enemy. Just the previous day, the Marine Major Pablo Barry had flown in for a visit, and the entire officer community, on sea, air, and land, was now looking to him for guidance. Major Barry had, after all, been the commander who conquered the damn place in the first case.

But he was as bewildered as any of them, and, generally speaking, was greatly concerned that the enemy, whoever the hell it might be, would probably be considering flattening the only Argentine military base on the Malvinas they had not already eliminated: that is, the very ground on which they stood.

The news from Pebble was plainly terrible. But the news from Mare Harbor was much worse, given the heavy loss of life. Major Pablo Barry stared out at the airfield in silent rumination. Lined up were Argentina's all-conquering Skyhawks, Daggers, and Etendards, the most dangerous air combat force in South America. And he did not have the slightest idea at whom to unleash them.

The entire situation was, in his opinion, extremely unnerving. Here they were being smashed to pieces by an enemy who was refusing to identify himself, an enemy they could not see, nor even discern. Only one thought evolved in his mind: **Those ships were not hit by incoming bombs, nor missiles. And, given the near-simultaneous attack on Pebble Island, there was no question of sabotage.**

No, thought Major Barry. **Those ships were blown up inside the harbor, by bombs that must have been attached to the hulls**. Nothing else fit. Nothing else made the slightest bit of sense. Someone, somehow, had crept into the little dockyard, underwater, and planted bombs under the surface, all timed to go off bang at once.

Major Barry now knew that someone had done something very similar to the fighter aircraft at Pebble. The question was, who? Which country hated Argentina so badly they would do such a thing? And did it all have anything to do with the sheep stealers up at Port Sussex? And, if so, where the hell were they? Why had they not been found? And where was the missing patrol? Major

Barry had about a thousand questions and no answers to any of them.

But shortly after noon, someone provided him with just one answer. Luke Milos, wandering among his sheep up in the high pastures above his house, had found the Jeep, and all four men inside had been assassinated, shot to pieces, dozens of bullet wounds. What's more, they had been dead for at least three days, probably since Sunday night. The Goose Green garrison had a medical team up there already and were towing the Jeep out, bringing its grisly cargo back in body bags.

On the face of it, the Argentine military had now been slammed three times, and Major Barry considered it inconceivable the three were not, somehow, connected. Although what the sheep stealers had in common with possibly two highly trained groups of Special Forces...well, heaven alone knew the answer to that.

But the Major was aware the sheep stealers were very possibly a British SAS assault team trapped, and surviving, on East Falkland after the surrender. Were the bombers of Pebble and Mare somehow connected? Did Great Britain have an ally who was prepared to fight on when all seemed lost?

None of it stacked up for the Major. And deep in his soldier's soul, he sensed the perpetrators of these atrocities had already left. They did not, he pondered, come in by air or road. And they did not land on the Falklands in a surface ship. Therefore they must have come in by submarine, and if they did, they'd most certainly gone. He considered a massive air and shoreline search by Argentina's military forces to be a waste of time. Except for the sheep stealers, who may be still in residence.

They might be caught, if a search was concentrated for long enough in the correct place. And if they were, that might shed substantial light on the source of the other two attacks. Argentina was still in control of several hundred British prisoners of war, and that gave them some heavy leverage.

The key was to catch the sheep stealers. That was Major Pablo Barry's opinion. And the Marine Commander, conqueror of the Falkland Islands, was very certain about that.

But, judging by the events of the morning, it was entirely possible the entire airfield was mined and seeded with timed limpet bombs like Mare Harbor and Pebble. The Major advised a general evacuation to the outskirts of the area, with all personnel warned to stay away from the airfield.

He also decided that a search of Pebble Island was a total waste of time, and that the helicopters of Goose Green and Mount Pleasant should all return to the Goose Green garrison and launch their search for the SAS men from there.

Meanwhile, he took a large chart of the Falkland Islands and stuck the point of his compass into the hill behind Port Sussex. From there he described a thirty-mile radius that ran way out to sea and took in all the little near-deserted harbors down the west coast of East Falkland, Kelp Harbor, Egg Harbor, Cygnet, Port King, Wharton, and Findlay.

"They're in there somewhere," said Pablo the Conqueror. "They're either in the hills or, more likely, on the coast. But we **will** find them."

CHAPTER TWELVE

WEDNESDAY, APRIL 27

At 1400 Major Pablo Barry ordered all aircraft out of the Pebble Island area and back to base, three helicopters to Goose Green, the rest to Mount Pleasant.

At 1500 a military aircraft bearing General Eduardo Kampf, and the C-in-C Fleet, Admiral Oscar Moreno, landed at Mount Pleasant for a high-emergency meeting with the commanders on the ground.

Major Barry spent a couple of hours debriefing them about the devastating events of the past twenty-four hours. And at 1700 they convened in an Army situation room, inside the old Mount Pleasant Airfield passenger terminal, to formulate a plan.

Each one of them was in agreement, the key to discovering the secret enemy was to round up the rustlers, and grill them, metaphorically, of course, before executing them all for the murder of four Argentine military personnel, several days after hostilities with Great Britain had formally ceased.

General Kampf was certain any SAS group would make for the coast, in order to seize their only possible chance of escape. The occupied fortress island of East Falkland had much in common with Alcatraz. It was surrounded by wide, dangerous waters, with no other way out.

"To remain here would mean certain capture," said the General. "These men are well trained and likely to be ruthless. I suggest they now have one aim in this life, and that's to beg, borrow, or steal a boat. They have no other option, and even that might not work."

"I agree," said Admiral Moreno. "If we want to find them, we have to comb the shore by land and air. It will require a lot of troops, but we have a lot of troops. And we have as many helicopters as it takes."

He glanced at his watch, and said quietly, "It's heading for 1800 and growing dark. We must prepare to launch this manhunt at first light tomorrow. Therefore we should start to get organized right now, gas up the aircraft, establish pilot and aircrew schedules. That way we can go to work as soon as it's light over the airfields."

If solutions were becoming simple in the front line of the Argentinian military, back in Buenos Aires they were becoming highly complex. The President of Argentina, in company with his principal ministers, had received this afternoon a somewhat perplexing note from the United States Ambassador Ryan Holland.

It came directly from the White House, and it was signed by the President himself, even though the letter itself had been crafted by the delicate hand of Admiral Arnold Morgan.

It read:

Dear Mr. President, Needless to say, we in Washington have been deeply saddened to hear of your recent losses of aircraft and warships on the Falkland Islands mainland. These were most unexpected attacks, and apparently without either reason or an obvious culprit.

You will by now have received our electronic communiqué, with regard to reaching a satisfactory agreement with both Great Britain and the U.S. oil companies over the future of the new Malvinas. Perhaps you may feel inclined to furnish us with a reply, with a view to opening negotiations with all interested parties.

The United States would be more than happy to both broker and host such talks. Yours Sincerely, Paul Bedford, President, United States of America.

The Argentine President at first read the letter with equanimity, but as he did so, he was aware of a certain sense of foreboding. The letter contained only three paragraphs, and the third was an expression of goodwill.

The first two were enormously more important, and they each seemed, at first sight, unrelated to the other...(1) Sorry about your mysterious losses of fighter aircraft and warships, (2) Perhaps you would now like to talk about an amicable solution.

"Jesu Christo!" he breathed. "Is this a threat? Because if it is, there's no way I'm going to condone any kind of a conflict with the USA."

His Defense Minister, the trusted veteran Vice-Admiral Horacio Aguardo, asked to read the communiqué from Washington once more. And he took several seconds to make a comment afterward. But he said, very firmly, "Two things, **Señor Presidente**. First, the letter is almost certainly a veiled threat. Second, we are most definitely not going to have any kind of military altercation with the United States."

"Are you telling me the United States of America was responsible for the atrocities on the Malvinas?"

"Sir, I cannot say that. But that letter suggests the perpetrators of these military strikes against us may somehow answer to the United States."

"As indeed, we ultimately will do, if we are not very careful."

"Sir, I thought we were all agreed before we went into this conflict with Great Britain, it would be a straight fight between us and our very weakened opponents. With just a little help from our friends in the frozen north. We did not anticipate any U.S. involvement."

"And until now, we were right," replied the President. "And even now we cannot be sure they had anything to do with the actual attacks at Pebble Island and Mare Harbor."

"Nonetheless, there is an undercurrent in that letter from the U.S. President," said Admiral Aguardo. "You don't read it, you feel it. Because it is telling us if we don't come forward and toe the line, as laid down by the White House, something else will happen and we will not like it."

"I know. I know. The feeling is hiding between every line of the letter."

"Remind us, sir. What did that other communiqué from Washington suggest?"

"Well, the first one delivered ten days ago made it clear the USA did not approve of our military action, and when the time was right, Washington would step in on behalf of ExxonMobil."

"Yes, of course," said Dr. Carlos Montero, the Minister for Industry and Mining. "But was there any indication of Washington's solution to the problem?"

"Absolutely," replied the President. "The President of the United States proposes that Argentina and Great Britain enter into a joint governing and handover period of two years. After that, with proper institutions put into operation, the Malvinas become a solely owned sovereign territory of the Republic of Argentina.

"At that point we wave good-bye to our friends from Great Britain, and Spanish becomes the official language of the islands, which will be ruled from Buenos Aires."

"And the oil?"

"As a part of the agreement, that will immediately be handed back to ExxonMobil and British Petroleum, on a fifty-year contract between them and the Argentine government. The Americans will negotiate us a very fair royalty deal long into the future."

"And how about for the next two years?"

"We will share that royalty with the government of Great Britain, sixty-six percent for us, thirty-three percent for them. They did, after all, manage the exploration and licensing for many years."

Admiral Aguardo nodded gravely. "And how about our friends in the Kremlin?" he said.

"Well, they will understand the sudden intervention of the Americans has rather changed the game," replied the President. "I've had a private word with the U.S. Ambassador, Ryan Holland, and he thinks the Russians will be happy to fade away, once they know we do not own the oil free and clear."

"Yes, they probably won't want to raise their heads above the parapet," said the Admiral. "After all, the entire exercise cost them no more than a couple of plane fares and two torpedoes, I believe."

"Perhaps," said the President, "but I don't much like being manhandled into a corner by the Americans. And quite frankly I do not think we should jump just because Uncle Sam has growled. And he's done that pretty quietly."

"So he may have, sir," said the Admiral. "But he has big teeth, and he can be very vicious, especially when someone runs off with a couple of billion dollars' worth of assets that belong to a U.S. Corporation."

"I am aware of that," said the President. "Nevertheless, I believe we have one chance, only one, to come out on top in this thing. We need to capture that Special Forces group that is rampaging around the Malvinas. If they will talk...under... er...duress, we just might be able to hang the Americans out to dry in front of the United Nations...you know, launching clandestine attacks on us, murdering our seamen in Mare Harbor, assassinating our soldiers in Port Sussex.

"But I am inclined to agree. If we don't capture these men, we would have a very difficult time persuading the Americans that the Malvinas, and the contents of the islands, rightfully belong to us."

"Yes," said Dr. Montero. "And then they might get very, very angry, and that would not be to our advantage, either economically or militarily."

"So what do you think?" asked the President. "Do we continue to defy them, refuse to answer their communiqué, and double our efforts to catch those renegades in the islands?"

"That's a possibility. But if things do not work out, and the Americans demand justice for Exxon, what do we tell the United Nations?"

"We tell them as a result of a long-running territorial dispute between the Republic of Argentina and Great Britain, and as a result of broken-down negotiations, we found it necessary to assert our rights over our own sovereign territory.

"When the government of Great Britain decided to send a battle fleet down here, plainly to attack the brave servicemen of Argentina, we were obliged to sink it. This was a fair fight between two nations with very entrenched positions. In the end we won, the British were defeated, surrendered and went home. End of story.

"The assets of the Malvinas plainly belong to us in the ancient traditions of the spoils of war. And we are always open to talks with the Americans. However, we are not prepared to be blackmailed by them."

"One thing, sir," added the Admiral. "What happens if our mysterious enemy strikes again, in secret, and vanishes just as comprehensively, as he has done this week? What then?"

"Well, that depends on the degree of damage."

"Well, say he wipes out the Mount Pleasant air and military base—destroys everything?"

"That would be very serious. And if we still had no idea who the culprits were, I think we would have to give very serious consideration to the proposals put to us by the President of the United States. Assuming, of course, he possessed sufficient influence to put a stop to these...er... most unfortunate events."

Admiral Aguardo smiled a slightly lopsided smile. "I don't think you'll find he has much trouble doing that, sir."

"No. Possibly not. But I think we should try to bring this entire business to a close as soon as possible, perhaps do nothing for a week, and then consider our position...but, Admiral, it is imperative you urge our forces to catch those intruders on the Malvinas. And catch them fast."

2000, SAME EVENING, WEDNESDAY, ABOVE EGG HARBOR EAST FALKLAND

Douglas Jarvis and his team were tired and hungry. Tired of roast lamb, and hungry as hell. The problem was, however, academic, because they had run out of lamb, and with the sudden increase in military activity in the air, the Captain had decided their regular evening pastime of rustling sheep was unwise.

All day long aircraft had been coming and going, and the SAS team was still unaware of the events on Pebble Island or Mare Harbor. Douglas was certain the Argentinians had now discovered the bodies in the Jeep, and this plainly made their position ever more dangerous.

So far he surmised they were confining their search to the immediate area around Port Sussex, but he expected the manhunt to intensify tomorrow morning at first light. He was confident in the camouflage that covered the hide. At least he was confident they could never be seen from the air. But they were vulnerable to a massed ground search by hundreds of troops.

The trouble was they had nowhere to run. They had no access to any aircraft, or any ship to get them off this confounded island. They had one chance, Sunray and his team, and if **they** did not show up in the next few hours, tomorrow might be their last day on this earth, since he neither hoped for nor expected mercy from the Argentinians.

Quietly, lying back on the ground sheet, he watched Trooper Syd Ferry switch on the satellite radio and pull the big padded headset down over his ears, like he did every night at this time. He saw Syd shake his head miserably, at the same old, same old—just that mushy background electronic noise.

Suddenly, at six minutes past eight o'clock on that chill Wednesday evening, Trooper Syd sat bolt upright. "Fuck me," he snapped. "I'm getting something...there's a voice, sir...it's a definite voice...and I'm bloody sure it's not Spanish...wait a minute...it's American...**Yes, this is Foxtrot-three-four receiving, Sunray...Foxtrot-three-four receiving, Sunray...please hold for Dougy...**"

He whipped the headset off and handed it to Captain Jarvis..."It's an American, sir, asking for Dougy...dunno how he knows your name..."

Captain Jarvis came across the trench like a mountain lion, grabbed the headset and spoke into the comms system...**This is Foxtrot-three-four receiving, Sunray...Dougy here...repeat, Dougy here...**

The response was all business. **Free-range dockside 2200...left or right main jetty query?"**

**My right two hundred yards looking at
you.**

**Signal us in...flash three slow...two quick...
copy?**

Copy. Roger out.

The newly heightened radio surveillance system at Argentina's nearby Goose Green garrison picked up the signal. But it was heavily encrypted, both to and from the satellite. Doug Jarvis could hear a voice and its American accent, but the electronic words had been automatically dismantled, jumbled, and put back together again when they hit Foxtrot-three-four's receiver. It was a voice, but an unrecognizable voice, machine made, belonging to no earthly being.

Nonetheless, the radio operator at Goose Green had heard a transient satellite transmission at 2007, received not far away, somewhere on East Falkland. Of course, it could have been a straightforward communication from one farmer to another. Many of the islanders had quite sophisticated radio systems, but this had been encrypted, and sheep farmers did not need codes.

The operator reported the transmission to the duty officer, who reported it to the Mount Pleasant Air Warfare HQ. Immediately, the entire Argentine military surveillance system went on high alert, island-wide, with every possibly electronic sensor tuned to pick up and possibly identify the approximate position of the receiver, or maybe the transmitter, even if they could not decipher what the words were.

If Commander Hunter even looked at that comms system again, the entire island would quiver with electronic antennae. Commander Hunter, however, had no intention of even switching on his transmitter, much less speaking into it.

He and his team had cleared Many Branch Harbor at 1930 under cover of darkness, moving through the narrow seaway into Falkland Sound and making a hard right turn down the shoreline. When they contacted Foxtrot-three-four, they were running the inflatables south, with no navigation lights, three miles off the settlement of Port Howard, which housed a massive 200,000-acre sheep station, the oldest farm in the Falklands.

There was a slight chop to the water, but nothing of any consequence, and the helmsmen held their speed at seven knots, making for North Swan Island, which sits more or less in the middle of the Sound eight miles northwest of Egg Harbor.

Commander Hunter knew that one mile off the north coast of the island there was a submerged wreck, marked by a flashing white light. When he saw that, they would change course to one-three-five, which would take them directly down the two-mile bay into the free-range dockside. There might be a slight southward pull from the tide, but he would compensate for that, and keep one eye on the GPS, watching for the five flashes from Captain Jarvis's light.

He'll probably faint when he sees me, thought Rick.

They chugged on through the deserted water for another twenty minutes, until Rick's lookout man, Mike Hook, thought he saw something way up ahead.

"I thought it was a green light...but it's a bit difficult through the night glasses...hey, wait a minute...there it is again...Christ! It's a green running light about two miles south..."

Commander Hunter reached for the glasses and peered through the darkness into the greenish hue of the night glasses. "I can't see anything," he said. And then, "Oh, Jesus. Yes I can. Mike, that's not just a green running light, I can see a red one as well. Whatever it is, it's coming dead toward."

"Do we fight or run?" asked the Petty Officer, tightening his grip on his machine gun.

"Right now we run," replied Rick. "Because we can't just wipe out a local fishing skipper, who's English."

"What if it's an Argentinian patrol?"

"We wouldn't have time to take 'em all before someone hit the panic button to HQ. That would probably make life very tricky. That's why we run."

"Where?"

"We make a right swing, leaving that flashing light up ahead to port—we'll get into the shelter of North Island and hope to Christ no one sees us."

"Fast or slow?" asked Helmsman Segal.

"Slow. I just want to disappear quietly from their radar, which will be switched on for certain. Fishermen have radar as good as warships."

"Please God it is a fisherman," said Ed Segal.

Nine minutes later, tucked into the lee of North Swan Island, they could hear the beat of the oncoming diesel engines. They would not see the vessel until it was past. That's, of course, if it didn't come looking.

Well, it didn't. It turned out to be a local trawler with better things to do, and it kept right on going, almost certainly into Port Howard on the West Falkland side of the Sound.

They waited for another five minutes and crept out, line astern, creeping past the marked wreck on the ocean floor, and then southeast toward Egg Harbor. The trawler had not been a problem. It was the time that was bothering Rick. The last thing he wanted was for Captain Jarvis and his boys to be exposed on a beach, a couple of hundred yards from the three houses close to the harbor jetty. Especially at this time in the late evening, when fishermen might be leaving for their night's work.

And yet he dared not hit the throttle, simply because he had no idea of the Argentine surveillance in Falkland Sound. **Jesus, twenty-eight years ago they lost a war right here...right now they gotta have something listening to all traffic through here...**

As it happened they did not. But still, Commander Hunter could not risk it, and the two SEAL inflatables just kept going at seven knots, knowing they would be nearly twenty minutes late at the RV.

Meanwhile, Captain Jarvis was leading his men softly down the hill to a point only thirty yards from the houses on the harbor. From there he would lead them down onto the beach, beyond the wall of the jetty, and out to the deserted stretch of waterfront where the SEALs would come in.

The curve of the shoreline was not perfect because it could be seen from the houses. But the other side was worse, because the beach angled outward and was in plain view of the occupants from their living rooms, never mind outside the front door.

And, unknown to Douglas, there was another much more serious problem. Major Pablo Barry had ordered four patrols out of Goose Green to drive to each of the harbors on that west coast, from Kelp Harbor twenty miles south to Flores, taking in Egg, Cygnet, Port King, Wharton, Findlay, and Danson.

At each of them Major Barry had ordered two armed troopers to disembark and take up station on the waterfront. He would deal with the rest of that long lonely shoreline at first light, with search helicopters, but for now the conqueror of the Malvinas was positive he had sealed up the most likely points of escape for the sheep stealers.

And he was no fool militarily. Guessing his quarry was in hiding somewhere in the rough hill country up behind one of the tiny seaports, he had the Jeeps pull up two miles east of each waterfront and make the two-man patrol walk the rest of the way.

Douglas Jarvis and his team, heads down in their hide, had no view of the ground to the south, no immediate view, that is. And the track along which the Argentinian guards walked was completely obscured from them. They might have spotted them on the jetties, but there had been a half dozen locals down there at various times, presumably waiting for the returning fishing boat.

And the two soldiers had arrived at twilight and somehow slipped into Egg Harbor unobserved. The SAS, however, moves very quietly in the dark, and Captain Jarvis had no intention of being spotted by anyone. They came down the hillside with the utmost stealth, in single file, staying low, crouching almost double, reducing any silhouettes that might be seen should the moon make a sudden break from behind the cloud.

They reached the hard-top along the dock without being detected and made their way carefully down the rough track to the beach to the right of the jetty. There was light in the houses, but no sound, and Douglas led his team along the beach, trying to walk slowly, to avoid the crunch of the shingle.

It was five minutes before ten o'clock. The night was pitch-black, and there was as yet no sign of Sunray. Douglas let three more minutes go by, until they reached the spot he had chosen, two hundred yards from the jetty.

At 2159 he pulled out the flashlight, and with his back to the houses, shielding them from the beam, he aimed out to sea, and flashed the light five times, three long, two short. He did not expect a response, he expected a boat. And with his heart unaccountably pounding he strained his eyes into the night, strained his ears against the soft breeze for the sound of an engine. But there was only silence.

Like Rick, he had switched off the comms system, knowing the danger of the last transmission. If anything had gone wrong he could not have been informed. Troopers Wiggins and Goddard stood on either side of him. Joe Pearson, carrying the radio, was right behind, in a huddle with Fermer, Posgate, and the two unarmed combat experts, Syd Ferry and Dai Lewellwyn.

And the clock ticked on. At five past ten, Douglas again signaled the five flashes. And again there was nothing, no sight, no sound of Sunray.

Sternly trying to control his anxiety, fighting down a feeling of dread, Douglas Jarvis said quietly, "They're just a bit late, only five minutes, but retreat up the beach a bit. I'll stay here by the water with Syd and Dai, the rest of you get into those rocks behind. I'll signal again in five."

They dispersed quietly, Trooper Wiggins positioning himself alone halfway between the three men on the shore and the four men keeping watch behind the beach. At ten minutes after ten o'clock, Douglas signaled again. And this time the three long flashes were a little longer, and so were the two short ones. Douglas Jarvis was praying the SEALs would somehow see the light.

And, in fact, they did. Rick Hunter had ordered both engines cut, and the eight SEALs, about a mile offshore now, were paddling in, hard, with firm sure strokes, and they all saw the signal, the five distant quick-flicking lights, like a warning buoy on submerged rocks.

The trouble was, Argentinian Trooper Ernesto Frasisti, staring out the window of the house nearest the beach, also thought he saw a faint light on the water. He had seen nothing the first two times, but he most definitely saw something now.

"Carlos," he snapped, "there's something out there. I saw a light on the water, along there, right of the jetty." The two elderly residents of the house, who had made coffee for their visitors, both stood up. The old Falkland Islander, Ben Carey, a retired seventh-generation fisherman, walked to the door and stepped outside, staring along the beach into the dark.

"Can't see anything myself," he told Ernesto, who spoke not one single word of English. "Might have been the moon or something."

But Ernesto was certain. He called to Carlos. "Come on, we must check this out, bring a cell phone."

The two Argentinian soldiers walked down the track to the beach, following the same route as the SAS men. And they crunched along the shingle, both of them carrying flashlights. Out at sea, Rick Hunter and his men, closer now, could see the extra lights.

"What the hell's that?" muttered Rick. "Unscheduled lights. Don't like it."

On the beach Douglas was horrified, as the lights drew nearer. "Must be local residents," he whispered. "I'm going to try and bluff this out, especially if they're English."

And he stood in the glare of the light as the two Argentinians approached, dazzled by the beams, and unable to see who was carrying them. But Trooper Goddard, using the night glasses, could see.

"Fuck me," he muttered. "These guys are Argentinian military. Peter...Peter...they're armed soldiers."

Trooper Wiggins did not hesitate. Ernesto Frasisti was almost level with Douglas, who still could not see his uniform. And the Argentinians were baffled by the sight of this unkempt beach-comber. And that bafflement, that split second of confusion, cost them both their lives. Trooper Wiggins cut them down in their tracks with two bursts from his machine gun. And the only other sound was the dull crunch of the pebbles as they fell.

But now all five of the rearguard SAS ran forward and gathered around the two bodies. Douglas, who was slightly shaken at his obvious brush with death, could only think, **What if they'd fired first?**

Instinctively he swung around and shook the hand of Peter Wiggins. But other thoughts were cascading into his mind. **What if Sunray was out there, and had seen the lights and even heard the gunfire?**

He grabbed for his flashlight and hit the buttons, firing five more quick beams out to sea. Still pulling hard on the oars in the inflatables, and still more than a half mile from the shore, Rick Hunter caught the message and made one of those decisions that had made him a legend in Coronado. Every impulse he possessed was telling him, **Speed, nothing more, just go, go, go!**

"Fire up both engines!" he yelled. **"And floor those throttles...make straight for that last signal...Now! Now! Now!"**

Segal and Wallace hit the ignition and rammed open the throttles. The bows of the Zodiacs arched upward as the engines howled, as the two Yamahas forced them through the water. Seconds later both boats surged up over the stump and settled onto their fastest angle, flying across the top of the short, choppy waves. Don Smith and Bob Bland were both upside down, legs in the air, flung back by the sheer force of the power-drive to the beach alongside Egg Harbor.

The SAS men could now clearly hear the roar of the motors as Commander Hunter gunned his SEALs into the shore. Douglas hit them with five more quick-fire beams as they reached the shallows.

"Engines up!!" roared the SEAL chief. **"Engines up!"** And the two Zodiacs came slicing into the beach, where Troopers Ferry and Lewellwyn, up to their thighs in water, grabbed the painters and hauled the boats in.

"Okay, guys...grab your stuff and get aboard...four men to each boat...eight of you, right?"

None of the SAS men had any idea who he was, this giant officer, with his face painted black and drive-on rag wrapped around his forehead. He looked like Geronimo's personal trainer.

"Captain Jarvis...your very bossy sister sent me to get you...and I've crawled through broken glass to make it!"

Douglas Jarvis stared in amazement at the mighty figure, whom he had met only twice in his life, but who now most certainly stood before him. "Ricky?" he said. "Jesus Christ! Is that you? I thought you'd retired. What the hell are you doing here?"

"Damn good question, old buddy. But I just told you. Di sent me to get her kid brother home."

"How'd she know where I was?"

"I think she phoned the Prime Minister. You know Di. Fearless."

Doug Jarvis flung his arms around his brother-in-law. "Jesus, Rick, you'll never know how glad I am to see you."

"I bet I do," chuckled the big SEAL leader. "And by the way, those two guys right there spread out on the beach, are they just resting, or are they dead?"

"Dead. Argentine military. Kinda jumped us. Had to blow 'em away before they blew us."

"Yeah, I know the feeling," replied Rick. "Better load 'em in the boats. One in each. Don, Brian... give the guys a hand. Dump 'em inboard and then let's go. Fast, before someone comes looking."

"You don't wanna just leave the dead guys, Rick?"

"Hell, no. If we do, they'll get found in an hour, if they came from one of the those houses. If we take 'em out to sea and dump 'em, it'll probably take a week. Missing soldiers are nothing like so urgent as murdered ones, right?"

"Right," said Doug. "Let's dump 'em, like the man says."

And so they all clambered aboard. Two of the SEALs shoved the boats out, stern-first into the tide. The helmsmen dropped the engines and backed out into deeper water, while the two boatmen, Mike Hook and Don Smith, hauled themselves up onto the bow.

Moments later they were heading directly out to sea, back into the south-running channel of Falkland Sound, all sixteen of them, eight to a boat, plus the late Ernesto and Carlos, whose journey would be somewhat shorter.

"How far, Rick?" asked Douglas, when the introductions were more or less complete.

"Thirty miles. We'll be running down the Sound between the islands at around ten knots all the way to our meeting point. That's a spot just south of Elephant Cays, north of Speedwell Island. Way down at the south end of the Sound. You probably saw it on the map."

"I did," said Douglas. "What are we meeting?"

"U.S. Navy submarine. USS **Toledo**. She had another pickup around at East Cove at 2100. That's a hundred miles away from our meeting point. She'll be there, right off the Elephants, at 0200, in about two hundred feet of water."

"Beautiful," said Douglas. "They got any showers on board?"

"That submarine's got more bathrooms than the Waldorf-Astoria," said Rick. "Get you guys smartened up. I forgot to mention, Dougy, you look like shit."

"And of course you look absolutely fucking wonderful, all dressed up for the enclosure at Royal Ascot, right?"

Everyone laughed at this typical exchange between the two brothers-in-law, until Ed Segal asked, "Rick, you got any idea what's up ahead?"

"We got a clear run steering course two-two-five," said Rick. "For about nine miles. Then we have to jog left through a narrow seaway off Great Island. There's a wreck to the south, and a god-damned sandbank the size of the Sahara."

"Two-two-five?" asked Bob Bland, checking, like all good navigation officers.

"Right. Just gotta be careful around the island. It's uninhabited, unmarked, and totally fucking unnecessary, but it's there."

And so they slipped quietly across the pitch-back waters of Falkland Sound, unseen by any-one, making a steady ten knots. It was a little after 2300, and simultaneously, USS **Toledo**, making a swift twenty knots 150 feet below the surface, was somewhere off Sea Lion Islands, the most southerly point of the Falklands, fifteen miles off the mainland. On board were the twelve U.S. Navy SEALs who had blown to smithereens every ship in Mare Harbor.

And right now, this particular Dirty Dozen had it all over the sixteen backs-to-the-wall warriors from Egg Harbor. Because it was beginning to rain, a violent, gusting squall coming up from the southwest, freezing cold, lashing rain sweeping sideways over the surface.

Inside the **Toledo** no one even knew. The big L.A.-class submarine moved serenely through the depths, no swell, no chop, no wind, perfect temperature. Excellent soup and steaks for the SEALs, clean dry clothes, and a large selection of movies.

Out in the Zodiacs the rain was awful, pelting down on the rubber hulls as they made their way south. The SEALs, who still wore their wet suits, were best equipped to cope with it, but Douglas Jarvis and his men were not so well insulated, huddled down inside their waterproof smocks, wearing hoods and Gore-Tex trousers. It was a wet and cold ride through seas that grew rougher every mile as they approached the open waters of the Atlantic.

Nonetheless it beat the hell out of being trapped in their hide trying to get off the island without a boat.

Meanwhile, back in Egg Harbor, Ben Carey and his wife were wondering what had happened to Ernesto and Carlos—"such nice young gentlemen."

Eventually, shortly after 11:30 p.m., Ben decided to go out and take a look. He knew where they had gone, and he had seen their flashlights along the beach, but they ought to have been back by now, especially in this weather. So while Mrs. Carey went quietly to bed, Ben went down to the beach, using his stout walking stick to help him along the shingle.

Of course he found nothing, certainly not Ernesto and Carlos. So he walked back to the house, but decided to make radio contact with the Goose Green emergency number, which they had been broadcasting all day on FIBS (the Falkland Islands Broadcasting Service), which is heard **everywhere**.

Hello, this is Ben Carey over at Egg Harbor...had a couple of your boys in here this evening...

Yes, sir. Please go on.

Well, around ten o'clock one of 'em, nice young man called Ernesto, thought he saw a light out on the beach. So he and his colleague, Carlos, went out to investigate. I saw their lights along the water, but I haven't seen either of 'em since. And that was an hour

and a half ago. I just took a walk along there,
but I found nothing. The place was deserted.
And now it's rainin' pretty hard, and I was
just beginning to wonder if they was okay.

Mr. Carey, thank you for your call. I think
we'd like to send a helicopter up there and
make a few checks. Could you listen for us,
and maybe give us a flashlight guide down
onto the jetty?

Oh, sure. Be glad to. How long?

No more than fifteen minutes.

I'll be out there.

Ben poured himself a cup of cocoa, put another log on the fire, and sat down comfortably to
wait. Nine minutes later he heard the steady beat
of a low-flying helicopter.

He grabbed a big golf umbrella and his flashlight, and headed out into the belting rain, closing the door behind him. He aimed the flashlight
up and began turning it on and off.

He could see the lights of the aircraft up there,
and he saw it bank around and come into land following the position of his light. It touched down on
the wide blacktop along the jetty. And he saw the
pilot motion his thanks through the windshield.

What he saw next, however, surprised him.
The load doors burst open and one by one Argentinian frontline troops, dressed in waterproof
combat gear, came swarming out, machine guns
ready. There must have been twenty of them.

The commanding officer shouted, "Which way, Ben?" in English. And he pointed out along the beach, at which time the entire group headed down onto the shingle and began running along the shoreline. The CO walked across and asked him again what time the two young troopers had left the house, and Ben confirmed ten o'clock.

He went back inside and sat by the fire, until the CO knocked and came in. "No sign of 'em, Mr. Casey. We're quite worried. But there's not much we can do until it gets light.

"Just to check, you saw nothing else out there, or heard anything?"

"Not really, but I did see lights on the beach. And come to think of it, I thought I heard a very dull crackling sound at one point, kind of like a firework, but not so sharp. The walls in here are very thick."

"Could it have been gunfire? Machine-gun fire?"

"Well, I don't really know what that sounds like. But anyway there was not much of it. Just lasted a few seconds. Never thought any more about it."

"Okay. Thanks very much, Mr. Casey. And good night."

With that he was gone, and Ben heard the chopper clattering up into the skies. What he did not hear was the Argentinian CO open up the line to HQ Mount Pleasant **...Bravo Four**

Six...we have an emergency in Egg Harbor...two of our men missing after reported gunfire...possible SAS bandits now on the run in this area...suggest broadcast warning to islanders, and prepare for first light search...weather conditions right now very bad, and these men are clearly dangerous. Lt. Colonel Ruiz, CO, Goose Green.

Weather conditions might have been bad in the helicopter, but they were a lot worse in the Zodiacs. For mile after mile Ed Segal and Ron Wallace drove the boats forward, their backs braced against the driving rain and cold. They made their sweep around Great Island, and set sail for the last twenty miles, now head-on into the wind, and against the tide, a buffeting combination.

By 0100 they were running down into the wide waters surging in from the Atlantic. Wide and deep, that is. They were driving into the wind and sea, using the kind of speed that would normally hold them at fourteen or fifteen knots, but here it just kept them at ten knots over the seabed.

At 0140 Rick checked the GPS and ordered a two-degree course change at five knots only, to bring them onto the precise position of the RV—two and a half miles west of the kelp-strewn Elephant Cays...52.11 South 59.54 West.

Ten minutes later the numbers on the little handheld GPS correlated. "Okay, guys, we gottit. Any moment now the submarine should make contact, but I don't want to transmit anything above the surface of the water...I'm just gonna keep watching this thing...make sure the tidal drift doesn't drag us off our numbers."

And there they sat, in the lashing rain, the pitch dark, the chill gusting wind off the South Atlantic. There were sixteen of them in the two inflatables, the bodies of Ernesto and Carlos having been heaved over the side a mile off Ruggles Island more than an hour earlier.

The eight Americans, even Dallas, were pretty fed up and wanted nothing more than to get off the decks of these freezing-cold, soaking-wet Zodiacs. Douglas Jarvis and his boys were as happy as any eight men could be, finally off the hellhole of East Falkland, where they had been effectively marooned since April 8, that Friday night below Fanning Head, nearly three weeks ago.

They were there for fifteen minutes more before Commander Hunter ordered a two-hundred-yard turn to the north. "We're getting dragged off," he said. But as the helsmen made the course adjustment, there was a sudden, massive roll on the surface of the water, as the 7,000-ton, 362-foot-long jet-black shape of USS **Toledo** came shouldering out of the deep, not forty yards from the Zodiacs.

It was as if a full-sized destroyer had suddenly materialized from nowhere. Nuclear-powered, on a single driveshaft thicker than a telegraph pole, the submarine broke cover at an angle, its massive propeller thrashing below the surface. Then it seemed to lunge forward with a mighty **s-w-i-s-h-i-n-g** sound in the long swells, before coming to rest, its deck casing only eight feet above the waterline.

Captain Jarvis only just had time to mutter, "Jesus Christ!" before the bulkhead door at the base of the sail opened wide, and the submarine's deck crew emerged carrying boarding nets, rope ladders, and harnesses..."**Okay, you guys! Make it real sharp now...get the hell out of those rowing boats...harnesses on, four at a time...**"

Dallas, Douglas, Ron, and Peter were first aboard the Los Angeles–class ship, being half hauled and half climbing out of the Zodiacs, which were now moored tight alongside. Four at a time was right, and the boarding operation took less than fifteen minutes, before Commander Hunter took out his combat knife and slashed four great gashes into each of the rubberized hulls on the port side.

Then he leaned out and cast off the second boat before stepping onto the rope ladder, no harness, and hauling himself up onto the casing with a shout of, "**Cast her away!**"

With one of the Zodiacs already sinking, the other began to ship water at a fast rate. Before Rick was inside the sail, with the door clipped shut, and making his way down the companionway, both the boats, which had served them so well, were on their way to the bottom in thirty-five fathoms, leaving no trace.

It was an expensive way to run a Navy, but not so expensive as it might have been hanging around on the surface for a half hour, trying to drag the heavy-engined boats inboard, and being picked up on Argentine radar. Submarines like the **Toledo** cost a minimum $500 million apiece.

Nineteen minutes after she had broken the surface, USS **Toledo** made her turn to the south and was about to vanish with all the Special Forces safely on board ...**"Down periscope...and bow down ten...five hundred...make your speed twenty...steer course one-three-five..."**

Captain Hugh Fraser had one thing in common with Douglas Jarvis. He just wanted to get away from the Falkland Islands, or whatever the hell they were now called, as fast and as silently as possible.

1200, THURSDAY, APRIL 28
THE WHITE HOUSE

Admiral Arnold Morgan had seen a few angry men in his time. But rarely had he sat in the Oval Office, in the presence of a leading U.S. industrialist, who was, quite literally, fit to be tied.

"Mr. President, I just cannot understand how this goddamned banana republic can ransack a massive U.S. oil and gas field, march my men out at gunpoint, and not raise as much as a squeak from the world's so-called superpower…not a threat, not even a goddamned postcard. Nothing.

"And you want me to go back and tell my shareholders, the Americans who actually own ExxonMobil, that not only have we just been robbed of two **billion** dollars—the President of the United States of America is not prepared to raise one goddamned finger to help us get it back."

"Steady, Clint," said Arnold, a fellow Texan. "This is not quite as simple as it seems. We **are** doing something; we've got guys out there risking their lives to get this thing resolved in our favor. Two days ago we sent a communiqué to Buenos Aires, direct from the President, suggesting we all meet, right here in Washington, DC, and come to terms as laid down by us."

"What kind of terms?"

"The kind that will give you back both of those big oil and gas fields along Choiseul Sound, and the one in South Georgia."

"But we don't have any leverage down there, Admiral," replied the President of ExxonMobil. "No warships, no big guns, no goddamned muscle. That's the only language these guys understand. Jesus, we could raise an army out of Texas shareholders who'd go down there and do **something**.

"I keep saying we just can't sit here, losing millions of dollars a day, not to mention our entire investment in cash, time, expertise, and plain ole Texas know-how. Goddamnit, President George Dubya would not have put up with it."

And now President Bedford stepped into the conversation. "Clint," he said, "I have decided to take you into our confidence. You just have too big a stake in this to be kept on the outside."

Clint nodded. Vigorously. "Sure do, Mr. President. Sure do."

"Well, are you sworn to secrecy? Because there is no one outside this room and the U.S. Navy Special Forces who knows what's going on. You will tell no one, not your wife, your children, your neighbors, your best friends, your fellow directors, or even your dogs. Because this is about as highly classified as it gets. So tell me, are you sworn to lifelong secrecy, so help you God?"

Arnold thought those last few words, delivered by the most powerful man in the world, had a resonant, damn near holy ring to them. He liked that.

"As my old granddaddy used to say," replied Clint, **"To the grave, guys, I'll take this one to the grave. Swear to God."**

"Okay," replied Paul Bedford. "Just so long as you remember, one word of this ever leaks out, the Secret Service will come looking for you, because you're the only person outside the military who could have leaked it. Right here, I'm talking treason against the United States of America. It's that serious. No one must ever know."

"Like I said, Mr. President. To the grave."

"Right, I'll tell you what's going on. In the past few days, our Special Forces have obliterated an entire Argentinian air base at the north end of the Falklands, taken out all fifteen fighter-bombers on the ground, and blown sky-high probably the biggest storehouse of bombs and missiles in South America.

"A second team of U.S. Special Forces has hit the Argentinian naval base at Mare Harbor on the Atlantic side of East Falkland and wiped out the entire Malvinas defensive fleet, two destroyers and two guided-missile frigates.

"Basically, Clint, we're gonna go on kicking the shit out of Argentina until they come around to our way of thinking. I probably do not need to inform you this entire strategy was created by Admiral Morgan here."

"That's good. Now you're talking my kind of language. Takes a Texan, right? Big **T**, little **e**—little **x-a-n**."

Arnold chuckled. So, for that matter, did President Bedford, who continued, "Our suggestions to the Argentinian President have bordered on blackmail, intimating, somewhat elusively, that we may be in a position to have this wanton destruction of their naval and military capability stopped. Although, we of course have no idea who the culprits may be.

"But our last communiqué was very...well, arched...though I imagine the Mafia have a more graphic way of expressing it. And I should tell you that if the Argentinians have not come to heel within the next twelve hours, we'll hit 'em again. Until they do."

"Jeez, this is beautiful," said Clint, beaming. "Really beautiful. And I'd like you both to accept my apologies, for my presumption in assuming nothing was happening."

"It's happening, all right," said the Admiral. "We're just waiting for a communiqué from Buenos Aires, confirming the Argentinians agree to our solutions. And, as the President explained, one of the critical points of the agreement is the return of all the oil and gas on both islands to ExxonMobil."

"Gentlemen, you can't say fairer than that," said the oil chief. "And I'm real grateful to you both. And I wanna thank those brave guys down there for all that they're doing on our behalf. By the way, you said Special Forces...did y'all mean those Navy Sea Lions?"

Paul Bedford smiled. "They're SEALs, Clint. SEALs. And not even I would dare to tell you whether they're involved."

"Will there be any announcement of the next mission, I mean after it's completed?"

"Not a word, Clint. Ever. Like you, we go to our graves."

"Well, gentlemen, this has been a very informative and uplifting discussion. Your confidences are safe with me, and I must wish you both good afternoon."

He stood up and nodded politely to them both... "Mr. President...Admiral Morgan...it's been my pleasure." And with that the Chief Executive of Exxon left the Oval Office, cheerfully whistling that Lone Star classic, "Get Your Biscuits in the Oven, and Your Buns in the Bed," originally performed by Kinky Friedman's Texas Jewboys.

"What the hell's that song he was whistling, Arnie?" asked the President.

"I couldn't tell you that," replied the Admiral. "But that was one happy oil driller when he walked out of here."

"Probably feels he's won the state lottery after being two billion down," said the President. "Anyway, on behalf of Big Clint, what's our next plan in the South Atlantic?"

"Well, we got twenty Special Forces on their way into Punta Arenas, and Bergstrom is in favor of an attack on Rio Grande, Argentina's most southerly air base. In the past eighteen months they've taken delivery of a squadron of brand-new Dassault-Breguet Super-Etendard F5 fighter-bombers from France.

"According to the National Security Agency surveillance pictures, they're all parked at Rio Grande, twelve of them. These things can deliver an air-to-surface laser-guided missile with a nuclear warhead. They're lethal and could be launched from that new carrier they just ordered from France. Well, according to Ryan Holland they just ordered it. I'd say those Super-Es would be the Argentine military's pride and joy."

"You want to send the guys in again?"

"Only if I can be absolutely sure no one's likely to be caught—and so long as Chile remains onside to help us."

"Okay, Arnie, you're calling the shots on this one. Even if those shots are ultimately in my name..."

2200, SAME DAY, THURSDAY, APRIL 28 SOUTH ATLANTIC 52.19S 67.35W

USS **Toledo** came smoothly out of the deep to make her rendezvous with the 3,000-ton Chilean Navy transport auxiliary **Aquiles**. They were sixty miles north of Rio Grande, twenty-five miles east of the Atlantic entrance to the Magellan Strait.

All twenty-eight of the embarked Special forces—SEALs and SAS—gathered up their kit and left the submarine on board two Chilean Naval launches, which transported them fifty yards to the light-gray, almost empty troopship, sent especially to bring them in by the President of Chile himself.

Before them was a 130-mile journey, firstly into the 20-mile-wide entrance to the channel, and then on down the long left-hand sweep of the strait to Punta Arenas, the great Chilean seaport that sits at the foot of the Andes.

Once the **Aquiles** passed the headland of Point Dungeness, three miles off their starboard beam, the rest of the shoreline, on either side of the seaway, was Chilean. They expected to dock in Punta Arenas at 0700 on Friday morning, April 29.

It was a relaxed, uneventful journey, conducted almost entirely in the dark, the Chilean CO following the buoyed ten-fathom channel for a hundred miles. The SEALs and the SAS team had dined the previous evening on board **Toledo**, bowls of excellent minestrone soup and steaks.

But the spread laid out before them in the dining room of the **Aquiles** brought joy to their hearts—the CO had laid on a banquet for the **Americanos**—it was called **curanto**, a hearty stew of fish, shellfish, chicken, pork, beef and potato, accompanied by both **chapalele** and **milcao,** delicious Chilean potato breads. Douglas Jarvis and the sheep stealers had found their heaven on a twenty-three-year-old former hospital ship with German diesel engines.

They all slept for six hours and prepared to leave shortly after 0630. They were showered and shaved, with freshly laundered clothes, and carried further clean stuff in their bergans. In fact most of the SAS shirts, trousers, vests, and undershorts were incinerated, and Captain Fraser had instantly come up with a new supply, the way Americans do.

It was a long time since Captain Jarvis and his men had felt quite so good. And when they finally docked in the Chilean Navy's Punta Arenas, about an hour later, on a cold crisp morning, there was a spring in the step of the SAS men for the first time for two weeks.

Commander Hunter's men felt very good too. And so did their leader, until he saw with some dread a hideously familiar figure standing at the bottom of the gangway to greet him. He was standing in front of a long black Chilean Navy staff car, the unmistakable figure of the head of SPECWARCOM, Admiral John Bergstrom.

Good grief! thought Rick. **There's only one goddamned reason on this earth he could be here. Where the hell does he want us to go now?**

A voice right behind him muttered, "Holy shit, that's Bergstrom. What in the name of Christ does he want now? Blood?" Dallas MacPherson was thinking precisely the same thoughts as his leader.

"Morning, Rick, and very well done," said the Admiral, holding out his right hand. "Everything went according to plan?"

"Most of it," smiled the SEAL leader. "You'll have received the signal that Captain Jarvis is safe...he had a few difficult moments, but he's right behind me, if you would like to meet him..."

"I'd like to meet him very much."

"But I can tell you did not come all the way down here just for that."

"No. I guess not. And perhaps you and Captain Jarvis, and your deputy, Lt. Commander MacPherson, would like to have breakfast with me for a very highly classified chat."

"Admiral, I would very much like to do that. But first I need to know what's happening to my guys."

"Rick, everyone's flying out of here this afternoon...Chilean Navy aircraft to Santiago. It's about thirteen hundred miles from here, 'bout three and a half hours. A United States Navy aircraft is already waiting there, and everyone flies directly back to San Diego North Island."

"Everyone?"

"Nearly everyone."

"Jesus," said Commander Hunter. And just then Douglas Jarvis, dressed now as a submariner in his new clothes, walked down the gangway and joined the two Americans.

"Dougy, this is Admiral Bergstrom, the man who masterminded your escape...Admiral, this is Captain Douglas Jarvis, Diana's kid brother, my brother-in-law, and a very, very fine Special Forces officer. Got his guys out alive, all of 'em."

Admiral Bergstrom offered his hand. "I'm very privileged to meet you, Captain," he said.

They shook hands, and Douglas Jarvis replied, "I want to thank you. I didn't do much. The U.S. Special Forces got us out, and if they hadn't arrived when they did, we might not have made it."

"Very British," smiled the Admiral. "But right now I'm talking to the guy who went into the Falkland Islands, operated undercover and took out an entire Argentine garrison with all of its weapons, including guided missiles...then kept his guys alive for almost two weeks more, behind enemy lines, on an occupied island, in very bad weather, with half the armed forces of Argentina conducting a manhunt by air and land. Correct me if I'm wrong."

Captain Jarvis grinned. "Well, you're on the right lines, sir. But I'm not much of a hero, just stumbling around, doing my best."

"Very British," replied John Bergstrom.

By now the underwater SEAL boss, Lt. Commander Chuck Stafford, was leading all twenty-five of the assembled Special Forces, in company with a Chilean Navy Captain, to a long low building two hundred yards from the jetty, where breakfast had been organized in an accommodation block where they could sleep and relax before the flight.

Commander Hunter, with Doug and Dallas, climbed into the staff car with the Admiral and were driven to the officers' mess, about a half mile away. Inside, they were escorted to a private room, somewhere between a U.S. situation room and an ops room.

It was without windows, painted bright white, with a large computer display screen on the wall, plus a line of consoles and keyboards. More important, for the moment at least, there was a group of silver-covered dishes on the long central table, which contained bacon, fried and scrambled eggs, sausages, mushrooms, and toast. Two navy orderlies were already placing large glasses of orange juice at the four set places, and filling the coffee cups.

The Special Forces commanders helped themselves to breakfast and sat down at the four places. Before Dallas had time to attack even one of the three sausages on his plate, Admiral Bergstrom said, "Gentlemen, we have little time, and I would like you to know what precisely we have been doing...in the broadest terms the U.S. government has decided to conduct a series of highly destructive raids on Argentina's most expensive military hardware—that's warships and fighter aircraft.

"Simultaneously, the President is demanding that Argentina sit down and negotiate a peace settlement with Great Britain, which will include the restoration of two billion dollars' worth of oil and gas to ExxonMobil and BP.

"Failure to comply with this represents a deal breaker. And it may cause the United States to take military action against Argentina. However, no one thinks that's going to happen. Indeed, the President's close friend Admiral Arnold Morgan is suggesting the attacks on Pebble Island and Mare Harbor may already have brought them into line.

"However, if that has not been enough, we intend to launch a further assault on their most prized military possessions. And that, according to Admiral Morgan, will surely do it, because Buenos Aires does not wish to end up in combat against the USA."

Finally, he came to the point. "Gentlemen," he said, "I have been asked to discuss with you the possibility of your undertaking this operation... the good news is that it should be swift, requiring only a very small team of eight men, operating in great secret, direct action."

"And the bad news?" asked Lt. Commander MacPherson, an edge of resignation to his voice.

"Er…it's going to take place on the Argentinian mainland," replied John Bergstrom.

"Oh," said Commander Hunter. "Interesting. Do they know we're coming?"

"Of course not."

"Just checking."

"Well…again, to come to the point…the objective of the attack is on the air base at Rio Grande…close quarters, if you understand me."

"Rio Grande?" exclaimed Rick. "That's the place down on the island of Tierra del Fuego, I believe. A full-sized military air base…home of the Mirage jets, and the Skyhawks and the Super-Etendards?"

"Yes. That's the spot."

"Well, Admiral, for the moment let me assume you have a way of getting men in there? But rather more important, have you thought of a way out?"

"Not really. We'll bring them in by helicopter overland from Punta Arenas. And we had rather assumed, after they had done their business of course, they would walk out to a safe point and we'd pick them up somewhere. Probably with another helicopter."

"I see," said Rick. But he did not look as if he saw. Not even one little glimpse. He sipped his coffee, and rubbed his chin, before saying quietly, "And what would happen, Admiral, if the men should have to fight their way out, and found themselves on the run, pursued, as it were, by very irritated Argentinians. How then would they fare?"

The Admiral looked uncomfortable. "Ricky," he said, "I know this is difficult. But this is just an exploratory talk. Let's go over and have a look at the chart and see what you think after that...I'm not asking the chaps to blow the fucking airfield up, merely to take out a dozen aircraft—delayed bombs of course—then vanish...our great specialty, correct?"

"Well, yes, sir. It is. But this is a big air base and it's pretty tricky to walk into the lions' den when there are too many lions on the loose."

"I was rather hoping most of the lions would be asleep when the guys arrived."

"Yes. But if they woke up, and the guys were caught, they'd be tortured."

"We know that. That's why we're giving it a lot of thought."

They finished their breakfast thoughtfully, and then walked to the chart table and stared at the great triangular island, dissected by the wide desolate waters of the Magellan Strait right at the foot of South America. Almost through the center on the eastern side of the terrain ran the dead straight north-south line of the Chile-Argentina border. "Hostile to the right, friendly to the left, correct?" said Commander Hunter.

"Correct," replied the Admiral. "Now, up here... right on the coast, is the port of Rio Grande...

situated at the mouth of the river, forty-two miles southeast of the Bay of San Sebastian. That's this big inlet, twenty miles across."

Then he pointed to a cross he had made eight miles inland from the airfield, and thirty-five miles from the Chilean border. That's the drop-off point, and from there it'd be a pretty straight, easy walk in at night."

"And what do you want the guys to do? Once they're in?"

"We essentially want them to take out these twelve Super-Etendard strike fighters, and then get out."

"How?"

"Initially it's a walk, through very lonely country. But the guys will carry a satellite communication system. As soon as we receive the signal, right here in Punta Arenas, a Chilean helicopter will fly in and pick them up."

"And what if the guys come under attack—or they are pursued in a serious way by Argentinian forces?"

"I must admit, we have not quite considered that."

The Admiral smiled briefly, and then his face clouded, as the SEAL leader asked: "What's your timing on this?"

The hesitation was obvious. John Bergstrom stood up, turned away, and said quietly, "Tonight."

"**Tonight!**" Rick Hunter nearly jumped out of his chair. "Tonight? A team of eight, ready to go, into almost uncharted land in the teeth of the Argentine enemy, on a mission that could get everyone killed? Christ. Are you serious?"

"I am, Rick," replied the Admiral. "Because right here on this base, right now, I have some of the best covert Special Forces in the world, experienced veterans, experts in the black arts of SPECWARCOM, men who have done it before. And I'm not liable to have this much expertise, not this close to our objective, ever again."

Well," said Commander Hunter, "I guess we may as well give it some thought...by the way, any idea who might lead the mission, as if I didn't know?"

"I was rather hoping you would."

Rick gulped, not for the first time in this war. And then he said, without emotion, "Yessir. Do I get to pick my own team?"

"Of course."

"Well, I'd like to take Dallas MacPherson as my number two, and I would select Chief Petty Officers Mike Hook and Bob Bland, because one's an expert with a machine gun and a radio, and one's an expert at breaking and entering. I guess I'm looking for volunteers for the final four spots. And I'd be happy with the two Petty Officers First Class who came with me to Pebble Island, that's Don Smith and Brian Harrison.

"The final two would need to be explosives guys, trained men who know how to set a timed charge and place a tailored charge right into the guts of an aircraft engine. I'd like Stafford's 2I/C if possible."

At which point there was a minor interruption. "Admiral, I should like to volunteer my services, if I may?" said Captain Douglas Jarvis. "I owe my life to you both—and if, God forbid, anything happened to Rick, I don't think I could face going home without him. I want to come on this mission."

The words he spoke were a true and faithful summary of his feelings. It surely would have been shocking to turn up at Blue Grass Field, to be met by Diana, whose husband had been lost trying to save him. But there was another drive inside the soldier's soul of Douglas Jarvis. Like his brother-in-law, he could hear the sound of distant bugles, and, as in the long-ago Sandhurst Cadets Boxing Championships, he was ready to come out fighting.

"Thanks, kid," said Rick Hunter. "I appreciate that, but you're not even a trained SEAL."

"Well, I'm a trained British sea lion. And they're pretty good in a tight spot."

"But you're not in the United States Navy. And I'm damn sure you have to be for this kind of work."

"Well, maybe Admiral Bergstrom could second me, just for a couple of weeks?"

"Well, I could most certainly make out a case for a decorated British SAS Commander to become a United States Navy SEAL on a short-term commission. But, Douglas, you'd have to take a very searching examination…"

"I would?"

"Sure, you would. We don't just take anyone."

"Neither do we, sir."

Admiral Bergstrom, a man with probably the most flexible command in all of the Navy, grinned. "I know you've trained with our personnel before, at Hereford. But I must ask you, how are you at those rare skills just outlined by Commander Hunter? You heard him, setting timers on specially tailored TNT charges?"

"Expert, sir."

"Excellent, Captain. You're in. Rank of Lt. Commander, like Dallas. Two-week commission."

"Thank you, sir. I'm honored."

"And does he pass your selection board, Commander Hunter?" asked the Admiral.

"He does, sir. Though I'm not completely certain what his sister, my wife, would say if she heard that."

"Well, I'm afraid the lovely Diana is not going to hear that. As from this moment, gentlemen, you are a part of one of the most highly classified covert Special Forces missions the U.S. Navy has ever mounted. No one leaves here today, not until the helicopter is ready for the flight in tonight. Cell phones are banned. There will be no further communication with the outside world."

Admiral Bergstrom stood up and walked to the sideboard to collect the coffeepot. And before he turned back to face them, he added, "By the way, gentlemen, failure is unthinkable."

CHAPTER THIRTEEN

0900, FRIDAY, APRIL 29
THE WHITE HOUSE

There was no diplomatic communiqué from
Buenos Aires the previous evening. And nothing
arrived this morning either. Paul Bedford stared
hard at his friend, Arnold Morgan, the kingmaker
who had effectively made him President of the
United States.

"Do we wait longer?" he asked.

"Absolutely not," replied Admiral Morgan.
"When someone's going to give up a fight, they
give it up quick, before something else happens.
These guys are rolling the dice, one more time,
hoping we're bluffing."

"And, of course, we're not."

"No, sir. We're not." And he picked up the interior telephone and instructed the President's
secretary. "Okay, send that e-mail right away, direct to the Chilean naval base at Punta Arenas, address I gave you. Attention Admiral Bergstrom."

The e-mail was of course coded. It read: **"Good-bye, French flock. Proceed this day."** Admiral Bergstrom was still sipping his coffee, talking to his three senior assault commanders, when it arrived. "Gentlemen," he said, "we have clearance to go tonight."

Back in the White House, the President looked quizzical. "Arnie," he said, "what do we do if the Argentinians still don't react, even after this next attack?"

"We get serious," replied the Admiral.

"Meaning?"

"We take out the entire Rio Grande air base and everything on it. And if anyone finds out it was us, we come clean and say that Argentina's armed forces seized the Falkland Islands, including our oil fields, in an act of international piracy.

"After repeated attempts to negotiate a fair settlement, we were driven to remove from this planet their air warfare capability, because it happens to represent a threat to the fair-trading nations of the world.

"And in this, we will be joined by the governments of Great Britain and Chile, and anyone else we decide to press-gang into assisting us with our case."

"And how, Arnie, do you propose we conduct this mass assault on Rio Grande—nuke it?"

"Oh, I don't think it will come to that...think about 1976, when Israel's elite commandoes stormed another nation's main airport and took it…remember they smashed their way into Entebbe in Uganda, completely overpowered a big force of guards, blew up ten MiG fighters, rescued a hundred Israeli hostages, and took off back to Tel Aviv. Not bad, right?"

"No, not at all bad," agreed the President.

"They came in by air. In four darned great Hercules C-130 transports, landed in the dark, taxied right up close to the airport buildings, and the next thing Idi Amin's men knew, the Israeli commandos were on them, gunning down the terrorists and anyone else who got in the way. Twenty Ugandan soldiers were shot down in their tracks because they were not ready… frankly, I doubt the Argentinians would be much sharper."

"You mean you actually have a vision of one of our big transporters coming in to land at night in Rio Grande, taxiing over to the main building, where eighty of our guys exit the aircraft, rush out and open fire, blowing up the building, getting rid of the Argentinian guards, and then demolishing the aircraft?"

"Subject to adequate reconnaissance, yes. I think it would work well. Very well."

"And from where does this mythical U.S. military transporter take off?"

"Oh, I think our very good friends in Chile might help there, eh?" The aircraft would, naturally, be redecorated, a nice shade of light blue and white."

"And what do you think are the odds of it coming to that kind of a crunch?" asked the President.

"About one hundred to one against," replied the Admiral. "If the guys remove all twelve of those brand-new Super-Es tonight, we'll have the Argentine government on the phone tomorrow morning asking for terms."

1700, FRIDAY, APRIL 29
PUNTA ARENAS NAVAL BASE, CHILE

Rick Hunter's team was huddled in the embarkation area, faces already blackened, ready for the insertion into Rio Grande. Each of them carried a personal weapon, the light, compact, and terminally deadly CAR-15 assault rifle, which is close to perfect for work behind enemy lines. The CAR rapid-fires an extremely-high-velocity .223-caliber cartridge, which is sufficiently light for each man to carry six thirty-round magazines.

The SEALs' rucksacks were carefully packed with standard combat gear, insect repellent, water, purification tablets, power food bars, a little regular food, wire cutters, battle dressings, knife, medical kit. Already stowed into the helicopter was the C-4 explosive with detcord and timers, one M60 E3 machine gun, ammunition, two patrol radios, the PRC319 rescue communicator, which could send encrypted short-burst satellite transmissions, in particular the one from Rick that would probably read, "get us the hell outta **here**!" There were also two handheld GPS systems and a dozen hand grenades.

Standing with Rick were Lt. Commanders Dallas MacPherson and Douglas Jarvis, Chief Petty Officers Mike Hook and Bob Bland, the beefy combat SEAL who would carry the machine gun most of the way. There were the two Petty Officers First Class, Don Smith and Brian Harrison, and the new man, the twenty-six-year-old explosives wizard, Lt. R. K. Banfield, from Clarksdale, Mississippi, or as the young SEAL put it, "from raht down there by that **big** ole river."

By late afternoon conditions were beginning to deteriorate. There were reports of claggy conditions over the Argentine coast, but the pilots were confident in the ability of the high-tech instruments in the HH-60H Sikorsky Seahawk, one of two purchased from the United States in the past year.

By 1800 they were ready, and in a rising wind, with rain sweeping across the airfield, the SEAL team jogged out toward the helicopter, ducking instinctively below the great whirring blades, and clambering on board, weighed down by their heavy packs, but ready to carry out the mission.

It was dark now and they took off, clattering straight up to their cruising speed of 120 knots and heading southeast over the Magellan Strait. Rick Hunter sat up in his small private cabin poring over the chart, wishing they had a better map, wondering what the terrain would be like between the airfield and the Chilean border, both west and south of Rio Grande.

Like everyone in the SEAL planning team, he regarded the getaway as infinitely more dangerous than getting in. That should be simple...**but if we should get caught, and have to fight our way out, that's not going to be so simple...I just wish I could tell what this ground is going to be like.**

Doug Jarvis, one of the best night navigators who had ever worked at Stirling Lines, had brought up an interesting point..."Let's say, for argument's sake, sir, we get caught and we have to take out a few Argies. I know Coronado thinks we should immediately make our way west following the river, making a beeline for the Chilean border, but I'm not too sure about that."

"Why not? It's the fastest way to friendly territory," said Rick.

"Exactly. And if I was an Argentinian officer in charge of the pursuit, that's the way I'd go, sir. Right along the river with helicopters, looking for the filthy intruders trying to get into Chile the fastest way they could."

Rick stared at the chart. "What would you do, Dallas?"

"I'm with Dougy, sir. I'd go south, straight for those hills, and the border at the Beagle Channel. No doubt in my mind. That's the way the Argies won't go, sir. They'll try to hunt us down along the short route, along the Rio Grande River."

Rick allowed his eye to wander down the chart, noting the several rivers that rose from the mountains south of Rio Grande. He stared at the high peaks all the way down to the Beagle Channel, trying to hold a mental picture of the very last segment of land on this earth before the icy wastes of Antarctica.

"It'd be a walk of almost eighty miles, south to the Beagle Channel. And it would be over a range of mountains, some of 'em ten thousand feet."

"I know," replied Douglas. "But where would you rather be, sir—fighting your way through the mountains to safety, with a chance of rescue at any moment, or dead on the banks of the Rio Grande."

"I'll take the mountains."

"Good thinking, Ricky baby. Let's hope we don't have to do it, though."

The one-hour flight passed swiftly as they flew down the Magellan Strait, and then turned east up Inutil Bay, crossing their first land fifteen miles south of Lake Emma, still in Chile. Less than a half hour later, they crossed the border into Argentinian airspace, thirty-four miles east-northeast of Rio Grande.

Twenty minutes later they saw their first fog bank, drifting in off the Atlantic Ocean. They flew right through it, as they began to lose altitude, and almost immediately ran into another, and then another.

"These conditions are a damned nuisance," the pilot called back. "We keep flying in and out of the fog, and I can only just make out the coastline...those lights up there are San Sebastian."

The pilot's observer was following his chart, and right behind them Rick and Doug were following theirs.

"Here we go, sir...here. We're looking for the river..."

"Gottit," said Rick. "Then we go over another couple of small rivers...then this lake...then land here...53.48S 67.50W...eight miles due west of the air base."

"Fifteen minutes, sir..."

And now the team began to muscle up, zipping up their padded, weatherproof Gore-Tex jackets, checking waterproof boots, pulling on gloves, as the helicopter slowed down to eighty knots, the pilot trying to cut out the noise as they flew in over the cold deserted landscape below. All of them wore thick, heavy-duty woolen hats, and all of them could feel the helicopter swaying in the gusting breeze as they came on down toward the

Rio Grande River. This made it slightly awkward for their final gulps of hot cocoa from the specially provided flasks, but somehow they managed.

"GPS showing 53.47S, longitude correct."

"Two minutes."

"There it is, sir. Dead ahead. Break left... not too close in case it's marshy...longitude correct, 53.48 right now, sir."

"Coming in."

The chopper swayed to a halt, hovered and then touched down softly, the rotors now beating quietly, but the engine still making an unbelievable racket in the night air.

The observer climbed out first, and Rick Hunter jumped down, setting foot on Argentinian soil for the first time. Dallas and Doug were right behind him. Then Mike Hook, Smith, Harrison, Lt. Banfield, and Chief Bland, who had manhandled the machine gun and the communications system into the hands of the SEALs.

Then the observer jumped back on board, slammed the door tight, and all eight of Rick Hunter's team watched as the helicopter took off, keeping low as it edged its way west toward the border. From there it would head out over the strait back toward Punta Arenas.

The wind that was backing south gusted hard over the rough damp ground, and it whipped away the sounds of the retreating helicopter, leaving Rick's men alone in the silence of the South

American wilderness. The dark was all-consuming, as more cloud, drifting in from the Atlantic, brought down a wet night mist, blotting out the stars.

Rick and Doug took a long careful look at their compasses, confirmed their route was due east, and set off on course zero-nine-zero. In the absence of a path or track of any kind, the rest just stayed on bearing and followed the firm marching of their leader out in front, going with the gradient, sometimes clambering over ridges, sometimes moving easily down thick grassy hills, but always moving forward.

Every fifteen minutes they all paused and strained their ears for any sound, perhaps a car, maybe even an aircraft, but there was nothing. Only the wind, which was now southeasterly.

Mike Hook heard it first, a dull rumble in the clouds to the north. **"Sir! I think it's an aircraft...coming in...can't see it yet..."**

"Great," snapped Rick. "It'll give us a fix. Right now, everyone hit the deck..."

The eight men went down, secure in their heavy camouflaged jackets, trousers, and hats, facing due east, peeping up over the grass, watching for the aircraft. They could hear it way behind them, and then, suddenly, it was on them, howling down the flat plain, right above, possibly only a couple of hundred feet, its landing wheels outstretched for home.

They watched its lights all the way, even catching the slight bounce as it touched down bang in front of them, less than a mile away.

"Okay, guys," said Rick. "A few decisions have been made for us right here…the first one being we don't wanna be stuck directly under the flight path of every incoming jet. I just don't wanna get caught here—that's all. Because then we'd have to fight and kill, and if they did subsequently catch us…well, don't wanna think about that, right?"

Without further talk, they made their way left, to a point about a mile and a half off the outer perimeter of the airfield. They had some cover, and a fair view, between two huge rocks, of the takeoffs and landings. They would also have a chance to observe the guard patrols. So far as they could see, there were no guard posts out here in this most remote part of the field, which, according to Dallas, was assessed as "good to totally fucking excellent."

And so they sat the night out, watching through their field glasses, sleeping in turns, one man always at the machine gun. They started their little Primus stove, found some fresh water in a stream, and boiled up some powdered vegetable soup, which they ate with bread and cheese. They did not dare to try any sustained cooking, nor did they intend to do so until they were safely on their way out.

The next evening at 1930, with night now casting a pitch-black darkness over the air base, they stowed their camp, leaving Don Smith to clear their gear into exit mode, and then maintain guard with the radio active in case of an emergency. Rick's seven-man team moved off in light rain at 1945, toward the Rio Grande base, home of the Super-Etendard aircraft.

Rick and Doug had taken the view that the two checkpoint gates, one out on the right and one adjacent to the main buildings, would be heavily guarded, but they did not know the extent of the wire that certainly surrounded some of the field.

Rick led them forward, walking through the high grass into the teeth of the freezing wind. They all noted with satisfaction it did not penetrate their jackets, nor their waterproof camouflage trousers. And in some ways the wind was their friend, because their enemy was upwind of them, and the SEALs would hear everything as they approached the field.

Rick again ordered them to hit the deck, but this time with rifles in their hands. And they crawled through the thick ground cover, making the final two-hundred-yard approach on their bellies, almost in a canoeing action, just as Doug had been taught at Sandhurst, out on Barossa Common, thirteen years ago.

When they reached the outer border of the base they ran into a heavy wire fence. And they could not tell how far it stretched in any direction. "No sense hanging around to find out either," said

Commander Hunter. "Wire cutters, Bob...let's go straight through...then we'll take some kind of a mark inside, and this hole right here will be our way back to the rendezvous point...hit the hole and head due north on the compass for one mile and a half...that way we can't miss if we get separated."

Bob Bland made short work of the fence, cutting a hole two feet high by four feet long, virtually unnoticeable in the grass, unless you were looking. Rick made a note of the GPS position at the hole, and radioed it back to Don Smith. One minute later the team was inside the perimeter fence, hurrying over to the main runway on which they had seen aircraft coming and going. Once there, they turned left down the blacktop and went in search of the Super-Es, which, according to Coronado, were four hundred yards down the main runway to the right.

They had traveled almost three hundred yards when they came to the first group of aircraft, out on the left, nearest the buildings. They counted eight of them, all identical, A4 Skyhawks, the single-seater American-built low-altitude bomber, distinctive by its high, curved top fuselage. And by the heavy clips for the thousand-pound bombs it could carry under its wings.

"That's not the ones," said Dallas, who had spent much of the afternoon studying aircraft shapes.

And in the darkness, they moved on down the runway, to the next group—twelve sleek, black, strike fighter aircraft, a slight tilt to the nose cone, the tail fins set slightly higher than the aft fuselage.

"Jesus, guys…this is it." Rick Hunter stared at the dark shadows of the supersonic French-built Dassault-Breguet Super-Etendards. "This is the bastard we're after."

Dallas and R. K. Banfield immediately moved in to check the location of the hatches that cover the engines. They were simple to find, and even simpler to open. Within two minutes, the SEALs had their extremely stable C-4 explosive ready to cut and shape like modeling clay, with two men assisting Dallas and two more helping R. K.

The two young officers placed the charges and inserted the fuse that would detonate the explosive. They then attached the detcord and ran it out to a position on the ground midway between four aircraft. Rick Hunter was waiting there to splice the four lengths of detcord into one pigtail, which he screwed into the timer and set for four hours. All four aircraft engines, and much of the fuselage, would be obliterated at precisely the same moment.

The entire four-aircraft project took the biggest part of one hour, each team sabotaging two aircraft. And then they repeated the operation twice more, ensuring that, barring a miracle, not one of Argentina's brand-new Super-Es would ever leave the ground again.

Only once did the SEALs need to hit the floor, when a big Hercules C-130 came in, and the lights at the end of the runway lit up half the field. The rest of the time they were more or less undisturbed, although they did notice a guard patrol, traversing the entire field in a couple of Jeeps at irregular intervals, once at 2030 and again at 2115. Rick thought they were going too fast to notice anything.

By 2300 they had completed their task. A pale moon now cast light on the secondary blacktop strip, which ran north-south at the far western end against the ocean. They could see it was a parking area for helicopters, five of them, in plain view now that the night was less dark.

This operation, thought Rick, **has been a whole lot less trouble than it might have been**. And he led his six teammates back up the main runway, walking fast, anxious now to get out through the fence, back to their base camp, and out of there as fast as possible.

Up ahead they could see the great dark shapes of the wooden telegraph-pole piles that supported the wide gantry of runway landing lights, the ones they had seen light up only once this entire evening, over two hours ago. Far away to the right they could see the lights of two vehicles speeding along the southern perimeter, though from this range they could not tell whether they were inside or outside the fence.

Either way, it scarcely mattered. If the security guards were driving right around the base, the SEALs troop would just flatten out in the dark grass two hundred yards from the outer track, until the Jeeps had passed. No problem.

But one minute later, with the Jeeps now only a half mile away, there **was** a problem. With a sudden devastating flash of voltage, the runway landing lights came on, catching the SEALs full in their fluorescent glare, lighting them up like small black figures on a milk-white background. Rick froze. He could not tell whether the distant guards had seen them. If they had been seen, with the fence still one hundred yards away, and they hit the ground now, they were finished.

Rick only had one choice. **"Run! Run, guys, for fuck's sake, run! Straight for the fence... I'll see you there..."**

Dallas, Douglas, and R. K. needed no second instruction. They set off like Olympic sprinters, with the other four right behind them, Bob Bland running with the M60 machine gun. The two Argentinian Jeeps were now bearing down, probably six hundred yards away, as the SEALs hurtled across the high grass, led by Dallas and Dougy, still in the full glare of the runway lights.

They could see the hole through the wire now, but the ground was very rough, and every one of them stumbled and fell, fighting their way back upright, racing, falling, getting up, charging on, trying to escape the lights, an air of desperation adding fleetness to their strides. It was not possible to move any faster over that ground than those six men traveled. They were now lining up to get through the hole.

But, with absolute horror, Doug Jarvis realized the CO was no longer with them. "Rick... Ricky!!" he yelled. "Answer me. Where are you?" But there was only the revving of the Jeep's engine to be heard, and no sign of the Commander.

He was back in the grass, lying prostrate, facedown, the light on his back, but still, he guessed, hard to see. If the Jeeps kept going, fine. He would wait 'til they had passed, wait 'til the plane had landed, wait 'til the lights were out, and then make his way back to the rendezvous point.

But if the guards in those Jeeps had spotted them, then they would slow down, and make for the fence, with their radios, and lights, and instant access to helicopters, maybe even dogs. And in a race across country, Rick's men would have hardly any start on them. In his opinion, they might very easily be looking at the last hour of their lives. Rick knew he needed to stay still and then move in from the rear, machine gun blazing, if the guys were caught.

And now he could see the Jeep coming on, fast, two yards away. **Jesus Christ! Are they slowing?**

Fuck me. Yes, they are. They're stopping. Oh, shit. They're getting out. At least three of them are...headed for the fence.

Rick lay still, making his preparations, squirming his way toward one of the big wooden pylons supporting the gantry. He felt the pin of his first grenade in his fingers, pulled, and ran forward. He saw the soldier in the rear Jeep turn toward him and raise his rifle, and then he hurled the grenade, diving sideways back into the grass, the bullets ripping into the ground two feet to his right. The grenade sailed high and landed in the back of the Jeep, and the explosion lifted it into the air, killing four men and blowing the second vehicle forward onto its nose.

Rick came to his feet again and hurled the second grenade, which hit the underside of the upturned Jeep and blew it, and its driver, to smithereens...and Rick came running in behind the blast.

The three Argentinians at the fence had turned around, staring at the destruction, uncertain what had happened, half blinded by the massive lights, stunned by the closeness of the explosions. Not one of them had even seen Rick Hunter, and for a split second they just stood there, mouths open, bathed in a light that was brighter than the flames.

And now they ran back toward their burning vehicle. And as they did so, the SEAL leader stepped out from behind it. Rick's CAR-15 fired three lightning bursts, and all three Argentinian guards fell instantly dead in the illuminated grassland in front of the fence. And the runway lights were still so shatteringly bright, neither the explosions nor the fires had made any impact upon the darkness.

Without a second glance, Rick bolted for the fence, diving underneath, picking himself up and running straight into the arms of Doug Jarvis, who had come back for him. "Christ, Ricky...I thought you'd bought it..."

"No. Not me, Dougy. The only thing I bought was about thirty minutes for us to get the hell out of here...come on...back to base...before we all get killed."

0120, SUNDAY MORNING, MAY 1
AIR TRAFFIC CONTROL,
RIO GRANDE BASE

Acting Sub-Lt. Juan Alvarez, his eyes glued to the screen, was watching for the second Hercules C-130 of the night to make its approach from the north. He had been talking to the pilot, calling out height and distance, when Rick Hunter wiped out the entire mobile guard patrol. Juan saw nothing.

His only other colleague in the control tower was Jesus de Cuelo, aged twenty-one, who had been trying to read a book above the interruption of Juan's jargon with the Hercules, and was just about to tell him to keep it down when the Jeeps were blown.

Jesus thought he had seen a bright flash way down at the end of the runway, and he stood up to see what was happening. However, at that moment, the Hercules came in, thundering out of the sky, its landing wheels hitting the blacktop with their usual heavy impact. Both men watched it taxiing in, but it was not until the Hercules came to a halt that Jesus took another look down the runway.

"You see something way down there near the big lights?"

"No. Where? What kind of thing...?"

"Sudden bright light...almost like an explosion...I think I can still see something...turn out the runway lights...there's nothing else coming in 'til tomorrow, hah?"

Juan hit the big switch, plunged the distant part of the airfield back into darkness, and there, quite clearly now, were two flickering lights, almost a mile away.

"What the hell's that?"

"Can't tell...maybe a plane crash. Ha ha ha."

"No. That couldn't be. We'd have seen it."

"Just joking. But it has to be something...can you see the guards' Jeep? We could get 'em on the radio...tell 'em to go have a look."

"Wait a minute...I'll get 'em..."

Two minutes went by. "That's funny. They don't answer...I'll try the guard room."

"Fat chance. They're all asleep."

"Well, I'll have to wake 'em up, hah?"

And they took a lot of waking. It was five minutes before the duty officer came to the telephone and listened to Juan Alvarez report that he thought he could see two small fires at the end of the runway, that he could get no reply from the patrol, and would one of the hundred lazy pigs in the guardroom kindly get down there and find out what the hell was going on, or else he'd call the air base commandant.

The guard knew better than to argue with the night chief of Air Traffic Control, who wore on his sleeve, he knew, the tiny gold crossed anchors and thick single stripe of a junior officer.

"Right away, sir," he growled. But it was not right away. It was about ten more minutes before he and his three colleagues were in a vehicle and ready to go. Five minutes later they stood staring at the burned-out wrecks of the two patrol Jeeps, in which it was obvious that several people had died.

The area around them was pitch-black, save for the headlights and the dying embers of the fires, and they called into the tower for Lt. Alvarez to switch on the runway lights.

When they were finally illuminated, the first thing they saw was three dead guards, lying faceup in the grass, slammed backward by the impact of Rick Hunter's bullets.

"Jesus," muttered one of the security men. And he was not referring to young de Cuelo. He crossed himself, and said, "We better get some brass out here. These men have been shot."

Twenty minutes later the area around the still-smoldering Jeeps was occupied by fifteen people, one of them Commander Marcel Carbaza, the camp commandant, two of them doctors, plus the head of security, Lt. Commander Ricardo Testa.

"No doubt, sir. All three men were shot. I'd say from a burst of expertly delivered fire. The bullets were less than 6mm-caliber, and they all hit in the central chest area..."

"Hmmmm." The camp commandant was thoughtful. "Obviously military?"

"Oh, I'd say so, definitely."

"Well, gentlemen. If that's the case we should perhaps stand by for the entire air base to go up. This looks like Pebble Island all over again. Special Forces, eh?"

Two men laughed. Nervously.

"But if it doesn't go up...then I ask myself many questions...how did they get here? What were they doing here, shooting guards and vanishing? Or are they still here?"

And then his tone hardened. "Lt. Commander Testa. I want this camp searched from end to end. Every building, every aircraft, for signs of a Special

Forces raid. Meanwhile, get the helicopters in the
sky, eh? If they're on the run, they're making for
the Chilean border. Heading west, down the river.
There's no way they'd want to stay in Argentinian
territory. Whatever it is they've done.

**"Take dogs if you have to. Then we catch
'em. Make 'em talk, hah? Clear up a few
mysteries. Now get moving!"**

Dutifully, the guards on the big Argentine
air base moved into action, not what you'd de-
scribe as urgently—at least the SEALs would not
have regarded it as such. But it was activity. They
turned on every light on the base, runway, field,
service area, fueling area, and inside the buildings. Then they began the two-hour-long process
of searching every yard of the place.

Patrols circled the airfield, drove up and down
the runways, then, at 12:25 a.m., the order was issued to begin a ground search on foot, lines of men
moving across the airfield into the parked aircraft.

Which was roughly the time the detcord,
placed with such unerring precision by U.S. Navy
Lieutenants MacPherson and Banfield, blew all
twelve Etendards to pieces with shuddering si-
multaneous explosions that shook the outer field
of the air base—especially the area in which four
of the engines had blasted upward and crashed
to the ground, courtesy of Dallas, who was apt to
be a bit heavy on the gas pedal when placing C-4
explosive.

Lt. Commander Testa, who had been gazing out at the airfield from the control tower, almost had a heart attack. He knew a career-threatening explosion when he saw one, and he roared somewhat hysterically into the air base Tannoy system, **Action stations! Action stations! We are under attack...repeat, under attack!! Air search patrols, go!! Action stations!! Action stations!!**

0240, SUNDAY MORNING, MAY 1
SOUTH OF THE RIO GRANDE RIVER

Rick Hunter and his men had a start, so far, of one hour and twenty minutes, which was not much of a match for a pursuing helicopter. But they had used the time well, and the rising moon caught them jogging steadily across flat country, more than seven miles south of the base, Don Smith and Bob Bland carrying the machine gun between them, Mike Hook with the communications system. Thankfully, they were light now of their heavy loads of explosive and detonation gear.

Their years of training made the going easy and their feet beat out a relentless rhythm on the soft grassland, their breath coming effortlessly. They knew that up ahead the ground would begin to rise, up into the mountains. But that way lay cover, and shelter, and a chance to get the satellite system into action, a chance to call in rescue. Out here on the bleak coastal plain, with little tree cover, there was nothing for it but to run, south, literally heading for the hills, away from the Argentinian pursuit teams, which would surely not be far behind.

And now, in the far distance they could hear the muffled beat of helicopters, the unmistakable clatter of those big engines echoing through the night. Doug Jarvis thought they would probably be French-built Pumas he had seen on the north-south runway. These patrol aircraft were never heavily gunned, but they could carry pintle-mounted machine guns, which Rick Hunter thought was not a reason for real overwhelming joy.

However, the noise of the helicopters was growing fainter, disappearing away to the northwest, and Dallas confirmed what Captain Jarvis had thought in the first place..."They went down the river, sir. Straight for the border."

"Dallas, you'll probably end up an Admiral, with that fast brain of yours," said Rick.

"Very likely, sir. Very likely. I was hoping to mention that to the President soon as we get back."

"If we get back," muttered Chief Hook, jogging along on an easy stride right next to Rick.

"We'll be all right," said Dougy. "Remember, they've got a thirty-five-mile stretch of land to check out all the way to the border, and they don't have a damn thing to go on. They don't know if we're in a vehicle. Whether we've been rescued... whether we had a helicopter. They don't even know if we're a force of two, six, or twenty.

"They don't even know whether we have a Stinger to knock 'em right out of the sky. My guess is we won't see those helicopters for several hours, not 'til they get sick of the river route into Chile. Then they might run a check to the north, and to the south, but it won't be yet. Mark my words."

Acting Lt. Commander Jarvis was correct, as it turned out. The Argentinian search troops thundered up and down their stretch of the river, all the way to Chile's eastern border and back, all through the morning. And it was not until 1500—when Commander Hunter and his men had been running and jogging for fourteen hours and were on the verge of exhaustion—that Commander Marcel Carbaza's men finally switched their attack, first, briefly, to the north. Then to the south.

By now the SEAL team had covered a truly phenomenal thirty-eight miles. They were still moving steadily forward into the long, snow-capped mountains that guard the northern approaches to the Beagle Channel. This is the five-mile-wide waterway that flows ultimately into the Atlantic, dividing Argentina and Chile in the extreme south, the final seaward fragments of windswept mountainous land, which includes Cape Horn, and belongs to Chile.

The total distance from Rio Grande to the shores of the channel was eighty miles, and the SAS men were just about halfway when they spotted the helicopters, battering their way up the foothills of the mountains, searching not only with high-powered naval binoculars, but also with heat-seeking infrared. None of the Argentinian searchers believed that a British assault team could possibly have got this far, but they were under orders to cover a fifty-mile-radius, and they were doing it, flying back and forth, covering every yard of the ground.

Rick thought his best chance was to deploy among the rocks and lay low, try to get under the lee, away from the sights of the helicopters. And right now they were moving through a bowl-shaped valley, which they had reached through a rocky pass, where they encountered their first snow. And so they walked down the slope and turned into a crevasse, staying low, listening for the chopper to come clattering through the pass.

It took half an hour, and when it did show up it made enough din to start an avalanche, roaring above them heading south, its search sensors out in front, missing them completely. The trouble was a second helicopter was coming the other way, and its search sensors, seeking heat, could hardly miss them. Nor did it. It hesitated right over their lair, hovered, and then edged away, looking for a landing spot right in the middle of the bowl, not three hundred yards from them.

"Stay still, but get that machine gun ready," snapped Rick. "Dallas, Mike, come with me. We'll try and divert them."

The three soldiers set off, running up through the rocks along the western edge of the valley. They were still able to see the big Puma, now on the ground, its blades whirring. But what they next saw was very bad news indeed. Three heavily armed soldiers had disembarked, and they were hanging on to three big, black-and-brown Doberman pinschers, straining at their leashes. Rick could see their hideous pointed ears from where he stood. He did not have to imagine their salivating mouths.

"Fuckit," he muttered. "Let's keep going."

But then he heard the dogs bark, and realized they were loose, running on ahead of their handlers, searching for the scent. Rick, Dallas, and Mike Hook climbed higher, but they could not make it high enough, and the first dog was around the corner of the rock, its long powerful paws skidding, its breath coming in short eager bursts, a low growl of anticipation in its throat, as it spotted the SEAL Commander. The Doberman instantly adjusted course to the higher ground, and charged straight at him, barking now, fast as a racing greyhound, teeth barred, ready to tear Rick Hunter apart.

The SEAL chief, off balance, trying to hang on to the rock face, tried desperately to draw his pistol, struggling to get a bullet away, in any direction, just to slow the raging beast down.

But it was too late. For the dog, that is. Captain Doug Jarvis blew it away with his standard issue CAR-15, the bullets smashing into its head. And as he did so, the other two came charging up the stony hill, and Dougy felt obliged to treat all dogs equally. "Fucking things," he muttered. "Anyway, I always preferred Labradors."

However, the machine-gun fire that had wiped out the dog pack had attracted everyone, and now the three Argentinian troopers were racing after the dogs, light machine guns held before them.

Back in the crevasse, Don Smith had heard the gunfire but could not make out who was alive and who wasn't. But he could see the pursuing Argentinians, and he opened up with a withering burst from the big M60 machine gun, cutting all three down on these cold remote southern mountains of their homeland.

Dallas never missed a beat. He could see the chopper still revved up on the ground with just the pilot remaining inside. He ran toward it from the blind side, right on the pilot's seven o'clock...200 yards...150 yards...100 yards...he still kept running...only eighty feet now...**"First base!"** he yelled.

And he hurled his grenade, underarm, hard, low and straight, a real frozen rope, clean through the open door. And he heard it smack into the instrument panel, breaking glass. A split second later it exploded with a massive echoing roar around the valley, obliterating both helicopter and driver. "I shoulda played for the Braves," he muttered. "This stuff is getting fucking crazy."

The question was, where was the first helicopter, which seemed to have gone? Commander Hunter had no idea, but he thought it might be making another search line out to the right.

"Anyway," he told the troops, "if our luck holds, the damned thing will return to base, and they might not work out the other one's...er...crashed, at least for an hour or so, by when it'll be just about dark...we better put a few miles between us and this burning wreck...then we'll stop and eat and get the communications fired up...I don't think the Args will conduct a rescue operation until it's light."

And so they pushed on, weary now, taking turns carrying the gun and the satellite system through the valley, then climbing some more, up through the snowy passes. For leadership at these heights Rick handed over to the unerring instincts of the mountain man, SAS Captain Jarvis, a man who could follow the contours of the slopes and

peaks, picking his way through the lower gaps, trying to restrict their climbing, staying east where
the escarpments were less formidable, going for
the Atlantic end of the giant Lake Fagnano.

By 1930 the GPS was telling them they had
covered fifty-four miles in eighteen hours, a su-
perhuman feat of endurance and stamina through
this kind of terrain. And right now they were enjoying two real slices of luck. One, it had been an
unusually mild autumn, with snow not so bad as
it might have been, even up here; and two, the
Args seemed to have gone home for the night.

Thus Rick Hunter's tired band of warriors
found a dry spot under the lee of a rocky hill, un-
packed their rucksacks, lit the Primus, and fired up
the communications system. Mike Hook had sent
their message away in a fast satellite burst while
they were waiting for Commander Hunter on the
airfield, and now he was recording a new one.

This would give their current GPS position—
54.30S, 67.25W. **Have come under attack from
Arg helos, anticipate further action first light.
Heading Beagle Channel as per last signal.
Staying east Mount Cornu. Rescue 54.51S,
67.20W, app 1100. Our course 180.**

Chief Hook projected the signal into space,
praying it would reach Coronado off the satellite. Which it did, and the ops room immediately
signaled the ops room at the Chilean naval base
at Puerto Williams, right on the south shore of

the Beagle Channel, eleven miles away from the rescue point. Parked right here was one F/A-18F Boeing Super Hornet strike bomber, primed with its AIM-9 can't-miss guided missiles, heavily loaded 20mm Vulcan cannon, and prepared for takeoff at a moment's notice.

The pilot, Lt. Commander Alan Ross, wore the sinister patch of VFA-151 **Vigilantes**, a red-eyed skull with a dagger in its teeth. He had been in residence for just a few hours, having flown off a diverted U.S. aircraft carrier in the Pacific, and arrived via refuel stops at Santiago and Punta Arenas.

That Hornet 18F was all that stood between the SEAL team and certain death. Because even graduates from Coronado could not fight an entire country's national defense system, not if that country was determined to hunt you down on its own territory.

And no one was more concerned than Commander Rick Hunter that after traveling so far, he and his team were still on Argentinian soil.

Nonetheless, they cooked the last of their food, baked beans, ham, three steaks sealed in foil. They finished the bread with the rest of the cheese, drew straws for first watch and camped out for five hours, after which they would once more head south, through the light shallow snow that, at this medium level, barely covered any part of the mountains.

Sleep came easily, and the watch keepers found it hard to stay awake. But the danger up here was minimal, and they were all rested when Chief Bland summoned them back to duty. He had already made coffee, and with some reluctance they crawled out of their sleeping bags, in the dark, and began to pack, pulling on their boots. Dallas found a couple of packs of ginger cookies he had been hoarding, and they shared these before picking up the machine gun and the radio and setting off south over relatively flat ground, with Dallas out in the lead. Still munching boldly.

They had five hours marching through the darkness, and much of it was surprisingly easy going, because the ground began to slope downward as the mountain began its long dip down to the channel. The first fifteen miles went by before they could see the dawn breaking, way out to the left. And as it did so each man began to feel the tension of impending attack.

Because, as Commander Hunter told them, "There are two possibilities for us. The Args either believe they lost us, and that Puma simply crashed into the mountain. Or they have found out that it did not crash, and that we probably hit it."

At this point Lt. Banfield lapsed into deep Mississippi. "In the first case, our worries are over and we're just gonna be walking in t-a-a-a-ll cotton. In the latter case, them boys gonna come lookin'."

Dallas and Doug Jarvis chuckled, even though they knew it wasn't funny. And they pulled down their hats and kept going, and no one said anything as they tried to walk home across this freezing territory right down here at the end of the Western world.

Two miles farther on, the mountain seemed to come to an end. In front of them was a long green downward slope, still thick grass, with some copses of trees, and a broad area of woodland at the bottom. Beyond that, out by the horizon, maybe seven miles from where they stood, was the thin, shiny ribbon of the Beagle Channel. Except that it would not be thin when they arrived there. Five miles never looks all that thin, even across water.

"Well, this bit should be pretty easy," said Brian Harrison. But the Commander stood and stared down the hill, frowning. "Not too easy if they decide to come after us in the next hour, while we're walking over that exposed ground. What time is it?"

"0930, sir."

"Okay, let's get another message off, Mike, before we get going. Give 'em our GPS position, and tell him we may come under attack. And that if we do we will fire in a short SOS burst to the satellite, and then use our little TACBE to try and guide help in. If there is any."

"Okay, sir. I'll prepare the SOS so we can wing it off in seconds."

"Good boy. Let's hope we don't have to."

Three minutes later, they were on their way, still walking through enemy territory, albeit deserted, still carrying the big machine gun and the comms system. The wind was getting up a little as they made fast progress down the hill, but it came out of the south, bitterly cold, obscuring the sounds from the mountains—obscuring the sounds of two Argentinian military helicopters that suddenly appeared, flying high and slow, way above the peaks, plainly searching.

The SEAL team had traveled almost three miles downward, with perhaps four hundred yards still in front of them before the long beech wood, when they finally heard one of the choppers swoop in low, maybe a thousand yards behind them. There was no point hitting the ground, not here. Their only chance was to run for the woods.

Rick's voice rang out in the lonely grasses. **"Go, boys, go!!! Run for your lives...Take the gun and the radio, but run...For fuck's sake, run..."**

They charged toward the wood, racing over the flat sloping ground. Out in front they could see the leading helicopter making a wide turn right over the trees, and then banking hard in a tight starboard turn, coming back in, behind them now.

The Puma swooped low, and now it was on them, raking the ground with its mounted machine gun, the bullets spitting into the soft ground, making lines in the grass. The second burst seemed only yards away as the SEALs pounded over the ground, and suddenly there was a terrible cry from Lt. Commander Dallas MacPherson. The most dreaded cry in the Navy SEALs' vocabulary. The leader's hit.

"Jesus Christ...Sunray's down! Stop! Oh, Jesus...Sweet Jesus...the CO's down..."

Dallas ran back, and he could see Rick, face-down, blood pouring down his camouflage trousers. He couldn't tell if the boss had been hit in the stomach or the leg, but there was a lot of blood.

He looked up to see where the helicopter was, couldn't find it, and yelled to Mike Hook to get to the wood and send the SOS message, and to open up the TACBE. He told Don Smith, **"Run, but leave the gun!"**

Out on the horizon they could see the Argentinian helicopters, flying together now, making a long circle. They were plainly on their way back. And Dallas banged a new ammunition belt into the machine gun, cranked open the tripod, then swung around, lying in the grass, adjusting the sights for the approach of the choppers. Dallas was trained, and he was ready to face the enemy.

Doug Jarvis tried to lift Rick to check the injury but could not do so. And within one minute the Arg helicopters were on them again, streaking in low over the grass, both firing now, and Douglas Jarvis flung himself over Rick Hunter to take the impact of the bullets himself.

Dallas hammered back at the Args with the machine gun, aiming every one of the two hundred 7.62mm bullets in the belt straight at the nearest cockpit. And as they overflew the embattled SEALs in the grass, Dallas rolled right around, swiveling the gun with him. Somehow he kept on firing, scarcely realizing he had already smashed the entire windshield of the lead helicopter with the sustained fire from the SEALs' most trusted weapon.

The pilot, unsighted, too low, plummeted into the ground in a fireball, and Dallas leaped to his feet, only now seeing the blood streaming out of Douglas Jarvis's jacket as he crouched over their Team Leader.

Dallas roared in fury. And a thousand memories stood before him, memories of how he and the CO had fought together before. And he stood upright, trembling with rage, shaking his right fist, tears streaming down his face as he screamed without reason at the retreating helicopter, **"You bastards!! You bastards!! Well, come and get us…Come and fucking get us!!!"**

Unhappily, that was precisely what they were doing, and the surviving Argentinian helicopter, with its deadly machine gun, swung around for yet another attack. Worse yet, there was a new helicopter lifting up over the mountaintop, and briefly it joined the first one, and they flew together some five miles east of the SEALs.

Captain Jarvis was hit, but not badly, high up on his right arm, which was pouring blood but had only been lacerated by the shell. He climbed to his feet and temporarily left the CO on the ground. They were totally exposed, effectively facing two incoming helicopter gunships. But for the moment the Argentinians seemed to be taking their time, hovering out above the snowy foothills. But then they made up their minds and started in again toward the stricken Rick Hunter and his men.

Rick had just opened his eyes when Dallas spotted another aircraft, plainly a fighter-bomber, in the sky, bearing down at high speed from the western range out by Mount Olivia. "Jesus," he said, "now we're in real trouble. They got half the fucking Air Force here."

And this one was not hesitating. It was traveling like a bat out of hell, racing low along the foothills of the mountains.

"Jesus Christ!" yelled Douglas. "I think they're going to bomb us…"

"Hit the deck now!" shouted Dallas. **"Heads down…For Christ's sake, heads down!"**

But neither Dallas nor Doug Jarvis knew this aircraft was not on a bombing mission. Its attack was more precise than that, and Lt. Commander

Alan Ross, from Springfield, Massachusetts, had his finger right next to the missile button. The SEALs, peeping up through the grass, gazed in astonishment as the Hornet 18F came racing in at five hundred knots and fired its first AIM-9 missile.

They saw the bright, unmistakable winged dart shape glinting in the morning light, fizzing in at just below supersonic speed, low over the mountain, and then slamming into the newly arrived helicopter, blowing it in half. Two sudden fireballs roared toward the ground.

"It's ours," bawled Mike Hook. **"The fucker's ours!!"**

And they stood up, Douglas helping Rick to a sitting position, to watch the split-second bright fire in the sky that signaled the second missile was on its way, lasering over the foothills, a fiery trail behind it.

They couldn't see Lt. Commander Ross's fist clench in triumph as he banked the U.S. Navy strike fighter hard to the southeast, but they saw the missile streaking over the grassland, swerving at the last second, and then smashing into the first helicopter with such thumping force it spun the aircraft right over before detonating like a thunderbolt, high over those lonely pastures.

"You little darling," bellowed Lt. Banfield. **tight-assed, French-fried little dar-**

"You

And now they could see Brian Harrison charging out from the wood to help. And, half running, half walking, and laughing, they manhandled Rick Hunter into the safety of the trees. In the distance they could see the Hornet way over the wood, slowed down, somewhere out over the Beagle Channel.

But that was not their immediate concern. What mattered now was the amount of blood their leader was losing, and the obvious pain he was in. With the three Argentinian helicopters all destroyed, and the cover of the trees, they probably had a half hour to get organized.

They wrapped two field dressings on Douglas Jarvis's arm, which in the end might need stitches. But Doug himself took charge of Rick Hunter, resting him down on a sleeping bag, with another one covering him, trying to stop the violent trembling that had set in.

He and Brian cut away the trousers to try and see the extent of the wound, and to Doug's great relief there was no further injury. The Commander had been hit in his right thigh, not in his stomach. The bullet was probably still in there, but the wound was toward the outside, and it had missed the main artery—the one that always kills matadors when the horn of the bull rips it open.

Nevertheless, the leg was bleeding heavily, and Douglas stripped off his jacket, pullover, and

ripping up the shirt to make a tourniquet,
he bound around the Commander's upper
He then injected morphine into Rick's arm,
ressed the gaping wound as well as he could
a combination of field dressings and the rest
shirt.

looked as if the blood might have stopped,
may have still been bleeding inside. Doug
they had to get help, fast; and he told Mike
:ord a new satellite message, giving the pre-
GPS at the point where they would reach
ide Beagle Channel. Staring at their chart,
his small ruler, Doug called it…**"54.52N
W…Tell 'em we'll be there in two hours,
we'll have the TACBE turned on…"**

allas MacPherson also knew they would ei-
be there at that time or they would no longer
ive. It just depended on whether the Argen-
is realized there had been a minor battle out
in these desolate lands, and that the foreign
ilt group they were seeking was still on the
, heading for the channel.

i the considered view of Dallas, there was a
good chance the Argentinians might not re-
what was happening, because there had not
a fourth helicopter, and the destruction of
hree searching choppers had been so sudden
almost certainly had made no report back to
. At least not one that stated categorically they

were being wiped out by a mad groundhog with a machine gun, and a fighter plane they wrongly assumed was Argentinian.

Nonetheless, he thought they had a couple of hours maximum to get the two wounded men to the meeting point. Because one of them was seriously hurt, and they had nearly four miles to walk, and they did not have a stretcher. Dallas assumed a loose command, ordered Mike Hook to fire off the satellite message immediately, and went to help Bob Bland cut or break two fairly straight beech branches, which took ten minutes.

While this was happening, Don Smith made a mug of coffee, principally to give to the Commander, and then they all helped to force the two poles through a couple of sleeping bags and form it into a stretcher that could stand up to the relatively short distance they must travel with the boss.

They rested it on the grass and lowered Rick onto it, and Douglas was really concerned to see the mission's CO drifting into unconsciousness. They had to get him some medical help, antibiotics, and someone to remove the bullet. Doug was afraid there might be two of them in Rick's right leg.

And so they hoisted him up, Dallas and Brian holding the front poles, Doug, using his good arm, with Don Smith, at the rear. The mighty Bob Bland carried the heavy machine gun, with the ammunition belts around his neck. Lt. Banfield

d the main satellite transmitter. Mike Hook
now held on to its other parts. And they set
through the wood, walking slowly, carrying
heavy burden through the trees, then out
the light. And still there was no beat of Ar-
nian helicopter blades.

hey rested after a mile, placing the Com-
ler on the ground, trying to give him water,
te seemed unaware and his head kept falling
, and Doug was worrying the morphine had
how had a bad effect.

ut they could see the channel out in front
and the remainder of the walk was down-
and they hoisted up the stretcher again and
ed on down toward the water. Rick's eyes
open now, but it was obvious that some kind
lirium was setting in, and he was murmuring
ething none of them could make out.

'Come on, guys, keep going...I'm afraid
re losing him...if that poison gets right
his system we will lose him...'' There was
rgency to Doug's voice now.

They all knew the clock was ticking for Rick.
as 1105, and they could not expect any res-
r, whoever it might be, to hang around in this
tile Argentinian territory for long. Doug said,
imme one of the ammunition belts round my
k...that's about all I can manage.''

They reached the riverbank and stumbled
he steep slope toward the water. Mike

was aiming the TACBE everywhere along the shore. But there was a light mist over the water and they could not see more than about fifty yards. And they waited for five minutes and then ten...and then Mike Hook heard it, the unmistakable growl of big engines crawling along the shoreline.

Two minutes later they saw it, a gray, 450-ton fast-attack naval patrol craft, flying a national flag off its mast, red and white horizontal halves, with a white star on black in the top left-hand corner.

"It's Chile," said Dallas.

But now the craft had seen them and the helmsman held her on the engine in the fast current. The SEAL team waved, and they could see a big rubber inflatable being launched, and then heading into the deep rocky shore. On board was a young Chilean officer, who just said, "No speak, yet. Just hurry. Get injured men in right now. I come back for last two."

Five minutes later they were all on board the Israeli-built gunboat **Chipana,** speeding across the channel toward Chilean waters and the Navy base at Puerto William on Chile's own south side.

The young officer smiled and said, "I'm not too sure who you are, but you must be real important. Orders came down from very high, right from HQ at Valparaiso...very simple...get you guys out of Argentina no matter what. GPS ve accurate...good, eh?"

hey all shook hands at last, but Rick Hunt-
s now unconscious, and the Chilean Sub-
enant Gustavo Frioli told them, "Doctor
ng. We get messages."

nd they made it just in time. The naval doc-
Commander Cesar Delpino, had trained at
ton Medical Center, and he recognized a
emergency when he saw one. They took the
mander immediately into a spotless, white-
ed emergency room, and he administered a
rful dose of antibiotics, and placed him in-
ly on an IVD.

y the following morning, Tuesday, May 3,
was stabilized, the poison in his system un-
control. He was still extremely feverish, and
mander Delpino thought they should wait
her twenty-four hours before removing two
hine-gun bullets embedded in his thigh.

Rick asked him if he would perform the op-
on himself. But the Chilean doctor told him
someone else had arrived.

'A top Chilean specialist, I hope," said Com-
der Hunter, grinning.

'No. Your surgeon will be American."

"American!" said Rick. "Where's he coming
g!!" ?"

don't know, but he's here. They arrived
hours ago."

How?" said Rick, sounding much like
down ase vaiter.

"The American submarine. It's right out there, beyond those buildings, alongside."

"What submarine?"

"Well, Major, I can see it's a U.S. Navy L.A.-class nuclear boat, maybe seven thousand tons...it's called **Toledo...** I hear the plan is for her to wait here for a few days and then take you all home."

"How's she going to do that, straight along the Beagle Channel and up the Atlantic?"

"No, Major. They'll go the other way, slowly west through the much deeper water around Gordon Island and then Cook Bay, out into the Pacific. They can go deep there and then turn north up the coastline to your aircraft carrier."

"That's a long way, eh?"

"Ah, yes, Commander. A long way, but a safe way. Out of shallow enemy waters, not on the surface."

"How about the doctor?"

Commander Delpino laughed. "I don't know about him."

The following morning Lt. Commander James Scott met Rick Hunter for the first time, in the operating room. They shook hands briefly, and the U.S. Navy surgeon said, "This isn't going to take long. You've been in good hands. No infection. We're leaving for home this afternoon."

"Thanks, Doc," said Rick.

"I'm going to give you a shot of Pentothal...in your forearm...try to count to ten, but you won't get there…then I'm going to take those two bullets out."

Rick counted, made it to three, and the world went blissfully blank for just thirty minutes. When he awoke, it was done. The leg was strapped, the pain bearable, and Dallas MacPherson and Douglas Jarvis were standing by his bed.

"Well done, sir," said the Lt. Commander from South Carolina. "We all wanna thank you." And, with an obvious air of admiration, he offered his hand to the SEAL Team Leader. Dallas himself would never comprehend the majestic embrace of that compliment.

And Rick Hunter's war was over.

0930, THURSDAY, MAY 5
CASA ROSADA
BUENOS AIRES

The military communication from the commandant of the Rio Grande air base had been decoded and presented in hard copy by Admiral Oscar Moreno to the President of the Republic of Argentina.

It read:

Rio Grande, Wednesday, May 4. Attack on this base on the night of May 1 and the subsequent air and ground

pursuit of the heavily armed intruders has resulted in the total loss of twelve Super-Etendard fighter-bombers, two military patrol Jeeps, eleven guards, four Puma attack helicopters, and twelve aircrew. The identity of the enemy remains unknown. None have been killed, wounded, or detained. Lt. Commander Ricardo Testa, head of air base Security, is currently under arrest awaiting court-martial.

The President of Argentina could hardly believe his eyes. And yet, somehow, he could. And his mind flashed back to the veiled threats contained in the communiqué from the White House that had arrived the previous week, the one to which he had not replied.

He turned to his Defense Minister, Admiral Horacio Aguardo, and then to Admiral Moreno and General Eduardo Kampf. "Gentlemen," he said, "either directly or indirectly we are being sucked into a war with the United States of America…and, by any means, we have to stop it."

All three of them nodded in agreement. "Further defiance from us," said Admiral Moreno, "may very well mean the Pentagon will come out into the open and slam the entire Rio Grande base, not to mention Rio Gallegos and maybe even Mount Pleasant...and there appears to be nothing we can do about it."

"Also, we scarcely have a leg to stand on," said Admiral Aguardo. "The USA will plead its case to the United Nations, explaining that Argentina committed an act of international piracy, smashed the Royal Navy Fleet in international waters, and stole a legal British colony, plus two billion dollars' worth of U.S. oil and gas."

"I think we are of accord, gentlemen," said the President. "I shall accept the American terms for the future of the Islas Malvinas. Not because I want to, but because I have no choice."

Again, all three men nodded their assent.

0900, THURSDAY, MAY 5
THE OVAL OFFICE

Admiral Morgan liked what he saw. He liked it very much. President Paul Bedford was just smiling and shaking his head. The communiqué from the President of Argentina was perfect:

> **My regrets for the delay in replying to your previous dispatches, and I trust you will understand my government has been totally preoccupied in**

reestablishing normal working and living conditions among the good citizens of the Islas Malvinas.

Now, in the interests of peace and trade, we are prepared to accept your terms and suggestions for a lasting treaty, and a thoughtful handover of the islands from Great Britain to the Republic of Argentina over a two-year period.

We do require international acceptance of the Islas Malvinas becoming a sovereign territory of Argentina by the year 2013, and we call upon both Great Britain and the USA to ensure this is understood by the Security Council of the United Nations.

We regret the unfortunate events that led to the expulsion of the innocent personnel of both ExxonMobil and British Petroleum from the legally owned oil and gas fields on the islands. And we agree to their immediate restoration—under fair royalty considerations for the Republic of Argentina.

I will be joined by my senior envoys and advisers in Washington next week, beginning May 9, and look forward to a cordial meeting with you in order to bring these matters to a mutually agreeable conclusion.

"Thank you, Admiral," said President Bedford.
"My pleasure," replied Arnold Morgan.

MONDAY, MAY 16
EASTERN PACIFIC OCEAN

The Nimitz-class aircraft carrier USS **Ronald Reagan** steamed steadily north, a thousand miles off the coast of Peru. The eight-man Navy SEAL team had been on board for almost a week, and would remain so until they docked in San Diego, 2,640 miles and five days hence.

Commander Hunter was still recuperating from his thigh wound, and was undergoing daily therapy in one of the ship's gyms. The Navy surgeon had decided to insert ten stitches into the gash on Captain Jarvis's upper arm.

The two of them were watching a satellite broadcast of the evening news before dinner when the anchorman announced that terms had been agreed for the peaceful transition of power from Great Britain to Argentina over the Falkland Islands. He added that executives of ExxonMobil and British Petroleum had been present at the talks in the White House and that the two oil giants were returning to the oil and gas fields in both South Georgia and East Falkland.

There was a film clip of the men arriving at Mare Harbor in an ExxonMobil tanker, and a further clip of Exxon's President, Clint McCluskey, saying what a privilege it had been to work with the President of the USA and reach a "one hundred percent oilman's deal." **Fair but firm, that's the Texan way, the way George Dubya himself would have done it. Yessir.**

"You think we had something to do with all that, Rick?" asked Captain Jarvis.

"Wouldn't be surprised, kid. Not at all," said Commander Hunter, knowingly.

SATURDAY, MAY 21
SPEED 7, DEPTH 400, COURSE 360

Captain Gregor Vanislav was tiptoeing slowly north up the Atlantic. They'd been running for five weeks now, and **Viper K-157** was 8,000 miles north of the Falkland Islands, 8,000 miles north of the sunken war grave that was once HMS **Ark Royal**.

He had been ultra-wary all the way, sliding quietly through the deep waters, slowing and listening for the sounds of a U.S. or British attack submarine, staying clear of the land, following the line of the North Atlantic Ridge.

And now he was beyond the ridge, 450 miles west of southern Ireland, headed for the shallower waters of the Rockall Rise, and then 600 miles farther to the northeast, into the GIUK Gap.

Right now, moving stealthily in deep waters, west of County Kerry, Captain Vanislav was entering the most dangerous waters of his long journey. This was the business end of the North Atlantic, where the U.S. Navy's underwater surveillance system (SOSUS) was likely to miss nothing.

It was right here, many weeks ago, when **Viper** had first been detected, but then lost. If Gregor Vanislav could negotiate the next eight hundred miles safely he would have a trouble-free run home to Murmansk. If he were picked up on the grid of SOSUS wires on the seabed, he could expect the navies of the U.S. and UK to come looking.

The Russian submarine commander assumed that by now, someone, somewhere, knew that the **Ark Royal** had been sunk by torpedoes, and not by bombs delivered by the Argentine Air Force. The key to the safety of his ship and his crew was stealth, slow, quiet running.

And the farther north he went, the less suspicion there would be. Any Russian ship had the right to run through these international waters. Indeed, they had to run through here, since it was the only way the Russian Navy had to reach the rest of the world.

"Just get through the gap," he muttered. "That's all. And then we're safe."

SIX DAYS LATER, FRIDAY, MAY 27
LEXINGTON, KENTUCKY

The U.S. Army's latest Bell Super Cobra helicopter came clattering out of the sky above the long lawn alongside the main house at Hunter Valley Farm. It had traveled eighty miles from Fort Campbell Military Base on the Tennessee border, and it was carrying just two passengers.

Diana Hunter had been worried almost senseless for the past five weeks, because the rigid secrecy surrounding highly classified Special Forces operations had made it impossible for her to discover anything, not even whether her husband and brother were dead or alive.

She watched the Cobra land with her heart missing every other beat, half expecting to see Admiral John Bergstrom emerge personally to break the worst possible news to her. But the first person to disembark was the unmistakable Captain Douglas Jarvis, lean, athletic, hatless, wearing a short-sleeved U.S. Navy white shirt.

She saw him raise up his left arm to assist the second passenger down the steps, and she watched the mighty figure of her husband step carefully down onto the grass, betraying only the slightest limp. And then she literally ripped open the French doors, flew down the wide stone steps, and ran across the grass, hurling herself into the arms of Commander Hunter, tears streaming down her face.

She could manage no words except, **"Thank God, thank God!"** over and over. Until finally she turned to her beloved little brother, who was standing there grinning, a picture of health, his profession betrayed only by the bandage still covering his upper right arm.

Helplessly she shook her head, and asked lamely, "Are you both injured? Were you in the most terrible danger?"

"Nah," replied Rick Hunter. "But I guess we had our moments."

EPILOGUE

Viper K-157 ran slowly northeasterly up through the GIUK Gap, heading stealthily for Mother Russia. At times Captain Gregor Vanislav cut the speed even more, to only five knots, which was just sufficient to make the surface on emergency propulsion, without wallowing, should the nuclear system fail. He was a very sound submarine CO.

And he understood fully the perils of the GIUK, where the U.S. and Royal Navy listening systems were so electrifyingly sensitive. He knew he might be detected, at whatever speed, and simply concentrated on trying to bend the odds in his favor.

They were west of the Faeroe Isles now, just east of the central dividing line between the UK and Iceland, heading into the Norwegian Sea. And Captain

Vanislav did not consider they had been detected. But in this he was wrong. The U.S. listening stations on the east coast of Greenland and the one on the southeast coast of Iceland had both detected a transient contact moving slowly northeast.

They had each assessed the tiny paint on the screen as a submarine, and in Iceland they had sufficient data to list it, **"Russian nuclear, probably Akula class. Nothing else correlates on friendly or Russian nets."** The clincher came from the British, from the ultrasecret surveillance station near Machrihanish on Scotland's far western Atlantic shore of Kintyre.

The sonar operators there, positioned considerably nearer than their American colleagues, had picked up **Viper** two days ago and identified it immediately, **a Russian nuclear boat, running deep, slowly, almost certainly an Akula class, series II.**

They immediately had the submarine positioned in a wide hundred-mile square, but over the next forty-eight-hours, by process of elimination, and two further detections, they now had the submarine in a ten-mile square. The SOSUS system was on red alert for her predicted position the next time she crossed the undersea wire.

In the blackest of all possible Black Ops, two U.S. hunter-killer submarines, fifty miles apart, guided by the satellites, were patrolling the northern reaches of the GIUK, closing in as the **Viper** moved unsuspectingly forward.

1800, SATURDAY, MAY 28
ON BOARD USS CHEYENNE
NORTH ATLANTIC

"Stand by, one."
  "Last bearing check."
  "Shoot!"
  "Weapon under guidance, sir."
  "Arm the weapon."
  "Weapon armed, sir."
Two minutes...
  "Weapon two thousand yards from target."
  "Sonar...switch to active...single ping."
  "Aye, sir."

1804, SATURDAY, MAY 28
ON BOARD VIPER K-157

Captain—Sonar...one active transmission... loud...bearing Green one-three-five...United States SSN for certain...close...really close.
  Captain Vanislav reacted instantly, attack, not defense...**Stand by, tube number two... set targets bearing Green one-three-five... Range three thousand meters...Depth one hundred...shoot as soon as you're ready.**

Hard right...steer zero-three-five...shut off for counterattack...full ahead...ten up... two hundred meters.

Captain—Sonar...Torpedo active transmission!!... Possibly in contact...right ahead interval nine hundred meters!!"

Captain Vanislav was going for the classic but reckless standard Russian defense of driving flatout into the direct path of an incoming torpedo. But, too late, he shouted his last command, **"Decoys!!"**—just as the big wire-guided Gould Mk 48 American torpedo slammed into the bow of his ship just forward of the fin.

It blasted a massive hole in the pressure hull, and the thunderous force of the ocean smashed through the bulkheads as if they were made of cardboard. Along with his entire crew, Captain Vanislav died instantly, much as the crew of the **Ark Royal** had done forty-two days before.

She went down in 750 fathoms of ocean, just a few miles short of the Norwegian Basin, where the North Atlantic shelves down to a colossal depth of 12,000 feet, more than two miles.

**FOUR WEEKS LATER
0900, SATURDAY, JUNE 25
CHEVY CHASE, MARYLAND**

Admiral Arnold Morgan smiled a thin smile as he scanned the front page of the **New York Times**.

The single-column story at the top left hand of the page announced the resignation of the Prime Minister of Great Britain.

Basically, Arnold quietly rejoiced in the demise of any left-wing leader of a Western country. And, anyway, that particular PM was never going to survive the catastrophe of the Falkland Islands.

What caught his eye far more sharply was a front-page cross-reference to a story on page three, concerning the loss of a Russian nuclear submarine.

It was an agency story, credited to **Tass, Moscow, Friday;** the headline over two columns described it as "missing, believed lost."

The Admiral read it carefully:

> **The Russian Navy's 9,000-ton nuclear-powered Akula-class submarine** Viper, **hull number K-157, has been lost in the North Atlantic.**
>
> **Naval officials believe it sank in the Norwegian Basin northeast of the Faeroe Isles, where the water is more than two miles deep. Both the search area and depth are so vast no rescue operation is planned.**
>
> **According to Russian Navy sources,** Viper **missed first one then a second satellite call sign. Every effort was**

made to make contact, but the submarine was patrolling hundreds of miles offshore.

When it missed its third call sign, Viper had been missing for possibly three days and the search area, given a ten-knot average speed, would have been 360,000 square miles. There has been no further contact between the submarine and its base, and Russian naval authorities now accept the submarine has sunk, with all hands.

A spokesman for the Russian Navy's Commander in Chief, Admiral Vitaly Rankov, said last night: "Sadly, we have no information as to what caused the accident, and at this stage we are presuming a nuclear reactor failure, possibly at great depth. In Admiral Rankov's opinion, we may never know the answers."

Admiral Morgan betrayed no emotion. He set the paper aside, just as Kathy came in bearing coffee and toast.

"Did you read about that Russian submarine?" she said. "I saw it on CNN just now."

"I sure did," he replied. "Took 'em long enough to admit they'd lost her."

"You're always so critical of the Russians," she said, smiling. "Poor Admiral Rankov, he's such a jolly man…and anyway you don't know when she sank, any more than they do."

"Don't I?" grunted the Admiral, darkly.

About the Author

PATRICK ROBINSON is the author of seven international bestselling suspense thrillers, including **Nimitz Class** and **Hunter Killer,** as well as several nonfiction bestsellers. He divides his time between Ireland and Cape Cod.

www.patrickrobinson.com

Visit www.AuthorTracker.com for exclusive information on your favorite HarperCollins author.